The Body in the Wake

ALSO BY KATHERINE HALL PAGE

The Faith Fairchild Mysteries

The Body in the Casket

The Body in the Wardrobe

The Body in the Birches

The Body in the Piazza

The Body in the Boudoir

The Body in the Gazebo

The Body in the Sleigh

The Body in the Gallery

The Body in the Ivy

The Body in the Snowdrift

The Body in the Attic

The Body in the Lighthouse

The Body in the Bonfire

The Body in the Moonlight

The Body in the Big Apple

The Body in the Bookcase

The Body in the Fjord

The Body in the Bog

The Body in the Basement

The Body in the Cast

The Body in the Vestibule

The Body in the Bouillon

The Body in the Kelp

The Body in the Belfry

Short Fiction

Small Plates

The Body in the Wake

A Faith Fairchild Mystery

Katherine Hall Page

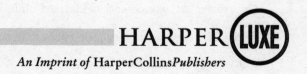

An Imprint of HarperCollins*Publishers*

THE BODY IN THE WAKE. Copyright © 2019 by Katherine Hall Page. All rights reserved. Printed in the United States of America. No part of this book may be used or reproduced in any manner whatsoever without written permission except in the case of brief quotations embodied in critical articles and reviews. For information, address HarperCollins Publishers, 195 Broadway, New York, NY 10007.

HarperCollins books may be purchased for educational, business, or sales promotional use. For information, please email the Special Markets Department at SPsales@harpercollins.com.

FIRST HARPERLUXE EDITION

ISBN: 978-0-06-291213-8

HarperLuxe™ is a trademark of HarperCollins Publishers.

Library of Congress Cataloging-in-Publication Data is available upon request.

19 20 21 22 23 RS/LSC 10 9 8 7 6 5 4 3 2 1

For my husband, Alan, and my son, Nicholas
From the luckiest woman in the world

Wake n.

the visible track of turbulence left by
something moving through the water

Wake n.

a vigil for the dead

Till human voices wake us, and we drown
—T. S. ELIOT, "THE LOVE SONG OF
J. ALFRED PRUFROCK" (1915)

Acknowledgments

My thanks to the following for help ranging from a pot buoy plot device and medical expertise to navigating the currents of getting this book published: Dr. Robert DeMartino; at Greenburger, my agent Faith Hamlin, Stefanie Diaz, and Edward Maxwell; my editor, Katherine Nintzel, and other Harper treasures: Danielle Bartlett, Vedika Khanna, Gena Lanzi, Shelly Perron, and Virginia Stanley; in Maine: Jean Fogelberg, Steve and Roberta Johnson (Bert and I Charters), Stephen Pickering, Elizabeth Richardson, and Tom Ricks.

Special thanks to Holly and Trisha Eaton for their high bid to name a character at the Maine Center for Coastal Fisheries auction fund-raiser, which gave me a chance to include their adorable son Sam!

Throughout the series so far, I have been fortunate to have had the following editors: Ruth Cavin, Carrie Feron, Zachary Schisgal, Jennifer Sawyer-Fisher, Sarah Durand, Wendy Lee, and Katherine Nintzel. Their expertise and friendship have been treasures.

The Body in the Wake

Chapter One

If one more person tells me to relax and stop thinking about it, I swear I will commit murder. I'll get myself off. Justifiable homicide. Why else did I go to law school? It will be a win for women everywhere who are *trying*—and I hate that word with its suggestion that you just aren't *trying* hard enough—to get pregnant!"

Sophie Maxwell set the glass of iced tea she had been drinking down on the small table next to her with such force, the lemon slice shot out onto the floor of the porch where she was sitting with her friend Faith Fairchild. Sophie scooped it up and set it next to the pitcher, which had been full an hour ago when the two women had come outside hoping for a breeze off Penobscot Bay's Eggemoggin Reach. It was the third day in a row of record-breaking heat. The sailboats, colored dots of varying sizes, were either not moving at all, or motoring with sails down.

The wraparound veranda of The Birches, Sophie's family's turn-of-the-twentieth-century summerhouse, sported the usual Down East assortment of Bar Harbor rockers made famous by John F. Kennedy and wicker of all sorts and vintages. Sophie and her great-uncle Paul had been almost living on the porch, taking meals there and sitting in the dark until the mosquitos, made even more vicious by the heat, drove them inside. Sophie hadn't had a decent night's sleep in ages, tossing restlessly on top of the sheets and searching in vain for a cool spot on her pillow. Uncle Paul was relying on an ancient dangerous-looking fan with blades as sharp as a guillotine. He'd offered to search one out for her in the attic, but she had declined. On Sanpere Island a few people From Away had air-conditioning, but natives and longtime summer people considered it unnecessary, as it usually was, or showy.

"And when you are pregnant," Faith said, "you'll face even more personal comments from family and strangers alike. That carrying high means a boy, except when it means a girl. Or even worse, pats on the belly once you show, getting beyond the plum stage to melon. Where did the fruit comparisons come from I wonder?

One woman actually put both her hands on my honey-dew bulge while I was in line at the post office and told me she was transmitting her aura to my unborn infant." Faith was trying to distract Sophie, keep things light. "That aura thing was a bit creepy, though. For weeks after Ben was born I found myself looking for telltale signs of possession—not mentioning the whole thing to Tom, of course. When the Linda Blair phase arrived, it turned out to be colic."

"I would never bring up something as intimate as, well, I guess family planning is the best way to put it," Sophie continued to fume. The heat and lack of sleep was making her cranky. "I mean, when they say 'trying,' you know what they really mean!"

"'Roll in the hay,' 'shagging'—I'm told that's Old English, by the way—'nookie,' of course, and then there's 'mattress dancing.' I prefer 'making love' or just good old 'sex.'"

"Faith, for a minister's wife you seem extremely conversant with all these terms." Sophie laughed.

The two women had known each other for a long time—Sophie had been an occasional babysitter for the Fairchilds when she was in her teens—but they became more than close during their unwitting involvement in solving two murders. The first was several summers ago on Sanpere. In the course of those dark days, the bright spot was Sophie's meeting her future husband, Will. After the wedding the following fall, performed by Faith's husband, the Reverend Thomas Fairchild, the couple moved to Will's hometown—Savannah, Georgia. The new bride had barely mastered which square was which when she was caught up in the kind of ghost story that fit right in with Savannah's reputation as the most haunted city in the South. When Will had suddenly disappeared, Faith came to Sophie's aid as they learned the spirits were all too real. It wasn't the type of bonding common between most female friends, particularly since Faith was older and in a different place in life, but as they now sat in companionable silence drinking sweet tea—the Savannah influence—Sophie thought that aside from Will, there was no one she was closer to than Faith, who knew what was dominating Sophie's thoughts now. The big three oh was looming closer and closer, weeks away, and her biological clock was ticking at warp speed.

"It must be hotter than Hades in Savannah," Faith said. "When is Will going to be able to get back here?"

"He says he should tie things up in another two weeks, three at the most. I feel a little guilty leaving him, but the house and his office are air-conditioned.

He says he's used to the heat. And what little work I need to do can be done from here." Sophie had become a partner in Will's family firm while he opted to stay independent with his PI agency, which specialized in investigating white-collar crime.

"In that case, you really *can* put all this out of your mind. If you get pregnant it's going to be a second immaculate conception or an indecent scandal."

Sophie stretched and stood up, smiling. "Thank you, Faith, I knew you'd cheer me up. Not that I'm at the stage where a Pampers commercial makes me sob, but I *have* been blue. The heat hasn't helped. Let's go to the Lily Pond for a swim. I know you won't go off the dock here no matter how hot it is." Sophie had learned in the past that Faith considered a plunge into Sanpere's cold salt waters unthinkable unless she found herself at the end of a plank with the tip of Captain Hook's cutlass between her shoulder blades. The Lily Pond was fresh water.

The Fairchilds had bought a small piece of land on Sanpere some years ago and put up a cottage of their own, but it wasn't a cottage like The Birches, which had more in common sizewise with the "cottages" in Bar Harbor and Newport. Sophie's great-grandparents,

Josiah and Eleanor Proctor, had built at the same time as other rusticators from Boston, New York, and Philadelphia, selecting the large scenic site overlooking the Reach on a sailing trip as newlyweds, captivated by the nearby lighthouse, the rough granite ledges, and a deep-water mooring. Once the house was completed, they never missed a summer. They came up from Boston by train, changing in Portland for the coastal steamboats that carried them to Sanpere, where they indulged in early-morning bracing swims, yachting, long walks in the woods, and other Teddy Roosevelt–type roughing-it activities while making do with plenty of servants to help them lead such simple lives.

Except for the outdoor activities, this way of life had vanished. The rusticators' descendants now arrived by car, usually four-wheel-drive Subarus—the Maine state car—with kayaks on the top. The army of servants had been replaced by part-time help like Marge Foster, a local island woman, who was pushing the screen door to the porch open now.

"Thought you'd need more tea and I've got some molasses cookies I made this morning," Marge said. Sophie jumped up to get the tray and was glad to see that Marge had brought a glass for herself.

"You have to stop baking in this heat—not that we

don't appreciate it. But, sit and relax please! It's a little cooler out here."

Marge was an ample woman and filled the rocker Faith pulled up for her. "With just you and Mr. Paul there is scarcely anything for me to do. Might as well bake, as you only want cold suppers," Marge said, taking the glass of tea Sophie had poured for her.

Sophie had insisted that she take care of meals, but Marge in turn had told her that cooking was part of the job, and they settled on having Marge leave what she called the "fixings." She also considered cleaning the house and doing the wash part of what was supposed to be a half-time job. Sophie occasionally found herself in a race to get to the housework before Marge. However, she was a godsend when the house was full, as it had been over the Fourth of July. Sophie's Uncle Simon, her mother's only sibling, and his family were a throwback to an earlier era and considered anything more than mixing a drink "not my job."

Marge drank thirstily. "That was some good, and yes, thank you, I'll have more. Missed seeing your mother, Sophie. It's not like her to skip the Fourth, or be this late coming."

Babs, Sophie's mother, was a favorite of Marge's— and of the whole island. She started life as Barbara

Proctor, Josiah and Eleanor's granddaughter, never missing a summer either, and Marge was right. To Sophie's almost certain knowledge her mother had rarely been absent for the Fourth.

Sophie was the happy result of Babs's brief marriage to Sandy Maxwell, one cut short by the discovery of a receipt from Firestone and Parson for a diamond bracelet Babs never received that Christmas, opening the promising small box to find a silver one from Shreve's instead. Babs didn't have any more children but did have plenty more husbands. Her current full name was Barbara Proctor Maxwell Rothenstein Williams Harrington. She'd told her daughter that in her day you married your beau rather than "jump between the sheets." Yet, with this current marriage, which had lasted the longest, Sophie was pretty sure that her mother had finally found "The One" in Ed Harrington, an easygoing venture capitalist with a good sense of humor and his own hair (one of Babs's requirements). They traveled a great deal, as Ed liked to golf in exotic places and Babs liked to shop in exotic places. They'd been to the Mission Hills Golf Club in Guangdong, China, and others from New Zealand to Abu Dhabi. At the moment they were in Greenland. She imagined her mother would be restless by now, as Greenland was not known as a shopping destination once you'd purchased something fashioned from musk ox wool.

"She's planned to be here for a few weeks before Samantha's wedding, so I'd say soon—early August— although she'll probably spend some time at the Connecticut house when she gets back from Greenland," Sophie said. Babs may have changed husbands the way other women changed nail polish, but through them all she'd held on to her magnificent house overlooking Long Island Sound on the Connecticut shore, where Sophie had grown up.

"The wedding's over Labor Day weekend, right?" Marge asked. "I told Mrs. Miller I could help and she's about asked every other woman on the island to keep the dates clear."

Pix and Sam Miller were the Fairchilds' closest friends and neighbors in Aleford, Massachusetts, and on Sanpere, and their daughter, Samantha, was marrying Zach Cohen. Pix had been in panic mode since the couple announced their engagement the previous fall. No matter what Faith, or Sophie, also a friend, said, Pix was sure they'd run out of food or there would be a Nor'easter or there would be a flu epidemic or a meteor would crash down on the venue, Edgewood Farm . . . the list was endless.

"You two better get that swim in before it rains," Marge said.

"But there isn't a cloud in the sky," Faith pointed out. "And the weather report didn't say anything about showers. I wish it would rain and cool things down."

"Oh, you can't trust weather reports," Marge said complacently. "My knee was acting up this morning and it's a sure sign."

"Leave everything, please," Sophie said to Marge. "You've stayed long enough. Go home and say hi to that nice husband of yours from me."

Marge's husband, Charlie, fished, like most men on the island, and he *was* a very nice man who turned up, usually unannounced, to help Paul with all sorts of tasks from splitting wood to repairing the roof. He just seemed to know. Like Marge.

Sophie's words brought a grin to Marge's face. "I'll tell him. 'Nice.' He'll get a kick out of that. Now, Sophie, I overheard what you were saying before. Can't say I ever had trouble in that department nor did Mumma. 'All you need to do is lay a pair of men's pants across the bottom of my bed' and nine months later the cradle would be full, she used to say."

"It's a thought," Sophie said. "Why not give it a try? I'll tell Will to bring some particularly sexy trousers up with him."

Marge gave her a look. "Silly girl, that's just an old wives' tale. Like sleeping with a piece of wedding cake under your pillow or planting parsley. What I'm telling you is to go off and have fun. And no, I did not say 'relax.' Don't want you turning into a murderer." She closed the door behind her with one last slightly wicked look over her shoulder.

Faith and Sophie dissolved in giggles. "Parsley! Wedding cake and pants. Those are new ones to me, and I thought I'd heard them all," Sophie gasped. "We are definitely not paying Marge enough."

Faith nodded. "Let's go swim. I have to get my suit back at the house so I'll meet you at the pond."

The Birches was actually located on Little Sanpere Island, a much smaller—only four miles long—piece of land connected to Sanpere by a causeway. As Faith crossed it now she noted the new guardrails that the state had finally installed on the narrow twist of road, a favorite for drag racers with often horrific consequences. Sanpere itself, with roughly two thousand year-round residents, was many times larger than Little Sanpere. The population in both doubled in the summer, a phenomenon giving rise to a local saying that you knew it was June because of the dual invasions of blackflies and summer folk. There were two towns on Sanpere, Sanpere Village and Granville, much bigger and home to the largest lobster fishing port in Maine. Last summer Sonny Prescott, a local dealer, told Faith the total year's haul was over seventeen million pounds. In the summer months, tourism coexisted with the working port. Newcomers expecting only quaint picture postcard fishing scenes were disabused by the first gigantic tractor-trailer truck passing them on a curve.

She turned off Route 15, which circled the island, onto the road that led to the Point, which she now considered home. She'd been in Aleford all her married life, but they lived in a parsonage that belonged to the church, not the current occupant. A few summers ago she and Tom had decided to buy a plot in Mount Adams cemetery, so the island would be her dwelling for a long time. The Millers had a large family plot not far from the Fairchilds' choice, and the Proctor plot already had a number of occupants, starting with Sophie's great-grandparents. Faith took comfort knowing that she could at the very least count on some good conversation in the hereafter.

She thought back to her first summer on the island. Ben, now entering his second year at Brown, was a toddler. The Millers had convinced the Fairchilds to rent a cottage on Sanpere, their beloved Maine island. Faith had given in, faced with such enthusiasm, especially Tom's. He'd grown up on Massachusetts's South Shore and thought exploring rocky beaches with side trips to canoe on the North River or hike in Myles Standish State Forest was heaven on earth. Faith's plan was to be a good sport—especially when she heard there was a bridge to the mainland—then call in her chips and head for the Hamptons or even Provence the following summer. Instead, looking back she was sure Tom and the Millers had slipped something in the well water at the farmhouse rental they'd found for them on a white sandy cove with a view straight out toward Mount Desert Island and sunsets more magnificent than Faith had seen anywhere. She found herself gathering wildflowers and sticking them in Mason jars, marveling at the number of varieties of ferns, listening for the cries of gulls and terns. Above all she cooked. The setting could not have been more different from Manhattan's Upper East Side, where she had grown up and chosen a more elaborate culinary path leading to her own catering firm, Have Faith, which became one of the most sought after in the city. It was at a wedding she was catering that she met Tom. He was in town to perform the ceremony, changing for the reception. Daughter and granddaughter of clergy, Faith was adamant about avoiding the fishbowl life of a parish spouse, but the heart knows not reason. Faith found herself in a small town west of Boston, the land of boiled dinners and soft bagels. But her feeling for New England changed definitively that first summer on Sanpere, with a richer bounty than Dean & DeLuca and Citarella combined at her fingertips. Lobster, mussels, clams, scallops, halibut, haddock, peekytoe crab, chanterelles and other wild mushrooms. Local goat cheeses and fresh eggs from Mrs. Cousins were a short walk down the dirt road. Maine meant a late growing season, but as first peas, then strawberries, blueberries, and all the rest of summer's bounty arrived, Faith found herself savoring each with renewed appreciation. She made things like blueberry buckle, green tomato chutney, and all sorts of chowders in the farmhouse's kitchen.

As she pulled into the empty gravel driveway, relishing the pleasant memory, Faith thought how different a summer this summer was from previous ones. First, no Ben, who had opted to stay in Providence and accept his professor's offer of a summer research spot. After entering college intent on linguistics, Ben had become interested in biochem, especially as it related to life in waters like Sanpere's, and had switched majors.

The other difference was having Tom on the island all the time rather than for sporadic visits. He had a contract with Harvard University Press to turn his divinity school thesis on the history and theology of the twelfth-century French Albigensians into a shorter and more accessible book. An editor had come across the thesis and was intrigued by Tom's conclusion that the successful, extremely brutal Crusade by the church to obliterate the Albigensians, or Cathars, was the first example of genocide in the Western world with far-reaching historical implications. He'd arranged to take a leave from First Parish for two months, working with the assistant minister and calling in guest preaching favors from fellow clergy to do so.

Faith had been delighted, picturing the two of them with free time for picnics, boat trips, and other fun they'd never had uninterrupted hours for, but Tom soon realized he couldn't work at the cottage because of both the delightful distraction that was his wife and the slow Internet. Friends with a techie's wired dream house who would not be on Sanpere until the fall had offered it as an office for Tom. This left Faith with daughter Amy, entering her junior year at Aleford High School. But Amy was following the time-honored Fairchild summer job tradition at The Laughing Gull Lodge's kitchen. Laughing Gull was now Sanpere Shores, a conference center. Last summer, its first, had proved very successful. The new owners, who had two other similar facilities in New England, had added tennis courts, a spa, and a pool. They had also changed the Rec Center that had served as a kids' camp and hangout space for families into a lounge with a bar, billiard table, Ping-Pong, and a flat-screen TV the size of Rembrandt's *The Night Watch*. The rustic cabins had been upgraded—no more knotty pine—and there was plenty of high-speed Internet. Companies used Sanpere Shores for training retreats, and professionals booked time to offer courses in everything from digital photography to how to trace your family tree. To distract herself From Here to Maternity, Sophie had signed up for a writing program starting soon.

Sanpere Shores provided three meals a day: a hearty continental breakfast, box lunches, and a full-course dinner with menu choices. Amy was determined to follow in her mother's culinary footsteps, despite Faith's admonitions—hard work, long hours, difficult customers, and so forth. Amy had left Nancy Drew and Lemony Snicket behind years ago for M. F. K. Fisher, Elizabeth David, A. J. Liebling, and Ruth Reichl. Sanpere Shores was close to the house Tom was using, so the two of them left after breakfast each morning like commuters. Faith didn't know what she would have done without Sophie and Pix. She was unaccustomed to the experience of free time.

She dashed into the house, changed into her bath-

ing suit, and threw one of Tom's old tee shirts over it—
Yankee thrift was part of the Fairchild DNA, and she
saved a couple of threadbare items from his wardrobe
she hadn't managed to spirit away to wear for times
like this. The tote she kept with towels, sunscreen, and
a book was already in the car.

Faith was surprised to see so few people on the pond's
small beach, or in its waters. Maybe it *was* going to
rain. She set her things down and realized that the
woman sitting next to a little girl filling a bucket with
sand was the mother of Samantha's best friend, Arlene, and the child was Arlene's three-year-old, Kylie.

"Hi, Marilyn," Faith said. "Wow, Kylie seems to
be growing taller—and cuter—every time I see her.
She looked adorable in the parade." The theme for this
year's Fourth of July parade had been "Our Island Paradise," and Kylie, riding on Larry Snowden's float, had
been a lobster with a grass skirt.

Marilyn gave a big smile. "Took me forever to sew
that thing. That Larry comes up with some foolishness
every year, but this took the cake."

"And the blue ribbon I heard," Faith said. "Is
Arlene swimming?" She shaded her eyes to look out
at the water. It was a long pond surrounded by birches
and other trees. Water lilies encroached upon the clear

water, and Faith didn't like to swim too close to the sides. Besides the lily pads there was an abundance of other aquatic plants that seemed to have tendrils waiting to grasp her ankles.

"No. She was feeling a little poorly today," Marilyn said, her smile dimming. "I said I'd take Kylie, but I've got to go now. I have to get supper on." Island meal times were considerably earlier than the ones Faith kept. She wondered if Arlene might be pregnant. If so, it would mean drastic alterations to her matron of honor dress. Kylie was also in the wedding party—the flower girl— and Sam Eaton, the little son of other island friends, was the ring bearer. The kids would steal the show, Samantha said when she showed Faith pictures of their outfits. They *would* look precious, especially if Sam could be persuaded out of his beloved rubber clammer's boots. Faith, however, knew all eyes would be on the bride. Samantha had selected a gown from Anthropologie's bridal collection that looked like something from *A Midsummer Night's Dream*, floral appliques over layers of tulle with a pale rose-colored satin underskirt. Instead of a veil, she planned to make a simple white floral wreath to crown her shoulder-length dark hair.

"Say good-bye to Mrs. Fairchild, Kylie," Marilyn said, and the little girl came over, planting a sandy kiss on Faith's cheek.

As she waved good-bye Faith remembered the car accident Arlene had been in late last winter and chided herself for not asking how Arlene was doing in more detail. On their way to pick up Kylie at Arlene's parents', Arlene and her husband, Mike, who was driving, hit black ice, and the car flipped over. They had been wearing seat belts, and both the front and side airbags deployed forcibly. Mike was tall and avoided injury, but Arlene's nose and left cheekbone had been broken; she'd sustained a hairline jaw fracture—plus several teeth had been knocked out. Samantha had told Faith that Arlene had worried she wouldn't be healed in time for the wedding. For months she had looked like someone from a horror movie. It had been a long process and many trips to various doctors, but Faith thought Arlene had looked amazingly good on the Fourth at the parade. No wonder she was "poorly" though. The long drawn-out recovery had to have still left her feeling tired, especially with a lively little one.

Sophie was coming down the path onto the beach, and after exchanging quick greetings with Marilyn and Kylie, she called out to Faith, "I'm dying to get in the water! Race you to the end of the pond and back?"

"You're on!" Faith said and sped into the pond. After a shallow dive took her to the deeper water, she quickly moved into a fast crawl, heading straight down the middle. She could hear Sophie closing in behind her and quickened the pace. She reached the end of the pond and flipped to return, then realized she was about to get tangled up in a reedy thicket filled with fallen branches and trash, a bundle of old clothes. She started to swim away.

Until she saw two bare feet sticking out of a pair of jeans.

"Sophie, come help!" she screamed and dove underwater, grabbing the legs to free the whole body from the tangled mess. Faith tugged hard, and it broke loose and slid across the water like a cork from a bottle. Facedown with pale blond hair.

At Faith's side in seconds, Sophie immediately grabbed the head and neck, lifting them above the surface. "I can't feel a pulse!! I'm going to float him over toward that mud flat and start CPR. Can't wait to get him to the beach. Go call 911!"

As Faith started toward the opposite end of the pond at a competition pace she tried to get her mind around what was happening. Sophie had said "he." The body was a man. He couldn't have been in the pond long. No discoloration. His slender feet and ankles were bare—no bloating. Nearing the shore, she started yelling for someone to call 911 and was relieved to see a man instantly take a phone from his pocket. The pond was near the new cell tower and one of the few reliable places on the island for a signal.

Getting out of the water, she cried, "A man has drowned! At the end of the pond!" Someone draped a large towel around her. Someone else gave her a can of sugary Mountain Dew and told her to drink it down. In what seemed like no time at all, she heard the ambulance's siren signal its arrival, and the volunteers instantly went into action, two of them swimming out to help Sophie transport the body ashore. As they closed in on her and the body, she yelled, "I think there's a pulse."

Onshore the EMTs strapped an oxygen mask to his face and then the ambulance sped off, leaving Faith, Sophie, and the other few who had been at the pond sitting close together. It was over.

"Anybody know him?" asked a man Faith recognized by his distinctive beard as Bill Haviford, the president of the historical society. They had all had a good look at the victim as he was taken away.

No one answered at first and then Sophie said, "I'm pretty sure I saw him and some other guys at the market last week. They looked in their twenties, maybe a little older. Around my age." One of the ambulance corps volunteers had tossed blankets out for Sophie and Faith to wrap around themselves, and despite the temperature Sophie was still clutching hers close. "They were buying beer. Four of them. I didn't really pay much attention until they left the parking lot. They were all on motorcycles—Harleys I think—and roared off."

"You gals need to go home and dry off," Bill said.

Faith nodded in agreement. "Yes, come to my house, Sophie. We'll get your car later." She was thinking dry clothes were in order plus some brandy. The image of the young man in the water like a grotesque Ophelia wasn't going to go away for a long time though.

"Give me your keys, and my wife will follow with our car. We don't live far from you," Bill said. Faith wasn't surprised he knew where she lived, although she had no idea where he did. It was the island after all.

"Thank you, that would be a big help," Faith said. Sophie was still shaking, and Faith was sure the young woman was in mild shock.

Since leaving the pond Sophie hadn't said a word, but now as they drove through Sanpere Village, she shuddered and, barely audible, said, "Did you see his tattoo?"

"Yes," Faith said. "I did." Tattoos were so common now and she'd thought she'd seen them all, but this one was unique: a lifelike green adder snaking up his right forearm, its fangs dripping blood and a few Gothic letters in red spelling something Faith couldn't make out before he was taken away. A *Y* at the end? And she was pretty sure the first letter was an *L*.

She stepped on the gas.

Pix Miller stepped out onto the porch at The Pines. She closed the screen door gently in case her mother, sitting in her favorite canvas sling back chair, was dozing. The Pines, built by Pix's grandparents next to the Proctors' Birches, was a large gray-shingled "cottage" with the same magnificent view of the Reach and lighthouse as its neighbor's.

"Pix? Is that you? Creeping up on me," Ursula said, turning to look at her daughter with a welcoming smile. Pix gave her mother a kiss. This year she had started bringing the mail from their post office boxes every afternoon along with the *Island Crier*, the weekly island newspaper, on Thursdays. Pix had thought Ursula, who had always fetched both for herself, would protest. Driving The Pines's 1949 Ford Woody station wagon, kept in perfect shape by Forrest "Fod" Nevells, had been octogenarian Ursula's particular delight. Pix knew giving this up was hard. She had friends who had had to hide elderly parents' keys and, in one case, declare the car stolen (with a buyer all lined up). But Ursula had never said anything except to say in the beginning that Pix must have better things to do than drive all the way from her cottage every day, that a couple of times a week would suffice. Pix had pointed out that Sam wasn't coming until August, nor were any of her children around, so she really *didn't* have anything to do. In fact, she treasured this quiet time with her mother.

"Get yourself something cold to drink," Ursula said. "I sent Gert home. Too hot to work. She insisted on baking cinnamon raisin bread this morning. Told her I couldn't have her passing out from the heat, and that convinced her." Gert Prescott was surely close to Ursula's own age, Pix reflected. She'd been working at The Pines since she was a teen, coming to give Ursula, with two small children, a hand. Pix disliked the kind of summer person who referred to the women and men who worked for them as "just like family" while underpaying and overworking them, taking advantage of the fact that these jobs only existed seasonally and were a much-needed source of income. But Gert truly *was* family, and a few years ago Ursula had hired a young woman to do the housework and tend the garden over Gert's protests. Gert was possibly more excited about Samantha's wedding than anyone. Arlene, the matron of honor, was a niece, and Gert was seeing to the refreshments at the shower that Arlene was giving close to the big event.

"I'll get you something, too," Pix said, noticing her mother's glass was empty. "Lemonade?"

"Yes, and hurry up. Want to see what's been going on this week."

Pix laughed to herself. While the paper was a news source, Gert knew what was happening on Sanpere before the island actually did and wasn't so much a part of the grapevine as the root itself.

When they were settled with their drinks, Pix opened the paper and as usual started with the column "From the Crow's Nest." Ursula had unearthed a Japanese fan and was wafting it to and fro in front of her face, sending puffs of air toward Pix, who was feeling extremely content until the thought of the wedding intruded. She sighed. Her mother waved the fan hard. "I heard that! I have half a mind to give them a large check and tell them to elope if you can't stop worrying. It's all going to be fine. Faith is taking care of everything, and what she isn't, Samantha is."

"I know, but I wish Samantha was here."

"She will be in a few weeks. In plenty of time for the ceremony, which is what counts. You know they can't get away from their jobs."

Taking the scolding in stride, Pix brightened up. "Maybe they'll be here sooner. Samantha loves Fishermen's Day even more than the Fourth, and Zach has never been. I wouldn't be surprised if they drove up after work tomorrow and back on Sunday after it's over. It never goes much past three."

"There now. Keep a good thought and open the paper!" Much as Ursula loved her one and only daughter, she was fast losing patience with Pix's wedding woes. This was a woman with such fine-tuned organizational skills that she was on the phone booking rooms at the inn and other lodging scarce on the island less than an hour after hearing the happy news from Samantha and Zach. "Now, what's going on?"

Pix started reading aloud. "'The Maguire family is having their reunion this weekend and expect seventy, one member coming all the way from Australia. Six generations represented.'" Ursula nodded. Family reunions were what kept those who left for whatever reasons closely tied to the island. No matter where you lived, you showed up. Pix continued, "'The Granville Community Center is having an auction to raise money for the Island Food Pantry and is looking for items.'"

"I'm sure we can find some things in the attic once the heat breaks," Ursula said. Clearing out the attic had been on The Pines to-do list roughly since the 1930s.

Pix read more—what was coming up in gardens and the Fisheries Log, which was pessimistic about the lobster catch equaling last season's. Lobsters liked cold water, and the increasingly warm Sanpere waters due to climate change meant many crustaceans were staying far from the traps in water more to their taste.

"Let's see. Your Sewing Circle Fair is featured in 'Coming Events.' No Planning Board announcements; they're not meeting next week." Everyone on Sanpere scrutinized these announcements. Fair warning if your neighbor was planning to put up a dock across your view or add an addition blocking your time-honored shore access.

She turned to the obituaries. "Oh dear." Her voice caught.

"Who is it? Tell me quickly," Ursula said.

"No one we know. But young. Only twenty-four. Fished, graduate of Sanpere High School, beloved son, father of a four-year-old. There's a picture of the two of them. Heartbreaking." Pix looked up at her mother and then out to the Reach. "It's another 'died suddenly' one," she said.

"We're losing a whole generation," Ursula said in despair.

Chapter Two

G in and tonic seemed to fit the weather better
than brandy. Once she had found dry clothes for
Sophie, Faith mixed two drinks with plenty of lime,
adding to the tray a plate of cheese and crackers plus
some smoked mackerel spread she'd made. Drink, yes,
but food at times like these was equally important.

They sat on the deck watching the tide come in.
It was swiftly covering the mounds of mud and deep
troughs the clammers had left after hours of backbreaking digging. The cove in front of the Fairchilds' was a
good spot. Tom and the kids enjoyed clamming, but
after getting her foot stuck and unable to free herself
because of the suction Faith opted to prepare the bi-
valves instead. Her rubber boot was still buried somewhere out there.

Faith took a swallow of the cool drink and looked over at Sophie. Her friend seemed fine now, popping a cracker with the mackerel spread into her mouth with relish. But obviously what had just happened was foremost in her mind, Faith's, too.

"It's quite shallow at that end of the pond, especially off to the side where he was. Maybe he couldn't swim?" Sophie said. "Although you keep hearing that swimmer or not, you can drown in your bath or in a teacup of water. Although why you'd be swimming in a teacup is puzzling."

Sophie was making jokes; the shock was wearing off. Faith smiled as her friend continued talking. "He wasn't dressed for a dip in the pond—not even shorts—although he wasn't wearing shoes or socks. He must have taken them off to wade and then slipped in too far? Then again, even though the bank is muddy, it's not all that slippery, especially with the recent temperatures."

"True, but there have been several other drownings in the Lily Pond over the years, fortunately not many," Faith commented.

"Will made me promise not to swim alone, although I'm not sure what Uncle Paul could do. He does like sitting on the dock when I go in. He unearthed an ancient life buoy that may possibly have come over on the *Mayflower*. He brings a thermos of martinis, and given that it's almost empty when I get out I don't think it's meant to be an emergency restorative." Faith laughed as Sophie made herself another cracker with the spread. "You have to tell me how you make this. A secret family recipe?"

"Nope, and so easy, it's embarrassing," Faith answered. "I get the Ducktrap smoked mackerel at the market in Blue Hill, take the skin off, flake the meat, and blend it with cream cheese plus a touch of mayo with a fork or the back of a spoon. It turns too mushy in the food processor."

"I'll never tell, but I will copy it." Sophie set her drink down, sat up straighter in the chaise, and said, "Okay. I've been doing a rewind of the guy from the market. He wasn't from Maine, or at least his bike wasn't registered in this state. He, and the others, had Massachusetts plates and a lot of gear strapped on the back. Maybe they'd just come here to ride because there's no helmet law and they wanted to feel the wind whistling in their hair. Or detouring onto the island on the way to Acadia is common. But if the others took off to Mount Desert, he obviously stayed behind."

"Or none of them went and are still on the island. When was it you saw them?" Faith said.

"Late in the week. Friday? Yes, Friday because

people were coming for dinner and I had to pick up a few more things."

"Anything else?" Faith asked. "Did you notice the tattoo then?"

Sophie shook her head and closed her eyes briefly to try to recall more details. "He was wearing a long-sleeved black tee shirt and a blue jean jacket with the arms cut out," she said slowly. "And one of them may have been a girl. That person was wearing a bright pink bandanna covering his or her hair and a leather jacket with a red rose stenciled on the back. Not exactly macho." She realized that she was remembering more and more. Maybe it was the gin.

"About how old were they?"

"One of them seemed older than the rest. Thirties, maybe even forty. But the others were mid to late twenties. Not kids."

"We know they were all over twenty-one. The market checks every ID unless you are very obviously old enough to buy." When places in both Maine and Massachusetts had stopped asking Faith for her ID it had been somewhat traumatic. Like the gray eyelash she'd discovered more recently. "Anything else?"

"They weren't talking much to each other and not to anyone in line or at the checkout. Nobody said hi, so probably not from the island."

"Or not favorites," Faith said. While she had always found Sanpere a congenial place, especially after coming for so many years, she knew that there were grudges that had lasted generations.

The two sat silently for a few minutes. The moon would be close to full tonight, and that meant a higher than usual tide. It was coming in at a steady pace, and Faith, as usual, found it calming.

"I didn't see motorcycle tire tracks at the end of the pond," Sophie said, "but then I wasn't looking anywhere but at him. Did you notice any?"

Faith shook her head. "Besides, you can't get a vehicle through the woods and brush there. Maybe a bicycle, but definitely nothing larger. The closest road stops well before that end—there are no houses nearby—and the surrounding area is pretty much acres of swamp. Seth Marshall and other builders have been trying to figure out a way to drain it for houses for as long as we've been coming."

"Maybe he left his hog on the main road?" Sophie suggested. "I was running late and wanted to jump in the water, so I didn't notice any vehicles except yours." To get to the Lily Pond, you had to park on the side of a road and then walk in on a wide lane created in an earlier era when the pond was a source of ice for icehouses. "Did you see one?"

"No, although it could have been parked under some trees. I did notice how few cars there were for such a hot day, but a lot of families like Sand Beach better—so much larger and real sand. And it would be cooler today, since it's on the ocean." Faith stood up. Their glasses were empty. "We need fresh drinks. I know you're driving, so lots of tonic, ice, and more fresh limes." She'd said this noting a slightly worried look that crossed Sophie's face. But it wasn't about driving.

"Faith, do you think there's any possibility he made it? I thought at one point I was getting a faint pulse."

"We can call the hospital in a while." Faith knew how much Sophie needed to hear that a life already in existence had not been lost.

When Faith heard a car on the gravel drive, she expected to see Tom's. He might have sequestered himself, but she was sure that by now someone on Sanpere had relayed the information that his wife had been involved in finding yet another body.

Except it wasn't Tom. It was Sergeant Earl Dickinson who got out of a Hancock County Sheriff's patrol car and strode toward the deck. Earl and his wife, Jill, were close friends of both Sophie's family and the Fairchilds. Earl was in uniform and looked as fresh as a daisy. Not a wrinkle, except the knifepoint crease in his trousers. He and Jill were still renovating one of the nineteenth-century houses in Sanpere Village that had been built by a schooner captain, and Faith hoped Mrs. Dickinson was ironing with all the windows open in this heat.

"Fortunately it was one of my days on the island," he said. The sheriff's office was the only police presence on Sanpere. There was no chief, force, or hoosegow. Earl pulled up a chair and sat down. "I am so sorry. It must have been a terrible shock. Sophie, I understand you did everything you could to revive him."

"I'm okay. Well, not really. I think you're saying he definitely didn't survive," Sophie said.

"Yes." Earl put his hand on Sophie's arm. "He was already gone when they put him in the ambulance. Bill Haviford told me you thought you'd detected a pulse and had started CPR in the water. I got in touch with him after I learned he was the one who had made the emergency call. He also told me where the two of you were."

Earl continued talking in his slow, steady voice. "We won't know until after the autopsy, but the guess is he'd been in the water for a while. Maybe most of today and even last night."

He took out his trademark little spiral notebook

and clicked a ballpoint. "If you feel up to it, could you tell me everything you two noticed at the pond? And, Sophie, Bill said you saw the victim at the market last week with some other people?"

"We've been sitting here going over it all," Faith said, "but let me get you something cold to drink and freshen Sophie's." She planned to make it a stiff one. Earl could drive Sophie home. And Faith herself wasn't going anywhere.

When she returned, Sophie was telling Earl what she'd already related to Faith about last Friday and the pond. She sounded calm—resigned.

"You've been a big help," he said, "but there's a lot more we're trying to figure out. Number one: What was he doing in that part of the pond? Number two: How did he get there? I knew about the motorcycle from what you told Bill, but there's no sign of one any-where there or on any nearby roads. We're looking all over the island now. What you said about the gear, pos-sibly camping gear, helps. And the Mass. plates. We'll send his fingerprints down there immediately."

"You know he was barefoot, right?" Faith said. "Walking through that part of the woods would have killed his feet. Unless you found his shoes near where we found him." It felt odd to keep referring to the dead man as "he." A man without a name.

Earl shook his head and reached for some crackers and cheese. "We haven't done a major search of the area, but there was nothing on the ground near the end of the pond except what you'd expect in the way of rocks, weeds, the odd broken bottle or two—didn't look recent. And there was nothing on him neither. No wallet, no keys, no phone. Tight jeans, so they couldn't have fallen out in the water. It's shallow and clear there. We raked it some and will go back, but so far no clues to his identity at all."

"Except the tattoo," Sophie said.

At first Pix thought an extremely loud mosquito had taken up residence in her ear. She brushed at it, but the noise continued. She opened her eyes and sat up. An early riser, this was early even for her. Not yet six. She shook her head. The noise continued.

Realizing that the sound was a chain saw—one close by—Pix jumped out of bed fully awake and headed out the door to the deck. The sound of chain saws was common on the island, and the ratio of males to that particular kind of machinery was probably one to three—that is three chain saws for every guy. Sam had one, although Pix lived in fear every time he decided to attack the alders or dead branches he claimed might hit the house. After a storm, the whole island buzzed as the opportunity to clear up the "damage," that is, expand your view, was seized.

After their first child was born, the Millers had bought their own summer place on Sanpere, an old farmhouse that was in good shape with shore frontage and surrounded by what Realtors always refer to as mature plantings—spruce, balsam, birch, bayberry bushes, *Rosa rugosas*, and juniper. A small meadow in front of the house was filled with blueberries and tiny mountain cranberries in season. When the Millers arrived each year, the space was a mass of lupine in a variety of colors. They'd added onto the house as their family increased, linking the small barn to the main house as well as extending a deck off the expanded living room.

There were only a few houses on their road, the nearest one a small cabin—what local people called a "camp." The Spoffords had built it in the 1950s when their children were small, and they moved there from their year-round one in "town" each summer. Ed commuted all of five miles to his job at the shipyard. When he retired they winterized the cabin and sold the house in Granville. Pix loved having them as neighbors, as did the Miller children, who called Edith the "Cookie Lady," returning from a visit next door with huge old-fashioned hermits and snickerdoodles clutched in their hands. Finally the day came when Edith told Pix sadly that they had to move closer to their daughter in South Portland—she made it sound like the other side of the moon, and it certainly would be different from the island. They'd get used to traffic and there was a big mall, she'd added. It had become too much for Ed to keep the cabin, small as it was, up to his standards and Edith had drawn the line at his plan to put on a new roof by himself. When none of the children wanted it, they regretfully put it on the market. It sat unsold for several seasons. The living space was tiny by most standards, and the house sat well back from the shore atop a narrow strip of land. There was a fine view at the shoreline, however, and their two Adirondack chairs overlooking the cove were a permanent part of the landscape. Most early evenings found them there enjoying the sunsets and the beer Ed brewed with a group of his friends. They called themselves The Old Hopsters.

Standing on the deck in the weak morning light, it didn't take long for Pix to pinpoint the direction of the noise that had awoken her so abruptly. The sound, louder outdoors, was coming from the Spoffords'. Only she knew it wasn't the Spoffords anymore. Edith had called in June to say they had finally found a buyer, a couple from New Hampshire who planned to use it as a vacation home. Cameron and Drew Crane. And no, Edith didn't know which was Mr. and which was Mrs. The Realtor had handled everything. She did know that Mr. was recently retired from owning some kind of business. Edith was a whiz when it came to island history, complicated family trees, selling things on eBay, and of course baking; but she could sometimes be vague as to other particulars.

Pix started down the short steps at the end of the deck heading in the direction of the noise. There was a path near the shoreline, well worn over the years, through the small stand of trees that separated the two properties. She stopped. Perhaps showing up dressed in well-worn PJs that originally belonged to one of her sons was not the way to make the best first impression on new neighbors. She dashed inside, threw on jeans and a tee shirt, shoved her feet into docksiders, and went back out. She wished she had a pie or some other offering to take, but the continuous noise meant serious cutting and Welcome Neighbor would have to wait.

A few feet from the property line she stopped again. In horror.

Mr. Crane had clear-cut a swath starting at the shoreline. He wasn't a large man, but he was wielding the biggest chain saw Pix had ever seen as though it was a bread knife. His wife was dragging the cuttings to a brush pile that looked like a prop for *The Towering Inferno.* They were both wearing the kind of headphones professionals wore, and Pix was forced to jump dangerously close to the man, frantically waving her arms in his face. Mrs. Crane put down the branches she had scooped up, but after briefly flicking his eyes in her direction, Mr. Crane kept on working. His wife walked over and tugged his sleeve. Pix could see both reluctance and irritation on his face as he turned the saw off.

"Yes?" he said.

"Hi, I'm Pix Miller. We live next door." She pointed behind her. When no one replied, she took a breath and soldiered on. "I'm a bit concerned about the clearing you are doing. The Shoreland Ordinance provides specific guidelines for what can and cannot be done in this zone. For instance, taking down a tree that size"—she pointed to a large pine already neatly cut into logs—"is not allowed."

"And your point is?" He had a crew cut—surely not done with the saw, but an equivalent—and the kind of face that was so bland you would never be able to describe it, say, after a robbery. Well, officer, he had two eyes, a nose, mouth . . . His wife was a bit more memorable. Short red curls were escaping from a craft brewery cap she was wearing. Good sign, Pix thought, then remembered that Ed Spofford had bought them in bulk and must have left a few in the cabin.

Mrs. Crane's face was shiny with sweat. Pix decided the best thing to do was invite them to her house for coffee. Mrs. Crane looked like she might want a break. Pix knew she had enough muffins left from the dozen Faith had brought over yesterday morning for the three of them.

"Why don't you come back with me now for some coffee and we can talk about all this?" she said brightly.

"Nothing to talk about," Mr. Crane said. "It's my land and I can do whatever I want with it. I'm exactly ten feet from the property line." Mrs. Crane had not uttered a word so far, but Pix did not think the smug smile that appeared on her face boded well.

"That may be so, but you are breaking other laws— and there are fines. Plus you are destroying both of our privacies!"

Mr. Crane's response took the form of switching the saw on and moving it menacingly close to Pix before limbing up a tree as far as he was able to reach, which was quite far. His wife got back to work, too. Pix started to stomp away and then remembered her phone was in her jeans. With a defiant glance at both of them she snapped photos of what they had done so far. She was so angry she felt sick to her stomach.

Back at the house she called Sam on the landline. The quixotic cell service on the island meant she could text him but not call. She sent all the photos as she waited for him to answer. He would still be asleep. When he picked up and heard her voice, it was a few seconds before she was able to assure him that she was fine—in body, but not in soul. It only took another few seconds for Sam to be as furious as she was. And this was before he saw the pictures arriving on his cell. Miles away in Aleford, his voice was so loud he sounded as if he were next to her. "Print out the regulations and go back there. No, don't go back there. We have no idea what this man is capable of." Pix knew they were both thinking scenes from a Stephen King novel. "Stay away. But call the Code Enforcement officer. Too bad Hubert's retired. Call him anyway if you can't get a hold of the new person this early."

Hubert Billings had been the island's Code Enforcement officer for more years than most current residents had been alive and knew every inch of it. He was fair, but strict. As he was wont to say, "Gone is gone." Whether it was a tree, acreage, or frontage. He had spoken highly of the woman who had taken his place after he told the town he flatly refused to keep going, having given in to their entreaties to stay just one more term too many times.

"I will," said Pix. "I'm going to the farmers' market in Granville and if I can't reach her by phone, I'll go to the town offices."

"Okay. I'll hit the road as soon as I can. The calls I have to make I can do pulling over. No one will be at work yet."

"But can you take the time off? I thought the case wasn't finished."

"All tied up yesterday. Thought I might come up for Fishermen's Day anyway."

Pix hung up, and despite the whine of the chain saw, which mimicked a never-ending dental drill, she felt better. Sam was coming. Sam and she would handle the Cranes, Cameron and Drew—he and she or she and he. Until then Pix wouldn't let herself think about what damage they would do before Sam's five-hour nonstop drive.

Chainsaw Massacre. Those were the only words for it.

Sanpere had a real farmers' market with vendors selling vegetables, fruits, eggs, cheese, smoked sausage, and other products of their own toil. No cardboard boxes shoved in the backs of pickups with places of origin far from Maine. The only craft items were wool from a woman who owned sheep and a man who made cutting boards and spoons from his woodlot. Therefore, it was smaller than some in the state, but as word had spread, Granville had had to open the ballfield behind the old elementary school now consolidated with Sanpere Village's to accommodate all the cars.

Over the years on Fridays, Faith and Pix left their families when they could to meet up at the Harbor Café before the market opened at ten. The late opening was to allow sellers who lived on the other side of the bridge a chance to get to Granville at the same time as island purveyors. Fair was fair.

Pix hadn't been able to reach the Code Enforcement officer, but she'd left a message. She'd also left a message for Hubert. Granville's Town Hall was next to the Café, and she popped in there to leave word, too, enjoying a few minutes venting with the sympathetic town clerk before meeting Faith.

Faith had scored a booth at the Café. "Sorry to keep you waiting," Pix said. "I'll explain in a minute. But first of all, how are you and how is Sophie?" Faith had called her after Earl and Sophie drove off, knowing Pix would hear the news about their grisly discovery—if she hadn't already—and worry. Pix had immediately walked over. She knew bringing any sort of food would be coals to Newcastle, so she arrived bearing a large bottle of Tanqueray gin. Tom pulled into the drive alone not long after. Amy was working late. Apparently, no one had wanted to disturb him with the news, so Pix had left it to Faith to fill him in. As she let herself out, she heard her friend say firmly, "I'm not going to be involved in any sleuthing."

Adding a splash of real cream to the Café's excellent coffee, Faith said, "I'm fine. Tom calmed down right away, and your gin helped. I owe you. I talked to Sophie this morning, and she's fine, too." Faith was sure that like her, Sophie must have been trying to push it all far to the back of her mind, answering "fine" to inquiries. And the one she uttered now, even to Pix, "A tragic thing, but we didn't know him. But you're not fine. What's going on? The wedding? Don't tell me Edgewood Farm has double-booked?" This, Pix had told Faith, was the kind of problem that kept her up at night no matter how many times she was assured it couldn't happen and had a contract to prove it.

"The wedding?" For a moment Pix had trouble remembering. What wedding? "Oh, no. Worse." And it was. If Mr. Crane didn't stop chopping, the Millers would be looking straight into his property and vice versa.

"Would you like me to go over and chain myself to his chain saw? Hug a tree?" Faith offered after hearing what had happened.

"I thought of doing both, but the noise stopped shortly after I left them. I mentioned fines, and maybe that was a deterrent. Although he also may have simply needed more gas."

"Let's go up to the market," Faith said.

Pix finished her grilled strawberry rhubarb muffin and her coffee—the fourth cup of the day, which might not have soothed her nerves, but holding the warm mug had been comforting.

It was much cooler than it had been all week, and the farmers' market was packed. The two women parted ways to stand in different lines. Pix figured that if Sam left Aleford when he said, he'd get to the island a little after noon or close to one o'clock with a stop. He'd want lunch. She knew he didn't consider salad of any kind a meal, so instead she got bread from Tinder Hearth and smoked gouda for grilled cheese. She stood in another long line for several kinds of Anne Bossi's delectable goat cheese and husband Bob Bowen's slab bacon and eggs. Dinner would be easy; she had steaks in the freezer and stood in another line for new potatoes, zucchini, peppers, and chard. She grew only patio tomatoes and herbs herself now, having declared the deer and slugs the winners years ago.

Seeing Faith in conversation with Sophie, she headed

over to them. Faith's trug was overflowing with purchases, including veggies Pix had no idea how to turn into something edible.

"I've been telling Sophie about your new neighbors from hell," Faith said.

"If you like, I can see whether there's some kind of injunction you can get quickly," Sophie offered. "I'm not familiar with Maine's environmental laws, but there must be a county or state tree warden's office. Unfortunately, I do know that people clear-cut and pay the relatively low fine. Still, there may be something about having to replant if it is too extensive."

"I'm relying on Sam," Pix said. "The only place he's ever lost his cool to my knowledge is on the tennis court. He should be here in a few hours and can reason with them."

Faith nodded. "I've seen him in action dealing with crazy-making questions at Town Meeting, so this should be a walk in the park—or woods." Sam was one of Aleford's selectmen.

Feeling better after both comments, Pix changed the subject. "I thought you two would be surrounded by groups of discreet individuals wanting to know all about yesterday."

"We have been a bit," Faith said, "but you know

how people are here. It's like when Julia Child used to visit her friend, and now Meryl Streep has rented on the Pressey Road. Live and let live."

"That's not to say there isn't a buzz," Sophie said. "Bob Bowen, never one to shy away from any topic, first commiserated and then related all the rumors of sightings of the victim on the island and the Hancock peninsula for a week or more—that he was here looking to buy property, make a movie, find a job, or compete in the codfish toss on Sunday. Take your pick."

Faith and Pix laughed. "And I'm sure that's only a few of the rumors," Faith said as she started to head for the ballfield where she had parked her car. Pix followed.

"Pix," Sophie said, putting her hand out to stop her. "Faith and Tom are coming for dinner tomorrow night. Why don't you and Sam join us?"

"I know he'd agree, so yes. And I can bring hors d'oeuvres. I bought a whole Fleur de Bossi, the cheese with herbs Anne makes that won best chevre in the state a while ago, and I'll pick up some smoked mussels at Clearwater Seafood."

She was glad to be free. Like the Fairchilds', Pix and Sam's social life in the summer was hectic as everyone took advantage of the proximity of friends who were spread out during the rest of the year.

"Great," Sophie said. "Uncle Paul wants to set some sailing dates with Sam, so he'll be very happy."

"See you tomorrow then," Pix said and went home to wait impatiently for her husband, a Daniel who would tame the lion in the den next door.

Sam didn't want to take the time to eat anything. Pix had returned to the sound of the chain saw and it was still going on when Sam arrived.

"I printed out the state handbook," Pix said, handing it to Sam. "Do you think it's better to go alone or should I come?" It was hard to think what the proper approach should be—nice couple living next door only concerned about a few, more than a few, trees or furious couple concerned about same. "I don't think I offended them, but you never know . . ." Pix really, really didn't want to confront the Cranes again, but if Sam thought it was best, of course she would.

"No, you've had a try, and we don't want them to feel threatened by two against, well, two but one problem. Give me the printout, and if I'm not back in an hour or you hear screams, call Earl."

Rather than take the shortcut, Sam walked up the road. He was back in ten minutes. It took five minutes to reach the cabin. The conversation must have been brief.

Pix quickly started lunch as Sam expressed his feelings using language never employed in front of the children, even though said children were now adults.

"He wants an open view," Sam seethed. "Oh, and he's Cameron, she's Drew. He said, 'Drew and I,' hence . . ."

"What can we do?" Pix realized she was letting the sandwiches burn and quickly took them out of the iron skillet.

"I don't know, honey. All I know is it will be expensive. We'll have to get Mainescape down here to put in a staggered row of evergreens twelve feet from the property line to be sure legally and maybe some sort of fencing up here by the house if that area is cleared, too." He sat down and eyed the oozing sandwich with obvious anticipation. "Now let's try to forget about it for now. Tell me about this body Faith and Sophie found."

"How did you find out?" Pix asked. "Oh, Tom, right?"

"Yes. He called last night. Wanted to know what I knew, which was nothing. However, I reassured him his wife wasn't getting mixed up in anything again or else you would have called me."

Pix gave him a brief description. She was distracted by the noise from next door. Sam's attempt at reasoning with them seemed to have only increased the volume.

"I just saw Sophie and Faith at the farmers' market,"

she said. "They seem to have put it all out of their minds. Sophie's invited us to The Birches for dinner tomorrow with Faith and Tom. Oh, she mentioned Paul wants to set a sailing date." As she'd predicted, Sam was pleased. "I'll call him right now," he said, "and see if he wants to go sailing during the day."

"He'd love that," Pix said. Delighted to have her husband sooner than expected, Pix cleaned up the kitchen while Sam called The Birches. Worries about the wedding and even the trees were pushed aside, and she looked forward to a lazy afternoon on the deck with a swim once the tide was high enough. Next door had grown blessedly quiet.

And then the noise started up again.

Sam stormed into the room. "Come on, let's go to Blue Hill and price out some trees! We can't stay here!"

Considerably out of pocket, but with assurances that the work would be done quickly, the Millers decided to stop at El El Frijoles in Sargentville on the way back to the island. Michele Levesque, the chef, and husband Michael Rossney had created a unique place—Mexican food goes Down East. Sam was addicted to their spicy lobster tacos, and Pix equally to their crab quesadillas. El El, as it was known, had a BYO policy and Sam had gone to the Eggemoggin

Country Store to pick up cold beers while Pix ordered. She remembered she'd forgotten to take the steaks out of the freezer and had a sudden yen for meat. She ordered the taco for Sam and a carne asada burrito for herself, deciding on an order of nachos to start. When Sam returned, they took the nachos—layers of beans, guacamole, crema, and salsa topped with melted cheese, a meal in itself—to the screened-in area with picnic tables behind the small restaurant. There were a few small tables inside, but it was beautiful out, and the screens took care of the mosquitos.

Sam took a long drink. "It will take a while for the trees to provide the privacy we had, but if we plant some low-lying junipers in between, it will look like a screen sooner." Pix nodded agreement—her mouth was full. She was feeling happier than she had for hours. Just getting away from the noisy reminder of the problem helped.

"Faith told me it took her a few summers before she got the El El Frijoles joke—L.L. Bean." Pix laughed. Sunday, the day after the wedding, Ursula was hosting a brunch at The Pines, and it had been her idea to hire El El's Michele to cater it. They would serve plenty of what was on the regular menu, but it would also be a showcase for Michele's considerable skills as a professional chef across many borders. El El's garden supplied much of their produce and the rest came from the local, high-quality sources they had discovered—even the black beans and, of course, the seafood.

By now the wedding really was as organized as Pix, mistress of the art, could make it. Faith was doing the rehearsal dinner Friday night, an old-fashioned clambake with a few of Faith's own touches. The guest list had expanded to include anyone who had already arrived from out of town in addition to the wedding party. The next afternoon following the outdoor—Pix said a silent prayer to the weather gods—ceremony at Edgewood, with its spectacular view across Penobscot Bay, there would be a sit-down dinner, catered by Blue Hill's Arborvine, followed by dancing. Samantha had told her mother that she and Zach were taking swing dance lessons at a dance studio in Cambridge. Reluctant at first, Zach had gotten into it and Samantha said now he was better than she was.

"I can't eat another thing," Pix said. "Home?"

"Absolutely—and I have a few ideas about what we can do for fun," Sam said with an attempt at a roguish smile.

The night was blissfully quiet. Since Cameron and Drew Crane were up with the lark, perhaps they went to bed with the birds as well.

The only thing that disturbed the Millers was the surprise arrival of their daughter and her fiancé shortly after one o'clock. The couple had crept in silently, but Pix—after years of fine-tuned awakenings if a child so much as sneezed—heard them, made sure they weren't hungry, and went back to sleep, elated to have so much of her family under one roof.

It wasn't a lark that awakened the Millers shortly after dawn the next morning, but loud banging on the front door and an angry voice shouting for them to get up. When Sam opened it, followed closely by Pix, he found their new neighbor on the other side.

"You bastard," Cameron Crane yelled at Sam.

"What are you talking about?" Sam was stunned. "I think you need to calm down!"

"Oh, you don't know what I'm talking about, do you?" Cameron grabbed Sam's arm and pulled him toward the drive, where Drew was sitting in a large Mercedes 4x4. "Get in."

"Now just a minute, pal," Sam said, wrenching his arm free.

Pix had never seen her husband so mad. Hastily she said, "Sam, put some shoes on and we'll go see whatever it is that's upsetting Mr. Crane." Somehow saying Cameron sounded too friendly, and he was frightening her. She pushed that feeling away and let anger take its place. Standing very straight, she said in a chilling tone, "We can walk over to your house. There are plenty of openings now."

As she'd intended, it was a red flag. The man looked as if he was going to deck her.

"Let's get this over with," he snarled, turned around and got into the car, backing out of their drive fast, scattering gravel.

"What's going on?" Zach came down the stairs. "Sounded like a fight."

"Go back to bed, dear," Pix said. "We'll explain later."

"Okay, but if you need me . . ." Zach rubbed an eye.

"If we do, we'll come back. We just have to go next door for a bit."

Pix followed Sam on foot down the path, and they arrived before the Cranes. "What on earth could have happened?" Pix wondered as the car pulled in.

"I have no idea, but this is not a person I ever want to have any dealings with and certainly not as a neighbor. We just have to wait and see what's triggered this, then keep a distance."

What triggered it was soon clear as Cameron virtually dragged them to the shed Ed Spofford had put up years ago for his tools and a small workbench. With his wife by his side, Cameron flung open the door and pointed to the cement floor. His chain saw was lying in a slick pool of something and covered with the substance as well. He didn't need to point at the cause, but he did, almost foaming with rage.

The floor was strewn with empty containers of Gorilla Glue.

Chapter Three

Both Millers were aghast. "You can't seriously believe we had anything to do with this!" Sam exclaimed.

Cameron Crane folded his arms in front of his chest. "And you can't seriously believe that last night some random passerby happened upon our shed armed with the stuff and thought destroying a chain saw would be a fun thing to do. Whereas you and your wife"—he made it sound dubious, Pix thought indignantly, as if she were something else—"had every reason in your perverted minds for committing this act of vandalism. I've called the police and my lawyer. That saw was an Echo thirty-six inch and put me back almost nine hundred bucks. I'll be expecting the replacement immediately."

Pix watched in alarm as Sam's face turned bright red. "Now just a minute! I'm not paying a dime and you can tell that to your lawyer. Judging by the way you've acted toward us, I'm sure there are plenty of people out there who would like to do this kind of thing to you!"

The windowless shed was feeling very cramped, Pix thought, even without the monster chain saw taking up room in pride of place. Plus the smell of the glue was nauseating. "Let's go home, Sam," she said. There was no point in continuing the conversation.

"Don't go far," Crane shouted after them. "The police are going to want to talk to you!"

"There goes that trip to Paris," Sam said sarcastically. He started to turn back, but Pix kept a firm grip on his elbow and moved him along.

Out on the road she said, "I think we'd better call Earl right away."

Going back to sleep was impossible, so she made a large pot of coffee and batter for blueberry pancakes. Zach and Samantha would sleep in, given how late they arrived, but Sam needed sustenance now. She was too upset to eat but poured herself a large mug of coffee.

"We know we didn't do it," she said to her husband,

who was sitting at the kitchen table staring gloomily out at the cove. "So who did?"

"They haven't been on the island long, but I'm sure with his attitude he's managed to piss off any number of people. You can get that glue at Barton's, although there was such a lot of it maybe it was from the Home Depot in Ellsworth." Barton's was the lumberyard and hardware store located between Granville and Sanpere Village. It stocked anything you could possibly need, but not in large quantities. "You said he started cutting early. Sound carries over water, especially that kind. Could have been someone on the other Point or farther."

Pix set a stack of pancakes and warm syrup in front of him.

"We don't have to find out who did it. The police will, and it won't be a secret long on this island. Eat your breakfast."

Sam shook his head. "No matter what, he'll never believe it wasn't us. Damn. We should have bought the place from the Spoffords ourselves. But I'd always pictured someone like them buying it, and it's nice to have neighbors."

Pix sighed. She'd been thinking the same thing since her confrontation with the Cranes yesterday. "It's annoying—more than annoying—now, but we'll plant and in a few years we won't see them and before that we *really* won't see them."

"So no inviting them for dinner?" Sam reached for his wife and pulled her onto his lap. "No bringing over crabs when we have too many from Ed Ricks?"

Ed Ricks, Dr. Edwin Ricks, was a well-known New York City psychiatrist, quoted in the *Times* and elsewhere, and often appearing on PBS. A few years ago he'd given up his practice and retired year-round to his Sanpere summer home. He had a license to put out a few traps and always dropped off the crabs that he caught with the lobsters, knowing they were favorites with the Millers and too much work to pick for other friends. Pix could not envision the Cranes at this time-consuming task. They seemed to prefer immediate results.

"I wonder what Ed would make of Cameron?" Pix said.

"If he wants to meet the man, it will have to be on other than our turf, what is left of it," Sam said. "And speaking of turf, I'd swear that lawn was new sod. Did you see there were no twigs or weeds marring the surface? Looked like a golf course, or maybe AstroTurf."

"The only flowers I saw were impatiens by the front

door in terra-cotta pots—fakes. I can always tell, no mold or chips." Pix tended a wide perennial garden along the front of their house but let nature supply the rest of the floral landscaping. After the lupine, the uncultivated lawn was covered with daisies and then black-eyed Susans. Queen Anne's lace was coming in now. They mowed occasionally to keep ticks away but tried to steer around the clumps of flowers. Pix liked marking summer's progression by looking out the window at what was growing. Goldenrod and wild asters marked its end. "I haven't been able to figure what Mrs. Crane, Drew, might be like. She hasn't said a single word so far, and her only facial expression has been the kind of smarmy smile that girl who used to bully Samantha in middle school had."

"*He's* certainly a bully, so two of a kind," Sam said, mopping up the syrup on his plate with the last bite of his pancakes. "I'm going to go check online what recourse we may have. Not about the chain saw but about reporting the clear-cutting and possible fines. We've made an enemy so might as well follow through."

"So nice to have legal counsel close at hand," Pix said, kissing the top of her lawyer husband's head. "Give a shout when the kids are up. I'm going to take Arty outside. Don't clean up. I'll do it all at once." The Millers were down to one beloved golden retriever,

Arthur or Arty. Pix hoped to have him by her side and at the foot of the bed for many more years.

"'When the "kids" wake up'? I don't think we can call them that anymore," Sam said.

"Well, the bride and groom then," Pix retorted. All three of her children and their significant others would always be "kids" in her mind.

Two pills. That was it. She shook them out of the vial into her hand and saw that it was trembling. She made a tight fist.

Two round white pills.

Nowhere near enough, but enough to make do for now. She closed her eyes and felt the tears. Hot tears that streamed down her cheeks.

He'd noticed she was losing weight, but she said it was so she'd look good in her summer clothes. Like a bathing suit. She almost laughed aloud. No way was she going swimming.

Her mother was worried that she was doing too much, because she was so tired all the time. Well yes, she was doing too much. She started to laugh again. Up. Down. Sunshine and tears. She'd never been that kind of girl. Miss Responsible. Steady as a rock.

She was alone in the house. It would be okay.

There was plenty of time. She could already feel the rush. Feel herself relax like a ragdoll. Soon all the bad stuff would go away. All the thoughts of the kind of person she really was. Poof. Gone like magic. Gone like her own personal Tinkerbell had waved a wand and sprinkled her with fairy dust.

She'd been sitting on the side of the bed and lay down, slowly stretching out on top of the quilt her grandmother had made for them. Wedding Ring. That was the pattern.

She opened her fingers. Only two. She had to get more. That meant going off-island. Too dangerous to score here.

The bad thoughts were starting to come. They were like snakes. Horrible snakes that wrapped around her brain.

She took the pills dry.

Sophie was sitting on the porch, watching the start of what promised to be a stunning sunset and waiting for everyone to arrive. Uncle Paul was taking a shower—getting "gussied up" he'd told her. Sam Miller had called early that morning inviting them for a sail. Sophie had declined, but Paul had enjoyed a long trip out to North Haven with Sam and Zach. Before he went up to change, Paul had given Sophie a quick version of the sticky chain saw incident, and she was sure she'd hear a full account once the Millers arrived.

So many angry people, Sophie thought, pushing world and national events firmly away. The island was never one big happy family, but the various groups—natives, people from away, and summer people—coexisted in a kind of surface harmony. But this summer she'd noticed some cracks. Not the same kind of mingling at the parade or chatting about the weather in line at the market between someone who had come out of a pickup and someone from a BMW. A local she didn't know yelled at her for parking in the post office lot, pointing to her out-of-state plates. Sophie had held out her post office box keys and started to say the family had had a box just about forever, but the woman got in her own car and slammed the door. Sophie had talked about it with Will on one of their late-night chats. He'd said it was the same everywhere and compared life now to a kind of large-scale road rage. Sometimes, he had said, you really were cut off, but mostly the rude gestures were because of what else was going on—nothing that had anything to do with the rules of the road. Worry, fear, not enough time or money. She'd agreed.

And now here was another island mystery—the title not *Who Drowned in the Lily Pond?* but *Who Glued the Chain Saw to the Shed Floor?* It would be funny if it were happening to people she didn't know.

As for the man in the Lily Pond, she had lied to Faith, Will, and others. She wasn't fine. Not now and not during the two long nights after her failed attempt to bring him to life. When she did drift off to sleep, she woke at once. The adder that slithered down his arm had slithered into her dreams. She could no longer picture what his face had looked like, but she could feel the texture of his hair as she gripped it, trying to breathe for him. Long strands. Down to his collarbones. Although wet, fine as silk. His eyes were closed. She remembered that and was glad. No stare to haunt her waking and sleeping thoughts. Will had sensed her true feelings and pressed to come. She had amped up her objections. The weekend would be tantalizingly short. She was surrounded by friends. She was fine.

I am fine, Sophie told herself again and put on a smile as her uncle came through the door.

"You cannot make this stuff up," Sam said. Pix was driving, so the martini Paul had offered—and he mixed the old-fashioned James Bond kind—plus the Peak Summer Ales Sam was having with dinner had created his jovial mood.

"What did Earl say when you called him?" Sophie

asked. She'd been putting the finishing touches to the seafood risotto and arugula salad with grilled pears that was the main course and had missed the law enforcement part of the story.

Pix picked up the thread. "Earl got the voice mail we left this morning and I spoke to him this afternoon when he called back. The Cranes had immediately phoned the sheriff's office, but Earl was in Ellsworth at the courthouse, so he didn't speak with them. Whoever it was took down the details, and said someone would come when they had an officer free and advised them to get a lock for their shed. Then they called twice more and their lawyer once in the next hour, so somebody drew the short straw and came down. Given what has been happening all over the peninsula, a vandalized chain saw was not a top priority on the department's list. If one that expensive had been stolen, that would have been another thing—and who on earth would pay that much for one? Anyway, Earl had relayed our message to the patrolman who went to the house. He took photos and even dusted for prints at Crane's insistence—there were none, which had them accusing us all the more, apparently."

"Pix is such a lady. She always wears gloves," Tom teased.

"Go on," Sophie said. "Then what?"

"Then nothing," Sam said. "Except the Cranes have now been reported by us and the sheriff's office for clear-cutting. The sheriff's office also reported them to the Bangor office of the Department of Environmental Protection for possible infractions. Guess there might have been some Cameron Crane attitude going on." He sounded gleeful.

Zach turned to Samantha, who was sitting next to him. "And you told me this was a peaceful place. I believe your words when you first told me about Sanpere were 'island of calm.'"

"It is," she protested. "Mostly. I mean, it's like anywhere else. Things happen. But calmly. They happen calmly. Look at the way my parents are taking this. Other people in other places would be suing the Cranes for slander or worse by now."

"Calm it is. A paradise. No problem." Zach put his arm around her. "And if you're not going to finish that risotto, I will."

"In your dreams!" she said and then put a big spoonful on his plate. "But no sharing my fried clams tomorrow on the pier. Or the fries and onion rings."

"Children, children," Paul said. "I happen to know for certain that there will be more than enough food. Marge told me this morning that the Rebekahs have been shucking mountains of clams and slicing a truckload of onions and potatoes for vats of chowder and the wickedly good food that is so bad for you."

"Are there that many women named Rebekah on the island?" Zach asked.

His future wife punched him lightly on the arm. "You went to the Blue Hill Fair with me last year and had strawberry shortcake. I know for sure I told you the women who cooked all those biscuits, hulled berries, and whipped cream were the Rebekahs, women's branch of the Odd Fellows!"

"It's all coming back." Zach did not sound convincing.

"What is?" Faith asked as she came through the door with a pan of Blueberry Buckle (see recipe, page 331) and a bowl of ice cream.

"Don't ask," Tom said. "If what you're bringing is what I think it is, it needs to be eaten immediately."

Faith laughed. "It's Blueberry Buckle, and I almost make it for the name alone! But what I think you're really talking about is the bowlful of the Ice Cream Lady's Madagascar Vanilla. And yes, both have to be eaten immediately while one is warm and one cold. Sophie, cut the cake and I'll serve the ice cream."

For years the Ice Cream Lady was another island mystery. A good one. Her flavors changed with what was in season—strawberries, blueberries, blackberries, peaches—but she always maintained a few classics like the vanilla, a dense dark chocolate, peppermint stick, and ginger. She was finally identified but still preferred a low profile and stuck to small batches at only a few stores. Happily the IGA was one.

After dessert, everyone helped clear and no one wanted coffee. The women shooed all the men from the kitchen back out onto the porch so they could talk about things of little interest to their male counterparts and vice versa. There wouldn't be port and cigars outdoors, but Paul did have some single malt on offer. In the kitchen while they were cleaning up, the women sipped mint tea courtesy of Pix's herb garden.

"Faith showed me a picture of your dress," Sophie said to Samantha. "It's a dream. I loved my dress, too, and they have a custom in Savannah and other parts of the South where you get to wear it on other occasions during that first year—and even longer if you push it. And Pix," she added, "yours is gorgeous, too. Just the right soft green for your lovely dark locks." Mother and daughter were brunettes, as Ursula—now snowy white—had been, too.

"I think my mother will steal the show—aside from the bride and those adorable children," Pix said. "She went to her lady at Saks and found a pale gold beaded cocktail dress, ballerina length, that looks like something Princess Grace would have worn during her movie career."

"What do you think Millicent will wear?" Samantha said. "I haven't dared ask her. I hope it doesn't smell of mothballs."

Sophie had heard about Millicent Revere McKinley, who was as much a part of Aleford as the town green. A distant descendant of the famous rider, she lived in a small clapboard house strategically placed with a sightline down Main Street. Claiming septuagenarian status for the last ten plus years, she was spry—and the arbiter of all things proper—in her opinion. "It's Miss McKinley, not Ms. Thank you very much." She was Ursula's closest friend and equally attached to the Millers and Fairchilds. Sophie loved hearing the tale about what happened after Faith dared to ring the Revere-cast bell in the Old Belfry her first year in Aleford. The fact that Faith, with baby Benjamin in a Snugli, had just discovered the still-warm corpse of a parishioner there cut no mustard with Millicent. In her very vocal opinion, Faith could have sped down the hill and screamed. The bell was tolled only on Patriots' Day and for the death of a president or of a descendant of those lucky enough to bear arms against the Redcoats that April day. Thinking about it now, she thought how New England it was and also that she couldn't wait to meet Millicent in person!

"She wore a kind of long velvet dress that may have been purple once to Ursula's eightieth," Pix said tentatively. "I think it may have been her mother's, judging from the style. Crushed velvet is in now, but I think Millicent's did not start out that way."

"I'll talk to Granny," Samantha offered. "She'll know what to do. Where is she tonight? I would have gone over to The Pines earlier but assumed I'd see her here."

"Her calendar is more filled than ours," Pix said. "Tonight she's at a friend's over in Sedgwick. It's the woman's camp reunion weekend—Camp Four Winds. Mother never went there nor did I, but she's always been considered an official Old Girl."

"How did Arlene like the matron of honor dress?" Faith asked Samantha. "I can't imagine she didn't love it—and look great in it. We saw her mother and Kylie the other day. Kylie is growing up so fast. It feels like we were just at that baby shower."

Samantha finished drying the plate in her hand. "Mike had to work and Kylie was running a low fever. Arlene's mother was working, too, so Arlene needed to stay home. I offered to bring the dress over but she didn't want me to catch anything if Kylie turned out to have that flu bug that's going around."

"There's always a flu bug going around in New England," Faith said. "No matter what time of year. Nobody ever had the flu in Manhattan when I was growing up."

Tom walked in on his wife's remark. "All the flu bugs were probably killed by exhaust fumes."

"Time to go?" she asked, exasperated as always for his lack of appreciation for any apples, Big or small, except New England ones.

"Yes, you know me and Scotch. My eyelids are getting heavy."

"Cheap date," she told the others and went to say good night to the men on the porch.

The Millers, Zach, and Samantha left soon after. Sophie joined Paul outside. It was still so warm she was tempted to swim. On a clear night like this the stars appeared as if an unseen hand had upended an overflowing astral basin. There was scarcely room among the points of light for the velvety dark.

Paul handed her a glass with a finger of Scotch. "Drink this. And I want you to sleep tonight. If you can't, come get me. We'll sit out here."

She reached across and took her uncle's hand, obediently sipped the drink, and felt its warmth travel down through her body. Maybe she *would* sleep. A star shot across the night sky. She closed her eyes and made a wish.

Pix was surprised to see Arty coming down the stairs the moment the kitchen door closed behind them. Normally the dog would be snoring softly at the foot of their bed. She went over, bent down, and stroked his soft head, noting how many more white hairs there were on his snout. "Doggy nightmare? What's the matter, sweetheart?" When she stood up, Arty promptly took her dangling sweater sleeve in his mouth and pulled her toward the stairs. Everyone laughed.

"Oh no, I think Timmy's in the well," Zach said.

"I guess I'd better go get him settled," Pix said. "I'll be down in a minute."

She was down in less than a minute with Arty at her heels. "There's a strange woman asleep in the guest room! Strange, I mean, as in I have no idea who she is."

"I'm assuming it's not Goldilocks," Sam said. "And I don't think we need to count the teaspoons if the perp stayed on the premises."

They all headed up the stairs quietly with Pix leading the way. She opened the door and they saw that there was indeed a woman fast asleep under a sheet and light summer blanket in the spindle bed. "Never saw her before," Sam whispered. "And even if I had I wouldn't recognize her with all that goop on her face and the mask."

Samantha poked her father. "It's an eye mask and moisturizer. Lots of women use a night cream."

"Not mine," he said. "Do most women wear that kind of eye thing, too? Never got that kind on a plane."

The eye mask was pink satin decorated with exaggerated long sequin lashes. Besides that, the woman had a kind of turban wrapped around her head, presumably to keep from getting bed hair.

"Why are we whispering?" Pix asked. "I don't want to seem inhospitable, but I think we should wake her up, ask her who she is and what she's doing here."

"Let her sleep," Zach said in a weary tone. "It's my mother."

After Zach's statement, Pix closed the door gently behind and they all filed downstairs.

Zach sat down on the sofa and Samantha snuggled close to her fiancé, putting her head on his shoulder. He stroked his fiancée's hair, then sat up straight. "You know my family situation. You could call me an orphan except my parents are both very much alive," he said. "Marrying into a family like yours is kind of like a dream. Samantha would be enough. But gaining sibs and parents-in-law like you is amazing—I'm getting sappy, but seriously, I didn't know what I had been missing. You don't miss what you never had. I last saw my father at my high school graduation because he happened to be in the area. Before that there never seemed to be the right time to go out to the coast and meet his new wife and their kids. Particularly since he wasn't exactly sending me a plane ticket. I'm a reminder of a very acrimonious marriage and worse divorce. As for my mother, she always made sure I was in the right boarding school and at the right summer camp, so problem solved year-round. She'd swoop in unexpectedly—like now—and then take off. I have an email address for her and at various times addresses for apartments she's owned in New York, London, and Paris, but I don't have an address for her at the moment. She could be living anywhere. She was in Mongolia at Christmas in some sort of luxurious yurt. I know because she sent a postcard. Once I turned twenty-one a trust—don't think millions—kicked in and has kept me in ramen."

Pix immediately got up and sat on his other side. "I knew you didn't have much contact with your parents, but I had no idea! Samantha never said." All her maternal juices were flowing. "You poor boy!"

He gave her a somewhat crooked smile. "I guess

I turned out all right though. Thanks to friends, especially the Fairchilds. Growing up on my own has made me stronger I think. Anyway, there wasn't much choice. At least my parents made sure I got a great education. The big question now is what is Alexandra Kohn doing here and how did she track me down? We have different last names, by the way—she changed *Cohen* to *K-O-H-N* for some reason. Pretty sure she didn't start life as 'Alexandra' either, but her birth certificate would be the last thing she'd let me see. She's in her thirties, which would make her about five when I was born. Now how about a beer and Scrabble? I play better when I'm slightly buzzed."

"Great idea," Sam said, standing up. "I'll get the beers and—" Whatever he was about to say was cut off by the sound of footsteps coming down the stairs. And they weren't doggy ones.

Everybody froze as the woman they had just seen asleep stood in front of them, hands on her hips. She was wearing an elaborately embroidered fuchsia silk dressing gown, and the sleep mask had been pushed up on top of her forehead, but rather than incongruous, the unsmiling figure was imposing.

"Do you have any idea the hell of a time I've had finding you, Zachary?" She didn't even pause for breath. "I get a computer invitation to your wedding—no earlier word that you were planning to get married. And not a proper invitation in the mail. What will my friends think?"

There *were* proper engraved invitations that the Millers had sent out. The evites went to Zach's and Samantha's friends, who were far more used to this form of communication. Zach hadn't had a snail mail address for his mother, he'd told Pix, so he'd sent the evite with a note about Samantha and her family, also reminding his mother that he had mentioned Samantha a while ago as a serious girlfriend. His mother either had not read it, had forgotten it, or was choosing to ignore its existence, possibly all three. He sent the formal invitation with a note to his father, whose address he knew, and received regrets with an Amazon gift card almost by return mail.

"I didn't have—" Zach started to protest, but his mother cut him off, actually putting her hand up, as if stopping traffic.

"We'll discuss this later." Her eyes swept the room, as if wondering who the interlopers into this one-on-one conversation were. "Fortunately I had your apartment's address, so I went straight there from the plane—don't even ask about that nightmare trip—they only had business class available not first. Your roommate told me you were on this island, so back to the airport I went and I ended up in Banger or some such place. No address for what I presume is the bride's family's house." There was another sweep of the eyes, but this time slower, taking in all three Millers and the rustic cottage with what could only be called mild distaste. "I had the cab take me to the venue on the invitation—a farm! What could you have been thinking?—and the people there directed me here. No one was in obviously and I'm terribly jet-lagged, so I'll be going back to sleep. Just coffee, dark roast, and wheat toast in the morning. Good night."

Zach jumped up. "Wait a minute. The wedding isn't for several weeks. What are you doing here?"

His mother sighed deeply, walked over, and patted her son on the shoulder. "To plan a proper one, of course."

She left bewilderment, anxiety, and the fragrance of Patou's Joy in the air.

It never rained on Fishermen's Day. At least not in the island's collective memory, which was extremely reliable when it came to weather. On this sunny Sunday morning, Samantha was sitting at the kitchen table with her future mother-in-law, wishing desperately that Zach or her parents were there, too. Her mother was already at the pier helping out with the festivities, which would start at ten o'clock. Zach and her father were grabbing some time on the boat polishing the brightwork, a never-ending chore. No one had expected Alexandra to be up this early.

"Alexandra." She'd immediately told Samantha to call her that, striding into the room dressed for the Hamptons or maybe the Riviera in snowy white capris, a turquoise silk shirt, wedged espadrilles that added inches to her height, and Jackie O sunglasses perched on her perfectly coiffed chin-length streaked blond hair—not the work of Supercuts and Clairol. A heavy gold-link necklace and several similar bracelets completed the look. She was carrying what Samantha knew was a Birkin bag. Whatever Alexandra was doing at night, and other times, to enhance her appearance was working. She was a striking woman who seemed much younger than Samantha knew she must be.

"'Mother Kohn' sounds like a patent medicine," Alexandra had added. "And I haven't been Mrs. Kohn for a very long time."

Samantha had been cleaning the cast-iron skillets they'd used for eggs and bacon. Alexandra had immediately observed that Samantha and Zachary might want to update their *batterie de cuisine* on their registry. "I'm assuming you have cookware listed? Calphalon and Creuset or my friends in Paris can send from Dehillerin," she'd said as Samantha hastily made toast and a fresh pot of coffee. Alexandra had looked on approvingly as Samantha ground beans, only asking whether they were fair trade or not. "Zachary can tell you that I am very concerned about the planet."

Now they were across from each other and Alexandra was grilling—there was no other word for it—her future daughter-in-law. Where had she gone to high school? What college? Job history? Why did she leave Manhattan for Boston? Why was she still living at home in—what was the place? Aleford? How many siblings did she have? What did they do? On and on and on until Samantha felt as if her skin were being peeled away layer by layer to reveal every fault, every defect minor or major. Shouldn't Zach's mother be happy that he was happy? About to marry the woman he loved? And simply accept her future daughter-in-law with open arms? Extremely well-toned and tanned ones Samantha noted.

Just when she thought she was going to crack and confess to shoplifting a bottle of glitter nail polish in sixth grade, Zach and her dad returned.

"Hi, honey," Samantha said gratefully. "Your mother and I have been having a, um, nice talk."

"Good," Zach said, and away from his mother's gaze, he raised his eyebrows and Samantha nodded, her mouth a tight line. "Well, Mom . . ." She didn't care for that name—"too Brady Bunch"—and had suggested Mater or Mother, even "Alexandra," but Zach had stuck with "Mom," claiming a tiny piece of his own territory. "We're all heading out to Fishermen's Day down on the pier in Granville if you'd like to join us. Granville is one of the largest lobster ports in the Northeast and every year they celebrate the industry and honor the fishermen."

"Sounds charming, but we don't have time," Alexandra said, pulling a Smythson leather notebook from her bag. "First of all, the place. Such a miracle, but I was able to pull some strings and get the Taj in Boston for the reception. The ceremony could be at any number of churches if you must, but also right there—so convenient. I assume you've already got some sort of dress"—she made it sound like a little number run up on the Millers' Singer—"but again, helps to have friends. Jenny, Jenny Packham, can send a toile as soon as I get your measurements and she'll do a custom rush job or Vera will. I think I'll have Vera do my gown and I can take your mother with me for hers. Men in morning coats I assume, unless you want an evening wedding and black tie? Really it would be best to move it to Manhattan. Florists to die for. Caterers, too. Glorious Food does such yummy things, but I suppose it has to be in Boston . . ." She was scribbling away as Zach sat down at the kitchen table next to her.

"Mom. Our wedding is all planned. For here. On the island. Everyone will be clothed just fine. The food will be delicious, and Mary, a professional gardener here, is taking care of the flowers. All you have to do is show up. I'm glad you'll be there." He put his arm around her, but she stiffened.

"You are my only child and I assume this is going to be your only wedding. I'm sure once I tell Samantha's mother the kind of wedding her daughter could have, one every little girl dreams of—you're very pretty, dear, and will make a lovely bride—all will agree that we need to change the plans."

Sam Miller had been listening quietly, standing away from everyone, and now he walked over to Alexandra. "We are happy to finally meet you and happy to have you as a guest, starting with the festival today. I'm sorry you had trouble getting here and that we couldn't welcome you properly last night. As for the wedding, I know my wife will enjoy telling you the details about what has been arranged."

Alexandra was savvy enough to recognize a stalemate when she saw one, equally savvy at knowing what biding one's time could accomplish. She looked at her son's intended. No girl in her right mind would turn down a wedding gown from Jenny Packham or Vera Wang, same for a reception at the Taj, formerly Boston's historic Ritz-Carlton.

She switched on a high-voltage smile. "Lead me to this fish thing, then. Just so long as I don't have to actually catch one."

Traditionally Fishermen's Day started with a moment of silence for those in peril and those lost at sea, following which individual fishermen were inducted into the Hall of Fame. The honorees had spent many, often colorful, years on the waters of Penobscot Bay. Occasionally the award was posthumous. As Faith, Tom, and Sophie walked past the photos posted on the fencing that lined one side of the pier they recognized, and missed, old friends.

The serious part over but not forgotten, the day started with a pet show ranging from tiny kittens to Great Danes with guinea pigs, hamsters, and the occasional iguana as well.

"It feels so odd not to have a kid with us," Faith said. "No one to cheer for in the watermelon eating or fish face contests."

"I'll enter," Tom offered, making an exaggerated one.

"I think not, Reverend. Too realistic!" Faith joked. "Besides, I would not be able to resist the temptation to text a photo to the church secretary for the next parish newsletter."

"The Wacky Row Boat Races are at noon," Sophie said. "Samantha and I are entered. I haven't seen her though. I hope she and Zach didn't decide to leave early."

"Who's rowing and who's signaling?" Tom asked. The race was aptly named, with the rower blindfolded and guided around a short course in the harbor only by his or her partner. It seemed simple enough, especially for an experienced rower. Just follow the commands, right, left, straight; but the roar of the crowd complicated the task. People shouted encouragement for their favorite team and made distracting comments like "My grandma could beat you without oars, just paddling with her hands!" The Fairchilds' neighbor on the Point, Freeman Hamilton, had told them years ago the trick he'd devised with his sister—a tap on one knee for right, double tap for left, and piercing whistle for straight.

The pier was packed, and Faith felt herself relax into the day as she greeted friends, stopped at booths set up by various island organizations, stocked up on Karen Cousins's beautiful photo cards, and bought, always in vain, still more quilt raffle tickets. One of these years . . . The air was filled with tantalizing smells—the chowder and fried seafood, fried dough, and kettle corn. At the very end of the pier people of all ages were dancing to the tunes of the Merry Mariners, who were set up on a flatbed trailer. The Mariners were known for their versatility, and so far Faith had heard and watched the twist, the macarena, and now an enthusiastic group of line dancers in synch to "Achy Breaky Heart." She was tempted to join, but her tendency to turn the opposite way from everyone else kept her where she was, humming along instead.

"Samantha!" Sophie cried. "I was afraid you had left. It's okay, though. The races haven't started yet."

"No way, this is our year," Samantha said, but Faith thought she didn't look too excited at the prospect. This was not the cheerful bride telling jokes at dinner the night before.

Sophie picked up on it, too. "What's wrong? We don't have to do this. No problem."

Samantha's eyes filled with tears. "Zach's mother was at the house when we got back last night. Asleep in the guest room, but she got up and then . . ." Samantha gulped. "We had a big talk this morning, just the two of us—or rather she talked and I listened. She's over there with Zach, Mom, and Dad. She's drinking a Diet Coke." Samantha pointed out a stylish woman Faith had noticed earlier, wondering how she had strayed so far from Seal Harbor on MDI, Martha Stewart country.

"She wants to move the wedding to Boston! To the Taj. She's 'pulled strings.'" Samantha made the motion with her fingers. "Everything has to be changed. Even my dress. She's ordering a toile and rush job from Jenny Packham, you know that British celeb designer, and 'Vera,'"—she made the quotation marks again—"as backup."

"But, sweetie," Faith said, putting an arm around Samantha. "It's *your* wedding. All the plans are set for here and it's going to be perfect. Nice of her to take an interest at last, but don't worry." Faith was inwardly furious. So Zach's mother, who couldn't be bothered to see him or even be in touch much for all these years, had decided to come steal his show.

Samantha was shaking her head. "I hope you're right, but you haven't met her. She's one of those un-stoppable type of people, a tsunami in the making. My dad tried to tell her the wedding plans were fixed and not going to be changed, but she wasn't buying it. Said she'd talk to Mom."

Faith hugged her. "Oh, I think Pix will be more than a match for her—and I'll be standing right next to her."

While they had been talking Sophie had been looking back and forth from Faith and Samantha to the other group, with Alexandra very much in the fore-front. "I think this may be a time for reinforcements," she said.

"Reinforcements?" Faith asked.

"Babs. I think this is a job for *my* mother."

Chapter Four

C orrectly divining that his mother would not be a fan of the two-person codfish toss—an occasional fish missed its intended recipient and veered into the crowd—Zach hooked his arm through hers and suggested they walk to the far end of the pier to look at the view of the Fox Island Thoroughfare and islands beyond. It earned him a big smile.

"I haven't had a chance to talk with you at all. Is there someplace I could get a latte?" Alexandra said. "I need some more caffeine."

"I think you're going to have to get your boost from the view. It's pretty spectacular."

They walked past the booths, some of which were already packing up. The only event left was the Granville versus Sanpere Village tug-of-war. Rivalry between the two towns had existed since each was incorporated. Granville had always been home to most of the island's industry—the quarries, sardine cannery, fishing fleet—while Sanpere Village's was a brief heyday around the time of the Civil War with lumber mills and easily accessible schooner landings along Eggemoggin Reach. For the most part the rivalry was a friendly one, but it flared up from time to time, most recently a few years back when the state had ordered the consolidation of the schools at a site in Sanpere Village instead of Granville.

"You know," Zach said, "that Samantha and I are driving to Boston in about an hour. I thought you could come, too. It would give you a chance to get to know Samantha better, and you have friends in the area you must want to see. Or we could take you to the airport if you wanted to go to New York."

Zach felt his arm tighten in hers. Tighten a lot. "Oh Zachary, that won't work at all. I had a long chat with Samantha this morning and she is very *nice* I'm sure, like her parents—although I must say her father seems like one of those men used to getting his way. Of course he's a lawyer."

Zach could feel his temper start to rise. The tone his mother had given the word *nice* was not nice. It was dismissive. It was a put-down. It was maddening. He wanted to tell his mother what an extraordinary person Samantha was, and her whole incredible family. How he was the luckiest guy in the world. In the universe.

"Samantha's—" But before he could get more than a word out, Alexandra cut him off.

"Oh, Zachary, you don't have to say a thing. She's your choice and you're old enough to make one. Certainly the phrase *making one's bed and having to lie in it* is apt here. No." She pulled her arm away from his. "I'm staying here. It's my job to see to it that the wedding is done properly. It's not always about you. A wedding is for the parents as well. To introduce the new couple to their friends and family and establish ties."

Zach felt like one of those cartoon characters with visible steam erupting from his ears. "First of all, when it comes to family, for all intents and purposes I only have one parent. Dad, whom I last saw before I was shaving I think, declined immediately. Both of your parents are gone, you don't have any siblings I've ever heard about or even cousins. Next, I have never met any of your friends. And last, Mom"—he stretched the disliked moniker out—"our wedding plans are not going to be altered in the slightest."

In front of them the late afternoon sun was streaming down, creating a mosaic of large and small islands surrounded by liquid gold water. His mother was silent, and for a moment Zach thought he'd won.

She took his arm again. "We'll see. Now we should be joining the others. I don't want to seem rude."

The moment Pix saw Zach's face she knew his very obvious plot to squelch his mother's grandiose plans had failed. Not that Pix had thought he would succeed. The tug-of-war was over—Tom and Sam had signed up to pull for Sanpere Village and were now crowing about the team's victory, the first in years. It had seemed to her that both teams were lacking the younger muscle usually displayed. Twentysomethings and even teens had dominated the teams in the past. Where were they all?

Pix heard Samantha call out, "Hey, Mike." The crowds were on their way up the steep hill to the ballfield where the cars were parked. She saw Arlene's husband, Mike, with their daughter, Kylie, on his shoulders. She was closer, so she quickened her pace and reached him first.

"Hi, Mike. Samantha is trying to get your attention."

"Hi, Pix," he said and stopped, swinging Kylie down. "Great day. I think this one may go to sleep before I can get her home."

"Not tired!" Kylie said, rubbing her eyes, smearing face paint that had turned her into a very colorful clown.

"I'm glad she was over whatever she had yesterday," Pix said.

Mike looked puzzled. "I didn't know she was sick."

"I think she was just running a little temp. Samantha had wanted to bring the dresses over and Arlene didn't want her to catch anything."

"Well, with kids it seems they're either getting something or getting over something," Mike said. "She's fine today."

Samantha caught up to them and Kylie immediately ran into her arms. "Wedding today? My pink dress? Mommy said pink."

"Very pink and you will look like a princess, but not today. Soon," Samantha said, hugging her. "Hi, Mike. Where's Arlene?"

"Nice to see you, too," he said. Mike and Samantha had been friends since Arlene first started dating him in high school. He was a foreigner, they'd teased him, since he was born in Brooksville on the other side of the bridge. "She had to help her mother. Too good a job to turn down. They're getting double time because someone took it today for family coming in tonight." Marilyn worked cleaning houses for one of the island vacation rental agencies, and Arlene helped her out on occasion. She was hoping to go back to her job at the bank once Kylie was in kindergarten. Mike Brown was a Marine Patrol officer. He'd been torn between being on the water fishing and law enforcement. This job, he said, made for the best of both worlds. Arlene had gone to Husson for an associate's degree in accounting. They'd both wanted to come back to live on the island and trained for jobs that would allow it.

"Zach, I know it gives us a late start, but could we drop the dresses off where Arlene is working, although she may be home by now, right?" Samantha asked. Her phone didn't work in Granville even to text. No cell tower.

"I think they were not going to be done until supper," Mike said. "And I'm sorry, but I have no idea where they're working."

Pix had been listening to the conversation. "Leave them with me, honey, and I'll bring them over this week. Don't worry. If either of the dresses needs altering we can do it. There's plenty of time."

Sensing that his mother was about to tell them to forget about these particular outfits, Zach said, "Good to see you again, Mike, and tell Arlene we missed her."

Samantha shook a finger at Mike. "Tell that matron of honor BFF of mine that I'm expecting the bridal shower to end all bridal showers! She'll know what I mean!"

Faith and Pix started to laugh before Samantha had finished talking. They'd seen the X-rated bridal shower lingerie catalog that Arlene had sent last spring. Pix had remarked at the time that her shower had been at Ursula's beloved Chilton Club in Boston, formed by a group of women in 1910 and named for Mary Chilton, the first woman to step off the *Mayflower*. As Pix had described the dainty finger sandwiches, white iced petits fours, and a bridesmaid appointed to thread all the ribbons from gifts through a hole in a paper plate to create a bridal bouquet—gifts that included four fondue pots and a bun warmer to "keep your Parker House rolls hot"—Samantha had commented it all sounded like the nineteenth not the twentieth century.

At the ballfield, Zach and Samantha said good-bye to everyone. They were stopping at The Birches for a short visit with Ursula before the long drive back. As he hugged her Zach whispered, "I'm sorry" in his future mother-in-law's ear. Pix whispered back, but in a very different tone. "Don't be silly. You have nothing to feel sorry about. Everything is going to be fine. Sam goes back Tuesday and I'll be all by myself. It will be fun to show your mother the island, and we can go up to Bar Harbor or even Canada if she wants to take a trip.

Marriage means not just the union of two individuals, but their families."

A few minutes later, waving from Zach's Mini Cooper as they turned onto Route 15, Samantha said, "Want to elope?"

"Got a ladder?" Zach replied.

When Faith walked into her house, she saw the message machine was blinking. Two messages. The first was from Ursula, inviting them to a welcome dinner the following night for Alexandra Kohn. She offered the next night if the Fairchilds couldn't make it, but she was hoping for Monday, since Sam was leaving Tuesday. Faith started to call her back and say yes, thinking how typical this was of Ursula. Not exactly making a silk purse out of a sow's ear, but some other image. From the amount of luggage she'd brought— Pix said it completely filled the guest room, and where it would all go when unpacked was a problem— Alexandra had been planning to stay for the month from the start. Filing away the question of why the globetrotting socialite would want to spend so much time on a small unfashionable island, Faith checked the other message. It was from Earl and markedly discreet. "Give me a call when you have a chance. I'm home for the rest of today."

Faith realized she hadn't seen either Earl or his wife, Jill, at Fishermen's Day. She called back immediately. Jill answered.

"Hi, Faith, I'll get Earl."

"Is everything all right? I didn't see you at Fishermen's Day."

"We went early for the Hall of Fame ceremony and then came straight back here. We started stripping wallpaper from the upstairs bath and discovered there are about seven more layers underneath. It's the kind of thing that once you start you just want to keep going."

Not a DIYer herself, Faith found it easy to envision stopping, particularly to call someone else to do it. "I'm sure it will look wonderful when you're finished."

"Here's Earl now, bye," Jill said, the eagerness to get back to her task unmistakable.

"Hi," Earl said. "Two things. We have the autopsy results and a positive ID. I think it's unlikely that it's someone you or Sophie know, but I'm assisting the state police, since the body was found—and seen alive—on the island. We'd like you to look at a photo."

"All right," she answered. "How do you want to do it? Should we go to Ellsworth? To the office there?"

"We want to make it as painless as possible for you, so I brought all the relevant material here. If you and Sophie are free tomorrow morning, how about coming to the house? I can guarantee a good cup of coffee, and Jill has picked so many blueberries she's been using the ones she hasn't frozen for baked goods. Muffins, pie, coffee cake—the works. I left word with Paul for her, but haven't heard back. He thought she could make it though. Nothing on the calendar in the kitchen, he said."

There was a Currier and Ives illustrated calendar with large squares next to the phone on a kitchen wall at The Birches. It even looked worn, but the dates were current. Faith had no idea where Sophie or someone else got it every year.

"Okay. Nine o'clock?"

"Fine. And, Faith, he didn't drown. There was no water in his lungs. He was dead before he went in."

She was good at this. Lying that is. But then she had always been good at everything. High honor roll, sports star, made most of her clothes, even her prom dresses, and the person friends came to when they needed a shoulder to cry on. She gave a little laugh. Not that she needed a shoulder now. She was handling everything fine. The trick she'd figured out right away was to make sure each lie had a large component of truth. Like today. She was where she'd told people she would be—just not for as long.

He'd been waiting at the McDonald's in Belfast and as promised he'd had a prescription he swore was real. She didn't care, just so long as it could be refilled and had her name on it. She had an old license that was still valid with that name, since she'd have to show it. The price had gone up, he told her, but it was cheaper to get the pills this way, even with what he charged for the script, than buying them directly from him. She'd started to protest but then was afraid he'd leave. Leave with that piece of paper she'd do anything to get. He offered to buy her a hamburger, but she told him she didn't have time. She wasn't hungry anyway. She was never hungry. Just thirsty. She'd been drinking so much water she was surprised she didn't make a sloshing noise when she walked. She bought a bottle now and headed for the big Hannaford. It had a pharmacy. She'd be all set and on her way home—back before anyone began to compare notes. Before they knew she was gone. Very gone.

The owners of Sanpere Shores, Sidney and Pamela Childs—he a retired dentist, she a Realtor—had developed a winning formula some years earlier. They'd started by purchasing a crumbling former resort in foreclosure near Gloucester, Massachusetts, and turning it into a luxury conference center that also served as a venue for special occasions. It had a view and enough outdoor space for tennis courts, a pool, even a croquet lawn. An eighteen-hole golf course was within walking distance. Their aim was to combine the best of the old—historic inn, lots of wicker, window seats, large public rooms, and high ceilings—with cutting-edge new technology, a spa and fitness center, plus gourmet food and plenty of it. The Gilmore Gloucester, named for the original owners, became the destination of choice for firms seeking a location for working retreats and for marketers as a place to pitch groups on everything from financial services to weight loss plans.

Once it was clear that the spinning-straw-into-gold strategy worked, the Childses turned to New Hampshire and found a similar derelict *grande dame* near Portsmouth, reproducing Gilmore Gloucester as Hampshire Haven. Sanpere Shores, smaller, was their third venture. This was its second summer of operation.

Amy Fairchild at sixteen, "and almost a half" she insisted—the age when she could get her junior driver's license—was going into her junior year at Aleford High, and the only conflict she had with her parents was her fervent desire to skip a liberal arts college and go straight to a culinary institute upon graduating. They wanted her to keep her options open and experience a wide range of subjects. The argument was on hold this summer, and Faith hoped that once all her daughter's friends began picking colleges she would change her mind.

At the moment Amy's long corn silk hair was in a braid and tucked up into a chef's pillbox cap. She was coating rounds of goat cheese with a mixture of fine bread crumbs and fresh herbs. Just before plating on a bed of local mixed microgreens, they'd go into the oven to bake briefly—crisp on the outside, runny in the middle. Being in the kitchen at the Shores—everybody shortened the name—was her dream job. And last week it got even better when the sous chef declared he couldn't stand the island's isolation any longer—"I mean, what kind of place doesn't even have a movie theater"—and left. Having watched Amy, the chef hadn't hesitated to promote her, especially since he didn't have to pay more than a token increase. Early on he'd realized Amy would work for nothing, or even pay, to be in a restaurant kitchen, and he took as much advantage of her devotion as possible—long hours, more work. She was in heaven and snapped at her mother's protest that the Shores was using her unfairly. "Welcome to real professional cooking, Mom! This is what chefs do." Slightly stung by the obvious implication that a caterer wasn't a real chef, Faith kept her mouth shut and made sure Amy took her day off and slept.

"The cheese is done, Chef," she said. "What next?"

"Add mustard to the leftover breading to make a paste and we'll use it for a crust on the rack of lamb."

Chef Dom, short for Dominic, had ruled each of the Childses' kitchens, another strategy that paid off for the couple. He trained staff and developed essentially the same menu for each location, so buying nonperishable ingredients was done in bulk. The manager at the Shores, Cindy, had also been at the other two places. Dr. and Mrs. Childs rotated among the three, never announcing their visits. It kept their employees on their toes. The big problem at Sanpere Shores, and the other two resorts to a lesser extent, was finding local staff for the dining room, housekeeping, grounds, and kitchen. There had been four dishwashers alone so far this summer, each fired or in one case just didn't show up the next day.

"How are you feeling tonight, Chef?" Amy asked. He had terrible allergies and kept a giant box of Kleenex in the small half bath off the kitchen.

"Fine and happy to have such a charming and talented chef in the making at my side," he said. Amy breathed an inward sigh of relief. There were nights when she swore he was related to Jekyll and Hyde. Hard to believe one person could have two such different personalities.

They continued to work rapidly. Breakfast was a plentiful buffet that Darlene, a local woman, took care of, baking the day before then cooking eggs and other menu items, like French toast, to order. Amy liked to come in early to pick up tips like using soda water for the lightest scones. She also liked hanging out with Darlene—the chef slept in. Depending on the group currently in residence at the Shores, lunch was either box lunches for excursions or served in the dining room. Dinner was formal for the island, with gourmet choices of appetizers; meat, fish, or vegetarian entrées; and desserts—one always chocolate in nature.

The air-conditioning in the kitchen kept it cool. During the day some of the staff nipped in for coffee, but the chef only encouraged a few favorites to linger— all of whom had worked at the other resorts. Chief among them was Cal Burke, head of maintenance. He was a favorite with others as well. Long, lanky, with rusty brown hair and deeply tanned from working outdoors, he looked like a handsome cowboy who should be riding the range instead of fixing them. He was island born and bred, although he'd left after high school and only returned when Sanpere Shores opened last summer. He projected an air of mystery—hinting at adventures all over the world, regaling Amy and others with tales of fighting pirates off the coast of Africa and leading perilous expeditions down the Amazon. He'd been working for the Childses for the last few years as a "vacation," he'd said. Keeping the grounds in shape and unclogging drains was nothing compared to fighting for his life armed only with a penknife—this yarn set in Snake Island off the coast of Brazil. Cal was popular with the guests, especially the ladies, and besides the thousand and one anecdotes had a well-rehearsed gig accompanying himself on the guitar after dinner while interjecting Bert and I–type Down East humor between Beatles songs and other oldies.

Cal walked into the kitchen now and grabbed a Coke from the fridge while snatching a brownie from a cooling rack.

"Hey," Amy said. "We need those for the brownie sundae special tonight."

"Aw, come on, you've got plenty, and I need to keep my strength up. Just saw the bosses. They want a firepit on the beach with a sing-along after dinner."

Amy liked the Childses the few times she'd had contact with them. They came into the kitchen several times during their stays and had always been appreciative of her work. She was sure they, and the chef, would write letters of recommendation for her. She gave the coating for the lamb a final stir.

"What next, Chef?"

As soon as she hung up the phone, Faith called Sophie. She was home and had just gotten Earl's message from her uncle about meeting in the morning. Faith told her that she had talked to Earl directly.

"Earl has a photo of the dead man that the police in Massachusetts sent," she said. "You saw him in the market, so I'm sure they want you to make a positive identification—that it was the same person. Other than that, I can't think what else Earl might want."

"Nor can I," Sophie said pensively. "We've told all we know."

Pix woke up early as usual, but to silence, except for the sound of her own rapidly beating heart. She'd walked past the Cranes' twice yesterday, early and late. It appeared that the couple was away. Their car, which looked more like a tank on wheels, was gone. For the rest of the summer, Pix hoped, but it was unlikely they would depart the scene of the crime, having taken such a firm stand on the chain saw incident's perp, that is, Pix's beloved Sam.

But no, it wasn't the new neighbors that caused her to wake with her blood pounding, but the new occupant of her house, who seemed to have settled in for the remaining summer days.

Alexandra had gone to bed early, claiming jet lag. Before that she'd taken a small bite of the halibut and vegetables Sam had grilled and outright rejected Pix's rice pilaf—"no carbs, nothing white." She did not turn down nourishment in the form of most of the bottle of pinot grigio Pix had put in the fridge to go with the halibut, however.

When she was sure the woman was upstairs and out of earshot, Pix had said, in a lowered voice just in case, "What on earth are we going to do with her? Me, mostly. And why doesn't she go to the inn?"

Once Alexandra had made it clear she was staying on the island, Zach had described the inn to his mother, extolling its high-end private en suite rooms furnished with antiques and mentioning some of the famous people who had stayed there. To no avail. "Thank you, darling, but this is family time," she'd replied with more than a hint of reproach.

Sam poured his wife a glass of what was left of the wine, looked at the dribble, and got another bottle. "I'm so sorry, darling. But we can be thankful that this particular apple fell very far from the tree. We're getting a wonderful son-in-law and everybody comes with some baggage."

"She's come with enough Vuitton to pack twice my entire wardrobe, throwing in yours as well," Pix snorted, reaching for the glass Sam was handing her.

"I'll try to get back as soon as I can, and remember Samantha will be here for more than a week before the wedding. And earlier for the shower."

Pix had tried to feel reassured. "I know. But, Sam! What am I going to *do* with her?"

She slipped out of bed gently, although it would take considerable noise to wake her snoring husband, grabbed clothes, and went into the master bathroom to get ready to face the day. Over the years they had added onto the original farmhouse, but it was still small by what she assumed were Alexandra's standards. At least there was a separate guest bathroom, although it didn't have a tub, and her future in-law struck her as the long-soak-with-bath-oils-and-maybe-scented-candles type.

Dressed, she crept downstairs. She needed coffee. A lot of coffee. Taking a steaming mug out onto the deck, she let the view settle her nerves and was just beginning to feel like herself again when she was startled by Alexandra's arrival. She was dressed in what Pix recognized from her yoga class as head-to-toe Lululemon, which she'd wanted for warrior pose and cat/cow herself until she discovered the price. Sleek as a greyhound, Alexandra's face was becomingly covered by a film of sweat that indicated her morning run had been much more than a stroll.

"Hi," she said. "I don't suppose there's anyplace more level around here? A track? Though dodging the potholes was great for my calves."

"There's a kind of track at the high school," Pix said, but she had no idea what it was like. "Could I get you some coffee? And I have some anadama bread for toast. Samantha said you didn't eat much breakfast."

"Such a thoughtful girl to remember. Anadama bread. How quaint. I'll just go shower and change first."

By the time she came back down, dressed in what Pix knew was called "cruisewear" from various catalogs, Sam was up and eating what he called a Full Maine in imitation of a Full English or Irish—bacon, sausage, eggs, home fries, and toast.

"A beautiful morning," she said. "Now, I have my notebook here and we can get started on plans. It's terribly late, but crunch time is my specialty!"

Sam put his fork down. "Kind of you to take an interest, but we're all set, thank you." He was using what Samantha called his scary lawyer voice and what Pix called channeling Perry Mason. "It's a fine day for a sail," he continued in a kinder tone, "and the tides are right for a good long one. We can pack a lunch. Do you like to sail?"

"I adore sailing! Richard—Branson that is—said I was a natural-born sailor, and of course when in the Greek Isles, a yacht is the only way—"

"Great," Sam interrupted. "So that's a plan. Leave in half an hour? Our *boat* is on the other side of the Point where there's deep water. Oh, and bring a jacket. It can get cold on the water." Pix noted the emphasis Sam put on the word *boat* with amusement. The *Owl*, their Hinckley Sou'wester Jr., a scaled-down version of the larger wooden Sou'wester sloop, purchased shortly after they were married, wasn't exactly a rowboat at thirty feet, but then again it wasn't in league with the yachts Alexandra must know.

Wondering what kind of picnic she could whip up that did not include carbs, Pix added, "We have caps and sunscreen on board, but you may have a brand you like." She was sure Alexandra had one and equally sure it wasn't from CVS.

"Jill went to the store early and was sorry to miss you," Earl said, opening the door to Sophie and Faith. Years ago, Jill Merriwether Dickinson had started a small gift and bookshop, The Blueberry Patch, in what had originally been her grandfather's cobbler shop. It abutted the parking lot for the Sanpere Village post office, and this strategic location—the mail was sorted, give or take, by ten o'clock—was one of the keys to the store's success. The Patch, as it was known, provided a gathering place, especially in bad weather, if the mail was late. In addition, the shop was the only place in town for newspapers, postcards, souvenirs, and most important, jars of penny candy for kids. Although nostalgic adults were known to dip into them for Bit-O-Honeys and Jujubes.

Sophie was feeling nervous as she followed Faith and Earl into the kitchen. She'd been edgy since she woke up and there was no reason for it, she told herself sternly. She'd been feeling this way most days, and it seemed a permanent condition.

Jill and Earl had accomplished wonders with the house. Sophie remembered it from her childhood as a tumbled-down eyesore built in the mid-1800s by a ship captain for his large family. The Dickinsons didn't have any kids, but their house was like a child—cared for. Lavished upon even, and much beloved.

Earl poured out three mugs of coffee and set a plate of blueberry scones with butter and blueberry jam on the table.

"This won't take long. Sophie, Faith probably told

you that we know the victim's name now or the one he's been using for a few years: Dwayne LeBlanc—and that he did not drown. There was no water in his lungs. Judging from some of the other results, we know he was an addict, and the assumption now is that he died of an overdose of heroin, possibly laced with fentanyl. Somebody, or several people, dumped him in that part of the pond, probably figuring he wouldn't be found for a while and when he was would be thought a drowning victim. The fact that he had no identification makes it likely that they didn't want him traced back to any individual, or again more than one."

Sophie nodded. "Good to know this, Earl. I appreciate it. But so sad. He must have been young, from what I remember of his face the time I saw him in the market."

"He was. Only twenty-five. Since you'd noticed the out-of-state plates on the motorcycle, we started by sending his prints to Massachusetts and got an immediate hit. I have his driver's license photo—and mug shots. He'd been arrested over the years for DUI, possession of controlled substance, daytime B and E—did a brief amount of time for that. At the time of death, he was on probation and not supposed to leave the state. He lived in Lowell and grew up there as far as we know." Earl saw the look that crossed Faith's face and said, "Yes, lots of fine people live there, but I'm guessing you know it is part of the pipeline that starts in Colombia and comes here through Mexico, the Southwest, and up to us primarily from Lowell and Lawrence through Portsmouth and Portland."

"Show me the pictures, Earl," Sophie said. She really wanted to get this over.

He pulled them from a manila envelope, and it only took a few seconds for her to recognize Dwayne. "Yes, his hair was longer, but that's the man I saw in the market."

"These are some of his known associates. Any familiar faces?"

Sophie looked longer. "Maybe that one." She pointed to a heavyset man with dark hair and a tattoo of something that covered his neck up to his chin. "I remember the tattoo, but a lot of people have tattoos like that and I can't be sure about the face."

Tattoo. The word triggered a question from Faith. "Did the Massachusetts police recognize the tattoo on his arm, the snake? Was it gang related?"

Earl shook his head. "It was a new one to them, and us, too." He put everything away. "Okay. Done. Now I suggest you two go have some fun."

"We intend to," Sophie replied, smiling weakly, "but no swimming today."

Arriving for the dinner party, Faith pulled Pix aside, letting Sam escort Alexandra to the front door of The Pines. She knew Ursula would not like the guest of honor to be ushered in through the kitchen door, the one everyone normally used. "How did today go?" Faith asked.

"Surprisingly well. She really is a good sailor, and that's a sure way to Sam's heart. Mine, too. Once she stopped talking about all the America's Cup ones she'd been on, even crewed when she was younger, and because whenever wedding talk came up Sam changed the subject, it was just another great day on the water."

"What did you do for a picnic?"

"Packed crudités enough for a fleet, hummus, and fruit salad. I also made two roast beef sandwiches for Sam and slipped in cookies Gert sent over once she heard Samantha was coming for the weekend. I kept Alexandra company, and I'm starving now."

"So, it's going to be all right?"

"Not really. As soon as she gets me alone she starts to twist my arm about changing from the island to Boston and other things."

"Like what?" Faith hoped she could mask the annoyance, no make that anger, she was feeling, over dinner. Pix had been worried about small things like hurricanes. Nobody could have envisioned the one named "Alexandra."

"She wants Samantha to register at all sorts of places that are so not the kids: Tiffany, for example. When I explained that they had registered only at Heath ceramics for dinnerware and that midcentury modern was more their style than Waterford and Wedgwood, she looked as if I had said they were going with the Dollar Store. She insisted they would need more than dinnerware to start married life and I said that registering even with Heath had only been because people were asking what to give. You know that on the invitation they requested gifts be made in honor of the occasion to organizations of guests' choice, like Doctors Without Borders, but some people have wanted to give them something personal in addition."

"Alexandra must have seen that on the evite Zach sent and sensed what they are like!"

"Faith, sweetheart, this is a woman who only sees what she wants to see. And gets what she wants," Pix added ruefully.

"Don't be too sure of that," Faith said.

Besides the Fairchilds—including Amy, who was off tonight—Ursula had invited Ed Ricks, Paul, and Sophie. As Faith looked around the dining room, she imagined that it had not changed much since Ursula's grandparents built the house. Beadboard wainscoting and William Morris Willow Boughs wallpaper, which had been renewed from time to time, a classic still being produced. The dining table was more than ample for the ten of them, and Ursula was using the best china—a simple white Haviland Limoges. It was obvious that Ursula wanted the welcome party to be elegant but not ostentatious. A hard look to achieve at The Pines—unless you examined the rooms and valuable decor closely. The Tiffany table and hanging lamps were authentic, the flatware sterling, and the paintings that vied with family photos and framed pressed flowers on the walls represented well-known artists of several periods, including contemporary painters like Fairfield Porter, John Heliker, and Jill Hoy. Hoy's exuberant view of the Reach, a gift for Ursula's eightieth, dominated the dining room, at home with the Arts and Crafts sideboard below.

Faith noticed that Ursula was wearing one of her good summer outfits, a cornflower-blue sheath that made her silver hair appear platinum. Candlelight cast a flattering glow on everyone. The room wasn't dark, however, thanks to Pix's brother's installation of subtle recessed lighting some years ago after he mistakenly tried to eat a papier mâché shrimp his small son had made as a decoration for the plates.

The evening started with champagne, local oysters, smoked mussels in a dill mustard sauce, and for those indulging in carbs, Gert Prescott's cheese straws. If Alexandra was surprised by the offerings—the champagne was Möet & Chandon—she did not show it.

Amy had offered to serve even though Gert wanted to stay—as much for a glimpse of the guest as to help out. There had been peas at the farmers' market, and Faith brought the first course, a cold fresh soup of pureed peas with a hint of mint. (See recipe, page 327.) Amy had asked if anyone wanted a dollop of crème fraîche, and Alexandra—the reason for the inquiry—had predictably declined. The rest found a delicate white spiderweb traced on the bright green surface, a trick Faith had taught her daughter—pulling a sharp knife from the middle to the sides and across.

After clearing the empty soup dishes, Amy served her grandmother and Alexandra, who was at Ursula's right in the place of honor, the main course. Ursula said, "I'm afraid we eat a great deal of fish here. I hope you like scallops."

"I adore fish. So good for us, too. The chef at the Taj does a marvelous poached salmon that could be one of the entrée offerings."

Ed Ricks immediately began talking about the scarcity of lobster in his traps. "And to think that at one time they were so plentiful on the coast, you could pick them off the rocks at low tide and prisoners in the state penitentiary refused to eat any more of them, demanding anything but, even oatmeal instead."

"I'm pretty sure that's an urban—or what's the equivalent? Rural?—myth," Faith said. "Not about how common they were back in the day, but the prisoners protesting. The food historian Sandra Oliver wrote a great piece about it as an example of how this sort of tall tale becomes fact."

With the subject changed abruptly, Alexandra gave in—for the moment—and said, "This looks delicious, but I'm afraid I don't eat pasta."

Amy grinned, setting another plate down in front of her mother. "It's not pasta, it's zucchini. With a little fresh basil and EVOO. The scallops are poached in white wine, not butter."

Sensing Sam's annoyance at the way they were catering to their future in-law's food foibles—he loved pasta—Pix explained, "Gert has a spiralizer. A pretty nifty kitchen tool that turns zucchini and all sorts of other vegetables into pasta-like strands. She saw one on the Home Shopping Network, and we've all become converts."

"We have one at the Shores, too," Amy said. "There are always going to be some guests—" A look from her mother stopped her short. "Some guests who want new things." She hastened to the kitchen for the rest of the plates.

"I'd like to have a look at that gadget," Alexandra said. "Although I don't cook myself."

As everyone ate, the conversation was genial, revolving around the great turnout for Fishermen's Day, the new coffee shop that was roasting its own beans in Sanpere Village, and of course the weather. Having finished her food, Amy put down her fork and joined in.

"So," she said, "did they ever find out who that dead body in the Lily Pond was?"

Chapter Five

As a conversation stopper, it was a lulu. Sophie looked across the table at Faith. Tom was looking at his wife as well. Faith did not always feel it was necessary to bother her husband with the details of her everyday life—as in meeting with Earl this morning, or even Earl's message on the machine, which got erased when she deleted Ursula's. She'd heard them both, she reasoned. Historically Tom took a dim view of Faith's involvement, however tangential, in crime. But clearly her daughter's question—note to self, talk to Amy about topics for dinner party conversation—had to be addressed. To wipe the look of absolute horror off Alexandra's face for a start.

Faith directed a reply to Alexandra. "We had a tragic, fortunately very rare, accident last week at the pond. I believe he has been identified. From out of state. Massachusetts it seems."

"Oh, Massachusetts," Alexandra said, as if that settled the question. "I know a few people in Boston and Cambridge, and dear friends near Lenox in the Berkshires, but as for the rest I'm afraid I would be quite at a loss." Faith avoided her friend Ed's eyes. She knew he was feeling what she was. If Alexandra didn't know the man or the place he lived, it was no never mind to her. "Drowned I presume. People are so careless," Alexandra continued.

"Dessert," Ursula announced. "We're having it in the living room or on the porch if the bugs aren't too bad."

The bugs were bad, so Faith, Amy, and Pix set the array of desserts that had been prepared for all tastes on the large round table in front of the bay window. With the porch lights off, the summer sky just past sunset seemed close enough to touch. The jigsaw puzzle, as well as other essentials like binoculars, bird guides, flora and fauna life lists, and whatever books anyone happened to be reading, had been cleared off the table to make way for two of Gert's famous pies, strawberry rhubarb and black walnut; dark chocolate brownies—Amy's contribution; ice cream for the pies and brownies; plus a large fruit salad for Alexandra with a pitcher of crème anglaise, which she ignored, unlike the rest of the party.

"One of my patients made me a needlepoint pillow that said LIFE IS SHORT, EAT DESSERT FIRST," Ed Ricks said, digging into his full plate with relish. "I took it as a good sign—she was a clinically depressed individual who had made great progress over the years—but it also could have been a hint that the shrink should loosen up. Which I have." He laughed, and Amy said, "I think I'll make one of those for myself. Dessert really *is* the best part of a meal. Samantha should just have desserts at her reception. I know she'll have an awesome cake, but I'll bet the s'mores station will be the most popular."

"The what?" Alexandra seemed to be choking on a grape. Faith quickly poured her a glass of water, which the woman gulped down.

"S'mores," Amy said. "You must have made them in Girl Scouts or camp. You toast marshmallows over the campfire, or in this case little braziers, and eat them between two graham crackers and a slab of Hershey's chocolate."

"Of course, there will be many other offerings," Pix said rapidly, "and I meant to mention that the string quartet that will be playing during the reception before the dancing starts is performing at Kneisel Hall in Blue

Hill next Sunday. It would be fun to get a group together to go."

Faith jumped in. Although her mind tended to
wander during classical music just as it did at sermons
by preachers other than Tom, she said, "Count us in."

"Me, too," Ed said.

Alexandra had regained her composure. "If we
move the wedding to Boston, Yo-Yo would play," she
said firmly. "I know what you're going to say, Sam. The
plans are all set, even the marshmallow thingy, but just
think of what a memorable wedding this could be."

"Oh, but it *will* be a memorable wedding." A familiar voice rang out from the doorway.

Sophie ran over and threw her arms around the
woman standing there, flashing a kilowatt smile on
everyone, in an outfit that rivaled Alexandra's.

It was Babs née numerous surnames, now Harrington, to the rescue.

"What have I missed? And I'm not talking about
dinner, although I will have some of that lovely fruit,
thank you. Oh, and Ed, bourbon and branch—you
know where Ursula keeps it." Babs sat down next to
Alexandra. "You must be Zach's mother. I believe
we have friends in the city in common—the Auchin-
closses? Connections of dear Louis—such a loss to

literature and so much else. And if you don't mind a personal comment, you must have been a child bride! Of course, people are always saying that about me—just look at Sophie, a grown woman and married, but more like my sister."

Ed Ricks appeared with the drink and Babs paused to take a sip—and come up for air. It was a bravura performance, Sophie thought, and had the intended effect. Alexandra Kohn was speechless.

Babs was on a roll. "Yes, memorable nuptials. They were so lucky to book Edgewood Farm. It's in such demand. Didn't Travolta have an event there? He lives on Isleboro, you know. And Pix has done such a fabulous job lining up places for everyone to stay, because sweet as it is, Pix dear, your house would not stretch to anything resembling Mother Hubbard's shoe." She took another sip and sighed. "Heaven to be on the island. When I saw that no one was at The Birches, I figured you'd be over here. Now, let's talk plans. Lovely to have a new face! Today's Monday—and damn I missed Fishermen's Day! Ed—not this one, but my husband"—she addressed the remark to Alexandra—"has gone to Scotland to play golf but will be back in plenty of time for the wedding. Do you golf, Mrs. Kohn? Quite a nice little course here at the Island

Country Club. Tennis is my game." She stretched her empty glass toward Ed, who took the hint.

Sophie thought it was time to let someone else get a word in edgewise, although she was enjoying the stun gun effect on the woman who was causing such problems for the Millers. "The weather is looking good for the rest of the week and I hear you had a good sail today, so we can definitely plan another soon. You might like to go down to Castine, which is a lovely historic spot. I think the garden tour may be this Thursday."

Ed had returned with a generous refill for Babs, who said, "This all sounds fine but we should do as much as we can early in the week—I for one want to go up to Bar Harbor and fill in a few wardrobe gaps." Sophie rolled her eyes at Faith. Babs had a closet at the house in Connecticut the size of many people's master bedrooms and had appropriated a small storage room on the top floor of The Birches for her Maine wardrobe.

"Our class starts Friday night, which doesn't give us much time. We'll be in memoir writing"—Babs shook her finger playfully at Alexandra—"and something tells me you have plenty of material, as do I. When we're finished, we can have a reading and everyone here can vote on whose is spicier!"

Alexandra was still looking dazed and a heavy dose

of bewilderment was entering the picture. "What . . ." she started to say.

"Oh, of course, you have no idea what I'm talking about," Babs said merrily. "Such fun. Sophie told me she was enrolling in a fiction-writing program at Sanpere Shores, a beautiful resort here—we may never write a word, just enjoy the spa—and I went online to see what we gals could do. I've always preferred fact to fiction—so much juicer. When I called them, they had two spaces left in the memoir program. We'll be day students, like Sophie. Tomorrow we can move you over to The Birches. So much easier to commute together. I must say I'm very excited about it all. After we move you in, we can go up to Bar Harbor. Maybe stop in Seal Harbor to say hi to Martha. If you haven't seen it already, you'll love Skylands. She certainly has the touch." Babs leaned back, drained half her glass, and shot her daughter a cat-finishing-cream triumphal glance. She also gave Pix a warning glance that Sophie understood. Pix was too good and was apt to protest that Alexandra should stay where she was and only take the course if she wanted.

Sam was cutting himself another piece of pie and there was nothing but glee on *his* face. "Well then," he said. "This does sound like fun. Want to write my own memoirs someday."

Alexandra still had not uttered a single word. She appeared to be considering the prospect of both moving to a much larger space and hanging out with someone so obviously on her wavelength. The choice was a forgone conclusion. Alexandra might as well have turned up at The Birches to start. The woman might be used to getting her own way, but Babs was a force of nature of substantially greater magnitude.

"Done and dusted," Tom whispered to his wife. "Now, let's get out of here."

Faith nodded, and as she went around saying goodbye, Ed Ricks said, "Come by for coffee? I haven't seen you much all summer."

"I'd love to," Faith said. "Tom and Amy are both working long hours, so I'm a free agent."

"How about tomorrow morning? Ten? You bring the baked goods, unless you want some admittedly old vanilla wafers."

"See you at ten and I'm sure I can drum up something a bit fresher."

The phone was ringing as the Fairchilds walked into the house. Amy grabbed it, a reflex inherent in all the teenagers Faith had ever known. "For you, Mom. Pix. I'm going to bed. Have to be at work early."

Kissing her, Faith took the phone. At first it was

hard to make out what Pix was saying. "Could you speak up? I can't hear you. Is Alexandra right there?" Faith asked.

"No, she went straight to bed. But, Faith, I love Babs and I know she just wanted to help, but do you think she well, railroaded Alexandra into all this? I feel a bit guilty, since it will be so much easier having her at The Birches and taking a course will keep her busy."

"And away from any wedding interference."

"Well, that, too."

Smiling, Faith said, "Now my best beloved friend, you have absolutely nothing to feel guilty about. Alexandra will be much more comfortable over at The Birches. There's plenty of room, and Babs redid the guest rooms last summer. The large one at the front has a gorgeous bath—you've seen it. It's not as if you're shunting her off to a shack with no indoor plumbing. And she'll love the Shores. Remember, you didn't invite her. She landed on you all by herself."

"But she's going to be family." Pix's protest did not sound all that strong.

Faith's answer *was*. "There's family and family. Once the wedding is over and she resumes her previous lifestyle, you won't see her. Not exactly family as in let's be sure to set a place for the holidays. Take her over to The Birches once she's packed up tomorrow and breathe a big sigh of relief. You've had enough stress this week to last for many summers to come."

"Mother said almost word for word what you just did."

Faith's smile broadened. She didn't mind being the second opinion and second call—they had a longer drive home and Pix was bursting with the kind of inbred Yankee guilt that only an old Yankee mother could assuage.

"Go to sleep, or maybe not. Sam's leaving, and it could be a while before you two are together again."

"Faith!" Pix exclaimed, but her friend had already hung up.

Day camp at the Community Center took care of the mornings into the early afternoons. And it's not like it wasn't a great place. No, she didn't feel guilty at all. The timing worked, and at the end of the summer when camp was finished, there was preschool. But by then it wouldn't matter. She was going to stop, wasn't she? This was the last dose. So what if there were two refills? She wasn't going to use them. Maybe wouldn't even finish what was in this container.

The pain had been a nightmare. Both at the

time of the accident and in the hospital before they treated it. Almost gone for a while except for an ache or two. No, it was a different pain. The one from trying to hold everything together. And pretty much alone. All she had for neighbors out here were trees and water. Not like growing up off Main Street in Granville with people around all the time. People she knew and they knew her. It would be okay to be where she was, except she didn't sign on to being with a guy she barely saw. She was proud of his job, sure—they were able to buy this place—but why did he have to work all the time? Yeah, he was the new kid compared to others, but what about her? What about dealing with all the stuff she had to do—the cooking, the cleaning, the garden they depended on to save money—and it all had to be done all over again the next day. Years from now she would be doing the same things, and when she thought about never being finished, never getting a break, she felt a kind of mist settle over her brain. If she was never going to finish, why not finish herself right now?

Ed Ricks and Faith were sitting outdoors the following morning on his bluestone patio overlooking Penobscot Bay. Built some years ago in preparation for living year-round on the island, his home was similar to Philip Johnson's Glass House in New Canaan, Connecticut. Ed's privacy was protected by evergreens and the fact that the house sat high on a bluff. The result was to bring the outside in and the reverse. There was a separate guesthouse with more solid walls for friends from his former very urban life.

Fishing boats dotted the water at varying distances. By this time almost a full day's work was done. Ed's small boat, moored at his dock, was tossing in the wake—a wall of water—that had just been created by a large lobster boat as it sped on to pull the next trap.

"Same boat every day," Ed said. "Lets it out full throttle. Think he may be practicing for the races. If so, he's a contender." All summer long, starting with the first race in Boothbay Harbor, fishermen traveled up and down the coast for the Lobster Boat Races on Sundays. It was a rare chance to play, and the captains let loose, revving up to over sixty miles per hour while competing in a series of classes. The boats ranged from small dinghies with outboards to thirty-eight footers with very pricey engines; the sole stipulation was that the lobster boat had to be a working boat. No ringers who had never hauled a single trap but converted lobster boats to pleasure craft. Onlookers lined the courses onshore and in boats celebrating the tradition with a

Down East version of tailgating. Freeman Hamilton, the Fairchilds' nearest neighbor, was still racing at seventy-five, even though his wife had insisted he retire from fishing a few years ago after what he called a "little episode" with his heart. He'd turned his boat, *Grandpa's Pride*, and the family's fishing territory over to his son, but not his place at the helm for the races. It was rare for Freeman to come in second in his class.

"Freeman told Tom he's entered again in Granville," Faith said. "He did well at Jonesport, and that's the toughest on the circuit. So much competition."

"Come on my boat to watch? Or are you and Tom already booked on someone else's?" Ed asked. "And I'm not just issuing the invitation because I know you'll bring your lobster rolls."

"We're not and I'd love to. Tell me how many people and I'll bring the whole picnic." Faith's lobster rolls were almost as famous as Freeman's legendary winning streaks. When it came to lobster rolls, Faith was a purist. No celery or other fillers. (See recipe, page 329.)

"I can supply the lobster if the catch gets better, otherwise I'll get them up at the Co-Op," Ed said as he pointed to his pot buoys, one on top of the boat, as required for identification. He'd told Faith he picked the colors—bright yellow with black stripes—so he could spot them easily. They were bobbing about like bumblebees in the wake's white spray. "I imagine as long as there have been men and boats, there have been races; but these didn't officially start until the 1930s, and I'm pretty sure it was because a lot of the skippers had souped up their boats as rum runners during Prohibition and wanted to keep going."

Faith laughed. "I'm getting a picture of all sorts of nautical contests, going back in history: Viking ships, Chinese junks, dugout canoes." She reached for another of the doughnut muffins she'd brought as Ed filled her cup with more coffee.

They'd covered last night's dinner—"Sophie was right. Alexandra could only have been outmaneuvered by Babs," Faith had observed—and Ed remarked that so many names were dropped there must be a number of new indentations in The Pines's living room floor today. They traded island gossip—Ed mentioned a possible split in his book group over bestsellers versus classics, and Faith said Nan and Freeman's niece from Massachusetts was living with them this summer, but Faith had yet to meet the young woman. She was a music major and singing at various spots on the peninsula. "We should go hear her," Ed said.

For a moment, they sat quietly and watched the activity on and above the water—boats, gulls, cormorants swooping down, even some porpoises breaking the surface. Faith was about to say she should get going when Ed started to speak.

"I don't think I ever mentioned that I first came to the island as a child. My parents had friends with a summer place that looked straight north out to Swan's Island. It had a small beach and plenty of trees to climb. I thought it was the most beautiful spot I'd ever seen. We came back only a few times more, but I never forgot it. When I was in medical school and thinking about the sorts of serious life questions a place like that engenders, I decided Sanpere was where I wanted to be permanently, as in forever, and planned my life back from there. Before I bought the land for my house, I bought a plot in Hillside Cemetery." He grinned. "It's got a great view, and by now I know a lot of the neighbors."

"I like that notion," Faith said. "The one of picking a place or even a way of being and backtracking. Sanpere's become the same for Tom and me, but if you had ever told me when I was in my twenties that a spot like this was my ultimate goal, I would have thought you were crazy. I didn't ever want to leave Manhattan and only Tom could have made me."

Ed put his mug down. "I kind of knew you both felt the way I do and I have to admit besides always enjoying your company I asked you to come by for another reason. Faith, I need your help. Tom's, too. All the talk I'm sure you've heard about the opioid crisis here isn't just talk. It's real and getting worse fast. I see it up much too close on almost every shift now."

Ed was a volunteer with the ambulance corps.

"Did you know that we carry NARCAN? And I keep extra gloves in my car to pick up syringes and other paraphernalia tossed along the roadside." He shook his head. "I was on duty when we took the young man you found to the hospital. It wasn't just the marks on his arms, but I could also tell by his teeth that he was a heavy user. Heroin causes dry mouth, and there's no saliva to wash away the bacteria. Users also tend to grind their teeth. He was probably into meth as well, which causes decay in a short amount of time."

"We are aware of it and talk a lot about what's happening," Faith said. "We've never locked our doors, but there have been so many break-ins that if both cars are out of the drive, we do now. From the kinds of things taken, you know it's not a ring of crooked antiques dealers like the thefts a few years ago. What we worry about losing are the computers, especially Tom's. Although, I was there when one of Ursula's neighbors told her he was locking his doors now, and her response was so strong, I didn't dare tell her we were also."

"I feel the same way," Ed said. "I don't want to have

to do it, but I do have valuables here I wouldn't want to lose."

"Increasingly Tom finds himself helping people in the congregation cope with a family member's addiction. One of the main problems is the shame they feel. He's been trying hard to make them understand addiction is an illness, a terrible illness—has preached about it—but it's still a skeleton that most people want to keep shut up tight in the closet. The drug epidemic in Massachusetts is bad, and it affects all ages, all incomes; but I know it's worse in Maine."

"You're right. And the hushing-it-up problem is deeply embedded in the Mainer's 'we can do it ourselves' independent way of life, the belief that to get help, ask for it at all, is letting go of that. Plus, it's none of anybody's business. Like alcohol addiction, which has always been a major drug of choice here, there's also the notion that a person should be able to stop when he or she wants to and that not doing so is the person's own fault."

"Long winters," Faith said. "Maybe that's responsible for this crisis as well."

"I don't mean to give you a TED talk—although there are some good ones posted about all this—on such a beautiful Maine day, but it's not the winters. It's the lack of programs, structured support, rehab facilities, and most of all it's because of the overwhelming availably of the drugs. Heroin is cheaper than a pack of cigarettes. Prescribed pills like oxycodone, which started it all, are heroin in pill form. Commercial fishing is the most dangerous occupation in the country. Injuries and constant pain are a way of life. Starting in the 1990s the solution in pill form was, too. And it's not just the fishermen, or young people who want the high, but also the elderly who were overprescribed pain medication and became dependent to the point where now that they can't get it from a doctor they're turning to the street, too. Impossible to contemplate. Someone's grandmother meeting up with a dealer in Granville."

Ed got up and began pacing back and forth. "As a physician and more as a human being, I can't sit this one out and blame the politicians or whomever for not doing anything. A number of us on the island—people from here and people from away—are forming a group to try to do what we can in our corner of the world. Education, starting with elementary school kids—they see the signs up close more than anyone else, a parent who can't care for them. We need more doctors who are willing to treat the illness with Suboxone—they have to take special classes and many opioid users are uninsured. Treating addicts is grueling and depressing. I'm training to be a recovery coach and am encouraging others to do so. I could go on and on, Faith. There's no one magic solution. Addicts aren't criminals, no matter what anyone says. No one would say that about someone who was diabetic or had cancer. Relapses are part of the illness, just like other diseases, and they don't mean the individual is weak. The name 'Heroin' was a late-nineteenth-century trademark for the drug, because it made the patient feel 'heroic.' We never needed heroes more than now. One of the saddest facts I learned recently is the largest number of addicts on the island are mothers with small children, and of course they don't want to admit the problem for fear they will lose their children into care." He sat down and slumped forward. The lengthy, emotional outburst over, he looked exhausted. Faith reached for his hand.

"Sign us up, Ed. We'll do whatever we can. Talk to people you haven't—Sophie and her husband, the Millers."

"I'll tell you when we're next meeting. We're using social media. Facebook. Whatever reaches people."

They both stood up and Faith kissed his cheek. "You're a good man. A lot of people are and will be thankful to you."

"Not necessary. You see, it takes one to know one. I was a drunk for twenty years, Faith. High functioning, but a drunk. So, been there, done that, and don't want the tee shirt."

Amy was worried. Tonight Chef Dom had had to leave before all the guests were served. He'd asked Amy to make sure the orders were correct and pulled one of the servers from the dining room to help her before departing. The Shores was full, and to keep people happy while they waited for their food, the chef had also asked Cal Burke to get his guitar and play. The music filtered into the kitchen, not Cal's usual oldie favorites, but what Amy recognized from her parents' CDs as classical guitar. Cal really was a man of many talents and she wondered where he had learned to play so well. And where he grew up on the island. She was sure she must know where it was.

Cal came in for a glass of water. "Good job, kid. Looks like almost everybody has been served."

Amy nodded. "And the desserts are all made and plated in the fridge. Only the fruit crumble will need heating, and most people chose the Baileys cheese-cake. I was thinking someone should check on the chef, see if he needs anything. Maybe you could do it during a break?" The chef and Cal shared a cabin that the Childses had deemed too far away from the main building and too small to refurbish, so it was used for staff who didn't live locally. Amy wasn't sure where it was and, in any case, didn't think it was appropriate for her to go check.

"Good idea. I can do it while dessert is being served," Cal said. "I'm sure he'll be fine by tomorrow."

"It's just that for the next two weeks we'll be having the most guests of the summer, so I hope he's completely better by Friday when they all arrive."

"I almost forgot," Cal said. "The scribblers and the number crunchers."

Amy smiled. "That's a good way to put it." She remembered that Sophie was taking one of the writing courses and now so were Sophie's mother, Babs, and Zach's mother. The other group, which was larger, was a team-building exercise for a national actuarial group. Fiction and faction, she thought and filed it away to tell her parents. It was the kind of joke they liked.

But what wasn't fiction was the chef's illness. Normally at this point in the day she would be feeling high at having spent time doing what she loved best and being where she knew she was meant to be. The chef had expressed surprise at her knife skills and overall culinary expertise. The rush of getting the food from raw ingredients to beautiful plating and the fun of thinking what they might make the next day and the next never paled. Tonight hadn't been like that. She went back to worrying.

"I'm taking the day off to spend it with my beautiful wife," Tom Fairchild said, rolling over in bed to pull said wife into a close embrace.

"Hmmm," she murmured. "This is nice."

"The work is going well, and this is one of those days the Lord hath made," Tom said, gesturing out the window. The sun was straight out of a kid's drawing, perfectly round and yellow, sending beams of light across the room. "Let's spend the day on the water. Maybe head out to Isle au Haut. We can stop at Green Island or one of the others where it's easy to tie up for lunch." Some years ago they had bought an eighteen-foot Grady-White powerboat, and Tom had been lamenting how little he'd been able to use it this summer.

"Besides," Tom said, "rabbit, rabbit—it's August first. We need to celebrate that." Faith's husband had never been able to explain this old New England custom—saying "rabbit, rabbit" upon awakening on the first of the month to ensure good luck and if one forgot, repeating it backward at bedtime, but Faith had adopted it. She murmured the phrase now. No point in taking any chances.

Last night after Amy had gone to bed, Faith and Tom had stayed up talking about what Ed Ricks had said. Faith had been restless since—thinking about it all. The idea of a day consisting only of keeping an eye out for harbor seals and avoiding pot buoys was a welcome one.

"We could ask Pix if you like," Tom added. "Zach's mother is over at The Birches now, right?"

"Yes," Faith answered, "but today Pix is going up to Bar Harbor with her and Babs. I tried to convince her that not only would she hate it—as you know, Pix would rather walk on a bed of nails than shop—but that they would probably have a nicer time without her. She's never been very good at hiding her feelings. But she feels she should make an effort to get to know Alexandra better."

"All right. Poor Pix. But just you and me, kid, is fine."

Faith got out of bed. "I'll pack the lunch. Chicken salad on sourdough? I can make deviled eggs, too."

"Fine." Tom smiled, not moving. "But what's the rush?"

The unusually intense heat of the past weeks had only slightly abated, but out on the water the temperatures always required layers. Faith had started out with a sleeveless tee and was up to a sweatshirt now. They'd passed close enough to the three-masted windjammer *Victory Chimes*, in full sail, for Faith to get what she hoped was a stunning picture. Lots of kayaks—or as the fishermen called them, "speed bumps"—were out as well as other pleasure boats, power and sail. And the working boats. Faith raised a hand in greeting to all. She'd learned from Freeman in her first days on the island that this greeting was a signal that all was well. She'd thought of it as a friendly gesture, waving heartily back each time. She still did, but now it was less energetic, one of a longtime sailor.

The sun was sending diamonds across the waves. There might not be as many lobsters at the moment as in years past, but Faith had never seen as many buoys, each with its distinctive markings and number. So far it had been a peaceful summer, no lobster wars. No one invading another person's territory to set traps. Retaliation was swift. First trap lines cut—and the loss of the trap and catch was a financial blow—and then maybe bait stuffed into a fuel tank, and finally shots fired across a bow. Fishing grounds were handed down from generation to generation and, unlike farmland, couldn't be fenced in. But those who fished it knew the boundaries, as did those trying to poach it.

Granville brought in more lobster than any port

in the Northeast and close to more than anywhere in the country. It was a lucrative occupation, and as Faith looked at the fields of brightly colored buoys she thought about something else Ed had said. That Sanpere's dependency on lobster and tourists was new. In the past there had been granite, boat building, the cannery, sawmills, and ground fishing—all virtually gone now. The amount of money even a weak season for the crustaceans poured into the island was significant, and in recent years a lot of that money was going for drugs.

Faith looked back at the boat they had just passed. Two young guys were opening a trap, throwing some lobsters—shorts—back and others into the plastic bins on board. Both had raised a hand in greeting— the royal-blue thick rubber gloves the fishermen wore were more spots of color. There had been a letter to the editor in the *Island Crier* recently from a young fisherman detailing the prevalence of drugs the fishermen were using while hauling and calling for more public awareness. He pointed out that he didn't want his boat to get smashed into by someone who was high and unable to control his boat. The day after the paper had come out someone had left a dead gull on his front step with a tag bearing his name wrapped around its neck.

She shook her head to clear away the dark thoughts and concentrated on the view. The day was crystal clear, and Mount Desert Island seemed a mere hop away. She thought of Pix traipsing around Bar Harbor from boutique to boutique. She hoped she'd manage to get herself her favorite Moose Tracks ice cream at CJ's Big Dipper on Main Street. Alexandra wouldn't want the calories and Babs was usually on a diet, too, but Pix, and Samantha, too, never put on an ounce no matter how sinful the dish.

The image of one of those luscious scoops in a waffle cone made her realize she was hungry. Being on the water always created an appetite, and though there must be a scientific reason for it—salt air as an appetite stimulant?—she never remembered to look it up. She went back and sat in the second mate's chair. "Time for lunch? We can eat on the boat or pull in somewhere."

"Let's go to Green Island. It's close, and don't worry, I won't make you swim in the quarry."

The old quarry filled with fresh water from deep underground springs was a favorite swimming hole for locals. The one time Faith had been convinced to give it a try she was so cold she thought she wouldn't be able to swim the few strokes back to the rock she'd jumped off. "We can walk across to the little beach on the cove facing the Camden Hills," she said.

There were two kayaks tied securely to the iron

stakes left from the days when the pink granite in this particular quarry was mined and prized. On a weekday the only people on Green Island would be vacationers. Two walls of the stone created a long, deep inlet, and the Grady-White just fit. Tom cut the engine and Faith tied the mooring lines to more spikes left in the rock all those years ago. Also years ago someone had attached a ladder up to the top of one wall.

They climbed up to the path, passing the quarry and the brave souls jumping in from the rocks, before crossing the top of the island. Low junipers spread on either side of a small trail that had been worn over time. The birds had eaten most of the blueberries and huckleberries, but the air still smelled of fruit. They scrambled down to the cove and Faith spread the checked oil-cloth table covering she used for picnics on the sandiest rock-free spot she could find. Tom started to unpack the cooler, handing his wife one of the stainless-steel drinking bottles she'd filled with iced tea. He took the other and, unscrewing the cap, drank. "Ah, that tastes good. Now for a sandwich . . . oh, look, Faith—we'd better get that pot buoy."

A bright neon-orange buoy was protruding from the rocks off to the side, tangled lines anchoring it firmly. They'd drop it off at the harbormaster's office. If she didn't know whose it was by the color, she could look up the owner by the number stamped on it.

Faith stood up. "There's a trap floating farther out. The tide is coming in, which will make it easier to save."

"True, but sandwiches first," Tom agreed.

They made quick work of what Faith had packed, including ripe peaches and white chocolate chip cookies. She flung her pit overhand back to what little soil there was behind them. "Someday people will be here having a picnic under a peach tree and wonder how it got on the island. Heavy for a bird to drop."

She pulled her husband to his feet. He'd been packing up the remains in the cooler, muttering, "Leave only your footsteps . . ." She gave him a quick kiss. "Thank you for taking the day off. I've been missing you."

"I've been missing you, too," he said. "Let's free the gear and head home. I'm thinking G and Ts on the deck."

They walked over to the buoy. It was bobbing freely in the water, and Tom grabbed the handle, rapidly pulling the green plastic trap onto the beach. "Must be full. Weighs a ton," he said. The reason was soon gruesomely clear. Pinned underneath was the body of a large man, faceup. He wasn't wearing either a survival suit or life vest of any kind, but too many fishermen didn't.

"Poor soul," Tom said softly. "He must have fallen in while hauling and drowned." Few fishermen could swim, many reasoning that the temperature of the water would kill you before you could take a stroke.

The body had been in the water a while, Faith realized, noting the green tinge on the face and general overall loosening of skin. A series of waves, possibly the wake from a boat not that far off, moved the corpse and trap up onto the shore.

That's when Faith noticed there were no lobsters, crabs, or any other sea creatures in the trap. It was filled with stones.

And then she saw what was on the man's right forearm.

"Tom, I'm pretty sure I know who this is."

Chapter Six

There's something very odd about this trap," Tom said. It appeared he hadn't taken in Faith's sentence.

Faith looked at her husband in shock and said, "Well, there *is* a corpse of a noncrustacean lashed to it." The sight of the dead man was making her giddy.

Tom straightened up. He'd been on his haunches close to, but not touching, the ghastly flotsam. "Wait, what do you mean you know who it is?" He *had* been listening.

"I think he's one of the motorcycle guys who were in the market with the deceased from the Lily Pond."

"But you weren't in the market, were you? I thought only Sophie was."

Now was not the time to mention the meeting with

Earl and the photos he'd shown her. Instead, pointing to the trap, she asked, "What's odd about it?" The ploy worked. Tom crouched down again.

"The pot buoy is battered and has rockweed clinging to it, but the trap is brand-new. Look at the wire. This trap could have been bought yesterday. No signs of having been in the water at all. Same with the netting inside and the bait bag."

Tom was right. "And traps are weighted down with a few bricks," Faith said, "but not loaded with stones like these. They look as if someone picked them up on the shore."

Tom was checking his phone to see if he had service. "There's enough bars for me to call 911. They'll get in touch with the Marine Patrol." As Faith heard Tom describe the situation, the unreality of it all hit her hard. Two bodies in less than a week.

Two bodies with the same tattoo snaking up their lifeless arms.

It had been a long, very long day. Pix had joined Babs and Alexandra that morning, leaving her car at The Birches, taking Babs's Lexus. Alexandra had looked at the Millers' beloved—yes it was old—Subaru as if it were an oxcart.

Pix had no idea there were so many boutiques in Bar

Harbor. She only went up once or maybe twice a season to meet friends passing through. The crowds and especially the sight of the behemoth cruise ships in the harbor were not her Maine.

They'd gone to Testa's on Main Street for lunch, and since they were eating late—Pix had been starving—got one of the upstairs tables with the view. Pix happily ordered the haddock Reuben with fries before the others predictably went for the Superfood Salad—kale, Brussels sprouts, sunflower seeds, and cranberries with dressing on the side of course and no, they didn't want bread. When the food arrived Pix's Reuben was delicious, and sloppy. Pix decided not to care and used her fries, every last one of them, to sop up the dressing and calories.

Ursula had called early this morning and said Gert would pick up the mail, so not to bother, stay away as long as she liked and have fun. Fun! The very long day had included precious little of that. Back at home now, Pix eased off her flats—not her usual comfy sandals in deference to the occasion—and took a long drink of the glass of lemonade she'd poured herself before heading out on her deck. There had been one very bright note today, however. Babs had convinced Alexandra that having the wedding on Sanpere was much more chic than what Alexandra was proposing. "So done, so yesterday," she'd said every time Alexandra mentioned the Taj or any similar ideas. Babs had followed up by reeling off A-listers who had had weddings similar to the proposed Sanpere plans, starting with Meghan Markle and Prince Harry's: "And if they could have pared it down even more they would have. I'm not suggesting a lemon and elderflower wedding cake—it must have had some secret significance for them, that Harry, such a rogue! But everything else Samantha and Zach have planned is straight from the royals' playbook."

It had worked, and knowing Babs, she'd have Alexandra opting for bare feet in the farm's meadow and daisies in jelly glasses for the table decorations.

Pix stretched out her legs and wiggled her toes in relief. *Bless Babs.* Later she'd call Samantha and tell her so she could relax, too, but right now Pix wanted to relish the peace of the late afternoon. With nobody to feed but herself, she didn't even have to plan dinner— she could have cornflakes if she wanted, her favorite fallback, much to Faith's horror. In fact, Faith thought Pix was joking when she'd revealed that cornflakes were what she had for dinner when alone. And when Pix added that Sam had been known to join her, Faith simply could not believe it. In any case, she didn't have to think about food for a while. She was still full from lunch and the ice-cream cone she'd sneaked away for when Babs and Alexandra were trying on endless tunic tops, most of which looked the same to Pix.

The tide was out and the air was still. It had been hot up in Bar Harbor, and in comparison it was blessedly cool here. A single great blue heron swept majestically past before landing in the mudflats, its raucous cry at such odds with its beauty. Pix felt her eyes close and was soon drifting off to sleep.

"Not there! Over here!" A commanding voice startled her awake. A pair of clammers farther down the cove. She shaded her eyes and squinted. It was the Cranes. She should have recognized Cameron's voice immediately. She could see him motioning to his wife to join him. Drew was lugging a clam hoe and wooden roller and not making much progress. No rest for the wicked, Pix told herself. Clamming was backbreaking work, and the equipment, even empty, was heavy. The spot Cameron Crane had picked wasn't a good one. That end of the cove had been overclammed and they'd be lucky to get enough for an appetizer. It was also close to the turn of the tide, and the mud would be increasingly soupy. A good neighbor would walk along the shore and steer them toward better pickings. A good neighbor would tell them the best times of day for clamming.

A good neighbor? No thank you, she decided. Not today.

It hadn't taken the Marine Patrol—and it turned out to be Mike Brown on duty—long to get to Green Island. If Mike was startled at the grisly sight, he didn't show it. He asked the Fairchilds approximately when they had gotten to the spot and whether they had seen any boats in the area close to shore. They were getting ready to cross back over the island and leave when Earl arrived. After carefully examining the body, he made the same observation about the new trap that Tom had. "Unless somebody was replacing an old one. That's a possibility. We'll know when we run the ID number and find out who owns it." He walked over to Faith and said quietly, "You saw the tattoo?"

"Yes, it's the same I'm sure. I also think he was the man Sophie thought she recognized in one of the other photos you showed us. Same hair, beard, and the multicolored tattoos covering all but the one on his forearm. The Massachusetts police didn't recognize that single tattoo as gang related, right?"

Tom was looking askance at his wife and Faith knew she'd have to explain it all to him later. Earl shook his head. "No. They'd never seen it before." He appeared lost in thought. "You found the other guy, LeBlanc, on

Thursday. He hadn't been in the water long. This body hasn't been on dry land for at least a week, I'd say."

Faith knew what he was thinking. The tattoos were no coincidence and now possibly the times of their deaths weren't either. This time the letters in red script were clear: *L F D Y.*

Were there any more snake-tattooed bodies out there?

The return trip home was a speedy one, and after Faith secured the boat to their mooring and Tom shut the engine off, she was surprised that he didn't get up to disconnect the batteries and do the other things necessary before they could row the short distance to shore.

"We need to talk," he said, motioning her to the second mate's seat. Faith sat down. Male or female, no one ever wanted to hear those four words.

"This has got to stop. When we exchanged vows, I pledged 'with my body I thee worship' and I meant only two. Mine and yours. Not a count of other ones over the years that I don't even want to tally up. Other ones that were dead. Yes, you've been helpful—"

She interrupted. "Helpful! More than that, Tom. You're not being fair!"

"Fair! Do you think it's fair to put your life and yes,

Faith, several times the lives of those near and dear, at risk?"

She had never seen him so angry. Not even when she'd had to confess she'd given his lucky Celtics sweatshirt to Goodwill. She had no idea what to say.

"Well?"

Apparently she was supposed to say something.

"I don't go looking for them. Do admit."

He sighed heavily and raised the engine. "We'll go to the sheriff's office in Ellsworth tomorrow so you can view the photos with Sophie again. We'll sign a report or whatever about today. And then, Faith, that's it."

His voice was so stern it was scaring her. "You have no idea what you could be getting mixed up in. It's likely the men are drug dealers—and whatever they did to get themselves killed means those responsible are not going to play nice with someone poking around in their business, even if you are a good cook and kindhearted person."

"And pretty great-looking right?" She could see that Tom's mood was starting to change.

"Okay, great-looking." He drew her toward him, but just before he kissed her he stopped. "Promise me, Faith. Promise you won't get involved."

"I promise," she said, leaning in for the kiss. Yet her thoughts raced on: *She wasn't planning on detecting any further. Tom was the one who noticed the trap's age. She would look at the photos, not ask Earl any questions, and since they were in Ellsworth, they could have a nice lunch at Martha's Diner before they came home. Done and dusted. Wasn't that what her husband was always saying? Done and dusted.*

Her parents and Sophie were going up to Ellsworth for some reason, so Amy was dropped at Sanpere Shores early—even for the breakfast shift. She didn't see Darlene's car and then remembered Thursday was her day off. There were plenty of baked goods, and if the chef was still sick, Amy knew she could handle the breakfast requests. It was the turnaround day in any case. All the current guests had to be out by twelve so the cottages could be cleaned and readied for the two groups coming in tomorrow. Darlene and Amy had packed box lunches yesterday for those who wanted to take one along.

The back door was open and she was reaching for the handle on the screen door when angry voices within stopped her. She recognized Dr. Childs. She hadn't known they were here. Maybe they'd driven over for the turnaround and to welcome the new guests tomorrow, something they did often. She didn't mean to eavesdrop, but he was shouting. "No more slipups!

You were supposed to keep an eye on him! If there's even a single one more, you know what will happen."

The voice that answered was lower, but Amy recognized it as Cal Burke's. She could just make out the words. "Hey, boss, it's been fine so far. Don't worry. He'll be okay by tomorrow. There's no dinner tonight, and the girl can handle breakfast and the box lunches."

Amy knew she couldn't walk in now. They were obviously talking about the chef's illness. It must be a chronic condition and Cal was supposed to keep him on his medication or some other treatment. She would have thought Dr. Childs would be more sympathetic. She backed away from the door and walked to the front of the lodge, entering there.

Cindy was at the desk. "Hi, Amy, thanks for coming in so early. We really need you today. Dom is still under the weather." She waved her toward the kitchen. "I forgot it was Darlene's day off and she has a doctor's appointment in Bangor, otherwise she said she would have come in. If you could begin breakfast service now for early risers and those leaving soon that would be great. I'll see if Cal is around—he can help before he has to pitch in on the turnaround."

Amy started to say that Cal was in the kitchen but

stopped herself. "No problem. There are plenty of pas-
tries, and what we make to order for breakfast is easy."

"Maybe for you." Cindy smiled. "I can boil water
for my tea and use a microwave. That's it."

The kitchen was completely empty and the only indication that there had been people in earlier were two
empty Sanpere Shores mugs on a counter. It was too
soon for the dishwasher to be in—and Amy hoped he
would show, since he was new this week—so she un-
loaded the last load from the night before and put the
mugs in before getting to work setting up the breakfast
buffet.

She loved being in the kitchen alone. Solely in
charge. Life didn't get any better than this.

Tom's swiftness at getting them in and out of the
sheriff's office was almost embarrassing. No, it *was*
embarrassing, Faith thought. She had been very much
aware of every word that came—or didn't come—
from her mouth. Fortunately, Sophie hadn't been sub-
jected to the same talking-to and asked the questions
Faith would have. She had called Sophie with the news
of their discovery on Green Island as soon as Tom
had left to get Amy the night before. Sophie had also
leaped to the conclusion that the two men were killed

around the same time and wondered whether the second man was also from Lowell. And she knew about the numbering system for pot buoys. It would be easy to find out who owned the trap. Happily, she asked the sheriff both questions.

"The second victim was living in Lowell," the sheriff said, "and may have grown up there. His last name was also LeBlanc. It appears the two men were cousins or maybe half brothers."

When Faith had heard this, she thought of the wake that would be held at some point down in Massachusetts. A family losing two members at once. No matter what the men had done or not done, it was still tragic.

The sheriff had appeared reluctant to answer Sophie's question about the pot buoy, saying only that it wasn't registered to anyone on the island or surrounding ones. Seeing that she wasn't satisfied with the answer, he added tersely, "It was from Gloucester, Mass." At that point, Tom had thanked the sheriff and walked toward the door. Faith had no choice but to follow.

The three stopped at Martha's Diner. It was the real deal. There was a Martha and first-timers as well as regulars got a warm welcome from her. The diner had opened in 2004, but the 1950s retro decor was no imitation. Faith thought Martha and husband, Peter, must scour yard sales and eBay constantly for all the authentic memorabilia—Elvis, Lucy, *I Dream of Jeannie*. The diner opened at six in the morning and closed at two, six days a week. Although Peter's Greek heritage provided alternatives like his delicious spanakopita, you went to Martha's for all-day breakfast.

Settling herself into one of the booths with their red vinyl-covered seats and Formica tables, Sophie started to talk about what they'd just learned. "They didn't look alike, but they could have been cousins certainly, even half brothers."

Tom finished the coffee that had automatically appeared when they sat down and motioned to the server. "I'll have the Northwest Harbor omelet, steak as rare as possible, with sharp cheddar please. Faith, Sophie, are you having omelets, too, or something else?" They got the message. "The spinach and feta, the Hancock one," Faith said quickly. "Your homemade bread for toast, thanks." It was extra for the bread but well worth it.

Sophie was scanning the menu fast. She didn't come here as often as the Fairchilds. "I'll have the Brewer— haven't had corned beef hash in a long time—Swiss, and the homemade bread, too. Also, some orange juice when you get a chance."

Tom was taking charge of the outing—timing *and* topics of conversation. "What did Babs have to say about her day out in Bar Harbor with Zach's mother? And is she looking forward to the memoir workshop?"

"They had a good day and came back loaded down with shopping bags. Alexandra did comment it was a wonder Pix wasn't as big as an elephant, given what she had for lunch and an ice-cream cone that had given itself away with a smudge of chocolate on Pix's lip," Sophie said. "Later Babs told me Alexandra grows on you. But she's used to people like that. I sometimes think my mother is a chameleon, adapting to whomever she's with. Thank goodness I know the real Babs and can laugh, or just be in awe of the other."

"Us, too," Faith said, happy to enter *this* conversation. She'd talk to Sophie when they were alone about the topic off-limits.

"As for the writing courses, I think we're all looking forward to them," Sophie said. "I've been procrastinating long enough and hope to get a short story that could be the bare bones of a novel done by the end." What she didn't say, but both Fairchilds knew, was that she also hoped the intensity of the writing would keep her mind off having a baby. "It will be interesting to see who's in mine. It was open to fiction writers at all levels of experience. And I guess for memoir you just have to be alive."

Faith shot her a warning look, and Sophie said, flustered, "I mean obviously you had to be alive. Have a life, I mean. Oh wow, here's our food."

Sophie looked around the room with interest the next evening at the writers with whom she would be spending quite a bit of time over the next two weeks. It was five o'clock and the Writers' Welcome, as specified in the booklet that had been sent out, was about to start in the largest room of the main lodge. Sophie had been here in the past, but the new owners had definitely opened up the space—floor-to-ceiling windows and a large outer deck now faced the view. In addition, the furniture was more comfortable, Arts and Crafts in style as opposed to the previous knotty pine midcentury-motel look that Sophie recalled. Sanpere Shores manager Cindy had urged the group to get a drink before she spoke, and as Sophie suspected, it was a group that needed no urging. Although the females outnumbered the males by far, they still seemed to regard imitating Fitzgerald's and Hemingway's alcohol consumption an authorship bona fides.

Watching a woman who looked about Ursula's age down a generous shot of Scotch before holding her glass out for another, Sophie wondered whether she was a memoirist or a fiction writer—from her Miss Marple appearance, possibly specializing in cozy mysteries with cats and more tea spilled than blood. Or she could be a mistress of bodice-ripper romances. One thing Sophie had learned, and not all that long ago, was you couldn't judge by appearances. Especially not books from their covers.

She leaned back, took a sip from the white wine she had asked for, and admired the way Cindy was skillfully herding everyone to the seats. Cindy introduced herself again—"Two hats, manager and head of housekeeping"—and went over a few rules: no smoking anywhere except in the designated area by the parking lot; meal hours; spa hours and services; and so forth. Sophie's mind began to wander. Back at The Birches, Babs and Alexandra had displayed all the attributes of kids before the first day of school, consulting each other on what to wear and whether to take laptops or just their phones for notes. Sophie felt quite maternal as she ushered them into the car. Maternal! Stop it! she told herself and then amended it—*she might as well get some practice in. It was going to happen . . .*

"And here is the most important person of all," Cindy was saying. "This is Cal Burke, the head of maintenance and all-around fix-it guy, including IT. If you have any problems with the plumbing, your Wi-Fi, or heaven forbid, an unwanted visitor in your cottage like a squirrel, Cal will sort you out."

Cal Burke looked to be in his mid to late thirties and was wearing Levi's and a well-pressed blue work shirt that exactly matched his Benedict Cumberbatch eyes. Sophie had no doubt he would fill many of the attendees' sorting-out needs. She looked across at Alexandra, who was tossing her hair back—she'd decided to go for casual and wear it down—and paying close attention. She caught her mother's eye, and Babs winked. If it came to that, a little flirtation would keep Alexandra busy, as well as possibly providing more fodder for her memoir.

It was the instructors' turn to speak next. Sophie tuned back in.

"Hi, I'm Patrick Leary, and while I have not yet written my memoirs, I teach a course in them," the first instructor said in a slight Irish accent. It was too hot for a tweed sport coat with leather elbow patches, but Sophie conjured one up for him. He looked to be about fifty and his wire-rimmed glasses had already slipped down his rather prominent nose, as she suspected must happen often. His baldness was camouflaged by a cut almost to the scalp and she applauded his choice as opposed to a comb-over.

After Leary finished telling his group when and where they would meet in the morning, it was the fiction writers' turn to meet their mentor. Sophie had thought the woman who stood up was one of the students, and an eccentric one at that. She was a dead ringer for Emma Thompson as Sybill Trelawney, the Divination teacher in the Harry Potter films—trailing multicolored scarves, owl-like glasses, the kind of hairdo achieved when one sticks a finger in a live electrical socket, and a caftan decorated with both beads and tiny mirrors. It was a look she had likely adopted in the late 1960s and never abandoned.

"Please call me Eloise. Professor Bartholomew is not only too long, but too open to amusement." She grinned. Sophie liked her immediately. Eloise ran down the schedule and further endeared herself to the students in her group by suggesting they all grab another drink and go sit on the deck. "The view is magnificent. No need to take notes. We can talk about how to avoid writing fiction that sounds like a travel or nature guide another time. For now, just go soak it up!"

They did not need any further urging. As Sophie passed her mother, Babs pulled her down and whispered in her ear, "I may have picked the wrong group!" Sophie took the hint and refilled her mother's glass before leaving. Alexandra was in a world of her own, striking a pose, her chin resting on one hand—future author photo?—as she sat facing the maintenance man, who was still in the room. As Sophie went to join her group she had second thoughts about Zach's mother's possible interest in the handsome employee. Could be tears before bedtime. But, she said to herself, Babs would be there to keep all in check. Although, glancing over her shoulder, Sophie saw that Babs was also looking at Cal. Babs, whose husband of the moment was far away in the land of golf and haggis.

Talk about all dressed up and nowhere to go! Tears of frustration streamed down her face, ruining the makeup she'd taken so long to apply. At the last minute he had to fill in for someone. Again. He'd make it up to them. They could go to the Fry next Friday.

No thank you! She'd been thinking about it all day. Going to the Café, the one restaurant they could afford. Friday's Fry, always crowded with people she knew, wasn't just a meal. It was a gathering. Seconds were free. She always went for the haddock and onion rings with plenty of coleslaw. Her mouth started to water. She hadn't felt hungry in a long time, but she could feel her stomach rumbling. Damn it! They had reservations—you had to on Fridays—and she'd have to call and cancel now.

Or did she? There was no law that said she couldn't go without him. The Café was more than kid friendly. On Fridays the kids often outnumbered the grown-ups. So big deal—there would be two instead of three. She didn't have to let them know. They could share a booth with friends.

It was hot, so no jackets. She looked out the window at the car parked in the yard. She hadn't been driving for a while. Didn't need to. Didn't want to. She closed her eyes, the panic starting. Her throat was closing up. In the pantry she was keeping a few pills in an old contact lens case buried at the bottom of her flour canister. Soon her hands were covered with flour. She didn't remember deciding, but she must have. Just one. Just to take the edge off. Just so she could breathe. She popped it, washed her hands, waited, and soon she was dancing out the door.

"Mommy's happy."

"Yes, Mommy's very happy." She laughed and buckled the car seat.

"Tree, Mommy!"

"Yes, honey, lots of trees."

The noise of the impact barely registered. The crying did.

It was dark when she woke up. She was on top of her bed and dressed. Not bedtime. Not in paja-

mas. She closed her eyes anyway and then sat bolt upright and ran into the other bedroom.

Thank you, God. Thank you God, she prayed as she heard the soft steady breathing.

Thank you God. She went outside and moved the car back to where it had been, backing ever so slightly into the alders to hide the smashed left rear light.

Thank you God.

She went back inside and took another pill.

The Memoir Group had joined the others on the deck. Amy Fairchild and a young man, in the black pants–white shirt uniform that indicated a server, were bringing trays of hors d'oeuvres out in the approaching dusk. Amy was wearing a chef's white jacket and checked pants. She looked much as Sophie imagined Faith would have at that age. She went over to her. "Hi! This all looks delicious," she said and was delighted with the big hug Amy gave her. Still a kid.

"Try the seafood pot stickers—crab, lobster, and shrimp with a little chive. Oh, and the ham and cheese puffed pastry squares with Kozlik's sweet and smoky mustard. It's Mom's recipe. I taught the chef. You make it on a sheet pan in layers and then cut it up into little squares after it comes out of the oven. There's also a platter of cut-up veggies from King Hill farm in Penobscot with dipping sauces. And freshly baked breadsticks that we wrapped in slices of prosciutto."

"I'm going back to make dinner for Uncle Paul, but I can't resist some of these first," Sophie said, reaching for one of the breadsticks.

The cost for day students included lunch and dinner, but Sophie had the feeling she'd want to go home after a full day. Babs and Alexandra, social creatures that they were, would probably stay most nights, and in the future they should probably take two cars. She'd come back for them tonight unless they wanted to go back soon.

"I'll let you know when we're doing something special for dinner," Amy said. "Although most of them *are*. Tonight prime rib is one of the choices. Dessert is going to be on the beach. The Childses invited everyone to a bonfire once it's dark. We've got citronella torches to keep the bugs away. You might not want to miss it. Cal will be singing and telling jokes. It's fun, and the fire looks beautiful so close to the water."

"Don't tell me Alexandra is going to find out about s'mores!" Sophie laughed.

"Oh yes, and Darlene, who does most of the baking, made a ton of Whoopie Pies, too. Besides the Marshmallow Fluff–chocolate cake wicked good traditional ones, she also does maple filling and blueberry with lemon cake, in case someone doesn't like chocolate, which I cannot imagine! Did you know Whoopie Pies are the official Maine state treat? Like the state bird and other stuff."

"No, I did not," Sophie said in mock solemnity, "but if I'm ever on *Jeopardy*, this fact could come in handy." They both laughed. It was wonderful to see Amy so happy in her job.

"I have to go and finish the dinner prep," Amy said. "If you don't make it to the beach later, I'll send some of the pies back with your mom."

"Those two ladies won't have touched them I bet. Think of the carbs!" Sophie hugged Amy good-bye and decided to fill one of the small plates with the hors d'oeuvres. Paul liked to eat on the late side, and Sophie wanted a chance to check out the whole group further.

Why, she wondered, were there so many more women in classes like this than men? If you looked at bestseller lists, male authors outnumbered female significantly, so *some* men were writing. Maybe it was the whole notion of taking a class. Not a manly thing to do? Something you didn't need?

When they'd first gathered on the deck Eloise had

announced that she was not a "Hello My Name Is name tag type," which did not surprise Sophie at all. "Mingle, mingle. Get to know each other without a label!"

Sophie had mingled and introduced herself to two women who looked to be somewhere in their sixties and had sat together during the orientation. She learned they were college roommates, Susan and Deborah, now living in New York and California. They had decided it was time to write the novels they'd never had time for before. "Of course, you always read about those authors who get up at four in the morning and write for two or more hours before their day jobs or taking care of their families. I'm afraid my muse didn't wake me," Deborah said. She revealed that she had four kids, a surprise set of twins filling out the roster at the end. The notes she'd been making for years on yellow legal pads had stayed in a drawer until now. Susan had much the same story, except it was aging parents living with them, added to the kids.

"We're the MacDonalds from Morristown, New Jersey," a lively-looking woman said as she pulled a man with a tolerant look on his face toward the group. Mrs. MacDonald was the outgoing partner, it seemed. "I'm Cynthia and he's Ross. We both took early retirement last year. I saw the ad for this online and it's perfect. Ross has been delving into our family trees, so he's going to write it all up as a memoir for our grand-children, and I'm going to do the same, except make it fiction. Let them decide which ancestors they want!"

It was a novel idea, Sophie thought. She introduced herself and then made her way across the deck to speak to Babs and Alexandra.

As Sophie expected, the two women were the center of a group. "Isn't all memoir a kind of fiction?" Alexandra was saying. "What we remember is not always reliable."

"Especially at my age," said a man who could have been in his seventies but was definitely well preserved—thick slate-gray hair and the only wrinkles were laugh lines at his clear hazel eyes. Seeing Sophie, Babs announced, "This is my daughter, Sophie. Sophie, this is Hans Richter, originally from Germany, and I'm sensing a major memoir. Sophie's in the fiction group. You can't tell from her accent, but she's a southerner now. Her irresistible husband lured her to Savannah, his home-town. But she's a New Englander at heart, since she has been on the island every summer of her life, as have I."

"I've only been here a few hours and I already plan to come back," declared a woman dressed much the same as Alexandra and Babs. Sophie followed Alexandra's glance and was sure she could read her thoughts—

maybe the island wasn't as tacky and unfashionable as she'd first judged if people like this were raving about it.

Sophie leaned closer to her mother, who had looped her arm through her daughter's. "I'm going to take off now. I'm assuming you want to stay? I'll come back later to get you, and Amy has convinced me not to miss the bonfire."

"Yes, darling, we're going to stay." Babs lowered her voice. "You know why I was taking the course, but I'm glad now. Patrick is going to be a terrific teacher and I'm already inspired."

"And how about . . . ?" Sophie nodded toward Alexandra.

"I think she's even more excited than I am." Babs gave a little smile. "And such a good chance to make new friends." Alexandra was offering to get a tall good-looking gentleman who it seemed was in Sophie's class another drink.

"You're terrible." Sophie gave her mother's arm a squeeze. "See you later.

As she left she passed a new arrival—a pretty young woman Sophie judged to be her own age. As a whole, the group was older. The woman had paused in the doorway. Sophie stopped. "Hi, I'm Sophie Maxwell and taking the fiction course. Are you here for that—or the memoir one?"

There was no mistaking the relief on the woman's face. "Oh yes. I didn't know where I was supposed to go and I heard voices so . . . Oh, I'm Ellen Sinclair." She put out her hand. "And fiction. I mean I'm taking fiction." She blushed. Sophie shook her hand. It was small, in keeping with the woman's diminutive size. "I misjudged how long the drive would be. I'm from Burlington, Vermont."

"My family has a house here," Sophie said, "so I'm a day student. My mother and a friend are taking the memoir course. They're over there by the bar." She pointed. "I have to run, but I'm coming to the bonfire."

"Bonfire?" Ellen said.

Sophie laughed. "An old-fashioned camp-type one. Not *Fahrenheit 451*." She spied Eloise making her way toward them. "Here comes our instructor. Perfect timing."

Ellen gasped slightly. "She looks exactly like Sybill Trelawney, you know the . . ."

"Divination teacher," Sophie finished and patted Ellen on the shoulder. A kindred spirit.

The original owner of what was now Sanpere Shores had been a retired botany professor. He'd built a main lodge with several cabins in the 1950s, attracting like-minded naturalists who thought the spot, walks, and sails were an ideal vacation. He'd used the site well. The buildings were up high above the beach, a long curve on deep water. Sophie was glad for the outdoor lighting as she walked down the wide path, but also glad it had been turned off at the end as she stepped onto the sand. The fire was sending deep red and orange sparks into the night sky, and she could hear someone singing over the crackling flames. As she drew closer, she saw it was Cal, accompanying himself on the guitar. The two writers' groups numbered around twenty-five, Sophie knew, but the actuaries were double that. So it was a sizable crowd that was obviously enjoying the rich desserts and Maine sky.

Cal stopped playing as a man and woman emerged from the shadows to stand directly in front of the bonfire. Cal clapped his hands for silence and said, "It's my pleasure to introduce Dr. and Mrs. Childs, your hosts and my bosses."

Sophie was surprised at their appearance. As the owners of three such high-end resorts she had pictured a couple much like her mother and Ed. Dr. Childs looked like a pudgier, slightly taller version of Mr. Bean and wore round glasses with black frames. Mrs. Childs, also rotund, appeared twice his height and had a dark brown Dutch bob. The doctor was wearing a seersucker sport coat and his wife a shirtwaist dress reminiscent of

June Cleaver. Maybe they had just arrived and hadn't had time to change into L.L. Bean–type clothes.

"Out of the three properties we are fortunate to have acquired, Sanpere Shores is our favorite. This is a very special island, and although you will be busy with tasks during the day, I hope you will get to explore a bit during your free time. Cindy, our manager, and Cal here can help you with suggestions. Cal can also provide transportation for those of you without vehicles."

He had an old-fashioned delivery, Sophie thought, but he wasn't that old—late forties at most. Same for his wife, who was echoing his advice. "Now, enough of us, enjoy!"

Cal proceeded to liven things up, starting a jazzy rendition of "Makin' Whoopee," presumably inspired, Sophie thought, by the Whoopie Pies going like hotcakes. "Another season, another reason for makin' whoopee . . ." He really had a great voice. He paused for a moment when a woman carrying a guitar walked onto the beach and went over to him. She picked up where he left off, their two voices complementing each other perfectly. At the end of the song, he nodded to her. She smiled and started singing "House of the Rising Sun" solo. She sounded like a young Joan Baez, that extraordinary range, the crystal notes. Sophie was spellbound and hoped she would keep on singing. She untied a pink bandanna, letting her long dark hair hang loose while shrugging off a black leather jacket, tossing both on the sand away from the heat of the fire. Sophie could see the back of the jacket clearly. A red rose, painted by an amateur hand.

The singer was the woman who had been with both LeBlancs in the market.

Chapter Seven

Sophie counted eleven people gathered in the Shores dining room the next morning, the tables cleared except for a small coffee and tea station by one window. There were four new faces, late arrivals last night she assumed—a man and a woman who had hitched their chairs close to one another, obviously a couple; a guy about her age wearing Diesel black jeans and a tight black tee, hair carefully spiked to appear casual; and finally a teenage boy dressed in tan work clothes, a bruised thumbnail that looked as if a hammer had landed wrong. If he had not had an open notebook, she would have assumed he was on the maintenance crew.

"Welcome, welcome! Hello everyone!" Eloise was

clearly a morning person. Sophie was not and got up to refill her coffee mug before sitting back down.

"You've all come with differing expectations. The first thing you must do is discard them. The novel or short story you plan to write will not get finished. You will not learn any secrets about how to get published. In short, there aren't any, except to write a good book, and even then it's a long shot."

Sophie looked around the room at her fellow students, noting expressions ranging from shock to outright despair. The exception was the man her age, who looked smug. No doubt he thought he was the one who was going to make it—National Book Award, Pulitzer, Edgar, etc.

"But, as they say in the land of my birth, 'Don't get your knickers in a twist.'" *Ah,* Sophie thought, *Ms. Bartholomew* was *British. Emma Thompson's stand-in?*

"I'm not sure writing can be taught." Eloise seemed to be musing aloud. "I mean you have it or you don't. The itch. The talent." Finally noting the looks on most of the class's faces, she hastily amended, "But I can jump-start you *and* help make your results better. My mantra is 'Rewrite, Rewrite, and Rewrite Again.'" She flung one of her scarves, turquoise with purple fringe, over her shoulder for emphasis.

"That sounds like Elmore Leonard," the man in black drawled in an accent Sophie found hard to place. Not southern, not anywhere distinctive. Very practiced, though.

"Ah yes, Elmore's rules. Miss him very much. If you want to look them up or any other's—I'm partial to Orwell's—go ahead, but I would highlight the one he shares with Mark Twain about avoiding weather. As in don't start with 'It was a dark and stormy night' unless it's satire. Twain left all the weather out of *The American Claimant*—'No weather will be found in this book.' And put it at the end in an appendix for those readers who absolutely had to have it. As for myself, I can safely tell you I have no rules or if I do offer some—avoiding adverbs totally for example—I'll tell you to break them, as I just have."

Sophie was enjoying herself. She'd read both Orwell's and Leonard's rules. Her favorite was Elmore Leonard's advice to "leave out the part that readers tend to skip." It occurred to her, however, that sticking to that could leave her with a very short book.

Eloise was continuing. "Now I said mingle last night and no name tags," Eloise continued, "but before we start this morning's exercise, please briefly introduce yourself, name and where you live will do. Leave out where you live or make up a name if you want, but I need something to call you. The class list didn't include mug shots."

This last brought somewhat nervous laughter from a corner of the room, but Sophie couldn't tell whether it was the couple or the woman she had already categorized as Miss Marple.

Louise Todd, "a Jersey Girl" she said proudly, went first, then Susan and Deborah introduced themselves. Susan was from La Jolla, California, and Deborah, Bronxville, New York. Sophie knew both places, and the women weren't going to have to rely on royalties to keep them in today's equivalent of typewriter ribbon. Miss Marple was Mrs. Joan Whittaker from Montreal, Canada, and as Sophie knew, Ellen Sinclair was from Burlington, Vermont. Sophie went next and mentioned both places of residence. The couple had different last names—she was Karen Mann and he was David Donaldson, both from Ohio, no specific town. The teen was George Finley from Portland, Maine, and a day student like Sophie. Last up was Jay Thomas, "from here, there, and everywhere," he smirked, adding, "published in—" But Eloise stopped him cold. "No prima donnas here. I don't care if you won the Nobel Prize for Literature or best editorial when you were in high school. This isn't a competition, and if it were, I'm pretty sure it would be an even playing field."

Ignoring the indignant look he shot her, Eloise said, "Now, let's get started with a seemingly simple exercise, but things are never what they seem." Sophie glanced over at Ellen Sinclair, who obviously shared the feeling that they were both in Divination class about to peer into a crystal ball. Sophie had to fight to stifle a giggle.

"*P-O-V.* Point of view. The ability as a writer to put yourself in another's shoes, or whole psyche, is key to developing voice. We'll get to that discussion this afternoon. Voice, I mean. Plots are an easy fix—usually. But only the writer himself or herself can supply voice." Eloise waved a small stack of index cards at the group. "I'm going to hand each of you a card with a character on it—a parent with a toddler, an alien visitor. You will have forty minutes—thirty plus ten to rewrite—to describe the place in which we are sitting from the point of view of what or who is written on your card. When we are finished, I will read each aloud and you will try to guess the character." She started passing them out. "Find a place where you can concentrate, outdoors if you like, and use the pads of paper that were in your course materials. No computers today. Too easy to cut, paste, employ a thesaurus, other tools. I want you to connect with the words directly, viscerally."

Someone let out an audible sigh of disgust, and it wasn't hard to tell who. Jay as in Jay K. Growling.

Pix was going to have to get over the feeling of foreboding that swept over her each time she woke up. Just the thought of the Cranes not so far from where her head rested on her pillow caused a knot in her stomach far removed from the nautical ones she was good at—learned from her father along with rowing a dinghy and hoisting the mainsail and jib.

She needed to get back to her old self. The pre-Crane self. It sounded like an epoch. Well, the way she felt placed her squarely in the Paleolithic. She got out of bed, relishing the metaphors. Faith would enjoy them. She'd call her and some other friends for a sail today. Maybe all women. A Girls' Sail Out.

It was quiet not only next door but also in the entire cove. Only the sudden arrival of a boisterous flock of crows jarred the peace as Pix sat on the deck enjoying her breakfast of homemade (not by her) granola, Greek yogurt, strawberries, and coffee. She was soon finished and made her calls. Everyone was busy today, but three, including Faith, were free tomorrow. When she hung up she was happy she'd arranged the outing.

She was also due for drinks and dinner in Blue Hill at friends' tonight, so it wasn't that she didn't have things to do, but she missed Sam in a way she never had other summers. She'd always packed the kids up as soon as school ended and Sam came when he could, taking a long vacation in August. But that pattern had ended years ago when all three went off to camp for part of the summer and eventually whole summers elsewhere after college. She never minded being alone at the house. It was this summer that was out of sync somehow.

Concentrate on joy. She thought she'd seen it on a poster or maybe it was from one of Tom's sermons. She thought of Ed Ricks's LIFE IS SHORT, EAT DESSERT FIRST pillow and thought she'd do one with this reminder. Or at least put it on the top of her never-ending to-do list.

She washed her dishes and decided to go for it right now. Joy. The wedding. She would bring Arlene's matron of honor dress over for her to try on and drop off Kylie's flower girl outfit. Arlene was like another daughter, and the thought of seeing her expression when she saw the dress in person undid the knot in Pix's stomach, leaving only the knot her daughter was tying.

Who could it possibly be? Her mother had al-ready been by as day camp chauffeur since the car was being repaired. It was drivable—only needed a new taillight and a little bodywork, but it wouldn't have been legal to drive it. If she'd heard that once, she'd heard it a hundred times, and how did it happen anyway? No one saw who backed into her in the market's parking lot? How was that possible? he kept asking. It was the busiest place on the island, especially at the time of day she said it happened—late afternoon, when the fishermen were heading home and stopping for beer, maybe pizza for dinner if they weren't married. Someone must have seen something. He'd asked around. She let him. What else could she do? It actually made her laugh.

But who was outside now? Coming toward the porch? The cabin wasn't a place you passed. You had to know the long dirt drive leading to it. For a moment she panicked. She'd been so careful not to let any of her off-island suppliers know that she even lived on Sanpere. And she didn't owe them money. Could it be Earl? Found out somehow? She raced to the window. No, it wasn't his patrol car or his personal one. She knew whose car it was and her heart sank.

Smile, Arlene, she said to herself. Smile—and get rid of your best friend's mother as fast as you can.

The variety in writing styles, and skill level, was noticeable, but Sophie was relieved that none of the pieces Eloise read aloud were duds. She credited the instructor with selecting a challenge that anyone could meet. She also was quite sure that Eloise had tailored the POV to each student, although how she could have known Sophie was surrounded by examples of the simple description on her card—"eighty-year-old person"—wasn't clear. Just eerie. Back to Divination.

Eloise read each without names, but Cynthia MacDonald had squealed, "Oh you're all going to hate this!" revealing herself as the author of an ant's point of view. Her piece was very funny, and Sophie decided that Mrs. MacDonald was much smarter than she let on. She wrote in first person and filled the space with Brobdingnagian creatures. The ant employed clever tactics to avoid getting squished. Sophie thought an expanded version would make a fun children's book.

Her own piece brought positive comments—although Eloise made it clear that if someone didn't have something good to say, a mouth should be kept shut. She was the only critic allowed. Sophie had imagined herself as an eighty-year-old woman who had come to dinner in this room, one she had not been in for fifty years. Most of it was a flashback—partly the room's appearance, originally heated only by the massive two-story fireplace still extant—but the rest recounted the woman's passion for her lover, as they secretly met here at the then old unoccupied hunting lodge for the last time, each unable to break their wedding vows. Sophie tried hard to keep it from being too sentimental, focusing instead on the wrenching nature of their choice. The last sentence returned the reader to the present and the woman's realization that her lover is there at the dinner. She hasn't recognized the old man nor he she. Or had they?

It was getting close to lunchtime, and Sophie saw Amy hovering at the kitchen door, peering out to see how the group was getting on. The memoirists were meeting in a large cabin up the hill, where the Childses stayed when they were on-island. The two groups would alternate spaces, and Eloise had also mentioned some off-site locations, specifically the Roland Howard Meeting Room at the Blue Hill Library with a side trip to E. B. White's lovely small hometown library in Brooklin.

So far all the guesses as to the identities of the names written on the cards had been close or spot-on. Eloise was now reading the last one. Glancing at her fellow scribblers, it did not take Sophie long to identify the writer. He was sprawled back in the leather Stickleytype armchair he had appropriated as soon as the group arrived this morning, and his eyes were half closed. She could see his thoughts clearly, like skywriting—"Words like jewels from the hand of a master."

And they weren't bad. He did have talent. Some. But they were so grim, so horrifying, that Sophie was afraid it might put the group off lunch. His last sentence, describing the final act of the card's "a killer—human or nonhuman," was doing it for her: "The adder's fangs like carefully honed shivs dripped crimson gore on the lifeless arm. His job was done."

Pix didn't see Arlene's car, but as she'd pulled up to the house she'd seen her face at the window. Carefully gathering the two garment bags with their precious contents in her arms, she went up the front steps. Arlene, Mike, and Kylie had moved into the log cabin a little over a year ago, and Mike was working on it when he had time. The steps had been replaced, she noticed, but Pix knew there was a lot to do inside. The former owners had bought it as a kit and only finished the shell.

Arlene was a passionate gardener—she was one of Ursula's acolytes—but Pix was surprised to see no sign of the blooms that had edged the front of the house last summer. Arlene must be concentrating on the vegetable garden in the rear. Mike had cleared enough trees to create a good-size sunny patch.

"Hi, Arlene?" she called. "It's Pix with your gorgeous finery!"

The door opened slightly more than a crack and Arlene said, "Hi, thanks. I'll take them and try mine on later. Kylie's at the Community Center day camp. She can try hers on when she gets home this afternoon."

Pix took a step forward. "I know she'll look adorable. Samantha sent you a picture, right? She's continuing the rose and ivory tones for the whole wedding party. Zach is wearing an off-white linen summer suit with a pale pink shirt and ivory bow tie. The ushers—Mark and Dan, his soon-to-be brothers-in-law—are wearing the same shirt with chinos and a pale green bow tie. The color of my dress." Pix knew she was babbling, but Arlene hadn't moved or said anything more. As the door opened a bit more, she added, "And of course Kylie's is pink, a tulle skirt and lacy top. Little Sam is going to be dressed like the ushers and best man, except Bermuda shorts, not chinos. And suspenders with little lobsters." She smiled but did not get one in return. "Samantha really needs you to try your dress on right away in case it needs to be altered . . ." Pix ran out of steam.

There was a brief silence. Arlene sighed. "You'd better come in."

The rooms had been partitioned off and a few walls were up. "We're going with 'open concept,'" Arlene said sarcastically. "Mike's never home to do any work and we can't afford to hire anyone. So our bedroom is closed in, but nothing else."

The house was tidy, but Pix imagined it might get depressing to live without a finished kitchen—just boards on sawhorses for counters, what looked like a hand-me-down stove and fridge plus no cabinets, only storage containers. Added to what must seem an overwhelming project was the fact that the cabin was in the middle of nowhere, even for the island, Pix reflected. No neighbors to commiserate with or lend a hand.

"Arlene, honey, is everything okay?" She chose her next words carefully. "You seem a little tired."

"I'm fine, absolutely fine. Why wouldn't I be? Let me take the dress into the other room and I'll try it on." She snatched the bag from Pix's hands.

"Samantha ordered shoes dyed to match from the same place she got all of ours, and she'll bring them when she comes up for the shower," Pix called after her. "And Susie Shepard is doing everyone's hair Saturday morning, plus she has a friend who will do mani/pedis."

Pix looked at her hands. The last manicure she'd had was for son Mark's wedding four summers ago.

Arlene didn't say anything, just walked out of the room and closed the only inside door. Firmly. Pix had known Arlene almost all of Arlene's life and had seen her in every stage of dress and undress. Well, she was a matron now. A matron of honor. It was fine if she didn't feel comfortable changing in front of Pix.

She was out almost immediately. Pix swallowed hard. "You look beautiful," she said softly. "The color is perfect for you and we just have to take a little tuck here and there." The suggestion was a huge understatement. The dress hung on Arlene like a tent. Arlene's arms, clearly visible extending from the short cap sleeves, were so thin her veins showed blue. She'd taken off her sneakers, and her bare ankles looked sharp enough to break through her skin. Pix had seen Arlene at the Fourth of July parade, but she'd been wearing a loose long-sleeved top and overalls. Pix remembered thinking Arlene must be roasting in the record heat. Now she knew it was so no one would notice how much weight she'd lost. It explained why she'd been dodging Samantha, too.

Pix couldn't help but walk over and hug the girl—she'd always think of the two as girls, these BFFs. Under the gown's beaded top she could feel nothing but bone—and a rapidly pounding heartbeat. "You know you can tell me anything. What's going on? You're so thin, darling."

Arlene pulled away. There were tears in her eyes—whether from sorrow or anger, maybe both, Pix couldn't tell. "I wanted to look good for the wedding, so I went on a diet. Leave the dress. I can take it in. Tell Samantha I love it and I'll see her soon. The shower is going to be great. I have to go weed the garden now."

It was a dismissal. Pix followed her out the back door and then detoured around the side of the house to her car. A quick look told her that there wasn't any garden to speak of—a few mounds of squash and a raised bed of what might have been lettuce before the deer got to it.

"Good-bye," she called over her shoulder.

There was no answer.

Samantha's shower! She had to do the shower. Invite people. Plan a menu. Who? What? For a moment she panicked. Then she remembered. Her aunt Gert was doing the food, and it was going to be at Samantha's grandmother's. She went back inside. The sunlight hurt her eyes. There was a stack of invitations on the table they used for everything—eating, paperwork, Kylie's art. She had stamped them with a heart stamp and she'd filled out the time, date, and place. She just had to address them. They could wait. There was plenty of time. Plenty of time now, too. She went into the bedroom and lay down on the quilt, wishing herself far away. And soon she was.

The two writers' groups ate lunch together. Sophie sat with her mother and Alexandra, both of whom were consuming a mound of salad greens, no dressing, and water. "You really should try the crab salad," Sophie said. "Amy told me it's made with a drop of lemon juice and scant amount of mayo. Very crabby. I know you won't go for it in the crab roll, but it's delicious." Sophie was savoring hers—the traditional flat-sided white bread hot dog roll had been grilled in butter, then stuffed with the crab mixture, no onion or celery fillers. It came with coleslaw and sweet potato fries, which she was also making short work of despite the looks both her mother and Alexandra were casting on the plate. "I'm drinking unsweetened tea," she said defensively.

"Darling girl, you're certainly old enough to decide what you want to eat," her mother said, eyeing the fries pointedly. "Now, tell us how your group is going? The instructor is certainly picturesque."

Sophie smiled. Trust her mother to assess Eloise by her wardrobe. She described the morning's exercise and said, "I think she's going to turn out—at least for me—to be excellent. We are each meeting with her individually after lunch. I like the others in the class, except for that guy over there all in black. I don't know why he would come to such an unknown program. Couldn't get into Iowa or Sewanee is my guess. His 'Too Cool for School' is already grating on me. What's your group like?"

Alexandra answered, "I'm not sure most of them would qualify when it comes to material for an interesting memoir, except perhaps Patrick. Married, by the way, even though he isn't wearing a ring. I heard him talking about his husband to Ross MacDonald." She turned her head away from the table quickly. Cal Burke had just walked into the room. Alexandra sat up straight. "There are other irons in the fire, so to speak," she said in what sounded to Sophie like a very adolescent sotto voce, then called out, "Cal, there's a place here." She patted the chair next to her.

Cal smiled back. "Sorry, ladies. I'm going to chow down fast in the kitchen. I have to get right back to work. That other group must be ditching old tax returns down the plumbing, judging from all the unplugging I'm doing. Another time." His smile, Sophie thought, really was pretty devastating. It crinkled his bright blue eyes and radiated across the room. She exchanged a look with her mother, who was watching Alexandra toss the scarf around her ponytail over one very smooth tan shoulder.

Babs picked up the thread. "Most of the people in our class have been doing research on the Internet about their ancestry and want to get it all down as a coherent story. Not really memoirs. Patrick is encouraging them to start with their own lives first. Childhood up to the present and then weave in the past or write it as a separate beginning or end."

Alexandra sniffed and continued to be derisive regarding her fellow classmates. "Take Ross for example. The man has sold insurance all his life. What kind of story is that going to make?"

"You never know," Babs answered smartly. "Didn't you ever see *Double Indemnity*? And come to think of it, Ross looks a little like Fred MacMurray."

Sophie swiftly changed the subject to Alexandra herself. "How about your memoir? I don't even want to think about Mom's. Possibly more of a list than a narrative," she teased.

"I don't know that I'll share it with anyone, except Patrick," Alexandra said. "We can opt out of having him read our works in progress." She shoved her half-eaten plate of salad aside. "It has been interesting to think back. Our first exercise was to write down our very earliest memory. Mine was very clear. I must have been only two or so, since my mother died when I was three. We had gone to a lake in northern New Jersey where relatives of hers had a summer place. The door from the living room onto the veranda had a bead curtain, strings of them hanging from the lintel. I suppose it was intended to keep flies from coming in. The room was dark, but it was a sunny day. I can still recall the sensation of that bright warmth as I pushed through and the way the light made rainbows of the jewel-like beads. I think that's why I've always been drawn to beautiful things." She stretched out her left hand. No wedding band, but a large square-cut emerald surrounded by small diamonds that would not have been out of place in the Tower of London's collection. "I like to rotate my rings and other baubles," she said complacently. "Today seemed like a green day. All these pine trees."

"What a beautiful memory," Babs said. "I'm afraid mine was quite prosaic. And I wasn't as young. We were at my grandmother's and I was bored, so I snuck out of the room and down into her preserves pantry in the basement. I did write about how cool it was—stifling upstairs and maybe the company, too. Anyway,

I opened up at least ten jam jars, stuck my finger in to see which I liked best, and knocked over a whole shelf of watermelon pickles before anyone missed me. Every time there was a family gathering after that, someone was sure to ask me if I wanted jam or a pickle."

Sophie laughed. "Did you get punished?"

"Of course. Those were 'spare the rod and spoil the child' days. My grandmother was pretty handy with a switch. I never did anything to provoke her again. Sadly she was gone before you were born and I'm sorry you never got to know each other." Babs sighed. "I'm afraid she wouldn't have thought much of my serial nuptials. I'm sorry to hear you lost your mother when you were so young, Alexandra. I was eleven when my mother died."

Sophie knew this and had often wondered whether Babs's adolescence spent in boarding school with a loving but absent father had caused her to seek so many "forever" partners. It also explained why Babs had been so close to her late aunt Priscilla, uncle Paul, and The Birches. The sole sureties in her life. Who had been there for Alexandra?

"People, people, I mean *my* people," Eloise said, standing up at her table and clapping her hands together. "Finish up please, and look at the list I've left with Cindy indicating times this afternoon for each of you to meet with me. And I've left you another exercise that should be both a challenge and fun."

Knowing that Sophie and George Finley were day students, Eloise had thoughtfully scheduled them early. First George and then Sophie. During the break before lunch, Sophie had spoken briefly to him. He worked as an elementary school custodian in Yarmouth, outside Portland, and lived in South Portland, he'd told her. He was attending night classes at Southern Maine, working toward a BA in English with enough education courses so he could teach high school someday. His dream was to support himself as a writer, but he was realistic about his chances and figured "I'll always have to have a day job." He'd enrolled in the Sanpere Shores class to get feedback on a detective novel he'd been working on, the first he hoped in a series. "People like a series. I do anyway. Watch the main character change, but also deep down stay the same guy."

He'd found a good deal on a studio Airbnb in Granville and was enjoying living on the island. He looked about fifteen—freckles and a carrot top—but he told her he'd graduated from high school two years ago, so that made him nineteen at least. When he came to tell her Eloise was ready for her, he grinned. "Don't worry. She was gentle." Sophie laughed. He called after her, "Does she look like that teacher in the Harry Potter movies to you? Maybe she can predict my future as a writer."

"**What do** you hope to get from me? From these two weeks," Eloise asked Sophie. They were sitting down on the beach. Eloise had spread out a woven mat and offered Sophie water or juices from a cooler. A large package of Oreos had already been opened. Eloise pointed to the cookies. "I always get very hungry when I write and assume other writers do, too. When we meet bring your snack and tipple of choice. Oreos and lemonade are mine, but you may have other preferences."

"I'm not a writer," Sophie said, "but a lawyer, and as for a tipple I'm afraid I drink way too much Diet Coke. I live in Savannah, Georgia, most of the year and it's a food town, but when I grab a snack it's a yogurt from the firm's fridge. My husband is trying to change my ways, though. He's introduced me to pimento cheese sandwiches, my new favorite."

They talked a bit about Sophie's background— Sophie stuck to the expurgated version, omitting her resignation from a high-powered New York law firm and her heartbreak in London. This wasn't memoir—or therapy. Instead she sketched out her idea for a short story set in Savannah during the time of the Underground Railroad.

"When I moved there I began to learn about the signals—hanging patchwork quilts with certain blocks whose names indicated a safe house on fences and the escape tunnels under the city, remnants of which remain. But what was most evocative for me was visiting the First African Baptist Church, the oldest African-American congregation in the country and a stop on the railroad. There are twenty-six sets of apparently random holes drilled in the pine floor in what is now the lower part of the church that provided ventilation for the men, women, and children who hid there. The pattern wasn't random. It was a Kongolese cosmogram symbolizing the four movements of the sun and the journey of the body from the physical to the spiritual world. So a sign of hope. I thought I could try to imagine myself as one of the people huddled there. Perhaps a mother with a small child . . ." Sophie's voice trailed off.

"Are you a mother?" Eloise asked.

"No," Sophie said. She started to add "not yet" but stopped and just said "no" again.

"Go for it. I love your idea." Eloise nodded her head firmly.

The exercise Eloise had assigned was an intriguing one. It was a bit like a menu that asked you to choose one from Column A and one from Column B. The instructor had listed a number of first lines and an equal number of last lines. The task was to select one of each and fill in the part in between. No word count was specified. Sophie took her laptop, permitted now, out to the deck where several others from both groups were at work. She was relieved that the rule of silence was in effect and no one did more than nod in her direction.

She sat taking in the view for a few minutes. The cove was a large one, and the land that marked it on either side was heavily wooded above the sloping granite ledges. And the beach itself was a single sandy crescent with few of the stony outcroppings common to others on Sanpere. Sophie imagined what a haven this sheltered landing spot would have made for the Abenaki, the original settlers on the island or, more correctly, the original summer people, traveling from the north to spend the months in the comparatively warm clime fishing and storing up essential foodstuffs for the winter.

She examined the list. One of the last lines was simply, "The End." She liked Eloise's sense of humor and decided to go with that choice. The first line was harder. What to write about? As she stared at the beach, the white sand seemed to be moving in front of her eyes, but she knew it was the effect of the harsh sunlight. The scene came first—the canoes landing, the occupants setting up summer quarters. No lightweight North Face dome tents. They'd have to first venture into the woods, much denser than now, to find saplings, strip the leaves and bark, bend them to support the animal skin coverings they'd packed. She looked at the first lines again. "Her tired face betrayed her words." And there she was on the beach: an exhausted woman, how old? Reassuring someone, a man? Another woman? That she was fine and could keep working.

Sophie's fingers flew across the keyboard and when she looked up, Sophie was surprised to see that only two people remained on the deck—Ellen and Jay. She glanced at the time on the screen. She'd been working for over an hour. So this is what writing could be like. She'd experienced the same intensity working on briefs, and it occurred to her that the process was the same. Eloise had said "Good writing is good writing, whether it's fiction, nonfiction, a letter to your mother, or a report for your boss."

Sophie stood up and stretched. She did a few yoga poses—"tree" seemed a natural—to get the kinks out.

She saw someone—no, it was two people—heading up the path at the end of the parking lot. Cal Burke was easy to spot. And so was the young woman with him. The red rose on her jacket a dead giveaway.

"Mom, you have to make her stop!" Samantha's voice over the phone was close to a shriek.

"Of course I will, just as soon as you tell me who it is and what's she doing to you? From the sound of it, pulling your hair out one strand at a time?" Pix thought a little humor was in order. She was pretty sure this had something to do with the wedding, but it couldn't be Zach's mother. That was all settled and she was far from Boston, plus from the sound of it she was deeply involved in her Shores class while enjoying The Birches's guest quarters.

Pix was wrong. The future in-law's tentacles were far reaching.

"I get like ten links a minute to items on wedding websites for the most ridiculous stuff you can imagine with demands that I choose at once or they won't be shipped in time!"

"Can't you just politely write back that everything's under control and already ordered?"

"I did, but she wanted to know what they were and

what our theme is. She's suggesting 'Modern Glam' or 'Beach Chic,'" Samantha said glumly.

"Theme? The theme is 'Getting Married.'" Pix had to stifle a giggle. Samantha was seldom this upset.

"Matchbooks, packets of tissues, Tic Tacs, pens, lip balm. Refrigerator magnets, golf balls—golf balls, Mom!—cocktail shakers, glassware, bride and groom rubber duckies, 'Measure Up Some Love' measuring tapes, fans! And all with our names or initials, the date. She knows I'm keeping my name and also not going to be a 'Mrs.,' but she's already sent us terry cloth robes with 'Mrs. Zachary Cohen' on mine and 'I'm the Groom' on Zach's."

"The fans might not be such a bad idea," Pix said. "It could be hot. And you don't have a terry cloth robe."

"Mom!!!"

"I know, sweetheart. Just trying to lighten things up. I'm assuming Zach has tried to get her to stop?"

"Total failure. And even worse, she hates what he's picked out for his best man and the ushers. 'Tacky' she said."

"Remind me what they are?"

"Zach's best man is as much of a geek as Zach is, and he found some very cool circuit board cuff links and a matching belt buckle. The ushers are getting belts with monogrammed buckles. How could you call that tacky?"

"Sounds elegant," Pix reassured her, "and the computer whatever is a very personal touch."

"Alexandra wants Zach to get the buckles in sterling. Even if we could afford that, we already have them in their sizes—the guys will be wearing them for the wedding. And speaking of tacky, she wants to order toilet paper with little stick figure brides and grooms on the rolls!"

"Surely she was joking. That doesn't exist, does it? I take that back. I'm sure it—and more like it—does. As for the belt buckles, I honestly don't think your brothers either care or could tell the difference between sterling silver and whatever you picked. They're just happy to be part of it all. I'll have a word with Babs—she can deal with Alexandra—but for now why don't you give in on a few items?"

After a pause, Samantha said reluctantly, "Okay, the fans. You seem really big on those."

"Exactly. Your grandmother is bringing one of hers anyway, and now we'll have plenty to go around need be. But I think you have to choose a few more items."

"She's picked out reusable water bottles, too. So fans, the bottles, and I don't know. The ducks?"

Pix did start laughing now. Samantha was still her little girl. Rubber duckies! "Go for them! Suggest date and initials on the other two and that way you avoid any Ms./Mrs. conflict."

"I love you, Mom," Samantha said in a voice now several octaves lower and unruffled.

"I love you, too, darling, and it's going to be a wonderful wedding. Can't wait!"

"That makes two of us. Gotta go. Another email coming in. Maybe you could do something to her computer?"

"I'll tell Babs instead. Way more effective. Bye."

Pix knew Babs would still be over at the Shores with Alexandra, and she certainly wasn't going to leave a message on the machine for anyone, that is, Alexandra, to overhear, so she'd wait until she could get Babs alone either on the phone or in person. In a way she hated to take away the fun Alexandra was obviously having searching out all these favors—the measuring tape could come in handy—and maybe the solution was to have her send the suggestions to Pix, explaining Samantha was in a crunch time at work, which was true.

The tide was right and the air was warm. Time for

a swim. The Cranes were in residence, so that meant a bathing suit. She didn't want them trying to have her arrested for indecent exposure. Her skinny dips would have to be on moonless nights.

Chef Dom told Amy to take a break after lunch, so she had walked the Barred Island trail the Island Heritage Trust had created in the woods on one side of the beach. It felt good to be outdoors.

The kitchen was empty when she returned and she was surprised that the chef wasn't there starting dinner preparations. Saturday night was prime rib with traditional sides, as well as grilled halibut and a tofu veggie stir-fry option. She got out the veggies from the walk-in and started to cut them up. The creamed spinach was done and just needed warming, but after she finished the veggies she'd better start getting the potatoes ready for baking.

The whole lodge was quiet. Amy put down the knife and went through into the main area. Cindy wasn't at reception and no one was inside, although she could see a few of the writers with their laptops out on the deck. Sophie wasn't one of them. She must have gone back to The Birches already. Amy went back to the kitchen and was relieved to see Chef Dom come in through the outside door.

"Oh hi, Chef, I've started some of the prep work," she said. Chef Dom sat down unsteadily on a stool. His face was ashen and his eyes were half closed.

Her relief became short-lived. Alarmed, she asked, "Could I get you some water, Chef?" He didn't respond, but Amy poured a large glass from the pitcher of ice water they kept in the smaller fridge anyway and tried to hand it to him. He didn't reach out to take it, so she left it on the counter where he could reach it easily.

"Chef, would you like me to start on the desserts? The meringues are made, so they just need some of the Ice Cream Lady's strawberry ice cream and fresh berries. We were going to do grapenut pudding with whipped cream, but I think we'd better do that tomorrow and maybe tonight just offer ice cream sundaes with various toppings." She could hear her words rush together in a long, agitated stream.

Chef Dom slumped over and Amy ran to keep him from falling, bracing him against the counter. He opened his eyes wide, but he didn't seem to recognize her. His pupils were huge, and she realized he was sweating, even in the cool kitchen.

"Chef, I think you need to see a doctor. I don't want to leave you alone, but I have to go find someone to take you to the medical center."

The words seemed to rouse him from his stupor. "No doctor," he shouted, straightening up.

Amy backed away, frightened. She slid her hand in her pocket to feel for her phone. She pulled it out and turned away, punching her mother's number on the favorites list. But before the call was answered, she heard a crash and whirled back around. The chef was on the floor, eyes closed. She could tell he was breathing from the rapid rise and fall of his chest. She ran over. "Chef, Chef Dom!"

He didn't answer, but her mother did.

"Mom, Chef Dom may be in some kind of a coma. He fell off the stool onto the floor and isn't responding to me! I'm calling 911."

"And I'm on my way."

Chapter Eight

He wasn't dead. Amy repeated the fact to herself several times. She knew the ambulance corps would be here soon, very soon if one of the volunteers lived nearby. Help would come in time. He wasn't dead . . .

She knew there were people on the deck, but unless one of them happened to be a physician she didn't want to alarm them nor want to leave Chef Dom alone. His face had lost all its color and his eyes were shut tight. She felt his pulse but had no idea what the rate meant other than that he had one.

The door to the dining room opened. It must be the dishwasher, she thought, but it was one of the students in Sophie's class. The guy who looked really young.

The sight of the chef cut off whatever he was starting

to say and he instantly went over. "I'm an EMT. What's happened? You called 911, right?"

"Yes. He just came in and sat down, didn't say anything except when I suggested he go to the medical center he got mad and said 'no doctor.'"

"From the look of it, he's had a heart attack. I'm going to start CPR. Why don't you go outside and tell whoever comes where he is? My name is George, George Finley."

"I'm Amy Fairchild. He's been kind of sick all week. Even before that. He has bad allergies," Amy said, pushing open the screen door and swiftly heading for the drive. It felt good to be able to do something.

She had barely reached it when the ambulance sped in. "This way!" she called and waved toward the door. "In the kitchen! It's the chef. He's—" The EMTs pushed past her.

Cal Burke came running from the conference center. "Who's been injured? What's going on?"

"It's the chef. He—" Cal didn't wait to hear whatever Amy was about to say but raced into the kitchen. She hesitated, not knowing whether she should follow or not. Then she saw her mother's car pull into the parking area and ran to it. As Faith opened the driver's door, Amy blurted out, "Oh, Mom, I don't know if he's going to be all right. He just fell over and he looked so bad when he came in. Not like himself!"

"Hush, sweetheart," Faith said, gathering her daughter into her arms. "They'll get him over to Blue Hill Hospital immediately. You did the right thing, calling so quickly." Over Amy's shoulder Faith could see the ambulance crew loading what appeared to be a very large man on a stretcher into the ambulance. They were giving him oxygen. A young man and another older one, neither of whom she recognized, were following close behind. She kept Amy nestled tight. This was not a scene she needed to see.

The ambulance took off in seconds, leaving the two men standing by the lodge. Both stood still for a moment and then the older man darted around to the front door and went in. The younger man looked over to where Faith and her daughter were standing. Amy pulled away from Faith, running toward him. "George! What did they say? Is he going to be all right?" Faith followed and said, "Hello, I'm Amy's mom, Faith Fairchild."

"I'm George Finley. I'm taking one of the courses here and I happened to go into the kitchen for some water right after your daughter called 911. I work in an elementary school and we're all certified EMTs."

"What grade do you teach?" Faith asked.

"All of them," he said. "I'm the school custodian."

Faith knew why he said that. The custodians at Ben's and Amy's schools in Aleford knew the kids better than anyone, and yes, they had lessons to impart.

George put a hand on Amy's shoulder. "Your chef will make it, but he's not going to be cooking for a while. I wouldn't want to give any kind of false diagnosis, but he was carrying a lot of extra weight. I'm sure the hospital will be in touch with Cindy." He looked at Faith. "She's the manager here. She'll be able to tell you more when she hears." He turned back to Amy. "This must be hard for you, since you've been working with him all summer, right?"

Amy nodded and Faith realized there were tears in her daughter's eyes. "He was an amazing teacher. Let me try new things. Treated me like a future chef."

George dropped his hand. "Well, future chef, at the moment you are the only chef. I'm pretty handy with the basics like scrambled eggs—except nothing more complicated. But if you tell me what to do, I might be able to help with dinner, and I'm sure the Shores will have a replacement by tomorrow."

What a prince, Faith thought to herself, perhaps though a prince in cloud cuckoo land. There was no way the owners of Sanpere Shores were going to find a replacement for the chef at the height of the summer season, especially as the resort/conference center promoted its gourmet cuisine as one of its attractions.

She looked at Amy. Amy was looking at her. "Mom . . ." "Amy . . ." Their words overlapped. Amy's prevailed. "You could fill in at least tonight, right, Mom? Dad has been working late. You don't have to be anywhere, do you?"

George looked puzzled, and Amy said, "My mom is a caterer. A pretty famous one in Massachusetts and New York City before that. But we might need your help, too. Almost nothing is ready yet. The chef said he would do it all this afternoon and told me to take a long walk." Amy started off in the direction of the kitchen.

Faith sighed to herself. What was she getting into? Motherhood meant a lot of things, but showing up when needed had to be number one. "Okay, let's go see what we have to do."

As soon as they entered the kitchen, they could hear loud angry voices from the dining room. Faith didn't recognize them, but George quickly said, "Amy, maybe you'd better tell Cal and Cindy tonight's dinner solution." As she pushed the door open, Faith could hear the woman saying, "This is totally your fault. If you think I'm covering for you, you have another think coming. Or like a few hundred. And you call. Oh hi,

Amy." Her tone changed markedly. The door swung shut behind Amy, muffling the rest of her words.

Amy was back a few minutes later. "This is pretty bad timing," she said. "We are fully booked and the actuary group is an important client of Dr. and Mrs. Childs. Cal is calling the two of them about what happened, but Cindy doesn't think it will be easy to find a chef for at least a few days and definitely not one close to here."

"Let's just get through tonight," George said. "I mean, who doesn't love a good rare prime rib? Doesn't need fancy sauces, so pretty simple. Shouldn't the servers be coming soon to set the tables? And there's a dishwasher, right? I talked to him last night while he was putting in the final load. I'm kind of a night owl. Good habit for a writer. Anyway, he's a good guy and will pitch in. And what about that lady who has added pounds to my body with all her baked goodies? Maybe she can work extra hours for the next couple of days?"

Faith looked at the young man. A prince didn't come close. George Finley should be bottled.

Even though Pix knew Sam wasn't coming this weekend, she'd kept listening for his car in the drive. He'd be here by Friday and would stay until after the wedding. Like shrinks, it seemed lawyers disappeared for most of August. Faith had called earlier and explained she wouldn't be able to go sailing today. "Or maybe not for the foreseeable future. The chef at Sanpere Shores is out of commission. Maybe a heart attack. It all happened yesterday afternoon. Amy and I handled dinner."

Pix had expressed her regret, but there would be other sailing days. "Be careful, Faith," she'd warned. "They will try to get you to take the job. I can't imagine where they'll be able to find an experienced chef at this time of year."

The other two women were still on for sailing, but with an hour to kill before going out, Pix decided to walk to the other side of the Point. She didn't know where all this nervous energy was coming from, but she found herself inventing tasks and outings for herself. It must be the wedding, she thought. Wedding jitters.

She took the long way around—the opposite direction from the Cranes' house—strolling through the remnants of an apple orchard. The Point had been home to several farmhouses, but aside from the Hamiltons', they were barely discernible cellar holes. When the children were young, they'd thought of them as buried treasure chests—digging up pieces of china and occasionally a deep cobalt medicine bottle. Mark had found a coin silver spoon once, and it now reposed in a case at the Historical Society with his name as donor.

A stand of slender birches was so beautiful, the trunks strokes of white against a backdrop of greens, that Pix stood still for a while. It was Sunday, after all, and this was as much a church as any. More, perhaps. Sunlight filtered through the branches, making patterns on the moss and pine needles below—a kind of stained glass window. She said a brief prayer of thanksgiving and, whether it was that or the surroundings, felt her previous unrest melt away.

"Hey! Is that you, Pix?"

It was Nan Hamilton, and Pix circled round the trees to where the woman stood, a basket on her arm. "I thought I'd find some chanterelles. This is usually the best spot, but it's been too dry. Instead I've found a large patch of wild strawberries. If you have time to help me pick, we'll drop some off at your house. Ever since Faith taught me how to make that Italian pudding with these strawberries on top, Freeman can't get enough!"

Pix laughed. The "Italian pudding" was panna cotta and so easy that even she could make it once Faith walked her through the steps.

"I'd love to help you, but with just me at the house now, you keep them all for yourselves." There was something very satisfying about picking any kind of berries, Pix thought as she crouched down to pluck the tiny ruby-colored fruits from their stems. Blueberries were best, especially when the can was empty and they made that *plunk* sound. "How have you been? I haven't seen much of you this summer," she asked.

"We've been fine. Freeman is ornery because his doctor won't let him smoke cigars anymore or eat pork rinds, but it's lobster boat racing season, so he's plenty busy. He's raced in Jonesport and is only going to race here besides, but he and the boys have been going to all the others. They're up to Winter Harbor this weekend."

Pix smiled to herself at the mental image of the "boys"—Freeman and his buddies were in their late seventies and beyond—cutting loose on the Schoodic Peninsula.

They picked in contented silence until Nan said, "It has been a little hard this past month what with Freeman's niece Jenny living with us. You may have heard. That she's with us, not that it's been hard."

Nan wasn't given to personal revelations like this. Pix *had* heard that the niece, whom she remembered visiting as a younger girl, was there. But nothing else. "She used to come up during the summers, right? Remind me where she lives the rest of the year?"

"In Massachusetts. She's Freeman's youngest brother Harry's girl. They lost her mother to cancer a few years ago and Harry remarried this winter, but Jenny and her stepmother don't get along. No blame on either side. Just oil and water. Maybe Harry spoiled the girl—she wouldn't remember a time when her mother wasn't sick, and I guess he thought he could make up for that."

"How old is she now?"

"Just turned nineteen and she's some smart. Going to the University of Massachusetts near where they live in Lowell. Music major. She wants to teach, but she could make a pretty good living singing. Voice like an angel. I still get goose bumps remembering how she sang 'Ave Maria' at her mother's funeral. Don't know how she got through it. I was crying like a baby. Freeman, too."

"So she's here to get a break from her home situation?"

Nan nodded. "She's no trouble. Helps out—even hauling traps with her cousin, always was handy on the water, could pilot the boat before she was twelve—but I worry about her on land. She's out at night a lot, singing at various places. Freeman fixed up that VW bug he found in Uncle Henry's for her to use while she's here." Pix smiled. Like many men, including her own husband, Freeman was devoted to Uncle Henry's weekly classified swap or sell guide.

Nan stopped picking. "Sometimes she's not back until early morning. I know because I lie awake until she's in. Of course, Bar Harbor, that's one of the places she goes to perform, is far; but Sanpere Shores is almost around the corner."

Having spent sleepless nights for all three children, Pix was sympathetic and gave her friend a hug. "Poor Nan. You must have thought you wouldn't have to cope with a teenager, especially a teenaged girl, again."

Nan gave her a sharp look. "My girls are all growed, and most of my grandchildren, but you know you're never done coping or raising, however you want to put it. Not until they're all tearful at your wake."

"Truer words never spoken," Pix agreed and added, "Why don't you tell her that you're worried and would appreciate knowing when she expects to be home? And why don't we go hear her? Maybe we can hire her to do a few songs at the wedding if she is still here?"

Nan looked a bit more cheerful. "Well, I'll ask her when she'll be singing at the Shores next. She goes over to the open mic nights at Tinder Hearth in Brooksville, too."

"Now let's get the berries to your house and I have to get ready for a sail this afternoon. Why don't you come with us? Elizabeth, my friend in Sedgwick, is coming, and Marcia Klein—you've met her. She's a friend in Massachusetts and rents here in August."

"Another day. Without Freeman underfoot, I'm getting so much done. Enjoy your sail—perfect weather for it."

"How about your niece? She might enjoy coming."

Nan looked straight at Pix. "She might, but I have no idea where she is today. Never do."

Dr. and Mrs. Childs drove up to Blue Hill, hired a private ambulance, and moved Chef Dom to a health facility in Massachusetts. They spent Saturday night at the Shores and early Sunday morning. Dr. Childs called Faith to ask if he and his wife could meet with her.

"Sure," she said. "But I know what you're going to ask and the answer is no. We have a family wedding coming up at the end of the month"—well, if the Millers weren't family, who was?—"and I can't commit to a full-time job as chef for the Shores."

"Would you please just talk to us for a few minutes? We'll come to your house if that's easier," he'd pleaded.

His wife had taken the phone at that point and Faith had realized from her brisk manner who was in charge.

"Mrs. Fairchild, if Amy were over eighteen we'd hire her in a heartbeat. She's an extraordinarily talented young chef—and a lovely young lady."

Faith had felt herself softening. It was all true. "Okay, I'll come for a brief chat. I'm driving Amy over now anyway. After yesterday's shock, we wanted her to sleep in, and I was sure Darlene's handling breakfast fine on her own with your manager and the servers."

Which is how Faith found herself sitting on the deck at the Shores with Dr. Childs, who looked a bit like a Teletubby, and Mrs. Childs, who had the tubby part down, but was an amazon. She towered over him, and Faith, too. As she shook each hand Faith noticed the contrast there as well. The doctor's grip was limp and flabby; his wife's could break a brick. Dr. Childs was wearing a dark suit; Mrs. had the kind of dress that Faith associated with old black-and-white TV shows. Where did one buy this garb now? Vintage stores? It had what she knew was called a Peter Pan collar, but there was nothing that wasn't very grown-up about both Childses. Their teeth, of course, were perfect.

All the way over to the Shores, Amy had begged her mother to take the job. "A week, tops? Less. They'll find someone soon. You don't have to do anything for Samantha's wedding until way closer to the time. Gert Prescott and Arlene are doing the food for the shower."

Then she delivered the coup de grace. "I'll be going away to college in another year. This would be a special time for us to be together doing what we love. A time we'd look back on all our lives, Mom!"

Hence Faith had given in before she took a single step onto the deck, where Darlene had placed a carafe of coffee, cups, milk, sugar, and a basket of mixed berry muffins on one of the tables. She kept the fact that she was going to take the job—for a short time—to herself and let the couple urge her, offering an extremely good wage and making promises to search the whole country as fast as possible to find a replacement. She negotiated a raise for Amy, whom she'd sent off to the kitchen—"My daughter will be acting as sous chef"—and endured final handshakes.

Before she left, Amy gave her a tour of the kitchen—it was impressive—and showed her the menus she and the chef had drawn up for this session. Also impressive. Faith left with the menus and lists of suppliers, and steeled herself for Tom's reaction.

She was very pleasantly surprised.

"That's great, honey," Tom said. "Gives you a chance to spend quality time with Amy." Faith was suddenly thrust back to the days when that phrase meant reading *If You Give a Mouse a Cookie*. Tom continued, "I know it's been lonely for you here without any of us and

I like that I can think of you two in the Shores kitchen making people happy with your great food."

You don't fool me for a minute, Thomas Preston Fairchild, Faith thought. You want me tucked safely away stirring pots instead of stirring up trouble, that is, bodies.

When Pix pulled into the drive at The Pines, she was surprised to see that Gert Prescott's car was still there. Her first thought was that something must be wrong. When Pix rushed in, she found Gert sitting at the kitchen table reading the *Ellsworth American.* "Your mother was resting, but she must have heard the car. I can hear her walking about."

"Is she okay? Just tired? Or . . . ?"

"More okay than almost anyone I know," Gert answered. "I knew you'd be along soon, so I stayed to ask you if you knew what happened to the shower invitations. No one I know has gotten one. I thought Arlene was sending them out, but she said Samantha or you were. I called her to talk about the food as well, but she had to run. Take Kylie someplace."

Pix frowned and sat down next to Gert after putting the groceries on the counter. "I'm pretty certain Samantha said Arlene was taking care of them. I know she gave her a list of names and addresses, because she gave me a copy, too. Most on the island, of course, but Samantha also wanted to invite some of her Wellesley friends who are coming to the wedding even though they probably wouldn't be able to make both."

"I asked the postmistress and she said she would have noticed them going out or in—the envelopes are blue with a big silver wedding cake sticker on the flap. And they have those LOVE stamps on them. Well, it's a mystery. That's what it is."

Ursula came into the room. "What's a mystery? Or maybe what isn't?"

Pix laughed. Her mother was in a good mood, well rested, and there was nothing to worry about. In the long scheme of things, missing wedding shower invitations were a mere sprinkle.

Gert told her about the invitations, and of course Ursula had the solution. "No one will care if she ends up with two invitations. You have the list, Pix. Go to Blue Hill tomorrow morning. I'll bet The Meadow has dandy ones, and we can call on Thursday to get the RSVPs unless they come in. Besides, it's only people off-island who haven't had it on the calendar all summer. Now, Gertrude Prescott, what are you still doing here? Go home and put your feet up! Unless you want to stay and have a drink with us. Paul will be over."

"You know very well I haven't had any alcohol since my friend Margie and I mixed ourselves a concoction from her grandfather's liquor cabinet that had us sick as dogs for days. Can't abide even the smell of the stuff."

"This is the first time I've heard about your wild youth and I'm shocked," Pix teased.

Gert walked toward the door, turning back to say, "I said I didn't drink, but Margie and I were devils in other ways—she started driving when she wasn't but fourteen and there were always rowboats we could 'borrow' and go out to Green Island for midnight swims."

After she left, Pix mixed drinks—gin and tonic for herself and martinis for Ursula and Paul, arranging crackers and cheese on a wooden bread board either Mark or Dan had made in shop in the shape of a fish. She and her mother went out onto the porch to enjoy the cool of the early evening. Paul would know where they were.

"What do you think happened to the invitations?" Pix asked.

"I don't want to think, so I'm not," Ursula answered. "We'll have a fine time. Gert has the food all set. You'll get new invitations out. Concentrate on that. Maybe go up to Ellsworth after you send them—won't matter if they are mailed from Sanpere or Blue Hill—and get some decorations. Some foolish-type favors, too."

Her mother may not want to think, but her thoughts were way ahead of Pix's.

By Thursday, Sophie was totally immersed in her characters—and the characters around her. After her initial visit to First African Baptist Church with her Savannah neighbor Lydia Scriven, who was a member and also a guide, Sophie had gone back often. Sometimes for services—the music *much* livelier than the Maxwell family's praises to the Lord—but often to simply sit and feel the events of those years, tangible echoes in her mind. She was drawing on these memories now for the story and found that even when she wasn't putting words down, she was thinking them during the day. Seeing scenes, hearing voices.

As for the other characters—her fellow students— they were providing mostly entertaining distractions, breaks when she came up for air—or in, as she had claimed a quiet spot out of the way on the deck to work. Eloise had not assigned any more group assignments but individual ones. She asked Sophie to write a full description of her main character—appearance, personality, background, and so forth—explaining that these were not necessarily words that would appear in Sophie's finished piece but would inform it. It had taken

Sophie hours, and then, dissatisfied, she'd started it all over again. Not trying to alter what she had written—heeding Eloise's cut-and-paste admonition—but starting from scratch. She felt a bit as if she were cooking and maybe that was what writing was—assembling ingredients. She was even more pleased with the instructor as time went on, writing down some of Eloise's advice: "If you want to be a writer, you have to like to be alone and indoors." And the most important: "You have to write every day. Not intend to write, but write. Something, no matter how short."

As she had first thought, Ellen was a kindred spirit and Sophie already knew the two would keep in touch once the course was over. Ellen didn't share what she was working on and Sophie didn't ask. She also liked George Finley, who was the opposite and entertained them with updates on his progress and possible plot twists in what seemed to Sophie a very complicated suspense novel. The three had formed the habit of eating lunch together.

The college friends, Susan and Deborah, had explained to Sophie they'd set themselves a word total each day and once reached, they wanted to enjoy this all too seldom time away from responsibilities. They'd told her the Shores spa was great, which Babs had also mentioned. Sophie kept her nails short and did her own manicures, but a facial, or even better, a massage, sounded like a fine idea.

Cynthia MacDonald was having fun fictionalizing the family tree, as evidenced by the occasional bursts of laughter while she typed. It occurred to Sophie that husband Ross might not find the anecdotes his wife was dreaming up quite so amusing. Babs had mentioned that he was taking his memoir very seriously and had not agreed with Patrick's suggestion that he include his personal reminiscences, but was sticking to the facts, ma'am, only the facts.

The Ohio couple had announced that they were collaborating on a romantic suspense novella and after Eloise greeted the group each morning, they retreated to their cottage to work—or "work." Several times Sophie had seen them drive off before lunch, and perhaps they wanted to explore the area for inspiration. They'd been very open about their plan, adding that they'd decided to set the tale on an island in Maine. They already had a title: *Tides of Love*. Now they just had to write it.

Joan Whittaker, the woman from Montreal, was also writing a mystery. She'd revealed this when Jay Thomas told the group he was working on one. "Me, too," Joan had said brightly, and the look he'd given her was appropriately poisonous. "I doubt they'll have much in common. I do 'noir,'" he'd said.

Eloise had jumped in at that point, interrupting Jay before he could describe his magnum opus. "I'm not surprised by the group's choices. Genre fiction"—Jay made a face that bordered on indecent, which she ignored, continuing firmly—"genre fiction is easier to sell, and market, than literary fiction, that coming-of-age breakthrough debut novel every writer has in the back of his or her head. Joan is writing a traditional mystery, and as he has said, Jay is going for noir. Big difference. Traditional mysteries end with the restoration of order. Noir sees the world, or universe, as chaotic. Impossible to fix. I enjoy both, all forms in the genre—I have catholic tastes, which is one of the reasons I enjoy teaching. I never know what someone will be writing. And romantic suspense has always been popular. I often think of those books as cinematic, like du Maurier's *Rebecca*. So we are running the full gamut here—humor, historical, several kinds of mysteries—George has me on the edge of my seat with his chapters." She laughed and told them to get to work, ignoring Jay's scornful glance at George.

Before she got to work, Sophie went into the kitchen

to talk to Faith. It was a bonus to have her friend so close by. As predicted, the Childses had not found a replacement chef, but Faith told Sophie she was getting regular texts telling her how hard they were searching. Faith and Sophie had laughed at the skepticism reflected on each other's face.

"Always smells great in here," Sophie said now. "What's for lunch?"

"Cobb salads—I know your mother and Alexandra will modify theirs—then, since I am cooking bacon, a lobster BLT, plus a quinoa bowl with edamame and other good stuff. What you're smelling is the biscuits in the oven for old-fashioned strawberry shortcake, one of tonight's desserts."

"*Real* strawberry shortcake, you mean. I remember the first time I ordered it in New York and it came on a sponge round. Ugh!" Sophie looked around the empty kitchen. "Where's Amy?"

"Chef Dom had the foresight to plant an herb garden when he arrived in June and she's picking basil for us to make pesto."

Sophie gave Faith a little poke. "You're happy that things turned out this way, aren't you? And the longer the Childses take to find a replacement the better. Admit it."

"I do. For two reasons," Faith said. "The most important is that I'm having fun cooking professionally with my daughter. We've cooked at home often, but this is very different. I haven't changed my mind about her college choice—I still want her to get a liberal arts education first—but I also have no doubt she's going to be a great chef. Far too few women in the profession. Just think of those competitions on the food networks and the most well-known restaurants chefs—all very heavy on the testosterone."

"Try lawyering," Sophie said. "Although that has changed since I started. But you said two reasons. What's the other?"

"I think something's wrong here." Faith frowned and stepped past Sophie to take the first batch of biscuits from the oven.

"As in?"

"I'm sure you wouldn't, but please don't let on to Tom or talk to me about it in front of him or Amy either. I'm uneasy. And it has nothing to do with what happened earlier, although I guess I'm kind of on high alert. I never met the chef, but from Amy's description of his behavior prior to his collapse, I'd say he was heavily into cocaine. She told me he kept a giant box of tissues in the half bath over there because of his allergies. He was leaving more and more of the food prep to her while he took a 'nap.' And his herb garden has a large, healthy crop of marijuana—yes, it's legal, but I'm not sure for as much as is there. I saw it when Amy showed me around Sunday. She's so naive, she had no idea what it was. It was gone Monday when I went to cut some parsley. Not that smoking weed would produce his symptoms or behavior, but it's another indication that something may be going on among the staff."

"I've heard that restaurant workers are often drug users. The pace, the intensity, and some kind of macho gonzo chef thing."

"Exactly, but I wouldn't have expected it in a place like this—at a conference center essentially. I've asked both Cal and Cindy separately how the chef is doing, telling them Amy is worried, and both said he's fine. Had become overtired and his weight put a strain on his heart. They both looked away when they were speaking—the way Ben always did when he told me he hadn't touched the layer cake on the counter with a slice missing."

Sophie had told Faith about seeing the girl who had been with Dwayne LeBlanc and the others at the market at the bonfire that first night. Now she recalled she hadn't mentioned that she'd seen her go off with him the other day. She did now.

"And you said she sang like a professional, right?

I wonder if she could be Jenny Hamilton, Freeman's niece who is living with them this summer. Nan told Pix she sang 'like an angel.'"

"That's a good description," Sophie said.

Faith stopped taking the biscuits off the baking sheet. "Pix also said she was having family issues— new unwanted stepmother, having lost her own mother to cancer. And Sophie, Jenny lives in Lowell."

After Sophie left, Faith kept thinking about the vibe she was getting from Sanpere Shores. Cal Burke had crossed off a number of the suppliers that had been on the chef's list, telling her that Cindy thought they were being overcharged and was finding new sources. At the time, Faith hadn't given it much thought. She got along with both Cal and Cindy, but she wished they would stay out of the kitchen more. It seemed they were in for coffee or a cold drink every time she turned around.

And she'd started to wonder about Cal in particular. She knew he was from the island and had left when he was either just out of or still in high school. Why did he come back? And she never heard him refer to any family members, even when she asked. The island was so interconnected that his answer—"No one around anymore"—didn't ring true.

Today Cal had asked Faith to prepare a range of snacks for a storytelling and sing-along tonight in the Annex, which had a lounge where there was a full bar. "We'll be showing a short film about the island on the big TV, then I have a few tales up my sleeve to convince them they really are Down East. After that we'll have some live music," he'd said. It was her daughter who asked the question Faith couldn't—she wasn't supposed to have heard of Jenny Hamilton. "Cal, is that lady who sang at the bonfire coming again? She was amazing."

"Jenny? Yup, I'm sure Jenny will show up."

After Cal left, Faith slipped around the lodge to the back steps that led to the corner of the deck where she'd seen Sophie working. On the way she passed a large covered woodpile and some other sheds. The smell of pot from behind one of them was so strong, Faith picked up her pace to avoid a contact high. Over her shoulder she caught a glimpse of someone dressed in a black shirt and jeans and another person, a woman, or at least someone with long hair down the back. She went up the stairs quickly and tapped Sophie on the shoulder, startling her.

"Sorry to break your concentration. I know how writers are."

"Not this one. I'm beginning to think that even though I have a good story to tell, I don't have the skill. But you're right, it is engrossing and I didn't hear you come up behind me. What's up?"

"You may want to stay for dinner tonight, or come back afterward. Jenny Hamilton is going to be singing."

"I will definitely be there," Sophie said. "Let's hope she wears a sleeveless top." Faith had told her about clearly seeing the tattoo letters dripping from the adder's fangs on the second body at Green Island. L F D Y. They had both recognized the pop culture initials representing the phrase, a credo: "Live Fast Die Young."

Faith had to shoo Amy out of the kitchen when Tom came to pick her up. "Two of the servers are staying on, and there's the bartender—you couldn't help there anyway. As soon as the program starts and I'm sure the food is covered, I'll leave, too. We're both tired."

Amy put up one more feeble token protest and left. They were working a long day. If she hadn't wanted to hear—and see—Jenny Hamilton, Faith would have left the last of the work for the others. The food was prepared—bar snacks: small Cubano sandwiches, nachos, pigs in a blanket, thin and thick pretzel sticks with various mustard dips, cheddar popcorn, and a mix Faith had created: roasted chickpeas with some cayenne for kick, mini corn chips, golden raisins, sesame sticks, and honey roasted peanuts. A sweet, salty, spicy combo for every taste. Having seen the way both the scribblers and number crunchers were going through the wine and beer plus mixed drinks before, during, and after dinner, she wanted more than enough food to soak up the alcohol.

She walked over to the center and slipped in next to Sophie, who had saved her a seat. The film was about life on the water—a day with a lobster fisherman. "Good thing this isn't smell-o-vision," Sophie whispered. "Will went out with Ed Ricks and it was only a few traps, but the bait got to him, and he was pea green for the rest of the day!"

When the lights went up, Faith looked around. Babs and Alexandra were in the front row, literally at Cal Burke's feet. The place was packed, whether from lack of alternatives or the open bar, Faith wasn't sure. Cal was telling a few stories Faith knew he'd cribbed from Bert and I, the original Down East yarns that Marshall Dodge and Bob Bryan had recorded so many years ago, but familiar to all Maineacs. The Fairchilds' friends Steve and Roberta Johnson had even named their lobster boat tours "Bert and I Charters," although Faith suspected the "Bert" part was also a nod to the lovely second mate.

"Are there many from your group here?" she asked Sophie softly. "Some," Sophie answered. "I don't see my friend Ellen, but her shyness would have kept her from a gathering like this. I also didn't see Jay, the obnoxious literary enfant terrible I told you about. This wouldn't have been his thing either, but for a different reason. What amounts to home movies, tired jokes, and a sing-along? I don't think so."

Cal had worked his way through "You can't get there from here" and was finishing with the "You're up in a balloon, you damn fool" answer to the "Where am I?" question from someone from away in a Montgolfier hot-air balloon from the Maine codger in the field below.

Faith yawned. "I don't think I can stay awake much longer. You check Jenny out and let me know. Everyone will be hitting the bar now for a while before the music. I'm going to be sure there's still enough food and leave."

"No worries. I'll move up next to Mom and try to keep Alexandra from throwing her panties at Cal."

Faith laughed and went over to the buffet they'd set

out. The servers had been keeping the platters filled and assured her there was plenty more. She also spoke to the bartender, as Cindy was nowhere in sight. It was the manager's job to remind him to cut anyone off who had had too much, watering the margaritas or whatever the drink was before it got to that point, but since she didn't see her, Faith took it on herself. It was all fine. "That guy over there has been happily drinking lime seltzer in a glass with a salt rim for an hour, and that lady"—he nodded in another direction, at a woman who looked like a member of Ursula's sewing circle—"has been steadily imbibing OJ and seltzer 'mimosas.'" Faith thanked him and headed for her car in the employees' parking lot up the hill past the larger lot for guests and visitors.

A darkened pickup truck was parked almost next to her car. As Faith got closer, the driver's-side window rolled down and a head wearing a gimme cap turned to see who was coming. She paused, not sure what to do. She was very aware how far away from the lodge she was. Before she could decide, the passenger door opened. Someone jumped out, slammed it shut, and sprinted for the woods. The truck backed up, narrowly avoiding Faith, and screeched off down the road.

Shaking slightly, she walked to her car. There was

something on the ground. Something that had been tossed out of the truck when the door opened.

It was an empty syringe.

Faith called Earl's home number. He told her not to touch the syringe and he'd be there right away. He also told her to get in her car and lock the doors. "Faith, I'm afraid finding these is becoming more and more common."

When he arrived, she started to tell him what Ed Ricks had talked to her about, but he cut her off. "We'll talk soon. Right now you need to get home and get some rest. If you remember anything distinctive about the truck or the people let me know, but don't stress yourself out." He patted her shoulder, the equivalent of a bear hug—Earl was not demonstrative.

"Thanks," she said and left him to his task. He'd put on gloves and was placing the syringe in a plastic evidence bag, shining his flashlight over the entire area.

As she drove down the long road from the Shores to Route 15, she tried to think about possible details. There had been nothing distinctive about the pickup. Black or navy. Not tricked out with loud mufflers. Not new. She was pretty sure about that. And the two men—if they had been men; she couldn't be sure of that either—were like cats in the night.

An hour later she got a long text from Sophie. "Long-sleeve peasant blouse and yes, incredible voice. More tomorrow, but during a break I accidentally spilled red wine on her right sleeve, rushed her to bar for club soda despite protests. No snake. But same letters L F D Y plus ."

Pix knew Sam was leaving work Friday as soon as he could get away. Samantha was coming with him for Saturday's shower. So after she made a run to Madelyn's for a haddock burger to go, extra tartar, she put on a well-worn pair of pajamas and sat at the kitchen table with a bag of salt and vinegar potato chips, the burger, and a beer. She propped the latest Mary Kay Andrews open and felt utterly content. Her near and dear would arrive in fewer than twenty-four hours. All was well with the world.

"Surprise!" Her near and dear were here now! "Don't worry, Mom, we stopped at Madelyn's, too. Don't you think we know what you get up to when you're on your own?"

Pix wasn't thinking anything except how good it felt to have Sam's arms around her, then Samantha's. She was, however, very glad they had brought their own provisions. Otherwise it would have been a cornflakes night.

"Honey, do you smell something?" Sam was shaking his wife's shoulder.

"Hmmm?" she said sleepily.

He shook harder. "Wake up! I smell smoke."

Chapter Nine

Pix was awake instantly. She sat up, and sniffed. "It's not here," she said, starting to lie down again.

"But I think it's near," Sam said. "I'm going outside to check. Stupid kids may have set off firecrackers at the end of the Point again, and it's been so dry."

Samantha was at their door. "Do you smell that smoke? I'm heading down the road to check."

Pix was alarmed now, too. She shoved her shoes on, quickly following her husband and daughter downstairs and out the door.

"It's coming from the Cranes' house!" Sam said as soon as he stepped onto the deck. "Call 911. I'm going over there."

"No need. Listen," Samantha cried. "Sirens."

All three took off toward the next-door neighbors', using the shortcut—very short, since the clear-cutting.

"Thank goodness," Pix said, emerging into the field. "It's not the house."

They circled to the front. The fire was contained to the shed, threatening a few pines next to it. Cameron held a dripping garden hose, his wife a household fire extinguisher. Her hands were black with soot as was her face. In contrast, Cameron looked spotless. Apparently, Drew had been the one to attack the flames.

The volunteer firefighters immediately went to work, training hoses on the structure. Cameron dashed over to the Millers, followed closely by Drew. But it was Drew who started screaming at them first. The woman who had been silent in their presence before had plenty to say now. Arm outstretched, with her finger pointed at Sam, she said, "I saw you!! You're not going to get away with this! The glue was one thing, but trying to burn us in our beds is attempted murder!!"

"What the hell!" Sam said. "I haven't been here! You think I set this?"

Cameron's voice was only a few decibels lower than his wife's. "You're denying it? We both saw you drive past early this evening. My wife has trouble sleeping and she saw you run away from the shed from our bedroom window!" Before an astonished Sam could say anything, Cameron went back to the almost extinguished blaze and began talking to one of the firefighters, gesturing toward the Millers.

"Come on, let's go home," Sam said. "This is more lunacy. I don't believe it. These are very sick people."

Drew had started to move away to join her husband, but hearing the last remark, she stopped. "*We're* sick? Take a good look in the mirror. I don't care what kind of fancy lawyer you think you are. You're not getting away with arson!"

"Come on, Dad," Samantha said. She pulled him in the direction of their house. Before they had taken more than a few steps, Seth Marshall, one of the volunteer firefighters, approached. The fire had been reduced to smoldering ashes; it had been a small shed, and the fire hadn't had much to feed on, no dry grass and even the nearby pines hadn't caught. It was a windless night. The Cranes had been lucky—in that respect.

"Hi, Sam, Pix, Samantha—good to see you, although not under these circumstances." Seth held something out toward them. "The couple found this by the side of the shed when they came to douse the fire."

It was a single glove, heavy-duty striped thick cotton with a leather palm and fingertips. It was charred, but you could clearly see MILLER written on the wristband.

"One of yours?" Seth asked.

"Obviously," Sam snapped. "Too big for Pix or Samantha. Have no idea how it got here unless I left a pair when I was helping Ed clear brush. I buy them in bulk from Barton's, keep them in the barn to lend out when we have roadside cleanup days."

The Cranes had come up behind Seth. "The house was totally empty, the shed, too, when we bought the place. No glove," Cameron hissed. "I knew you'd try to wiggle out of this! Not so smart, counselor! You left evidence!"

"I can swear that my husband has been home since he arrived last night and he hasn't been wearing or carrying gloves!" Pix said, her face drained of color in marked contrast to those of the enraged couple confronting them. "And it doesn't matter. Why on earth would he want to burn your shed down?"

"You know very well why and I'm sure you were with him. Probably lit the match. Just can't deal with our cutting a few twigs!" Cameron spat the words out.

Seth was looking more and more uncomfortable. "We'll stay for a while more. Be sure nothing more ignites. All fires get reported to the sheriff's office and they can deal with any suspicions you may or may not have. Did you store anything combustible in the shed? Gas for a mower?"

"That has nothing to do with what happened," Cameron said. "I might have known you'd stick up for your friends. Thought this was supposed to be a friendly place. More like friendly only for some. Good old Sam help you out of a spot or something?" he asked snidely.

"Now just a minute . . ." Seth was a big guy and not someone you wanted to antagonize.

Pix slipped between the two men. "It's time we all went home. Mr. Crane, I'm sure you will be calling the sheriff yourself. I'm sorry your property has been damaged and it must have been quite frightening when you saw the fire, but we came over to help. We won't make that mistake again."

The Millers left by the drive, stopping to say hello to the volunteer crew, all of whom they did in fact know. Out on the road, Samantha said, "Good job, Mom. 'I am woman hear me roar!'"

Pix smiled weakly. "More like 'I am woman hear me snore'—I'm exhausted."

Sam put his arm around his wife. "Me, too. Arson is tiring work." He put his other arm around his daughter. "Guess we won't be inviting them to the wedding, eh?"

The sheriff's office had called early. Pix felt as if she had just gotten to sleep when the phone rang. The

Cranes had wasted no time in reporting the crime, and two officers were coming to inspect the damage, which the fire department had reported, and "talk"—that was the word used—to the Millers. She waited until a more decent hour and called Faith. "I'm not going to be able to meet you for coffee," Pix said. "Sam and I have to wait for someone from the sheriff's office."

As Pix related the early morning events to a very surprised Faith—"Sheriff's office!"—she had gasped, and they took on an even more surreal aspect than when they'd occurred, which had been bizarre enough.

"Obviously he was storing something flammable in the shed," Faith said, "and I'll bet he's a smoker. Left a butt that ignited a drip. He can't honestly believe Sam would do this. He has to have someone to blame other than himself to collect the insurance. And his wife is in on it. Just 'happened' to look out the window and see her neighbor. I am so sorry, Pix. I wish there was something I could do. Slashing tires, keying their car might make me feel better, but ten to one they'd think it was you. Call me after the police leave. I want to get some things for the Shores at the farmers' market and then I'll be home until around eleven. After that you can reach me at the Shores kitchen."

Pix had smiled at her friend's indignant proposed actions. Feeling better for the imagery, she said,

"Thanks, Faith. It's been a lot to take in. The whole summer has been out of kilter."

"Well, some unexpected stuff, but eyes on the wedding, starting with the shower tomorrow! I've arranged for a Saturday night clambake on the beach for dinner here at the Shores, so not much prep. The weather is cooperating. And Amy is coming to the shower, too. Samantha has been like a big sister all these years. Hard to believe she's all grown up and getting married!"

"You're going to make me cry," Pix said. "Now what does one wear for grilling by police?"

"Avoid stripes and all will be well," Faith advised.

Earl accompanied the other officers, which was a relief to Pix. But he, and they, were all-business. "The Cranes have leveled a very serious charge: arson with intent to harm, bodily harm. Mrs. Crane did admit she couldn't make out your face from her window, but she described an individual your size, and then there's that glove."

Pix flinched, thinking of a different infamous glove.

So far Sam had kept quiet, but Pix could see it was a struggle. "I know you've had issues with the Cranes this summer over trees and they did violate the shore-front regulations," Earl continued. "They swear you destroyed a chain saw to protest what they claim was their right to do as they wished on their own property."

"That's correct," Sam said, addressing all three. "Correct that this is what they claimed. Incorrect in that I had nothing to do with that or any other destruction of their property. I believe that the tree cutting is being dealt with by the town Code Enforcement officer and we have deliberately kept out of it. We have planted new trees well within our property line and may put up some sort of a fence for further privacy. The only contact we've had with the Cranes was our initial protest over the clear-cutting. I've been in Boston all summer except for a day here and there. Last night was the start of my vacation."

Pix reached for his hand as she thought, *Some vacation.*

One of the other officers was shaking her head. "We've called in the state arson specialist and secured the area around the shed. Without a positive ID, all we have is a glove that may or may not have been there before last night. Could you write out a statement regarding your activities last night? You, too, Mrs. Miller. Sign and date it, then we'll be on our way. I should tell you that we have heard from the Cranes' attorney, and he's pressing to have you arrested."

Sam gave a hollow laugh. "Of course he is. Make it a criminal case, so they'll be able to sue us in civil court."

"I'm going to pretend no one in this room heard that," Earl said.

That's when Pix began to really worry.

Sophie came into the kitchen just before lunch. She'd just met with Eloise, who continued to be supportive and offer constructive criticism. Sophie wasn't ready for the instructor to read any of it to the group, but she was getting close. Several in the course had given permission and the instructor had read them during the morning meetings before they separated to work or meet individually with her. Sophie had been surprised by the quality of Joan Whittaker's mystery. The Canadian woman had hooked her with the character, possibly some kind of vicarious self-portrait—Persis Gray, a foul-mouthed, tough elderly spinster with a black belt and fondness for Jack Daniel's. Sophie was even more surprised by the Ohio couple's romantic suspense work in progress. She hadn't taken them seriously, making the false assumption that they were sneaking off for a dirty two weeks away from possibly a wife and husband.

She pushed the thoughts of her fellow would-be writers away—she had more important things on her mind—and said, "I don't want to get in your way, but wanted to say hi." She gave a nod toward the door to the outside.

Faith took the hint. "Amy, sweetie, I'm going to cut some lemon thyme to add to the vinaigrette for the grilled chicken salad. I'll be back in a minute."

The herb garden was in a sunny spot not far from the spa and pool. "Have to fit in time for the amenities," Sophie said, pointing. "There's a sauna in there as well."

"Definitely with you! Now tell me about last night," Faith said.

"Jenny could definitely go pro. She has the voice, the looks, and made an instant connection with the audience without a lot of superficial patter. Some of what she sang, solo and with Cal, were her own compositions. And yes, she has the tattoo. The lettering style was the same, but what does it mean? That she knew the LeBlancs or just happened to go to the same tattoo parlor in Lowell? There were a few people in the audience I hadn't seen at the Shores—I think she has a following—but none of them looked like bikers, and the person I saw her with afterward when things were breaking up was Jay Thomas. The annoying guy in my writing group I told you wasn't there. But he came in just before the singing and stayed. Afterward I saw them leave together looking very much *together*."

"Hmm, that's interesting," Faith said. "Doubtful she would have known him before—but I guess he's not bad looking under all that gloomy garb."

"I thought she might be with Cal when I saw them sing together at the bonfire. They played up the steamier songs to the hilt, but that could have been part of their act. He's attractive, but too old for her," Sophie said.

"I'm not sure age matters. From what Nan Hamilton said, Jenny is calling her own tune, and it's one that worries Nan," Faith said. "I told you she said Jenny stays out into the wee hours, so she's with someone, or with a group. Nothing here or across the bridge is open late, so has to be outdoors or someone's house. Nan would be even more upset if she knew Jenny was with those guys at the market."

Thinking of the fertility superstition Marge Foster had mentioned, Sophie had been idly picking some parsley while listening to Faith. She dropped the bunch. "Guys who are dead now."

She'd only had a few hours' sleep on Friday night. It was hot and the fan was broken. The sheets on her side of the bed were soaked with sweat. He'd promised to pick up a new fan at Home Depot, but of course forgot.

Today was the shower. She told him she had to go over early to help Gert get everything ready. He could drop Kylie off at his sister's on his way. No men at the shower, but he'd told Ursula he'd help Sam and Tom Fairchild set the mooring for her son Arnie's boat, make sure all the equipment on board was working. Arnie was a doctor, she remembered suddenly. She couldn't recall what kind, but he might have a blank pad he'd leave lying around. You never knew.

The shower wasn't working, only a small stream of lukewarm water. He could go help Ursula— and Arnie was rich, could afford to pay someone to do all this for him—but he couldn't use his day off to do what was needed at his own house. She felt her anger rise until it felt as if it would tear holes through her skin. Her whole body ached lately.

She threw on some clothes, not bothering to dress up. Samantha wouldn't care. She paused a moment. But the others would. Gert. Her mother. She changed into a loose bright pink top but kept her jeans on—the skinny ones, the only ones that fit. Kylie called the top "Mommy's Princess Shirt" *because it had bands of silver thread woven around the neck and cuffs.*

She'd told Gert she would be there at noon. Plenty of time for the start of the party at one. And plenty of time to get to the Walgreens in Ellsworth for a refill and back. She had two more. And after this one she'd be stopping. She might see someone she knew in Ellsworth, but there wasn't time to go anyplace farther. She could always say she was picking stuff up for the shower.

"So, did you have a wedding shower?" Amy asked Faith. They were hanging a sparkling BRIDE TO BE banner on top of the door between the living room and the porch. Honeycomb white bells were suspended from wall sconces and the beams on the porch. The buffet table was swathed in white tulle, and Amy had scattered paper rose petals on almost every surface.

"Yes, I had a shower. My friend Emma—you've met her—gave it at her mother's very nice house in Manhattan." Poppy Morris's town house had been more than nice, but the shower had taken an unexpected turn that Faith was not going to mention now or ever to her daughter. Her future sister-in-law had slipped Faith a mickey. The two eventually became close, but

Faith kept a curtain tightly drawn over that nightmare shower.

Gert came in with a platter of what she called "fancy sandwiches"—chicken and egg salad, crab and tinted layers of cream cheese, crustless, most cut in bell shapes. "I don't know what's keeping Arlene. I've called the house and there's no answer. Mike said she was going to leave right after he did. She had something for Samantha she wanted to wrap."

"I'm sure she'll be here soon," Sophie said. "If she's had car trouble we'd have heard. Probably decided we needed more juice for the mimosas or something like that."

Island time meant if you were invited for one o'clock, you arrived at one o'clock. Maybe even quarter to. The living room and porch were soon filled with women oohing and aahing over the decorations and the food. Amy and Faith had made cupcakes, piping wedding rings, bridal bouquets, and bells on top of the icings. Marge Foster made her layered cherry Jell-O, cream cheese, and graham cracker mold shaped like a wedding cake with three tiers. "Got it from the Internet," she announced proudly, making the last word sound like an actual destination akin to another planet. "My nephew is a whiz with a computer, and when I told him what I wanted he found it and it was at the post office two days later."

Besides the mimosas, Gert had made strawberry shrub—"my grandmother's recipe." (See recipe, page 333.) Faith was familiar with the tangy fruit drink, which dated back to the days before refrigeration, when vinegar was used as a preservative. The combination of macerated fresh fruit, sugar, and cider or white vinegar boiled and strained had a long shelf life. She was tempted to tell Gert that her grandmother's recipe had become the new happening menu item, especially when combined with alcohol, at upscale New York restaurants. It would be the only thing on the buffet that would meet with Alexandra's approval. Samantha's future mother-in-law had already cast her eye on the decorations and had been about to say something when Babs whisked her out to the porch to meet Samantha's godmother, whose last name revealed very blue blood. The two were soon playing the "Who Do We Know in Common?" game—Samantha's godmother was a good sport and knew exactly what Babs was doing, having heard from Pix about Zach's mother.

Sophie had told Samantha about Jenny Hamilton's performance and she'd invited her to come to the shower with Nan, mentioning the possibility of singing at the wedding. Jenny had accepted the invitation and said she'd bring her guitar and stay afterward to talk about what Samantha might want. She was going over to Brooksville at five and could leave from The Pines.

Amy excitedly pushed a button on her phone as Samantha walked through the door, filling the room with the strains of Mendelssohn's "Wedding March." Ursula, who seemed more excited than anyone, popped a fascinator she'd made on Samantha's head—a headband with white silk blossoms and wisps of lace—crying out, "Here comes the bride!" The party was officially in full gear.

The asshole pharmacist wouldn't fill the prescription! Said it was too soon and pointed to the date. Also questioned her ID. Same thing at Walmart and the Rite Aid. At Walmart the pharmacist told her to wait while he went to check, but something told her not to stay and she was out of there.

She had trouble opening the car and people in the parking lot were looking at her funny. "What's your problem?" she yelled at one woman, slamming the door as she got behind the steering wheel. She could feel tears on her cheeks. She didn't have anything. Not a single pill. Nothing. Her heart was pounding. She couldn't breathe. She was going to die.

Sleep. Maybe she could get some sleep. A little nap, and when she woke up she'd figure out what to do. Where to go. She had to score.

Not on the island. Not on the island. Suddenly she was wide awake. Her phone had service here. And she knew who to call. A name. She laughed. It was Mike who had told her their former classmate had been arrested for possession. Even if she was clean, she'd know where to score. She made the call. There were a gazillion missed ones, but she ignored them. They made arrangements, and it wouldn't take long.

Lucky. She was in luck. She started the car and headed for Denny's.

It was going to cost her more cash than she had, but she could give her the watch. A Christmas present from Mike. It had real diamond chips around the face. She only wore it for special occasions.

And this was a special occasion.

By four o'clock the guests had all left. No one commented on the absence of the hostess, but as soon as the last car pulled away, Arlene's mother, Marilyn, began to cry. "Something's happened to her! Mike, call the police!"

The men had finished their nautical tasks and turned up half an hour ago, assuming correctly that there would be food left.

Mike went over to his mother-in-law and sat next to her on the couch. "I would have heard if there'd been an accident. She's been so touchy lately that if I do something like call around she'll get upset. Her phone must be off or she's where it doesn't get service. Maybe she took a nap before she left the house and lost track of time. She's been awful tired lately. She's going to feel terrible about missing this and I'll bet she walks through the door soon."

Soon was a half hour later and she didn't so much walk through the door as fly. "Party! Let's party! This is for the bride!!" She rushed over to Samantha and thrust a bouquet of gas station flowers at her. "Come on, everybody. Let's have some music. We want to dance!!" She began to spin around and collapsed on the couch onto her husband's lap.

No one else had said a word and then Alexandra stood up. "This is your matron of honor?" she said scathingly to Samantha. "She's drunk or . . ."

Ursula stood up, too. "Hush. The child is sick." She looked around the room. "We need to take care of her. Marilyn, did you know?"

Arlene's mother had stopped crying. "I've been suspecting, but I can't believe my daughter would ever get involved with drugs."

Mike looked stunned. "What are you talking about? Arlene on something? That's crazy! I'm taking her home now. My sister can keep Kylie overnight."

Arlene jumped off his lap. Her face was flushed, and Faith could see that her pupils were pinpricks. Before she could say anything, Arlene did. "Prezzie, I have a prezzie for my BFF. Here in my purse." She began to dig into her bag, throwing things onto the floor—a juice box, tissues, makeup, one of Kylie's small stuffed animals, her phone, her car keys, receipts, and a pill container. She got down on her knees to sort through it all. Jenny and Samantha got down with her. "Don't worry about it, Arlene, you can give it to me later," Samantha said, covering the keys with her hand and pushing them under the couch.

Jenny was looking at the pill container. Empty. She picked up one of the pieces of paper. Faith was watching and saw a look of surprise cross the girl's face. She also saw her put both in the pocket of her denim skirt. "I'm very sorry, Samantha. We can talk about music for the wedding another time." She picked up her guitar case. "I have to be at a gig off-island soon."

Every eye was focused on Arlene as Jenny left—

except Faith's. She followed the girl out the back door. "I saw you take the container and a paper off the floor," she said.

Jenny started to run toward the VW Freeman had loaned her. "Not now, Mrs. Fairchild."

Faith ran, too. "Yes, now! What do you know about all this?"

Jenny stopped at the car. "Nothing. But I'm going to find out." Seconds later she was driving off.

"Nobody in our family has ever had a problem like this," Marilyn was saying firmly when Faith came back inside. "You know the doctor gave her pain pills after the accident. It was all legal and she needed them! Maybe she kept a couple and took them today. She's been nervous about the shower and the wedding."

Arlene was lying on the floor, her eyes closed. "I can hear you," she said. "I can hear every single word. Your good little girl would never do anything wrong, right, Mom? And I'm married to a cop, so I *really* wouldn't do anything illegal? I'm just going to relax like this a minute and we can all go home."

"Help me take her upstairs, Samantha," Ursula said. "She can stay here tonight."

"I'll sit with her," Gert said. "Things will be better in the morning."

Tom spoke up. "Actually, they won't. Arlene is going to need all of us. Need us to know what has been happening and not judge"—he directed a steely glance at Alexandra, who looked as if she had been sucking lemons. "And she needs to go into a rehab facility now. Come off what she's on, which since she was prescribed pain medication, we can assume is an opioid. It has to be done under supervision, and once she's through it comes the even harder part—support counseling for Arlene, the whole family, and her friends."

Mike was crying now. "She didn't want to move out of town. I was the one who pushed for the place in the woods. It was cheap because it wasn't finished. And I wanted Kylie to grow up away from some of the influences in Granville. And here it was under my nose. I'll never forgive myself for doing this to her. I love her, I love her so much . . ."

"We know, son. Come on out to the porch," Tom said. "We'll talk if you feel like it. But I'll tell you right now that you're not to blame. Nobody here is, least of all your wife. And in your heart, you know that, too. Any one of us could be in the situation Arlene is in now. She's not a criminal. She has a disease."

"I'll call Ed Ricks to come over if that's all right with everyone," Faith offered. "I don't think any of us want to be alone right now. Marilyn, you don't know him well, but he and some others have been working to educate and treat what is an epidemic. In every part of the country. It may help you to hear what he has to say."

Pix sat down close to Marilyn. "We've known each other and been friends a long time, since the girls were toddlers. Arlene has always been like a daughter to me, and I know Samantha is for you. But I can't think of any other way to put this except as one mother to another. I don't want to see her picture in the paper with 'died suddenly' in an obituary."

The room was quiet and then Marilyn took Pix's hand and nodded. "Whatever it takes to prevent that. I'll do it. Our whole family will. Faith, call Dr. Ricks."

Ursula's living room filled up quickly after that. Marilyn called her husband to come. Arlene's brother and his wife lived in southern Maine, but Mike called his parents, too. After a few words, Ed had praised them all for responding so quickly. "What Arlene will need most now is the support of her family and friends. You need to expect that she'll be doing fine and then most likely relapse. It will be hard to keep going—for her and you—but we have some wonderful individuals here on Sanpere and across the bridge who have trained as recovery coaches. Many of them have been through the cycle themselves. They are here to help her, and you. More and more people are stepping forward to be trained, or just involved, as word spreads. We already have a group that meets at the Community Center Wednesday nights for support and education."

Upstairs, with Gert at her side, Arlene slept. Tom and Mike had come in from the porch. Samantha and Sophie were making coffee.

"I should have guessed," Samantha said. "She's been avoiding me all summer—no even earlier, during Memorial Day weekend, too. And when Mom brought the dress over she told me how thin she was." Samantha's voice caught.

Sophie put her arm around her. "You couldn't have known. Addicts are very good at hiding what's going on. Arlene is a very smart cookie, and just as she was good at everything she did, she was a good liar. Having to be good at everything has probably played a part in all this. She couldn't admit any weakness. Samantha, you've known people with addiction problems I'm sure. Alcohol or drugs."

"Or both," Samantha said. "When I was working in Manhattan I tried not to know, but the pressures at work were horrendous. Must have been the same for you at your law firm."

Sophie nodded. "If you admitted to getting a full

night's sleep, you were a failure. The creep I followed to London thinking he was the love of my life did me a favor getting me off the corner office/partner track."

"What's going to happen now?" Samantha sounded very young, Sophie thought. She and Arlene were both still so young.

"Well, judging from the amount of time Tom and Ed have each spent on the phone," she said, "I imagine they'll get her a spot at an excellent detox facility that will transition to a longer stay there or someplace else. It may be in Massachusetts or here in Maine. Let's bring in the coffee. Mugs, not cups and saucers. People want something to hold."

On their way back in, Alexandra pushed past them. "Sorry, must dash. Clambake on the beach tonight and I don't want to miss it. Babs is staying here."

It didn't escape Sophie's notice that Samantha's future in-law had carefully redone her makeup and hair. After the door closed, she said to Samantha, "Remind me to tell you about my mother-in-law, actually Will's stepmother. Alexandra will seem like a prize."

"The question is 'prize what?'" The two stifled a giggle. Comic relief.

When they finally got home, Pix was surprised to find an envelope with her name on it stuck under her car's windshield wiper. They had all gone to the shower in Sam's car. Pix picked up the envelope and opened it. Inside was a single sheet of paper. "I need to talk to you. I'll be at the coffee place in Sanpere Village tomorrow at 9:00 A.M. Drew."

Could life get any more complicated? Pix wondered and started after her husband and daughter to show them the note.

"Maybe she wants to apologize," Samantha said after Pix read it to them.

"I doubt that," Sam said. "And I don't want you going. Looks like a setup to me."

"But what kind?" Pix asked her husband, overlooking his preemptory "I don't want you." "What more can the Cranes do? I think Samantha is right, maybe she's going to say she's sorry and tell me they're calling the whole thing off. That it was an accident."

Sam shook his head. "I love you both to pieces, but not everyone is as nice as you are—nor as gullible. At least let me come with you."

"But she specifically put the note on my car. I think she wants to talk woman to woman."

"Woman to harpy is more like it." Sam shook his head.

There were several messages on the answering machine. Freeman, who hated the "durn things," coughed and said, "Be at the dock at eight." Sam looked at Pix. "You forgot tomorrow is Granville's Lobster Boat Race day. We'll be out on their other son's boat with Nan and about a hundred other Hamiltons to watch Freeman tear up the competition. His brother Harry is coming up from Massachusetts special. So I'm afraid you won't be able to keep your date." He sounded pleased.

"I have the feeling Drew doesn't want Cameron to know," Pix said, "so I'll leave word at the Café. They open at seven." She was tempted to stick her tongue out and say, "So there," but the next message quelled the impulse. It was from the sheriff's office, advising them to get a lawyer.

Even though she knew they'd prepared everything for the clambake, Faith decided to stop by the Shores after leaving The Pines and make sure all was going well. They should have reached dessert at this point, and afterward it was movie night in the conference center with popcorn and a craft beer tasting. She'd been astonished to discover how many local beers there were—all with names appropriate to the region like "Rising Tide."

She parked in the guest/visitor lot, having no desire for a repeat of the pickup truck incident. Which brought her thoughts to Arlene. Faith had known

Arlene ever since the Fairchilds had started coming to Sanpere. Amy hadn't been born, so it was at least eighteen years. More. Arlene was a chubby little girl, playing at the Millers' when Samantha wasn't playing at the Prescotts'. She and Samantha worked summer jobs together on the island and were indeed best friends. Before she was married, Arlene often came down to Aleford or to New York to visit Samantha. When Kylie was born, Samantha was almost as excited as the loving new mom. Faith thought about the pain the young woman must have been in these last months since that accident. Physical and psychological pain. Mike was right. The location of the new—and very unfinished— house had isolated her from contact with friends and family in Granville. Support she had needed. People might think it ridiculous to think of the few miles as an impediment, but they were.

She wondered where Arlene had been getting the pills and then chided herself. Everything she'd been hearing this summer and last had indicated the availability of just about anything in just about every part of the island and peninsula. Arlene wasn't shooting up. At least not on her arms. The sleeves on her shirt had been rolled up this afternoon—she must have been feeling warm—and there wasn't a single mark. But addicts found other places in order to escape notice, even between their toes.

As Faith walked down to the back of the lodge and kitchen door, she passed a steady stream of guests heading for movie night or beer night, depending on one's interest. Maybe both. She was happy to see some of the maintenance crew pushing the oversize cart they used for beach events, fully loaded, toward the trash area. Another close behind was piled with cookware and other remnants of the feast headed for the kitchen. Cal followed the carts looking tired, but content.

"Hi," Faith said. "Looks like it all went well, from the smiles on the guests' faces."

He grinned at her. "Thanks to your organization. I don't know what we'd be doing without you, Mrs. Fairchild—and your daughter."

Faith gave a quick thought to what Amy had just experienced at the shower and was glad the job would be a distraction for the rest of the summer. Tom was planning to take her night kayaking in the double kayak, and Faith knew they would talk.

"Call me Faith, please. I'm glad I could help. Is everything off the beach?"

"Yes, I doused the fire myself. The tide's coming in, too, so even if there is a hot spot that will take care of it. We spread out the rockweed we used to steam the bake to be sure there weren't any embers."

"Great. I'll just check the kitchen. Maybe we can salvage any leftovers for lobster salad or quiche for tomorrow's lunch." As Faith moved away she noticed Alexandra coming from the front door of the lodge. She was about to ask her how she'd liked the clambake, but Alexandra wasn't looking at her. "Hey, Mr. Cal," she called out. "I believe we have a movie date."

Cal winked at Faith. "I believe we do. I picked the films myself. Hope you like Bruce Willis. We're having a *Die Hard* marathon."

Alexandra flinched visibly, but Faith had to give her recovery credit. "Bruce Willis? Oh but of course. Adore him. So, so—masculine."

The two went off toward the conference center and Faith indulged in audible laughter.

Faith let the crew go, maintenance and kitchen. It was a Saturday night after all. She definitely wanted to hold on to all of them, especially the dishwasher who had shown up for work every day, and more important, stayed. Without help, it took time to pick the lobsters and finish cleaning before she locked up and headed for her car.

As she looked up at the sky, the author Henry

Beston's words from *The Outermost House*—words she knew by heart as one of Tom's favorite quotations—came to mind:

For a moment of night we have a glimpse of ourselves and of our world islanded in its stream of stars—pilgrims of mortality, voyaging between horizons across the eternal seas of space and time.

Tom and Amy would still be on the water. Faith could see the white curve of the beach beckoning. It was the perfect spot to sit, think over the day, and appreciate Beston's words, which put things into perspective as sharply as if she had a telescope to focus on all that was above and around her.

It was warm, and she had no need of a sweater. Walking down the steep drive that led to the sandy crescent, she could smell the beach roses, *Rosa rugosa*. The only sounds were night sounds—crickets, the swoosh of a bird. Everyone was either away from the Shores or enjoying tonight's entertainment—not Bruce Willis she was sure. Something more like *Mamma Mia! Here We Go Again*, or the first *Mamma Mia!* Something with music.

She was sorry to miss the Lobster Boat Races tomorrow, since she and Amy would be working. She wouldn't have been on Ed's boat in any case. He'd called to tell her he would be driving Arlene to a placement he'd arranged outside Boston. He'd added it had been difficult to persuade Arlene to go. She finally gave in when he mentioned Kylie's name, which triggered what amounted to hysterics and Arlene told him she had hit a tree when Kylie was in the car. Mike and her mother wanted to go with her, but she asked Gert to come. Only Gert. "Steady as a clock," Ed had said, and Faith had to agree.

It had been a long day. The Shores beach was one of the only pure sandy ones on the island. Faith slipped her sandals off and felt the grains like silk on her bare feet. She walked a short way and sat on a log, a huge timber that had washed up during some storm and had served as a convenient resting place ever since. The moon was bright, its beams rippling across the incoming tide. Far out she heard the sound of a boat. It was coming closer and going fast. She thought of the one she'd seen at Ed's when they'd had coffee. A week ago? Two weeks? Time was collapsing this summer.

The boat's captain must be practicing for tomorrow, running his craft at full throttle. Even though it was far off, the wake was churning up the water, sending waves of foam toward the beach. The cove was deep water here and supposed to be one of the spots where the Abenaki summered. Faith had read the short piece Sophie had written imagining those first people and heard about the longer one she was working on. She hoped Sophie would finish the project, and it had already served its purpose. Sophie's mood had changed and she was no longer obsessing about an empty cradle. She'd told Faith that Ursula had asked her a question no one else had. "Do you and Will want to reproduce yourselves or raise a child together?" She'd emphasized that a yes to either question was perfectly understandable. Trust Ursula, Faith thought. Sophie had gone on to tell her she'd called Will right away and he'd responded, "With my gene pool? And you don't know the half of it—for example, great-great-grandfather Aloysius Maxwell was a notorious swindler and a crook. His name is even scratched out in the family Bible!" Their plan now was to begin an adoption process in the fall. "I've been so stupid, Faith," Sophie had said. "Approaching the whole thing the way I had to get a high score on my LSATs."

The log was a nice perch but hard, and Faith decided to head for home. The lobster boat was coming closer and closer at full speed and she wondered why. The race wasn't an obstacle course, so it wasn't practicing maneuvers. Just a straight shot like bats out of hell toward the finish.

She was only a short way up the drive when she heard a scream. It was coming from behind, not in front of her. She ran back to the beach where she could make out a person—or two people?—at the far end. The boat was heading just as fast, maybe faster, away from the cove now, the wake lapping the shore almost up to the high-tide mark.

Faith sped through the sand as fast as she could, grateful for the moonlight illuminating her path. The scream had given way to a loud wailing sound.

Two people, not one. Two people Faith knew. Alexandra had her arms around Cal Burke. It was not a romantic gesture. The water from the boat's wake was swirling about them. It was red. From the size of the gash on the maintenance man's skull, there was no question he was dead.

A husband about to be charged with arson; her future in-law who was not only found clutching a dead man but also the only person in sight who could have killed him.

Pix was not going to be happy.

Chapter Ten

S eeing Faith stopped Alexandra's piercing cries. She let go of the corpse in her arms.

Faith crouched down and put her hand on the body. Cal Burke was still warm, but there was no sign of even a faint pulse at his wrist. Despite the blood—bright red in the moonlight, sticky, oozing over his face, puddling at the neck—Faith pressed her fingers on his neck. Nothing. His eyes were wide open, but they were sightless.

She looked for signs of anyone on the beach or in the nearby woods. No one. She couldn't leave Alexandra, and Alexandra was in no shape to go get help. The woman was moving as far away as she could, backing away from the water, scuttling like a crab. She'd started screaming again. Faith understood why people like

Alexandra were always getting slapped across the face in old movies. Instead of acting on the impulse, she said forcibly, "Stop it! Shut up!" This produced lower-volume moans. Faith was able to catch the words "I didn't do it. It just happened."

It was then that Faith noticed where Alexandra was heading. A tartan picnic blanket—probably Barbour—was spread out on the sand. A large leather tote was off to one side, and the necks of two bottles of extremely expensive champagne were clearly visible. The scenario was clear. There certainly were crashing waves at this point. A cinematic tryst—a reenactment of Deborah Kerr and Burt Lancaster in *From Here to Eternity*—only something had gone very, very wrong.

Faith eyed the tote again. "Your phone. Do you have it? Is it in your bag?"

Alexandra nodded.

"Get it," Faith ordered. It was then that she realized the reason for the woman's odd choice of movement. Her legs were shaking so hard she couldn't stand. She tried and collapsed back onto the ground.

"Never mind. I will. Stay where you are."

Over the years, Faith had memorized Earl's home number and punched it in instead of 911.

Earl answered, clearly puzzled by the caller ID. "Mrs. Kohn?"

"No, it's me. Faith. I'm with her. Cal Burke has been murdered. We're at the far end of the Shores beach. However he was killed, I'm sure it's just happened."

"Okay. I'll be there soon. Tide's going to be a high one tonight and it's coming in. Try not to move him much, but you may have to. Aside from Mrs. Kohn, anybody else there?"

"No, but there was a boat, a lobster boat that came in fast and near to the shore. Caused a huge wake. Other than that, nobody on the beach or on the water."

"What's that noise? Sounds like a coyote. Could he have been attacked by one? Lots around this summer."

"I doubt it. What you hear is Alexandra Kohn."

Faith hung up and considered her options; the water *was* coming in fast and the waves had already obliterated possible evidence. She looked at the body more carefully. His clothes were soaking wet and torn in places. She didn't think it was a result of an act of passion. Switching the phone to camera, she took several photos, particularly of what had been revealed on his right forearm: a tattoo of a realistic green adder snaking up to the elbow, its fangs dripping blood, a few Gothic letters in red. *L F D Y.*

"Live Fast Die Young." But Cal had messed up when it came to the rest of the credo: "and leave a good-looking corpse."

Alexandra was sobbing softly. Faith sat down next to her, putting an arm around the woman's shoulders—a woman barely recognizable as the figure of the last month. Proving there is no such thing as waterproof mascara, her face, red and puffy from crying, sported black rivulets, and her hair was a mess. There was blood on her white lace camisole and more on her hands.

"Valium, I need some Valium," Alexandra said.

"I'm sorry, but I don't have any. Try taking deep breaths," Faith answered.

"There's some in my bag. Get it!"

Interested as she was to see what else might be in the bag, Faith knew to leave that for Earl or some other officer of the law. She'd already had to take out the phone. She repeated her breathing suggestion and Alexandra hiccupped several times and then got quiet.

"Can you tell me what happened?" Faith said.

"I don't *know* what happened!!" she whimpered. "We'd arranged to meet here after the program was over. He suggested we wait an hour. Make sure we wouldn't be disturbed. I told him I'd bring a midnight picnic. When I got to the beach, he wasn't waiting like he usually was." Faith filed that admission away for later, letting Alexandra continue.

"I spread the blanket out, and it was such a beautiful night, I lay down to look at the stars. I must have dropped off. This has been a very stressful day."

"Yes, we're all concerned about Arlene," Faith said.

"Arlene? Oh, that girl at Samantha's shower. No, my dressmaker called and she hasn't been able to get confirmation that the fabric I'm having woven in Italy for my wedding outfit will arrive in time for her to finish it. She has the toile and my measurements never change, but . . ."

Faith almost *did* slap her now. She took a breath herself. "Okay, so you fell asleep and then what?"

"I heard a noise. Like some kind of engine. Cal was nowhere to be seen. I looked at my watch. He was two hours late. Well, I thought, I'm not going to be treated like that by some hired help and I stood up to pack all the things away. And then I saw him." She gulped for air. "I saw him in the water. I thought he was drowning. Huge waves pushing him back and forth into shore. I ran down to pull him in and there was all this blood." She shivered and stopped speaking for a moment. Collecting herself, she said, "I thought he must have gone for a swim when he saw I was asleep and banged his head on a rock or something. Except why wouldn't he have just woken me up?"

"Was there anyone on the beach or over at the sides, near the woods or ledges?"

"No. I looked, because I needed help. I don't know how to do any of that rescue stuff. CRV or whatever. I turned him over on his side and saw . . ." Alexandra closed her eyes. Clearly she didn't want to recall what she had seen and she clearly also didn't want to talk about it anymore.

But Faith did. "So you have no idea how he was killed?"

Alexandra's eyes snapped open and she said briskly, "Well, it's obvious, isn't it? They killed him on that boat and threw him in the water. I'd like to leave now, Faith. You can tell the police whatever you want."

Mrs. Kohn's return to the guest room at The Birches wasn't quite as speedy as she wished, but after she'd been questioned by both Earl and the state police homicide officers who'd arrived soon after, Faith—who had also told them what little she knew—drove her back. The kitchen lights were on, and both Babs and Sophie were waiting up. Faith had called with a brief account of the events. She had also called Tom and explained why she would be late, emphasizing that someone else, *not* Faith herself, had found the body this time.

At The Birches, Babs took charge of Alexandra. "I've drawn a nice soothing bath for you—lavender salts and here's something to start on," she said, handing Alexandra a glass of chardonnay and shepherding her out of the kitchen. "You poor dear. What a horrible thing."

"It was! And the police have taken all my things, including my Fendi leather tote! They're probably swigging down the champagne I put in it right now! Dom Perignon!"

As soon as they were out of earshot, Faith filled Sophie in with more details. Shocked, Sophie said, "I can't believe it! Cal Burke had that snake tattoo? That makes three of them! No coincidence, but how do you think he was connected to the other two?"

Faith had been wondering the same thing ever since seeing the image on Cal's lifeless arm. "He's from here originally, but has been living all over the place apparently and worked in both of the Childses' other conference centers, near enough to Lowell to have formed some sort of connection. He was older, but maybe they were all bikers?" It didn't sound very plausible to Faith, and Sophie said dubiously as well, "I guess that's possible . . ."

Faith thought of something else. "Cindy went to tell everyone still up in the bar that there had been an accident and not to be alarmed if they heard sirens. I was there on the beach when she came down with one of the officers. I wonder if there was something going on between them? She was crying almost as hysterically as Alexandra had been—an extreme reaction for just a coworker?" Faith shook her head, trying to put her thoughts in order. "One thing is clear—the Childses are losing staff by the minute, and this staff member needs to get some sleep or I may end up confusing sugar with salt tomorrow—or rather today."

She was almost at her car when she realized she hadn't told Sophie about seeing Jenny Hamilton take the pill container and a piece of paper from the items that had spilled out of Arlene's bag. Jenny Hamilton, Cal Burke's singing partner. She went back and described what had happened. "I confronted her, but she wouldn't say anything. Only that she had to find something out. Wait, I just had an idea. Why don't you take my place on the Hamiltons' son's boat tomorrow for the races? Jenny is bound to be on it. Amy and I have to keep the kitchen going at the Shores, especially after tonight. People are going to be understandably nervous. And that means comfort food, plenty of it."

"I was going to skip the races and get some writing done, but I'll call Nan in the morning and see if there's still room. Oh, Faith, this was supposed to be a carefree wedding summer . . ."

Faith gave her a hug. "Try to get some sleep."

Sophie hugged her back. "My cell will work on the water, so if I have anything to tell you, I'll text."

"Totally unrelated topic that just occurred to me," Faith said as she let herself out once again. "How are Babs's and Alexandra's memoirs going? Have you read them?"

"Mom is being very secretive but said she was surprising herself—how much she remembered about growing up and then later all the wusbands. She also said that Alexandra was working sporadically, taking frequent breaks—we now know the reason—but that she'd read a passage to the group about growing up rich."

"Kind of 'Poor Little Rich Girl'?"

"That's what I was expecting. An only child lacking for nothing but love. Losing her mother when she was young."

"It would explain a lot," Faith said sympathetically.

"Except she wasn't! All she remembered about her mother was the smell of her perfume. A silver spoon childhood that was as happy as a clam at low tide! And more sunny days to follow apparently. Talk about mixed metaphors!" Sophie said. "Anyway, Mom reported Alexandra told them very seriously that it *was* possible to have it all."

"Are we happy to hear this or . . . ?"

"Not." Sophie laughed.

Faith said with mock gravitas, "I'm beginning to think Samantha's mother-in-law-to-be has hidden shallows."

It was hard telling Amy about Cal Burke. As with the chef, she had worked with him all summer and liked him. Faith described the death as some kind of accident, which was all she knew in any case. She also made a brief call to the Millers, and clearly Pix was as baffled as Faith about any role Alexandra might have played.

Hanging up she went back to Tom and Amy. Amy, although upset about Cal, was determined to do her best to keep the Shores' kitchen operational. "We can't let the Childses down—or the guests," she said. Thinking back to some similar situations in her own culinary career, Faith realized that there might be something in her DNA that she had passed down to her daughter. A version of "The Show Must Go On"—"The Meals Must Be Prepared."

Sunday the island awoke to fog, but old-timers like Freeman Hamilton were not dismayed. "It'll burn off," he told Sam Miller when Sam called to see whether the races were canceled. And by the time the

Millers plus Sophie boarded Roy Hamilton's lobster boat, the fog was gone, replaced by crystal clear sunshine.

Roy's boat was filled with people ready to cheer their favorites—and coolers packed with comestibles and drinks of all kinds. Pix had barbecued chicken yesterday morning before the shower and also made a vat of Faith's coleslaw (see recipe, page 330), the old-fashioned kind but with red and green cabbage and carrots for color. The enthusiasm of the crowd—those getting into boats to watch from the water and those staying on the pier—was contagious.

Sophie smiled at Pix. "I feel a little bit as if I've been on that ride at the Blue Hill Fair, the Tilt-A-Whirl, and despite all that happened at the shower and hearing about Cal Burke, I'm happy to be here, and the only thing on my mind is Freeman winning again."

"I know exactly what you mean. Whirling events. On the way I had to stop to leave a message for Drew Cameron of all people at the coffee shop in Sanpere Village. She left a note on my windshield sometime yesterday when I was at The Pines saying she wanted to meet me there today at nine."

"Any indication why?"

"None—both Sam and Samantha think I should ignore it, but I didn't agree. The message I left said

I'd be at the races. It's up to her now to get in touch again, or not."

"I'll bet she wants to apologize for her husband and tell you they're dropping the whole thing," Sophie said.

"That's exactly what I said. My family told me if I believed that, the next time we had a rainbow I should get in the car and find the pot of gold at the end."

"Don't pay any attention to them," Sophie said, glancing at Sam, who was helping Roy cast off. "I'm a tiger in the courtroom, but a lamb outside—according to Will—so I'm with you."

Sophie had watched Jenny Hamilton get on board. Her long dark hair was tied off her face with the pink bandanna Sophie recognized from the market and the campfire, but she wasn't wearing the leather jacket. She greeted everyone warmly, and it seemed she didn't have a care in the world. Sophie thought the engine noise would preclude any private conversation for now, but she intended to keep a sharp eye on the girl.

The boatload watched several contests and started in on the food and drink. Freeman's class was the last to race. Sophie realized there was plenty of time to decide how to approach Jenny. The races were an all-day affair.

After a while, Roy turned the wheel over to his cousin Norman. "I think she's pulling to the right. No problem when I hauled yesterday, but I could swear something went wrong overnight. See what you think while I grab some of that chicken before it's gone."

"You don't mean you think someone was on your boat last night?" Norman asked. His face registered more than dismay. Using—even stepping onto— another person's boat without permission was tantamount to a crime.

Roy shook his head. "I don't think so. Doesn't make sense. She was moored the same. Just have a funny feeling that's all."

"I'll check it out," Norman said. A few minutes later he called over his shoulder, "Seems all right to me. How about the fuel gauge? You'd know if she'd been taken for a spin."

Roy shook his head. "It read the same as when I left her."

The conversation ended as a tight race began to unfold between two friends of the Hamiltons. As most of the group loudly encouraged one or the other captains, Sophie took the opportunity to sit next to Jenny, who was sitting apart up on the bow. The captain had cut the engine.

"I was sorry to hear about Cal Burke," Sophie said. "I'm taking the writing class at Sanpere Shores and it was a pleasure to hear the two of you sing."

Jenny looked wistful. "It's hard to believe I won't be doing any more duets with him. I met him down in Massachusetts at an open mic night near where I go to school. Somehow we ended up doing gigs together when he didn't have to work. It was a coincidence that he was coming up here to Sanpere when I was. I hadn't even known he was from Maine." She looked away when she said this last, and Sophie wished Babs were on board with her innate "Can you look me straight in the eye and say that" skill.

"He was older than you, right?"

Jenny looked her straight in the eye. "Yes, why do you ask?" Her tone was cool. She didn't wait for an answer and stood up. "I'm going to get some lemonade. You want anything?"

A lot, Sophie said to herself—and I'm not getting it from you. Not yet anyway.

"Nothing like a day on the water to make a man feel full of good cheer," Sam said as they pulled into the drive.

"And also possibly because of the number of Sam Adams Summer Ales you imbibed," Pix teased.

"Had to keep my throat lubricated so I could yell loud enough. Freeman was happy as a dog with two tails. His best time ever."

They had all been thrilled when Freeman crossed the finish line well ahead of his archrival. Pix's throat was a little hoarse, too. It had been a lovely day. She was sorry Faith, Amy, and Samantha, who had set out for Boston that morning, had missed this year, but Tom videoed much of it. Samantha and Zach could at least get a feel for what had been a perfect Maine day.

The food was all gone and Pix felt a secret satisfaction. One disastrous year she had experimented with the recipe, glazing the chicken with her version of hoisin sauce. It was so salty that only Sam ate any—not from loyalty, but because he'd eat anything.

"How about I make Americanos and we sit outside?" Sam suggested. They had developed a taste for the Campari, sweet vermouth, and seltzer drink with an orange slice in Italy two years ago, and it was now a summer favorite. Although unlike James Bond, the Millers did not insist on using Perrier, but whatever club soda was at hand.

"*Grazie.* I'll clean the cooler and put the containers to soak while you make them," she said. Neither her mother nor Gert would be peering over her shoulder at leaving the dirty dishes for later, and Sam certainly wouldn't care.

Pix was feeling pretty cheerful herself. Even after

she spied the same kind of envelope under her windshield wiper as yesterday, it didn't quash her spirit. If anything it made her feel even better. Drew Crane had replied. Pix was right to be optimistic.

She tore the envelope open to find a brief message. "Could you meet me at the small park by the Mill Pond at five today? I'll be there and wait thirty minutes."

Sometimes the planets align and what drops into your lap is more than serendipitous. "Sorry, honey, we're out of oranges," Sam called from the kitchen. "Gin or vodka tonics it is."

"Oh, Sam, I was craving an Americano. I haven't had one since you were here for the Fourth. I'll go to the market and be back before you know it."

"Are you sure you want to bother?"

"Definitely."

"Okay, I'll stretch out in the hammock until you get back."

This was even better news than the lack of citrus fruit. Sam would fall asleep before her car was out of the drive. She had plenty of time now.

She made a lightning-fast stop for the navel oranges and was at the bench by the pond a little before five. Drew was already there. There was no question that the woman looked nervous. And pale. She was picking at a cuticle and dropped her hand when she saw Pix.

"You'd never believe I had a manicure every week before we came here. And a pedicure. Even if there was a place on the island I could get one, look at my hands." She stretched her fingers out, and yes, Pix could see that a few nails were cracked and several fingers had cuts.

It seemed unlikely that all this subterfuge was to get Pix to look at Mrs. Crane's hands, however. "I'm assuming you had something to say to me alone. Not my husband?"

"And not mine. He thinks I'm at the market."

"Mine, too." Pix smiled. The ice was broken.

"I don't know where to start," Drew said. She looked down at the previously displayed hands, which she was twisting in her lap, then looked up and burst out, "I never wanted to buy the place. When Cameron started talking about a vacation home in Maine I assumed it would be southern Maine. Someplace like Boothbay or Kennebunkport. Not on a damn island away from everything!"

Normally Pix would leap to defend her beloved Sanpere, but she kept listening.

"He bought it on the spot one weekend on what he called a 'scouting' trip when I was at my sister's. At Winnipesaukee. Right on the lake," Drew said bitterly. "I never saw this place except for some photos he took—and it looked kind of cute—until we arrived. I certainly had no idea how far away it was or that from the moment I set foot here I'd be slaving away, clearing brush, chopping trees, digging clams, laying new flooring, painting the inside, and now Cameron's ready to stain the outside—after we treat it with some kind of stuff you have to push between the cracks in the logs by hand. I tell you, Mrs. Miller, I am exhausted!"

Still wondering where this was going, Pix gave her what she hoped was a supportive look and said, "Well, summer houses can be a lot of work."

Drew shook her head, sending her red curls bobbing in the slight breeze. "Not for this girl. Not anymore . . ." She stopped abruptly and lowered her voice. "I did it. All of it. The glue and the fire. I took the glove from a stack in your barn."

Pix was stunned. "Wait a minute! You're telling me you destroyed your own property to get back at us for complaining about the trees?"

"No, no. I'm sorry about the trees, but Cameron wanted a better view, and as you've discovered, he can be pretty obstinate. When I saw how things were developing between us I realized how I could get him to leave. And he is. The house is going on the market tomorrow. He's had it with the island—no one has been sympathetic, he says. He's sure everyone, including the authorities, are biased against us. So, and it's a quote, 'I'm out of here.'"

"But what about the arson charge?" Pix could hardly believe what she was hearing.

"Once we're gone he'll have some new project. I'll give our lawyer a call soon, instructing it be dropped. I handle our legal stuff and finances, too. I was a CPA before I retired. Kept the books for his business and got some nice jewelry out of it."

She couldn't help it. Pix started to laugh hysterically.

"Are you all right?" Drew asked anxiously.

Pix gasped, swallowed, and replied, "Never better. We'd better get home from the market." It seemed appropriate to shake hands, so she extended hers. She could almost see Mrs. Crane as a friend in some other context. Or maybe not.

"Can't wait to get to a nail salon," Drew murmured as they headed for their cars.

Walking over the grass to wake Sam up, clutching one of the oranges, Pix knew he would be angry when he heard the tale—might want to take some kind of action—but she couldn't be. It was all over now, and even though Drew hadn't said she was sorry directly, Pix recognized a woman driven to the breaking point. She vowed to keep her secret, except for Sam and Faith—and also vowed to get on the phone to the

Realtor first thing in the morning and buy the place. She and Sam should have bought the property to begin with, although now it would be a bargain, what with the fire damage and lack of privacy. She felt herself starting to laugh again.

Hearing her, Sam woke up. "I must have dropped off. Meet anyone at the market?"

"Not today, but I did find that pot of gold you and Samantha were so sure I wouldn't."

Dr. and Mrs. Childs arrived at the Shores Monday morning dressed in black clothes suggestive of what Queen Victoria donned for Albert. Faith noticed that even Mrs. Childs's slip, which was hanging slightly below the hem of her dress, was black edged in somber black trim. They came into the kitchen just as Faith and Amy were starting lunch preparations.

"A terrible thing," Dr. Childs said soberly. His wife nodded, too overcome for words. "We've known Cal since he was a young man. What kind of monster would do such a thing?" He pumped his little fist in the air for emphasis. "The goal now is to keep the Shores moving along normally. We've finally found a very well-regarded chef. He's been working at one of these new luxury camping resorts, which is shutting down for the season, since so many schools open early. He'll be arriving Thursday. You will be able to stay until then won't you?"

Faith finished drying her hands, which she had just washed. Mrs. Childs interpreted the gesture as hesitation and quickly jumped in. "We'll pay double time for the hours."

Faith had been planning to agree before the offer but was glad she hadn't opened her mouth. "I can stay through dinner Wednesday." Amy piped up, "And I'll come early Thursday to show the new chef where everything is. It's the end of this session, so no dinner and just box lunches for those who want to take them along."

Both Childses appeared relieved. "Thank you both. We'll be leaving tonight. We are working with the authorities about notifying any family. So far as we knew he didn't have anyone—or at least people he was in touch with. We will see to all the necessaries, in any case."

Why didn't they just say "burial"? Faith thought. All these overblown euphemisms.

"He grew up on the island, Mom," Amy said. "I'll bet the Hamiltons will know if there's anyone here who's a relative."

"I can give them a call," Faith said. "Good idea, although Earl has probably already looked into it."

"Well then, Mrs. Childs and I will be on our way. We want a word with Cindy, who is of course distraught, as she knew him almost as long as we did. And then we have to see to packing up his quarters to make ready for the new occupant."

At that moment, Sophie came into the kitchen. Faith quickly said, "Did you want a glass of water? I believe you met Dr. and Mrs. Childs at the start of your course."

Sophie stayed where she was. "Yes, good to see you again, although I wish it were not under such sad circumstances. My class has been wonderful and I'm sorry it's ending so soon."

"We have always been fortunate to find gifted teachers," Mrs. Childs said. "Patrick's courses fill up immediately." Dr. Childs added, "We were happy to discover Eloise this season and she, too, has been equally popular at all our locations.

With those pronouncements, they left. Necessaries to see to, Faith thought ironically.

When she was sure the door had shut behind them, Sophie said, "I'll take that water, but I have to get right back and find out what we're doing the rest of the day. We spent the morning rewriting and this afternoon Eloise is meeting with us individually."

Sophie gave a slight nod toward Amy and Faith picked up on it. "Sweetheart, could you see if we need more supplies at the coffee station?" One serving tea as well had been set up in the main lodge for the students.

As soon as she left, Sophie said, "Early this morning I stopped by the Hamiltons' to see if Jenny wanted to get together later—come to The Birches for a drink maybe or go off-island—but she wasn't there. Nan said she'd left just after dawn but didn't say where."

"Maybe you could drop back after you finish today?" Faith suggested.

"That's what I planned."

"Did Alexandra come today?" Faith had almost forgotten to ask.

"Oh yes. Not grieving. A new bright blue outfit, or at least new to me, and she's sitting next to—and rather close to—Hans Richter. The woman is incorrigible!"

After Sophie left, Faith took Amy's suggestion and called Nan to ask about any family Cal might have had.

"I'll tell you what I told Earl, too," Nan said. "Calvin Burke left the island when he was a teenager. Didn't wait to go to graduation, and I hadn't heard a word about him since until he turned up last summer working at the Shores and singing with Jenny. His family wasn't from here. Aroostook County I believe. His father came to work in the shipyard and his mother stayed at home. Not very sociable, and only had the one child. But his father was one of those men who never growed up. Out on his motorcycle, off with drinking buddies in Belfast. Course he went off the road one night, leaving her a widow, and once Cal took off, his mother did, too. Probably up north. Earl is checking."

"Roy is about Cal's age right? What does he remember about him?"

"I asked him early this summer when Jenny started singing with him and he told me he couldn't say anything bad about him. Couldn't say anything good. Restless, but not wild like his father. Mother spoiled him wicked, Roy said. Whatever he wanted. Fancy guitar, new car for getting his license. He liked money that was for sure. Worked as a caretaker for summer people, so probably did all right."

"Jenny must be upset," Faith said.

"You know something? She hasn't shed a tear." She sounded puzzled. "And now she's gone home. Classes start soon. When I asked her if she was all right, she told me she didn't really know him, and from the look on her face I could tell the subject was closed. Now, wasn't that some great about Freeman winning?"

Faith knew the other subject was closed so far as Nan was concerned, too. After chatting a bit more about the victory, she hung up and concentrated on getting a lobster quiche in the oven.

Sophie meant what she had said to the Childses. The course had been wonderful, and she knew she would finish her story once she got back to Savannah. She wanted to keep writing and thought finding a writers' group would motivate her.

She looked around the room as her fellow scribblers settled in. She'd become used to, and attached to, this group. And was still learning things about some of the members. The biggest surprise had been that Jay and Ellen were a couple now—or at least headed that way. Sophie prided herself on her powers of observation, but she had not picked up even the smallest hint. They didn't sit or eat together. Whatever went on was after Sophie left for the day. Ellen herself had shyly revealed the attachment to Sophie and also that Jay was in fact a gifted writer. Ellen was even more so. She'd finally shared some of her work with Sophie. She certainly didn't need this class. Sophie hoped that Jay's hubris didn't overshadow Ellen, an obviously adoring acolyte. How many women writers married to male ones had seen their own promising careers eclipsed? Women artists, too.

"Time is always fleeting during this course," Eloise

was saying. "Only three more days together. I've written a schedule of our afternoon conferences and I'll pass it around. I must say that this has been an impressive group. Both your dedication and your skill. Cynthia, your factitious family history has made me laugh out loud often, but you never went for cheap shots. You made the various relatives both likable and funny."

"Once I started," Cynthia said, "I found I was remembering real anecdotes that I knew Ross would leave out. There's some embellishment, but not a lot."

"Everyone else is well on the way to a manuscript that could get you an agent or be published in a literary magazine in the case of the short stories. Sophie, your piece is both moving and an important historical contribution. I'm sure any journal, especially one devoted to African-American history, would be glad to look at it. And, George, if you don't end up with an Edgar from the Mystery Writers of America, I'll be very surprised."

Eloise looked straight at Jay. "And you, too, if you're willing to cut some of what you've fallen in love with—it's too long. I have to admit, though, that my favorite in the mystery genre is Joan's Persis Gray. Again award potential—an Agatha. I've been called a bit quirky myself, and we're both of a certain age. Elderly sleuths bring knowledge the young ones can't hope to imitate."

She glanced over her shoulder. "Oh dear, they're putting lunch out. I'll talk about the rest of you at tomorrow's morning gathering."

Sophie looked at the schedule. She wasn't scheduled to meet with the instructor for a few hours. Through the glass door in the manager's office she could see Cindy with Dr. and Mrs. Childs. Their plates piled high with food, they were sitting and seemed to be going over a ledger, with Cindy taking notes on an iPad with a keyboard. They'd be there a while, and this gave her the chance to do what she had been mulling over.

The police would have thoroughly searched the cabin Cal shared with the chef, so it was doubtful there was anything left to find. But Sophie kept thinking about Jenny and wondering about that relationship— and the significance of Jenny's tattoo. One that partially matched the others, specifically Cal's.

"I need some fresh air," Sophie told her mother as the groups broke for lunch. "I had a big breakfast, so I'm not really hungry. See you later."

"Alexandra is eating with Hans and for *some* reason doesn't seem to want me at her table," Babs said. "I'll join the MacDonalds. Cynthia and Ross are quite a delight together. Polar opposites, but devoted. Kind of like Ed and me."

"Glad to hear it," Sophie said to her mother. It was

time that Barbara Proctor Maxwell Rothenstein Williams Harrington found the One.

Sophie quickly made her way up the path to Cal and the chef's cabin, which was distant from the other updated ones. She hoped the door was open. It wasn't.

Walking around the outside, she decided the only choice was to break a window, unlock it, and carefully make her way in. There was a low one at the rear that already had a crack. She picked up a rock and heaved it. The whole pane fell into the cabin in pieces and she unlocked the window, lifting it up. Glad that she was wearing jeans not shorts, she stepped over the sill and was in.

The cabin was small with one room housing a kitchenette, table, chairs, and a sofa in front of a woodstove. She checked this immediately. No ashes with partially burned letters as clues. Then she opened the few drawers and cabinets. The contents revealed that no one had been doing much cooking—or eating—here. Next, she went into the tiny bathroom, where she searched the medicine cabinet—empty—and the cabinet under the sink. It contained a few towels, a plunger, and nothing else. She shook out the towels, hastily folding them back. The stall shower contained a bar of Irish Spring and Axe shampoo. Any other toiletries, even a toothbrush, were missing.

The bedroom had two twin beds, neatly made. Remembering Chef Dom's size, Sophie wondered how he possibly could have fit in one. A closet covered by a curtain was empty. Where were Cal's clothes? Taken by the police? No suitcase or backpack left, nothing personal from either man. The two nightstands had a drawer each, also empty. Sophie pulled them out and turned them upside down. Nothing taped to the bottom.

Ready to give up, she thought she'd give the old "under the mattress" hiding place a try. She was impressed by the Shores housekeeping. Not a single dust bunny. Each mattress rested on broad wooden slats, not springs. Methodically she slid her hand on top of each, getting a splinter from the first bed for her effort. Nothing. She turned to the other and close to the foot felt something.

Excited, she pulled out a small rectangular notepad. She sat back and turned it over. Excitement built to elation. It was a prescription pad! Each page had been carefully filled out for a wide range of opioid types, strengths, and amounts. The patient's name was left blank. What wasn't left blank was the doctor's information and signature. Dr. Sidney Childs D.D.S.

"What are you doing here? And what's that in your hand?"

For a big woman, Pamela Childs had a very soft step.

Sophie jumped up. "I wanted someplace quiet to think about my writing," she improvised hastily, "and remembered this cabin. I knew it wouldn't be occupied. I'm just jotting down some ideas."

Heavy footsteps in the other room indicated the good dentist was with his wife. "Sidney, get in here. We have a problem."

"What is it, my dear?" he said, out of breath and coming into the room. He was red faced and sweating. Not used to hiking in the woods. "What is she doing here? Isn't she in Eloise's class? Don't tell me she's another of Cal's conquests?"

"No," his wife said grimly. She snatched the prescription pad from Sophie's hand. "She's been nosing around, and look what she found. Cal was so careless."

The doctor glanced at the pad and his usually benign expression switched to Hyde—pure evil.

Sophie edged toward the door, but Pamela blocked the way. "Give me your handkerchief, Sidney," she barked. "And your belt." Useless to protest—or reason—with them. Sophie realized her only chance was to get to the front door. She aimed a swift kick at Mrs. Childs's kneecap and was rewarded with a howl of pain. The doctor was cowering on the other side of the room. Apparently violence was not his thing. Just hiring people to do his dirty work.

She ducked past the woman, who was screaming, "Don't let her get away, Sidney, you fool! Shoot her!"

Dr. Childs had a gun.

Before Sophie could get to the front door, which they had closed behind them, a bullet whistled very close to her head. She stopped.

Mrs. Childs, enraged, grabbed her and stuffed the handkerchief in her mouth, painfully tying Sophie's arms at the wrists behind her back with the belt. "We can't leave her here, Sidney. She'd be found eventually." Sophie felt a twinge of hope.

"I say we deal with her like the others," Dr. Childs said. "My bag is in the other room. I'll just get a syringe."

Hope died and Sophie felt herself start to faint. She struggled to stay upright.

"No, we don't want to do anything suspicious. We really only need her on ice for an hour or so. More if we want to be sure she isn't found until we reach the border." Pamela appeared to be considering alternatives.

"Not keep her on ice, my dear. Something warmer."

Which is how Sophie found herself in the spa's sound-proof sauna with the heat on full blast, after being frog-marched securely between the two down the path she had come up and whisked behind several out-buildings to the back door.

"You should have minded your own business," Pamela Childs chided. "I'm hanging the OUT OF ORDER sign on the door, so you won't be disturbed. Good-bye."

The doctor had some parting words, too. "I want my belt back. It's my Tom Ford, remember, darling." Sophie was positive this last did not refer to her. As soon as he'd freed her hands, she'd pulled the gag from her mouth and flung it at him. "You may keep that as a souvenir," he sneered and shut the door firmly.

She collapsed onto the cedar bench. As a place to stash her while the couple made their way to Canada, the windowless sauna was diabolically perfect. With the sign and the out-of-the-way location, by the time Sophie was found extreme dehydration would have killed her.

The three resort conference centers. What perfect covers for drug distribution. And the same staff, so well versed, rotating among the three, setting up operations. Plus the Lowell connection. The tattoo must have been the biker-dealers' own private one, Cal their leader.

The Childses and any accomplices were obviously

pulling the plug on the entire operation. Somehow Cal's death had triggered it. Cindy and Chef Dom, if he was still alive, were in on it, too.

The wooden bucket that held water to pour on the hot rocks was empty. Sophie didn't know whether it made more sense to strip down or keep her clothes on, keeping moisture in. She was burning up and her head was starting to spin. She started to lie down across the bench but sat up immediately and started pacing the room. She couldn't let herself fall into a coma.

Doctors and motorcycle gangs. She recalled reading about a New Jersey doctor running a similar scheme, caught only when he had one of his nonmedical associates kill his wife.

Jenny. What did she know and how involved was she? The pill container and the slip of paper in Arlene's purse must have been from Dr. Childs. That's what Jenny had seen. What did she plan to do? Or was she in on it? As soon as she got out of here, Sophie intended to find out. No, wait. *If* she got out of here.

That's when she started to sob. Will! Would she ever see her husband again?

"I'm sorry to disturb you. I know you must be busy, but I'm looking for Sophie Maxwell. She's a friend of yours isn't she?"

"Yes she is and no, I haven't seen her since before lunch," Faith said. She hadn't seen the writing instructor up close yet and she was every bit as eccentrically dressed as Sophie had described: today, a bright persimmon linen caftan belted with a plum-colored Japanese obi. Large hoop earring with tiny bells hanging in each and chains of the same bells around her neck reached below her waist. Somehow it worked.

"It's just that Sophie didn't turn up for her appointment with me, which isn't like her. I've taken the others after her and had a look around. I know she's a day student, so perhaps she went home, but I'm quite sure she would have left word. And she isn't answering her phone."

This *wasn't* like Sophie. Faith took her apron off. "Amy, honey, I'm going to find Sophie. If she comes here, tell her to wait. We're in good shape for dinner."

"No prob," Amy said, concentrating on turning out millimeter-thick radish slices for a rose-shaped garnish.

Sophie's car was in the guest parking lot. Faith touched the hood. "Cold. She hasn't been anywhere recently."

"I hate to be an alarmist, but I don't have a good feeling about this," Eloise said. Given that the woman was a dead ringer for the Divination professor in the

Harry Potter movies, Faith had to agree. Besides, she was feeling the same way.

Just then Faith's phone rang. Sanpere Shores had the best service on the island. Her heart leaped, but the ID said "Unidentified Caller."

"Hello?"

"Faith, it's Earl. A heads-up. Don't be alarmed, but all hell is going to break loose there in a few minutes. The state police and DEA are raiding the place. I want you and Amy to stay put together in the lodge living room. Sophie, too. And tell no one else."

He ended the call before Faith could respond.

"News about Sophie?" Eloise asked.

"Nooo, just a friend. But I need to go back and help my daughter with dinner. If Sophie is there or turns up soon, I'll tell her you're concerned."

With that, Faith took off almost at a run, leaving a bewildered Eloise standing by the cars.

She wasn't wearing a watch, so she had no idea how long she'd been cooking in the sauna. Her phone was in her bag, which the Childses had taken from her. It was probably in Penobscot Bay by now, flung from the bridge as they made their escape. Sophie had succumbed to the fatigue and was lying down. She'd also taken off her jeans, which felt as if they had melted onto her.

At first she wasn't sure whether she was hearing things or not. Someone was pounding on the door! Using both fists she pounded back. She yelled, too. There was a brief return knock and then silence. Her heart sank. Whoever it was had gone. She kept knocking until her hands were raw. After what seemed like hours, the door opened and she tottered out, determined to hug her rescuer to bits. Which was quite appropriate.

It was Babs.

Mom!

"However did you manage to get yourself trapped in there, Sophie? It could have been very dangerous. Good thing I decided to come for a nice sweat. Getting rid of all those toxins. I was about to leave because of the sign on the door, but I could tell the sauna was on from the gauge outside. You know how people are. Selfish at times. I figured it was someone who wanted it all to themselves. Then I heard the knocking. Fortunately, the key was at the desk."

"Mom," Sophie said, still clinging to Babs tightly. "It's a long story, but we have to call 911 and every police force in the state. The Childses are major drug dealers and on their way to Canada. They put me in here."

"The dentist? And that enormous wife of his? Well, as I've often told you, darling, people are seldom what they seem. Now drink this water. I'll make the calls. And do put your pants on."

Stepping outside, the two women could scarcely see the woods for the police vehicles. Calling in the troops wasn't necessary. Someone already had.

Uncle Freeman was a sweetheart. He hadn't said a word when Jenny asked to use the car to drive back to Massachusetts. "I'll return it soon," she'd promised. "Keep it as long as you need it, de-ah," he'd said.

She'd thought they were dealing only weed, maybe some coke. She didn't do any of it, so never paid much attention. Stupid. Or worse. The LeBlanc brothers were fun to be with, and Jenny had never been the frat boy type. She'd always preferred Harleys to Vespas. Her tattoo was a thumb of the nose at the wimpy butterfly ones. And it had been a kick hanging out with Cal, especially once they started singing together. She felt free for the first time since her mother died.

She couldn't go back to Lowell. She'd told her father the day of the Lobster Boat Races and she'd also apologized for being such a brat about her stepmother, who really wasn't all that bad. Just not Mom. Nobody could be. She'd told him she was going to transfer to the

University of Southern Maine's music school. The Portland music scene was great and she wanted to be closer to the island.

It was seeing Arlene that had opened Jenny's eyes. Seeing the result of what they were doing to people up close. Saturday night on her uncle's boat—she'd "borrowed" it more than once, carefully replacing the fuel—she'd confronted him with the bottle and prescription. The doctor's name. She'd hoped Cal would deny any part in it, but he'd laughed and started bragging. How rich it had made him. "And what about the LeBlancs?" Jenny had asked. She hadn't heard they were dead until then. She thought they'd gone back to Lowell. "Collateral damage," he'd said. "Got careless. Started using themselves. A big no-no. Chef, too, but we need him. He's in rehab."

"I thought all of them were your friends," she'd protested, and his response made her sick. "Friends? Guys like me don't have friends, little girl, and the sooner you learn what the world is really like the better." He'd put his arm around her, a gesture she'd always liked. It had made her feel wanted. That night, she felt her skin crawl.

"You take over. Need to take a leak," he'd said and moved toward the stern.

She was ready.

A long drive never bothered the operative. Just as the wildly different postings didn't. It was a second career. A radically new chapter. She liked to think of herself as a Mrs. Pollifax, the fictional amateur spy for the CIA.

Only she was very real.

It had been a near thing this time. She should have been keeping an even closer eye on them in Maine. Sophie Maxwell could have been injured—or worse. It was over now. Her part. Time for a new look for the next case. She could stop at the outlets in Freeport. Maybe L.L. Bean outdoorsy woman? Or preppy Ralph Lauren? A Talbots lady who lunched? She'd make pillows out of all those *ridiculous* scarves and caftans. But what to do with all those little bells?

Usually Faith's eyes stayed dry at weddings, no matter the size of the lump in her throat. Not this time. She'd started dabbing at her eyes the moment Kylie Brown came down the mown path in Edgewood Farm's meadow, past the seated guests, enthusiastically scattering rose petals from her basket with a huge grin. She stopped to give her father a kiss, then continued on, closely followed by Sam Eaton, who was as serious as a preacher, clutching the little satin pillow with two gold rings embroidered on it that Ursula had spent hours making. Faith realized Samantha was right when she'd said the kids would steal the show.

Zach, his best man, and Tom in his robes were waiting in the gazebo under an arch that Mary Cevasco had made from what seemed like all the flowers in her garden. Samantha followed the children, her mother and father on either side. She'd told Arlene, who had moved from the facility in Boston to a center near Portland, that a year from now she and Zach would renew their vows on the dock at The Birches with Arlene as matron of honor, and even Kylie and Sam in their roles all over again. The Miller clan was always up for a party, so the suggestion was heartily approved by all.

Pix took Samantha's bouquet and sat down between her mother and husband, her heart filled with joy. The weather was perfect. Not a hint of a nor'easter. She looked at her boys and daughter-in-law, Rebecca. Becca hadn't wanted any coffee since she'd arrived at Sanpere and had ducked out of the kitchen when the aroma filled the room. Pix was hoping they might have news. But all in good time.

She caught the eye of her brother, Arnie, and beamed at him and his family. Son Dana had grown a foot it seemed since last summer. Arnie gave a slight nod at their mother, resplendent in her gold dress. Pix knew he was sharing her thought, thankfulness for Ursula's good health and the hope it would continue so for many years.

Stunning as she looked, Ursula was outdone by Millicent Revere McKinley, who was wearing a turquoise-blue silk sheath and jacket, selected with Samantha's help one afternoon in town, followed by tea at the Copley. Millicent had also been to her safe-deposit box; her mother's long rope of pearls was luminescent. But it was the art deco diamond brooch, sending rainbows over the guests, that had caused surprised gasps. Who knew? If Pix had given any thought as to what might be stored safe and sound at Cambridge Trust she would have put her money on a brooch made from the hair of dearly beloved departeds and perhaps the secret recipe for the potent Revere family gunpowder punch.

Tom had included the seven traditional Hebrew blessings and the couple had read short vows they'd written to each other. Samantha, no veil, her shining chestnut hair crowned with a wreath of flowers, was breathtakingly lovely.

And now—"With this ring . . ." Pix reached for Sam's hand and squeezed it tight.

"What a beautiful wedding," Sophie said. "It makes me want to get married all over again."

"To Will, I assume," Faith joked. The couple had been inseparable since Will had flown up immediately after Sophie's escape from the sauna.

"You assume correctly." The two had grabbed a small table away from the rest of the wedding guests, kicked off their shoes, and were drinking champagne. Their husbands, and others, had settled into party mode—ties loosened or abandoned, heels exchanged for flats—greeting old friends; making new ones. Sam Eaton, Kylie, and some other children were playing tag. The farmhouse and barn sat high on a hill and the view across Penobscot Bay was spectacular.

After the truly cinematic climax at Sanpere Shores, Alexandra had accepted Hans's invitation to stay at his summerhouse in Cape Elizabeth. He spent winters at his Manhattan town house and traveled extensively. He'd come to the wedding as her "plus one," and Faith had overheard her tell him that she had planned the whole thing. Some people never changed.

Looking around, Faith thought she was glad those here didn't, cherishing the Millers and extended family, all the island friends, and Aleford out-of-towners just as they were. And her own Tom, Ben, and Amy. Although she couldn't say that Ben and Amy hadn't changed. Ben was an adult now or near to it, and the events of the summer had affected Amy. She would always be Faith's little girl, but she wasn't one anymore.

A few minutes later, Sophie asked, "Are you thinking what I'm thinking?"

"Probably," Faith said. "Something along the lines of hasn't this been an incredibly hard-to-believe summer? A terrible one?"

Sophie shuddered slightly and sipped her champagne. "Exactly. But they didn't get away with it. Any of it. The Childses hadn't even gotten as far as Ellsworth, thanks to the APB that had gone out."

"Which was before the feds arrived, right?"

Sophie nodded and took another sip. "Strange that. After I had been questioned, I was alone with Earl, waiting for Mom to get me—not exactly in shape to drive—and he told me he'd received an anonymous phone call, muffled voice—didn't know whether male or female—describing the operation. I think it may have been Jenny, or perhaps Cindy. She's talking now. Hoping to make a deal—a different kind from the ones she was involved in. He also said the feds were already watching the Childses and Cal, too. The raid on all three places had been in the works for a while and was moved up when Cal was killed. They figured the doctor and his wife might make a break for it. They had been stashing money in offshore accounts for years it seems."

"But didn't Earl also say they insist they had nothing to do with Cal's death?" Faith said.

"Is that so?" The man himself pulled up a chair and freshened their glasses with the bottle he'd brought. "I talk too much and you never heard any of this from me, remember. But I do wish I could tell you one thing and that's who the DEA had planted at the Shores. In one of the writing courses, not the actuaries. I do know that much. Any ideas? Sophie, you were in the best position to spot the NARC."

She shook her head. "Not a clue. The people in my class were highly individualistic. Not exactly undercover material. If it were two agents I'd go for the women who were supposedly college friends. Or the couple writing what the instructor was sure was going to be a romantic suspense blockbuster. But they clearly wanted fame, not anonymity. Same with George Finley and Jay Thomas. Sorry, it will just have to remain a mystery."

"Okay, ladies," he shrugged, adding, "happens a lot in my job. Keep the bottle. I'm going to go dance with my beautiful wife."

The sun was slowly sinking below the horizon and

the scene in front of her was filled with the kind of brilliant long light that always reminded Faith of a stage set. Earlier the photographer had gathered everyone together, bride and groom in the middle, and recorded the gathering forever from the top of a stepladder. Click.

Faith looked at Sophie, content now, and out at the dancers. Click. At the beginning of the reception, everyone had joined in the horah as the bride and groom were hoisted up on two chairs, linked to one another by a silk handkerchief. Click.

At the moment Tom had engaged Millicent for what looked like some kind of waltz to an arrangement of "All You Need Is Love." Click.

And there they all were in the amber of the moment.

Author's Note

*T*here are places *I remember*—the first line of the Beatles' song "In My Life," on the 1965 *Rubber Soul* album, has been running through my mind lately. I find myself humming the evocative tune. This year Faith and I have celebrated significant birthdays—and no, we're not telling—so perhaps that is why I have been thinking about all the places I remember. And yes, some have changed; some not.

Patrick, the memoir-writing instructor, asks the group to go back to a first memory as a starting point exercise. I gave Alexandra what was my own mother's earliest memory, significant for the brilliant colors of the beaded curtain that Mom, an artist, recalled. My first full memory is of sitting on a sofa in the New Jersey farmhouse my parents rented just after the war—our first home—holding my brand-new baby sister. I had just turned three. Hopscotching through the years I've come to realize what John Lennon expressed so poignantly. That the places are all tied with the people, and I've loved them all.

A trip to the Jersey shore with my cousins, Uncle Charlie lifting me onto a carousel horse, pointing out the brass ring. To everyone's surprise my tiny hand grabbed it the first time around. Flash forward many years later to a week on Martha's Vineyard with my four close college friends. We'd rented a house and gathered from both coasts, leaving all responsibilities behind to celebrate a milestone birthday (what was it again?). After Oak Bluffs Illumination Night, we went to the Flying Horses carousel, and as we rode, laughing together, I stuck out my hand only to find I had grabbed the ring once more.

Seven months after our December wedding, I stood holding hands with my husband on a hiking trail high in the French Alps in the sunshine and knew I had grabbed the ring again.

Learning to swim from my Norwegian cousin Hege in the Hardangerfjord. We children, the smalls like me on up, were a tribe that summer. We slept in an old sod-roofed granary and went to the main house for riotous meals when we could be coaxed indoors.

Sgt. Pepper summer, 1967, the Summer of Love, outside London with my sister working as au pairs, spending our days off at Hyde Park watching all the beautiful people. "When I'm sixty-four" was very far away. Thirty was a stretch. All those *Sgt. Pepper* songs and the others, too. For many of us, the Beatles were, and are, the soundtrack of our lives.

A cross-country trip with our newly graduated high school son. I snapped a photo of him with his dad arm in arm, overlooking Oregon's Gold Beach, a photo I look at on my desk every day.

Back to places . . . Hearth and home rooted here in Massachusetts virtually my entire adult life. Especially this house, our forever house. The walls echo. Many joyful gatherings, but the one we give each year for close to a hundred neighbors and friends, old and new, is special.

And this house holds another memory I go back to often. A private one of intense happiness when my mother was staying with us some years after we lost my father too soon. I fell asleep wrapped in the knowledge that the three people I loved most in the world were all under one roof.

And then there's Maine, always Maine. It is no accident that this twenty-fifth book in the series, a kind of silver anniversary, is set on the island I chronicle and created. The island where I have been going since I was eleven. I had intended the "Sanpere Island" location for this book quite a while ago. No place is more significant for me, nor the people. To list them—some are gone and some still living—would take another chapter. It is home in a way no other has ever been—and not just because we'll be there a while: our plot is at the end of King's Row in Mount Adams Cemetery, next to a stand of pure white river birch, the spot selected by my parents long ago.

Think back to your own places and the people. Often stop and think about them as Lennon says he will. Listen to versions of "In My Life" that other musicians have recorded. It is an anthem of the soul.

In our lives we've loved them all. *I've* loved them all. Thank you.

Coda: *Like the characters in this book, I—and my family—have been watching the drug crisis deepen with alarm for years. In Maine alone there was a 40 percent increase in drug overdose fatalities in 2017 over 2016, most due to fentanyl and heroin. The first six months of 2018 saw drug overdoses claim nearly one life each day. But also like the characters, we have hope for the future. This hope is due to the efforts of some extraordinary people at, to name a few, the Is-*

land Health & Wellness Foundation—https://island-healthwellnessfoundation.wordpress.com/, Healthy Acadia—https://healthyacadia.org/, Opiate-Free Island Partnership—https://www.facebook.com/opiatefree-island/, and one individual in particular, Dr. Charles Zelnick. Addicts are our friends, family members, neighbors—not criminals. Watch the documentary The Hungry Heart. Filmed in Vermont, it is every state, USA. https://www.pbs.org/video/the-hungry-heart-b1sfbh/

Excerpts From
Have Faith in Your Kitchen

By Faith Sibley Fairchild with Katherine Hall Page

Summertime recipes!!

CHILLED GARDEN PEA SOUP

1 tablespoon olive oil

2 scallions (spring onions), sliced thin

4 cups frozen peas (Faith likes Birds Eye Sweet Garden Peas)

1 cup water

2 cups chicken or vegetable stock

Pinch of salt

1/2 cup crème fraîche

Fresh mint (optional)

Place the olive oil and scallions in a saucepan over medium heat and stir briefly. Do not brown the scallions.

Add the frozen peas and stir.

Add the water, stock, and salt.

Cover and bring to a boil. Check to see if the peas are tender.

Uncover, turn the heat down, and simmer for approximately 7 minutes.

The peas should be quite tender now.

Remove from the stove and let cool for about 10 minutes.

Puree in two batches in a blender and pour into a bowl. Cover with plastic wrap and refrigerate.

This soup is best made a day ahead.

Before serving add a dollop of crème fraîche or, using a pastry bag, pipe thin concentric circles of the crème and using the sharp point of a knife, draw a line through them to the side of each soup plate to create a web. Garnish with the mint.

Of course, if you are lucky enough to have enough fresh peas in season to make this, use them. You will cook them a few minutes less. Faith also uses her precious fresh peas for traditional salmon and peas on the Fourth of July.

For a variation on this dish, try garlic-infused or another flavor-infused olive oil. You may also add 1/4 cup fresh mint leaves when pureeing.

A lovely first course or luncheon entrée.
Serves six.

FAITH'S FAMOUS LOBSTER ROLLS

2 lobsters, a pound and a
  half each
1/3 cup mayonnaise
  (Hellmann's or Duke's)
A squeeze of fresh lemon

Pinch of salt
Pinch of freshly ground
  pepper
2 tablespoons butter
4 split-top hot dog rolls

Cook the lobsters. (Faith steams them in a large pot of two to three inches of rapidly boiling water for 12 minutes.) When cool enough to handle, remove the meat and cut it into bite-size pieces, reserving the large claw meat for garnish if desired. Set aside.

Combine the mayonnaise (brand depends on where you live), lemon juice, salt, and pepper in a separate bowl. Season to taste, adding more salt, lemon juice, or pepper. When it's just right, add the lobster and mix well to coat.

Melt the butter in a frying pan—iron skillets are the best—and toast both sides of the rolls. Fill immediately and serve.

Other recipes call for celery, chives, parsley, scallions, and condiments like Tabasco. The Fairchilds are purists when it comes to lobster rolls, and this is the real deal. You may also use this recipe for crab rolls.

Serves four.

OLD-FASHIONED COLESLAW

1 1/2 cups grated green cabbage

1 1/2 cups grated red cabbage

1 large carrot, grated

1 1/4 cups mayonnaise

(Hellmann's or Duke's)

1 1/2 tablespoons sugar

1 tablespoon half and half

1 teaspoon lemon juice

1 teaspoon salt

After grating the cabbages and carrot (a food processor works well and saves your knuckles), transfer to a large mixing bowl and stir to distribute the ingredients evenly.

In a separate bowl, mix the rest of the ingredients and stir well before pouring into the bowl with the cabbage/carrot mixture. Using a rubber spatula or similar utensil fold the liquids into the slaw. Cover with plastic wrap and refrigerate immediately until served.

While this is tasty right away, it is even better made the day before.

Serves a crowd.

BLUEBERRY BUCKLE

Topping

1/3 cup granulated sugar

1/2 cup all-purpose flour

1 teaspoon ground
  cinnamon

1/8 teaspoon salt

4 tablespoons unsalted
  butter, softened and cut
  into pieces

Batter

1 1/2 cups all-purpose flour

2 teaspoons baking
  powder

1/2 teaspoon salt

4 tablespoons softened
  butter, cut into pieces

3/4 cup granulated sugar

1 large egg

1 teaspoon vanilla

1/2 cup milk

2 1/2 cups blueberries,
  preferably wild Maine
  ones

Preheat the oven to 375 degrees F.

Grease a 9-inch-square pan at least 2 inches deep, preferably with butter.

Make the topping in a small bowl by mixing the sugar, flour, cinnamon, salt, and butter with two knives or a pastry blender. Set aside.

To make the batter, blend the flour, baking powder, and salt in a medium bowl. Set aside.

In a larger bowl, cream the butter and sugar until

light and fluffy using an electric mixer or by hand. Add the egg, vanilla, and milk. Mix.

Gradually add the flour mixture from the medium bowl into the mixture in the larger one until blended. Fold in the blueberries. It will be a thick batter. Spread it in the pan and sprinkle the topping evenly on the batter.

Bake in the center of the oven for 40 to 45 minutes. Check with a toothpick or broom straw.

Serves eight.

A "buckle" has been described as a muffin that has mated with a coffee cake. The name comes from the fact that the cake "buckles" into a slight round when taken from the oven.

Buckles are an old-fashioned New England recipe. My friend and cookbook author Brooke Dojny—*Dishing Up Maine, Chowderland, The New England Cookbook,* and more—sent me the following about buckles: "In the same category as Crumble (also called crisp), which is fruit with crumb topping; buckle is like coffee cake, then there's cobbler and grunt or slump (love those names) with biscuit topping that is steamed rather than baked so it sometimes heaves a sigh (grunt) and sort of slumps down into the fruit."

Whether you buckle, grunt, or slump, these are all delicious. A dollop of vanilla ice cream or whipped cream on the warm dish takes the cake.

SANDY OLIVER'S FRUIT SHRUB

Stymied by attempts that were too bitter, Faith and I turned to Sandra Oliver, food historian, essayist, cookbook author, and founding editor of *Food History News,* http://www.foodhistorynews.com/, for what would have been a simple recipe used in colonial Down East and elsewhere for shrub. One of our country's first drinks, shrub is a mixture of fruit and sugar steeped in a vinegar. The name goes further back to the Arabic *sharab,* meaning "drink." Shrub has once again become a happening drink, added to vodka, gin, or other alcohols!

Fill a quart jar with fresh strawberries. Cover the berries with cider vinegar, put a lid on the jar, and set away to soak in a cool, dark place for two to three weeks. Do not refrigerate. The berries will get very pale.

At the end of the two- or three-week period, drain the berries, reserving the liquid and discarding the berries. Measure the liquid and put it in a saucepan. Add an equal amount of sugar as there is of the liquid (if you have one and a half cups of liquid, add one and a half cups of sugar). Heat until the sugar completely dissolves.

Cool and store in a bottle or jar, tightly covered, until you are ready to use it.

To serve, pour a few tablespoons of the syrup into a glass, add club soda or plain water to taste, and a few ice cubes. You can also add the syrup to iced tea, ginger ale, lemonade, or a similar beverage.

You can also use other kinds of juicy berries like raspberries or blackberries.

Note: Many of the recipes from previous books are found in Katherine's actual cookbook, *Have Faith in Your Kitchen* (Orchises Press).

About the Author

Katherine Hall Page is the author of twenty-four previous Faith Fairchild mysteries, the first of which, *The Body in the Belfry*, received the Agatha Award for best first mystery. *The Body in the Snowdrift* was honored with the Agatha Award for best novel of 2006. Page also won an Agatha for her short story "The Would-Be Widower." The recipient of the Malice Domestic Award for Lifetime Achievement, she has been nominated for the Edgar, the Mary Higgins Clark, the Maine Literary, and the Macavity Awards. She lives in Massachusetts and Maine with her husband.

HARPER LUXE

THE NEW LUXURY IN READING

We hope you enjoyed reading
our new, comfortable print size and found it
an experience you would like to repeat.

Well – you're in luck!

HarperLuxe offers the finest in fiction and
nonfiction books in this same larger print size and
paperback format. Light and easy to read, HarperLuxe
paperbacks are for book lovers who want to see
what they are reading without the strain.

For a full listing of titles and
new releases to come, please visit our website:

www.HarperLuxe.com

Using Your Chakras

Using Your Chakras

a new approach
to healing your life

Ruth White

SAMUEL WEISER, INC.

York Beach, Maine

*To Penny, who has for many years
been a dear and supportive friend*

First published in 2000 by
Samuel Weiser, Inc.
P. O. Box 612
York Beach, ME 03910-0612
www.weiserbooks.com

08 07 06 05 04 03 02 01 00
10 9 8 7 6 5 4 3 2 1

Library of Congress Cataloging-in-Publication Data

White, Ruth.
    [Chakras]
    Using your chakras : a new approach to healing your
life / Ruth White.
        p. cm.
    Originally published in London by Piatkus Books in
1998 under the title: Chakras.
    Includes bibliographical references and index.
    ISBN 1-57863-161-0 (pbk. : alk. paper)
    1. Chakras. 2. Healing. I. Title.
RZ999 .W48 2000
131—dc21   00-020481

Cover design by Kathryn Sky-Peck

Printed in the United States of America
VG

The paper used in this publication meets the minimum requirements of
the American National Standard for Information Sciences—Permanence
of Paper for Printed Library Materials Z39.48-1992 (R1997).

Contents

Acknowledgements

I should like to thank the groups I teach for their support and for asking the right questions at the right time, so that the work continues to unfold.

Names and identifying details in the case studies have been changed but I should like to thank all who gave such generous permission for their life experiences to be used in this way.

Once again I wish to mention my Jack Russell dog, Jackson, who has been a warm, constant and patient companion at workshops and beside me at my word-processor throughout the writing process.

Introduction

This book builds on the foundations laid in its predecessor, *Working With Your Chakras*. Though each book is complete in itself, it is recommended that you use them together to get the deepest understanding of the chakra system and how working with it can help your life and spiritual development.

Working With Your Chakras set out basic information about chakras and explained how to recognize chakra energies, to explore, heal and enhance the function of the chakras themselves. It gave information about chakra colours, fragrances and crystals, with suggestions as to how to use these in chakra work.

For easy reference, this book also has pages setting out the basic information required for working with each chakra but it moves on from the work on chakra sensitivity to look at ways in which deeper chakra knowledge can enable you to reach your full physical, emotional, mental and spiritual potential and give you the tools with which to improve or heal every life situation.

Working With Your Chakras explored each chakra systematically, from the root to the crown, whereas this book is arranged in chapters relating to different aspects of life. In this way, if you need help, with family relationships for instance, you can turn directly to Chapter 4 to find those chakras with which to work in order to build strengths or to bring healing.

Firstly, though, let us remind ourselves of how this particular system of chakra work has evolved and set the scene for the use of this book.

Chapter 1

About Chakras and Chakra Work

Gildas, my discarnate guide and communicator, has been in direct teaching communication with me for almost forty years, but I have been aware of his presence beside me since early childhood. He tells me that his last incarnation on earth was as a Benedictine monk in fourteenth-century France. He is now working with a large group of guides from 'the other side' in order to establish clearer connections between the dimensions and to give spiritual help and teaching to those of us who are in incarnation.

When I attune to his vibration, I hear his words and teachings like a kind of dictation which I can repeat onto tape or write down. As part of his communication, Gildas gives teaching about healing. He talks of the channelling of subtle energies through one person to another, in order to aid healing and growth. Awareness of the energy system long recognized in Eastern esoteric teaching as the Chakras is a tool which helps in working with healing growth. Gildas has adapted the original Eastern chakra knowledge to make it more understandable and applicable within the Western tradition and it is this system that I share in this book. Gildas encourages us to see the chakras as a Map of Consciousness, which enables us to discover more about our individual and collective purpose. Furthermore, it enables us to use chakra work to heal our lives and fulfil true potential.

Awakening to your chakras heightens and intensifies your spiritual awareness but, important as this is, spirituality cannot truly flourish unless you are also on a pathway to fulfilment and growth in life as a whole. Your spirituality cannot find true expression unless you are a whole being – healthy in mind, body, emotion *and* spirit.

Through chakra work you can improve your relationships with family, friends, lovers, partners, colleagues and bosses; release blockages around such issues as sex, money and authority; understand more about your sense of purpose in order to find greater satisfaction in your work and more certainty about the direction you want to take in life; nurture the courage to make major life changes; enhance your confidence and psychological stature and discover subtle tools with which to heal yourself and others so bringing you greater physical health and vitality.

ORIGINAL TEACHINGS

Original teachings about the subtle energy system known as 'the chakras' come from Eastern esoteric writings in which the language used is Sanskrit. The Sanskrit word *chakrum* means 'wheel'. Properly speaking, *chakrum* is the singular form and *chakra* the plural but in the West it is usual to speak of one *chakra* and many *chakras*. I follow this Western practice throughout my books and teaching work. When seen clairvoyantly, chakras are wondrous wheels of light and colour: shimmering, turning and vibrating, feeding and reflecting our subtle life energies.

Sanskrit descriptions customarily refer to seven chakras as forming the major system, with some teachers acknowledging an extra, eighth chakra. More recently much channelled information, including that from Gildas, has spoken of additional major chakras which are in a process of awakening. These extra chakras usually expand the major system to twelve.

THE AURA

Around every human being there is an energy field known as the aura. This may be clairvoyantly perceived in full colour or as a vague light. It usually stretches 4 to 6 inches or 10 to 15 centimetres out from the physical body. Though some of our basic aura colours never change, others vary according to our mood or state of health at any given moment and can be indicators of these. Once a person is truly dead there is no longer an aura or energy field. A vital essence is withdrawn.

Much of the colour and energy of the auric field is supplied by the chakras, which are wheels of light and colour interpenetrating with (affecting and affected by) the physical body. Chakras also carry links to specific parts of the physical glandular system and might therefore be described as subtle glands.

CHAKRA COLOURS

Each chakra is associated with a particular colour in the spectrum and needs to produce this colour for its energy field. The root chakra produces red; the sacral, orange; the solar plexus, yellow; the heart, green; the throat, blue; the brow, indigo; the crown, violet. The alter major produces brown. Healthy chakra colours are bright but transparent, like those produced by a rainbow or those seen when sunlight passes through stained glass.

In healing and chakra work, the primary colour notes may have to be modified. It will also be seen that more than one colour is important to each chakra, that any colour may healthily be present in any chakra and even that each chakra produces its own spectrum. Difficulties arise when a chakra is not producing enough of its 'home colour' for complete health and well-being. Much chakra healing work is dependent on the use and visualization of colour and there is full reference to the significant colours and their meanings in each section.

NAMES AND LOCATIONS OF THE CHAKRAS

On page 7 the diagram shows the seven major chakras, plus one extra (the Alter Major), and their positions in relation to the physical body. They are named in descending order as Crown, Brow, Alter Major, Throat, Heart, Solar Plexus, Sacral and Root. Semantic difficulties can arise simply because there is a variety of terminology, some of which is Eastern and some more Westernized. For instance, different teachers use the terms 'Sacral', 'Hara' or 'Spleen', to refer to the chakra which is two fingers below the navel. Confusion of terminology around 'Brow', 'Ajna' or 'Third Eye' also sometimes occurs. Problems arise if these terms are used interchangeably within the usual sevenfold system, when minor or additional chakras come under discussion, and when those newly awakening chakras which are now becoming a part of the major system are named. In Chapter 12 the new chakras are described and some terms which have previously been used interchangeably are used more specifically.

Most Eastern traditions describe a sevenfold major chakra system, while acknowledging varying large numbers of minor chakras throughout the body. Students of the famous medium and esotericist Alice Bailey (see Bibliography), will know that she spoke of an eighth chakra, giving it the Latin name 'Alta Major'. This chakra is included as an important one here, but with the spelling 'Alter Major', meaning 'other' rather than 'higher' major.

The expanded major chakra system suggests a total of twelve major points to which we should direct attention in order to

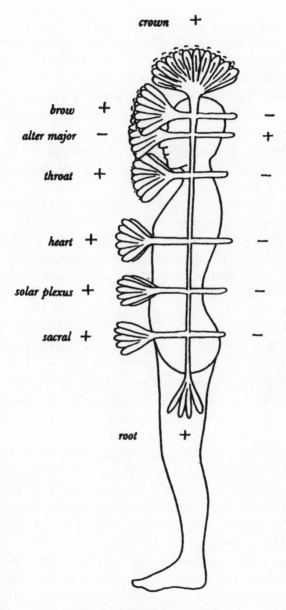

crown   +

brow   +   –

alter major   –   +

throat   +   –

heart   +   –

solar plexus   +   –

sacral   +   –

root   +

The seven best-known chakras, plus the alter major. Energy flows from positive to negative (+ = positive polarity, – = negative polarity) and up and down the central column. Note the reversed polarity of the alter major.

aid self-healing and growth. The number twelve is certainly important in other ways. We have twelve astrological signs, twelve calendar months in a year, and it is expected that twelve planets will eventually be discovered.

It is sometimes assumed that the words 'higher' or 'lower', in relation to Chakras, are used as terms of evaluation. But it is important to remember that these words are mainly descriptive of the chakra positions in the physical body when upright. There is no hierarchical system within the chakras – each one is a part of a team.

There is sometimes a lack of agreement as to whether the chakras are situated at the front or back of the body and its auric field. The diagram on page 7 attempts to depict the way in which chakras interpenetrate with the physical body, having 'petals' at the front and 'stems' at the back which project into the auric field.

CHAKRA PETALS, STEMS AND POLARITIES

There is a central subtle column of energy interpenetrating with the physical body and running from the crown of the head to the perineum (the area midway between the anus and the genitals). Each chakra has petals and a stem, except some of the new ones (see Chapter 12). The stems of the crown and the root chakras are open but contained within the central column. The other chakras have petals which open into the auric field at the front and stems which project into the auric field at the back. The stems normally stay closed but the petals are flexible, opening and closing, vibrating and turning, according to the different life situations encountered. A healthy chakra is a flexible chakra. Where there is dis-ease the chakra energies become inflexible or actually blocked, affecting our physical, mental, emotional and spiritual health.

Though normally closed, a healthy chakra stem is like a self-opening valve. It allows unwanted energy or reaction to pass through. It is part of the elimination system. Chakra stems can be damaged by shock or trauma, by over-use of drugs (medical or hallucinogenic), by lengthy or too frequent anaesthesia, and by abuse of alcohol or tobacco. In such cases they may stay open, rendering the individual vulnerable to outside influences of all kinds. This open state of the stems can be healed through an understanding of colour and energies, and by receiving the sort of healing which can be channelled through the hands. Much chakra work, though, is of a self-help nature. With a little knowledge you can do a great deal to change your life, with exercises which are almost as straighforward as breathing or through creative and colourful visualizations.

With the exception of the alter major chakra (see page 224), the petals carry a positive, and the stems a negative, polarity (see diagram on page 7). Again, these terms are not evaluatory but are rather used in an electrical or magnetic sense.

THE CHAKRA AREAS OF INFLUENCE

At the beginning of each chapter you will find a list of areas of influence. Besides the location and colours of the chakra under discussion, the list includes the following references:

Key Words

These words summarize the main aspects of life, feeling or spiritual development with which the chakra is connected.

Developmental Age

The first five chakras have a developmental age. This does not mean that a new-born baby only has a root chakra (developmental age 0–3/5 years), since every living person must have all the chakras for full spectrum functioning. Rather, it means that at certain ages particular chakras develop more strongly and their areas of influence are particularly operative. If childhood needs are met well enough at each developmental age then the chakras will strengthen and develop normally. Where there are difficulties at the developmental ages the chakras may be adversely affected. When, later on, you realize that something in your life is out of balance, healing the appropriate chakra will help heal the original trauma or imbalance as well as the existential discomposure (see also the inner child, page 91).

Element

Each chakra has its own element. Its areas of influence are affected by that element and related to it. Life issues connected with earth, for instance, will usually belong to the root chakra. Germane issues may also be connected to the element of the chakra through a more symbolic interpretation of the element. Thus, earth (root) is connected with the sense of smell, as well as matter, nurturing, rooting, basic physiological needs and the physical body. Likewise, water (sacral) is connected to the sense of taste, the emotions, the flow of life, flexibility, sexuality, creativity, power, empowerment; and the water and blood within the physical body. Fire (solar plexus) is connected to the sense of sight, individuality, identity, vision, symbolic digestion of life and the physical digestive system. Air (heart) is connected to the sense of touch, as well as tenderness, detachment, the symbolic breath of life and to breathing and circulation in the physical body.

Akasha, a rather esoteric element (throat), is linked to the sound and colour in the universe and is the layer around us on which personal and collective memory is engraved; it is connected with the sense of hearing and also with expression, communication, the ability to listen, making ourselves heard and responsibility. Radium (brow) is connected to higher vibrations, spiritual vision, refinement and inspiration. Finally, magnetum (crown) is an element given for this chakra by several guides. It is not yet included in any comprehensive list of the elements we know, as it is still to be scientifically discovered. It is connected to the pull between gravity and levity and the process of incarnation.

Sense

Each of the first five chakras is associated with a sense, which also connects with the element, as we have seen. The root is linked to smell; the sacral to taste; the solar plexus to sight; the heart to touch; the throat to hearing.

Body

We have already spoken of the aura and the subtle layers which it represents. Each layer of the aura and each chakra is connected to a subtle body or plane. The relationships between these bodies and layers can be immensely complex. At the risk of over-simplifying, here is a brief summary:

- **The root and the red areas of the aura** are linked to the physical body.
- **The sacral and the orange areas of the aura** are linked to the etheric body. This body, being closest in vibration to the physical, holds a subtle replica or etheric double of every organ in the body and of the body itself. The etheric aspect of an organ does not withdraw from the body when the physical organ is removed. The etheric body only totally withdraws when death occurs.
- **The solar plexus and the yellow areas of the aura** are linked to the astral body and plane. Our astral bodies are refined and fluid in texture. People who have near-death experiences move into their astral body. Sometimes anaesthesia, abuse, a shock, accident, or dream state will induce the experience of being able to hover above the physical body, seeing everything which is happening to it, but not feeling its pain or sensations. The astral body is connected to the physical by a subtle energy cord. At death this cord is finally severed and the animated spirit or being of the person is no longer able to return to the current physical body but moves

on to the astral plane to be welcomed and aided through
the initial experiences of death. The higher astral planes
hold many healing temples. The lower astral planes
(particularly at the interface between the etheric and astral
layers) hold thought forms, many of which are negative.

- **The heart and the green areas of the aura** are linked to the
feeling body. This is not to be confused with the emotional
layer of our beings. Used in this sense, feeling means the
ability to feel without being dominated by emotion and to
empathize to the degree where we actually feel that we know
how another person functions and what it is like to be them.
This state may be experienced during sexual intercourse. It
is also met when contemplating and empathizing with trees,
plants, animals or crystals. We enter the feeling body when
we are in true meditation, sometimes in dreams, when we
communicate with guides and angels, or experience altered
states of consciousness. Guides and angels use the feeling
planes as an interface to which they come in order to meet
us.

- **The throat and the blue areas of the aura** are linked to the
lower mental body or plane. These are the areas where we
experience the ability to name something. Once it is named
it becomes a part of our world and comprehension. Before it
is named it is too abstract for us to experience in the full
consciousness of the finite mind. The receiving of symbols
is one of the steps towards the naming process. The lower
mental body is the vehicle through which truths and insights
come from the personal unconscious, the collective unconscious and from the workings of the universe itself.

- **The brow and the indigo areas of the aura** are linked to the
spirit and the higher mental body, the stage beyond the lower
mental body or plane where there are energies and forces
which are beyond our finite comprehension. Part of the
angelic stream of consciousness exists on this level, as does
the pure energy of divine principles. Angels and guides help

us make the transition between the higher and lower mental planes to the finite mind.

- **The crown and the violet areas of the aura** are linked to the soul and the causal body. The soul carries the record of our evolution, knows the causes we have set in motion, and the effects we must balance, redeem and transcend. It is at this level that we make many choices which affect the conditions of our lives on earth. (see Chapter 2, page 24, and entry for 'karma' in the Glossary).

The Glandular Connection

Each chakra is related to a gland or several glands in the physical body. The chakras can therefore be seen as a subtle addition to the glandular system. Healing the relevant chakras will help glandular function.

In the system used by Gildas, the root chakra is connected to the gonads (ovaries in women and testes in men); the sacral is connected to the lymph system; the solar plexus to the adrenals; the heart to the thymus; the throat to the thyroid; the brow to the pineal; and the crown to the pituitary.

Quietening and Stimulating Fragrances

There are fragrances recommended for balancing each of the chakras. They are best bought in concentrated oil form, as used in aromatherapy. If mixed with a carrier oil, such as sweet almond or jojoba, they can be used directly on the body, for massage, or in the bath. Undiluted, a few drops can be added to water in a fragrance burner to perfume a room. Many of them can also be obtained in the form of joss sticks or incense cones. Suggestions for their use according to the specific concerns of this book are given in the exercise section of each chapter.

Crystals and Gemstones

There are specific crystals which relate to each chakra (see the Glossary, and the exercise section of each chapter, for suggestions about working with crystals).

Affirmations and Prayers

Affirmations are phrases which we reiterate mentally when we wish to change our behaviour or belief systems. Prayers are an appeal to a higher authority to help us to new realizations or to aid us in changing our lives. The words given for each chakra can be used as affirmations and/or prayers.

CHAKRA PAIRS

The important connections between particular pairs and groups of chakras are explored in depth, together with the areas of life affected by their interactions.

Firstly, each chakra needs to be considered as a pair with those which come before and after it in the energy system. Thus, in the sevenfold system, root pairs with sacral, sacral with solar plexus, solar plexus with heart, heart with throat, throat with brow, and brow with crown. With the inclusion of the alter major, throat and alter major become a pair, as do alter major and brow.

Other chakra pairings are linked with their colours. Each colour of the spectrum has its scientific complement. For example, if you look intently at something which is bright red and then close your eyes or look towards a blank wall, the 'after image' will be green, and vice versa. Thus red and green are known as complementary colours. The root chakra colour is red and the heart chakra is green, so the root and heart form an important pair in the chakra team. In the same way, orange and blue are complementary colours and the pairing between the sacral chakra and the throat is very strong indeed.

Yellow and purple complement each other, so the yellow solar plexus pairs with both the purple chakras – the brow and the crown.

The vital energy flow between root/crown and crown/root (see page 21) makes these two centres another key pair.

The crown chakra is the seat of the higher will, whilst the heart is the seat of incarnate wisdom. Much of our evolution depends on establishing a link between these.

The solar plexus is the seat of the lower will. Success in fulfilling our highest purpose is enhanced when higher and lower wills work smoothly together, hence crown and solar plexus form an interconnective pair.

The root and the alter major are both linked to our instincts, sense of self-preservation and early warning systems, and so form a pair that is essential in enhancing our connection with earth and the natural world.

With notable connections between root and heart, root and crown and crown and heart, these three also form a chakra group. Other groups include the solar plexus, brow and crown; the first five chakras (root, sacral, solar plexus, heart and throat); and the three main head chakras (throat, brow and crown).

Each of these pairs and groupings reflects a particular area of our lives.

ARCHETYPES

By dictionary definition these are 'primordial images inherited by all'. Each human society is affected by forces such as peace, war, beauty, justice, wisdom, healing, death, birth, love, power. The essence of these defies definition and we need images, myths, symbols and personifications to help us in under-standing the depth and breadth of them. Tarot cards, which have ancient origins, have twenty-two personified or symbolized archetypes in the major arcana. These cover most aspects of human experience.

We can come to a deeper understanding of the chakras if we study those archetypes which are most directly or deeply connected with them. In considering pairs and groups of chakras, working with certain archetypes can serve to clarify the chakra relationships and to give us a fuller comprehension of our life aims, drives and blockages. Archetypes can be great healers when we know enough about them to draw on their aid and use them creatively.

Higher archetypes are the pure energies emanating from the Divine, such as Love, Beauty, Peace. Lower, or degraded, archetypes derive from the higher qualities, are often personified and arise from our struggle to understand and come to terms with archetypal forces. Thus Love becomes The Lover; Beauty, The Maiden, Youth, Princess or Prince; Peace, The Peacemaker.

CLEARING THE CENTRAL COLUMN

Keeping the central column energetically clear is the first rule of chakra work. Each chakra feeds into, and is fed from, this central column. Using the breath to keep the energy free-flowing in this column prevents and heals chakra blockages and brings a new balance and vitality to life. Chakric energies need to move easily both upwards and downwards through your body. The following exercises are crucial in establishing this movement and in clearing the central column. They should be used as a preparation for meditation and healing and before doing any of the other exercises in this book. This form of breathing will subsequently be referred to as 'central column breathing'.

Exercise 1
Central Column Breathing

Stand or sit with your spine straight and your body balanced. Do not cross your legs if you are sitting in a chair, or your ankles if you are sitting on the floor, unless you are in the lotus position or a 'cross-legged' posture.

- Begin by being aware of the rhythm of your breathing and letting it slow down.
- Now draw the breath in as though it comes from just above the crown of your head; draw it down through the centre of your body. Change to the out-breath at a point which feels natural for you and breathe out as though right down and through your legs and into the earth. (The breath will not go down through your legs if you are in a cross-legged or lotus position but these postures automatically balance energies in the body and chakras.) Breathe in this way about five times (i.e. five in/out breaths = one sequence).
- Now, on the alternate breath sequence, begin to breathe up from the earth, through the centre of your body, letting the out-breath go out through the crown of your head.
- Continue to breathe in this way, without straining or forcing, for about five minutes. Always end on the downward breath sequence, repeating it in this direction more than once if you wish.
- Feel the balance of your body, resume normal breathing and pause for a few moments before meditating, proceeding to a guided journey or chakra exercise, or returning to your everyday tasks.

Exercise 2
Visualization for the Central Column

If the weather is favourable and there is a suitable tree that
you know, it is good to do this exercise with your back against
it and your bare feet on the earth. If this is not possible,
follow the posture instructions given for Exercise 1.

- Begin by being aware of your breathing rhythm; let it steady
  and perhaps slow down a little.
- Visualize yourself as a tree. Your branches stretch out above,
  your roots stretch deeply into the earth, your trunk is straight
  and strong. You are nurtured by the four elements. The
  sun (fire) warms you and the air refreshes you. Your roots
  are in the earth and they seek the underground streams,
  sources of living water.
- Breathe in through your branches, from the elements of
  air and sun; take the breath right down through your
  trunk and breathe out strongly into your roots, into the
  earth and the streams of living water.
- Breathe in now from the earth and the living water. Bring
  the breath up, through your roots, through your trunk,
  into your branches, and breathe out into the elements of
  air and sun.
- Repeat these two breath sequences for five to ten minutes.
  Gradually let the visualization fade. Feel your feet firmly
  on the ground and your own space all around you. Now
  proceed, with a sense of centredness, to chakra work,
  meditation or your normal activities.

Chapter 2

Being Here:
Finding a Sense of Purpose

Key Issues: Incarnation, Purpose and Choice

Chakra Pair: Root and Crown

Archetypes: The Sun, the Moon and the Stars

This chapter will help you to:
- be more in tune with incarnation
- be more aware of the elements
- prepare for and face life changes
- gain a better understanding of your life's spiritual purpose
- learn about the meaning and purpose of life on earth

AREAS OF INFLUENCE

The Root Chakra

Location Perineum (the area midway between the anus and the genitals). The petals face downwards, between the legs; the stem faces upwards into the central column and is naturally and healthily slightly open.

Colours Red; Brown; Mauve
Key Words Rootedness, Incarnation, Acceptance, Self-Preservation, Concept
Developmental Age 0–3/5 years
Element Earth
Sense Smell
Body Physical
Glandular Connection Gonads
Quietening Fragrances Cedarwood, Patchouli
Stimulating Fragrances Musk, Lavender, Hyacinth
Crystals and Gemstones Smoky Quartz, Garnet, Alexandrite, Ruby, Agate Bloodstone, Onyx, Tiger's Eye, Rose Quartz

Prayer or Affirmation

Through incarnation may spirit be brought into matter. Through rootedness may life-force be recharged and exchanged. We acknowledge wholeness and seek to gain and to reflect acceptance.

The Crown Chakra

Location At the top of the head with myriad petals (the thousand-petalled lotus) facing upwards and a stem going down into the central column
Colours Violet, White, Gold
Key Words Soul, Surrender, Release, Incoming Will
Element Magnetum
Body Soul, Ketheric or Causal
Glandular Connection Pituitary
Quietening Fragrances Rosemary, Bergamot
Stimulating Fragrances Violet, Amber
Crystals and Gemstones Diamond, White Tourmaline, White Jade, Snowy Quartz, Celestite

Prayer or Affirmation

Through surrender and release let the incoming will be truly the will of God working within us and through us, leading us increasingly to knowledge of mystical union and mystical marriage.

ROOT AND CROWN AS A CHAKRA PAIR

The breathing exercise central column also establishes the fundamental link between the root and crown chakras.

The developmental stage for the root chakra is from birth to 3/5 years. This does not mean that a baby only has a root chakra. The seven-layered energetic body of which the chakras form a major part is essential to life itself. A baby has a full chakra system, yet the early months and years vitally affect the functioning and potential of the root chakra. If these years contain all that the baby needs, and are full of love and nurturing, then the root chakra flourishes and the foundations for later strengths are fully laid.

Clairvoyantly seen, the root chakra is the simplest of them all. Its petals face downwards, from the perineum area into the earth and, ideally, are always at least partially open. The stem goes up into the central column. A direct upward flow of energy from the root, through the central column into the open stem and petals of the crown, and an answering flow from the crown, down the central column, through the stem of the root, out through its petals, into the earth, establish a vital interconnection. A question to ask yourself, linked to the sense connection of the root chakra, is: 'How do I smell the world and how does the world smell me?'

The root is the slowest and the crown the fastest in the chakra team in terms of movement and colour vibration. The crown has been described as 'the thousand-petalled lotus'. When balanced and healthy it is always open, moving and oscillating with high intensity. Red (root) has the slowest vibration in the colour spectrum and violet (crown) the highest.

The crown chakra is the gateway through which the energy of the soul and the higher self stream into our spiritual consciousness and inspire our incarnation. These energies have to be earthed and the root chakra is the complementary gateway through which this happens.

KEY ISSUES

The key life issues affected by the pairing between root and crown chakras at the spiritual level are incarnation, purpose and choice.

Incarnation

The word 'incarnation' literally means 'embodiment'. It therefore covers all the issues around the process of taking on a body, being born and finding our place in life. In addition to the spiritual implications there are emotional and physical factors to be considered.

The search for a deeper meaning to life leads us inevitably to the need for spiritual models or hypotheses. We need a *spiritual*, rather than a specifically *religious*, language to enable philosophical discussion and a wider comprehension. Chakras, as previously explained, derive their names from Sanskrit and Eastern spiritual philosophies, and so the context and function of each chakra naturally tends to be described using terms of mainly Eastern origin. Alongside 'incarnation' we need to use words like 'reincarnation', 'karma', 'the higher self', 'soul', 'spirit', 'destiny' and 'evolution', in order to widen our understanding of why and how we came to be here.

Gildas has summarized some of these concepts. He tells us that the impulse to incarnate comes from the soul, which is beyond the being in human form.

The soul, whose wisdom and experience is gathered by the overseeing intelligence known as the higher self, is intent on evolving into wholeness or perfection. Many lifetimes are needed for evolution and in each lifetime we become progressively more aware of the need for communion with our souls and for greater understanding of our purpose.

The spirit is the pure, animating, essence of being and is fully present within each one of us in every incarnation. The soul, however, remains on a different plane of consciousness, overseeing the process of evolution.

The goal of evolution is enlightenment, perfection or wholeness – a state of being in which we are beyond attachment and the limitations of the finite mind, no longer have any need to incarnate, and are journeying towards union with the Divine Source of All Being.

The pitfalls of the learning process mean that karma, the spiritual law of cause and effect, is activated (see also Glossary).

From karma comes the concept of reincarnation – or many lifetimes – in which to gain experience and learn the consequences of misuse or misinterpretation of the Divine Principles.

The Divine Principles (or higher archetypes) are pure, abstract forces affecting and motivating us all the time. As we interpret them so we name them: Love, Justice, Peace, Beauty, Harmony, Power, Service, Wholeness and Perfection. We struggle to live by these principles and, in order to understand them, we break them down into component parts and archetypes are created (such as the twenty-two archetypes in the major arcana of Tarot, see page 32 and Glossary).

The higher self takes an overview before and after each incarnation in order to assess progress, make choices, open opportunities or provide specific learning situations relevant to the soul's evolution. Consequently, each incarnating being carries the seeds of destiny.

Purpose

Destiny is the sum total of the choices made by the higher self for a particular incarnation. It includes the evolutionary lessons to be learned, the karma to be repaid, the imbalances to be rectified and the service we may elect to give to humanity or the earth. Our higher selves also endeavour to involve us particularly with one or more of the Divine Principles or archetypal themes. When we reach an understanding of the archetypal umbrella under which we live, we can work more consciously towards evolution and spiritual fulfilment.

Each of us incarnates with an 'incoming will to. . . ' – or under the influence of an overlighting angel. When we learn to live in harmony with this, the whole of life becomes more congruent. Thus our incoming will may urge us to teach, to learn, to heal, to create beauty or harmony, to govern, to be involved with justice or peace, to serve, to explore, to philoso-phize, to wield power, to bring love. . .

Knowing, identifying and acknowledging our overall 'will to . . .' or life theme, and making contact with our overlighting angel, is an important issue. (See Exercise 4, page 37). Many of us long to be relieved of the burden of choice. 'If only someone would tell me what I should be doing then I could get on and do it' is a plea which I constantly hear in my work. It is not as simple as this.

Choice

Even when we feel we have identified our incoming will or key word, or made creative contact with our overlighting angel, we still need to acknowledge that each area of possibility is a wide umbrella. We still need to make choices, find motivation and create our lives.

Many people who come for personal consultations with my discarnate guide, Gildas, ask the question: 'What is my life purpose?' Usually Gildas can see the incoming flow from the higher self and even contact the overlighting angel. He can then interpret and communicate the main key or task words for the present incarnation. He also firmly points out that, for each one of us, the overall spiritual purpose of life is evolution. In order to evolve we need experience and therefore every day, every hour and every minute of our lives is an accomplishment of life purpose. The main task is to become more conscious of ourselves and of the experiences we are having, in order to activate our power of choice. For many of us it is exactly this power which we find so formidable. How do we choose? What if we make the wrong choice?

Gildas informs us that there *are* no wrong choices. We agonize unnecessarily over some life decisions, telling ourselves that there must be a right or wrong direction to take at each of life's crossroads. Sometimes we stay stuck at the crossroads, unable to read the signs or make a decision about which way to turn. Influenced, as we are, by the Christian ethic (as interpreted by the Church), we tend to think that self-sacrifice and choosing the most difficult path must somehow be more virtuous than treading the way of true joy and inner fulfilment. We see God, guides, higher selves, angels and spiritual helpers as demanding killjoys and imagine that the most effective lessons can only be learned through pain and suffering. Unless the medicine tastes nasty we think it can't be doing any good! However, once we understand more of the mechanisms of the higher self, decisions and choices can be made more freely and creatively. We are often our own hardest taskmasters.

Gildas says:

Choice is a necessary part of life in earth incarnation. But in the widest sense there are no wrong choices. Before you come into incarnation your higher self has made selections which ensure that the scene for evolutionary experience is set. The historical time and culture for your incarnation are chosen, as is your initial social milieu. Children choose their parents. Parents choose their children. Gender, body type and mental orientation are

also decided before physical conception takes place. Even
the astrological influences at the moment of birth are
chosen and directed.

In this way your lives are circumscribed. Certain choices
will be impossible for the incarnate self to make, whilst
any choice which is within the realms of possibility will lead
to valuable experience which your soul still needs for
evolution. Therefore each time you are at a crossroads
different but *equally valuable* experiences are available
whichever direction you take. It is then for you, in your
incarnate personality, to decide which direction will bring
you the most fulfilment and how much or how little you
want to stretch yourself. Higher selves want each being in
incarnation to be self-actualizing [see Glossary] but no one
expects you to jump through hoops. All guides and
advisers on this side of life hope that you will find joy
and consciousness in incarnation and in connection with
the earth and what it has to offer.

The only wrong choices come when, with full consciousness, you turn to the dark or evil side of life and create
disharmony or wilful harm. The basic law of human nature
is harmlessness. There are multiple complexities associated
with the honouring of this law but if you try to live by it
to the extent of your conscious awareness at any given
moment then wrong choices are not part of the picture.
Embrace life's opportunities with confidence, neither fear
change, nor be addicted to it for its own sake, and you
will steer a true course through evolutionary opportunities
and concerns.

HIGHER ARCHETYPES AND THE
INCOMING WILL

A fuller list of key words which apply to the incoming will or
which describe the nature of the overlighting angel is derived

from the list of Divine Principles or archetypes of higher qualities. No suggested list can be comprehensive. We need to find the key word which really motivates and speaks to us at a personal level. This means that any given list will have room within it for creativity. There will always be additional words close to the meaning of others which are more pertinent or meaningful to a particular individual.

For some, like John (see case study, page 29), the key word will be more straightforward and easily related to the basic list of archetypal higher qualities. For others it will be more elusive or subtle, requiring considerable thought or meditation in order to arrive at the word which really encapsulates or enlivens the inner sense of life purpose. Here, I give some suggested lists of words arising from each of the archetypes of higher qualities, which may help you in your search to understand your incoming will and to have clearer contact with your over-lighting angel of purpose. (see also Exercise 4, page 37). Some words appear in more than one list as the archetypes can engender similar qualities. Yet it is subtly, but importantly, different to work with creativity under the archetype of love than to work with creativity under the archetype of power. Each has its place; one is not better than the other, but they fulfil a different purpose.

From the higher archetype of **Love** come: love of God, love of others, self-sacrifice, tenderness, mothering, nurturing, caring, creativity, dedication, vocation, commitment, healing, love of earth and growing things, love of animals, conservation, transformation, giving, contentment.

From the higher archetype of **Justice** come: equality, fairness, administration, law, order, guardianship, authority, leadership, reform, social conscience, politics, mitigation, arbitration, warriorship, human rights, debate, caring, idealism.

From the higher archetype of **Peace** come: peace-making, warriorship, arbitration, citizenship, defence, guardianship, healing, planning, order, freedom, relating, union, humanitarianism, safety, prayer, meditation, quietude.

From the higher archetype of **Beauty** come: preservation, creativity, shaping, artistry, skill, observation, grace, transformation, appreciation, colour, design, architecture, building, vision, assessment, perspective, awareness.

From the higher archetype of **Harmony** come: music, creativity, peace-making, dance, art, colour, design, symmetry, arbitration, counselling, inner searching, healing, friendship, empathy, rhythm, understanding, tolerance.

From the higher archetype of **Power** come: rulership, leadership, teaching, priesthood, government, self-empowerment, empowerment of others, self-actualization (see also Glossary), ambition, initiating, competitiveness, acquisition, responsibility, direction, inspiration, vision, hope, dedication, idealism, belief, courage, confidence, law and order, competence.

From the higher archetype of **Service** come: dedication, purpose, serving others, responsibility, administration, law and order, transformation, transmutation, healing, counselling, giving, self-sacrifice, social conscience, belief, social reform, improvement, idealism, patriotism, humanitarianism, love of others.

From the higher archetype of **Wholeness** come: self-growth, equality, balance, inclusiveness, healing, perception, blending, acceptance, seeking, exploration, assimilation, completion, vision, tolerance, breadth of knowledge, symbolism, creativity.

From the higher archetype of **Perfection** come: idealism, God consciousness, dedication, striving, healing, endeavour, vision, stoicism, industriousness, seeking the highest, goodness, belief, setting standards, aims, goal-setting, confidence, focus, advising, leadership, artistry, worth, conservation, preservation, following a prescribed path closely, application, diligence.

I have tried to avoid using words which have any negative connotations but, of course, almost anything which gets out of proportion can be seen as negative. All these aspects, in proportion and context, have positive and balanced applications.

Discovering the key archetypes and words which give you a

clearer sense of your incoming will or overlighting angel will not always immediately lead you to the perfect study, work or career. But they will give you a clearer sense of why you are here and a fuller understanding of the purposes of your higher self. Any combination of the key words can be applied to a variety of careers and will strengthen you in the style with which you approach the work you have chosen or from which, at present, there is no way out.

We are a *doing*-orientated society. Care must be taken to ensure that the key words are also considered in relationship to work or lifestyles which are more *being*-orientated. Creating and maintaining a beautiful home or garden and mothering children are, at one level, very active and demanding tasks, yet it is the happy homemaker's quality of being which deeply touches others. Some people also know that the actual nature of the work they do is less important than the quality of being which they bring to it. Some people learn to *be* through *doing* – others learn to *do* through *being*.

Case Study: Finding Your Incoming Will

John, in his early forties, was following a successful career as a teacher. He was a well-respected departmental head in a large secondary school. To all appearances he seemed to be the epitome of the career teacher, on the brink of further promotions and success. He was happily married to Ursula, also a teacher, who had recently become head of a local village school. They had a comfortable home and their son and daughter were both doing well at university. To the onlooker, they seemed to have achieved that rounded contentment in life which can be so elusive.

When John made an appointment to see me he had recently become interested in the transpersonal approach to therapy and counselling (see Glossary). He outlined his basic problem as 'disillusionment and loss of direction'. He felt that his life and career had lost their meaning and even wondered if he had ever known real meaning in its deepest sense. He regularly attended services at his local Anglican church but had begun to lose the comfort, solace and inspiration which he had earlier found in conventional worship.

John felt depressed, isolated and at a dead end. Outwardly he was trying to behave as normal but inwardly he was under considerable stress. The idea of changing his career or life direction seemed too awful to contemplate. Ursula and the children were settled and happy. John felt that if *he* changed the whole family would inevitably be adversely affected. He was unwilling to cause a family crisis and disrupt the lives of his loved ones. Furthermore, there was nothing John passionately wanted to do instead of teaching. But, if he remained in this career, he despaired of finding the inner and outer strength to maintain the high standards he had always set for himself and which were now automatically expected of him.

I felt that John was experiencing a spiritual crisis in the widest sense, as well as a degree of mental and physical burnout. This latter state needed to be dealt with at a practical level so that measures could be taken to alleviate or prevent the onset of physical stress symptoms. The long school holidays were not far away but John usually spent the major part of these reviewing previous work and preparing for the next school year. There would be two weeks for a family holiday. This year his student children were breaking from family tradition and had made their own arrangements. John felt that he and Ursula might just stay at home and attend to the garden. But when he had listened to what I had to say about burnout, John said he would seriously consider taking a longer break with Ursula, perhaps abroad, seeing this also as a celebration of her recent promotion.

Having emphasized that the physical needs were important, I then began to talk to John about archetypes of purpose. He felt that he had rather drifted into teaching, since at school he had not wanted to be a doctor, lawyer or priest and, at the time, teaching had seemed the only other alternative. Until recently he had been fulfilled in teaching. Now he found it difficult to maintain momentum but could not see any viable alternative. Somehow his relationship with the archetype of teacher had never been fully forged; he felt swept along by it; that it was in charge of his life and had cut off all other avenues. In some ways he felt he was the victim of the archetype.

In the end, John and Ursula decided to take a month's holiday abroad and, as he left, I asked him to think about teaching as an archetypal umbrella and to see whether any aspects of it excited him more than others. He also agreed to look at the other important umbrella archetypes to discover which seemed most energized for him.

With the start of the new school year John returned to our sessions. His thoughts around archetypes of purpose had proved fruitful. Deep reflection had convinced him that he had not so much drifted into teaching for lack of other choice but that teaching had subtly called him. 'I feel myself to be an educator,' he said. The aspect of teaching which currently excited him most was the work he did with younger teachers, helping them find their feet in their chosen career and supporting the development of their teaching skills and strengths. Whilst reading teaching journals his attention had been drawn to vacancies for lecturers in teacher training. He felt he would need to do some part-time courses before applying for such a post but becoming a trainer of teachers was now his clear goal.

In the interim, giving more lead to the young staff in his school would provide sufficient challenge for him to carry on where he was. He felt that he was forging a new relationship with the archetype of teaching or education, and could avoid becoming its victim in future, drawing on it, instead, for true inspiration and a sense of life purpose. A move into teacher training would be reasonably non-disruptive to the life of his family. He felt revitalized and that his dead end had become a crossroads, with him feeling confident now as to which direction to take.

John continued to come for sessions to discuss the spiritual side of life. He continued to go to church but also practised meditation and read widely in spiritual literature. His view of the universe and the purposes within it changed and widened.

Eighteen months later, when I was only seeing John for infrequent sessions, he phoned to say he had been successful in obtaining a post in teacher training and was full of eager anticipation. Everyone was thrilled for him. He was moving on with their blessing, even though his head and colleagues were sorry to lose such a valued staff member.

THE ARCHETYPES: THE SUN, THE MOON AND THE STARS

Whilst the qualities of love, justice, peace, beauty, harmony, power, service, wholeness and perfection are Divine Principles or archetypes of higher qualities, there are a host of other, more personified archetypes. They are often described as 'primordial images inherited by all'. Jung saw them as universal energy forces affecting each one of us by day and by night. They always represent principles, ideas or forces with which we need to come to terms in the course of life on earth.

The list of twenty-two archetypes covered by the major arcana of Tarot is fairly comprehensive, but there are always others which can be added. Reading the Tarot is a way of discovering which particular archetypes are most affecting our lives at any given time. The twenty-two archetypes of the Tarot major arcana are: the Fool, the Magician, the High Priestess, the Empress, the Emperor, the Hierophant, the Lovers, the Chariot, Strength, the Hermit, the Wheel of Fortune, Justice, the Hanged Man, Death, Temperance, the Devil, the Lightning-

Struck Tower, the Star, the Moon, the Sun, Judgement, the World.

Chakras have archetypal connotations and meanings. In suggesting archetypes for pairs and groups of chakras my aim is to help you gain greater insight into the subtle meanings and wide areas which they cover. Making connections between chakras, colours, gemstones and archetypes offers us a variety of ways of working with each chakra, pair, or group, one of which will seem appropriate to your growth.

The archetypes chosen for the 'Being Here' aspects of the root and crown chakras are: the Sun, the Moon and the Stars.

The Sun

The sun has been selected as an archetype for these chakras because, as it 'dies' and is 'born' again during each 24-hour cycle, it symbolizes death and rebirth.

The astrological glyph (or symbolic sign) for the sun is a dot within a circle. When we let go of old conditioning and find a true sense of purpose, we may need to let a part of ourselves die in order to be reborn. Gildas tells us that the higher self *circumscribes* our free life choices by the conditions it has already selected (see page 26). The dot within the circle is the part of each one of us which says 'I'. When we have explored the circle of choice more fully we can truly say 'I am', feeling confident in greater self-knowledge.

The sun can be seen as the higher self, shining in through the crown, fertilizing, enlivening and awakening the root chakra whose element is earth.

The symbolism of the root chakra is partly connected with the need to put roots deep into the earth so that the tree of the self may grow strong, tall, balanced and open its branches to the nurturing of the sun.

In most traditions the sun is the Universal Father, or the symbol for the masculine principle, whereas the moon is a major aspect of the Great Mother and the symbol for the feminine principle. The interaction of these primary principles produces creativity.

Psychologically the sun can represent the conscious, active mind, and the moon the unconscious, dreaming mind.

The Moon

The moon has been chosen as an archetype relating to the crown and root chakras because it represents the receptive, reflective, dreamy, unconscious aspects of ourselves. As we find our place on earth and evolve, these aspects need to be brought to fruition.

Universally, the moon is symbolic of the rhythms and cycles of life. As the moon waxes, wanes and goes into its dark time of withdrawal, it portrays the constant need for that which is unconscious to be brought into the light of awareness.

Reflecting the light of the sun, the moon represents the journey of the incarnate personality as, through the cycles of evolution, it seeks to understand and fulfil the purposes of the higher self.

The Stars

Stars have been selected as the third archetypal symbol of these chakras because stars in the heavens can symbolize our true or ascendant selves, fully in harmony with life and opportunity. They are also the eyes of the night, bringing hope and clarity when we are confused or muddled.

The pole, or north star, gives us direction; when it is identified in the sky we always know our path of travel. Stars are also connected with ancient wisdom. Since they have witnessed the whole history of the universe, they can inspire us to make creative decisions and show us where our true talents lie.

EXERCISES

Exercise 3
Considering Your Body

It is preferable to do this exercise lying down, on the floor, on a bed, or sofa. Make sure that you will be undisturbed, have writing materials at hand, and cover yourself with a rug for greater comfort or to avoid getting cold.

- Be in touch with the rhythm of your breathing. Do not try to change your breath rhythm, just observe it. Let your whole body relax. Starting at your feet and working upwards, be conscious of any physical tensions and breathe them out on the out-breath. On each in-breath, breathe in a sense of warmth and relaxation.
- Begin to make a mental note of, or ask your body to remember, the places where you hold most tension. Is it in your feet, knees, thighs, or the whole of your legs? Your genitals? Buttocks? Abdomen? Lower or upper back? Solar plexus? Rib cage? Arms, elbows, or hands? Shoulders? Neck? Head? Around your eyes? In your mouth, lips, tongue or teeth?
- Know that, throughout the whole of this exploration, with each outbreath you take you will automatically continue to breathe away tensions, and with each in-breath you will continue to breathe in warmth and relaxation.
- For five more minutes continue to be aware of your breathing, thus focusing on the **air** element in your body. Do you naturally breathe deeply or shallowly? Do you breathe relatively quickly or slowly? If you put your hands near the bottom of your ribs can you feel your diaphragm working as you breathe in and out? Feel the air coming in through your nostrils and being taken to your lungs. Imagine your body taking in oxygen, eliminating carbon

dioxide and other toxins, sustaining vital life energy for you. You can live for only a very short time without breathing. Appreciate the air you breathe and your body's automatic function of in-breathing and out-breathing. (If you want to make any notes before going on to the element of fire, take a moment to do so and then relax down again).

- When you are ready, begin to contemplate the element of **fire** in your body. Fire energy keeps you warm, digests and metabolizes your food, causes your blood to circulate, is your basic energy, your initiative, your 'get up and go'; brings you light and vision; makes you creative; affects your sexuality; and in chakra terms is mostly connected to your solar plexus. After five minutes considering the element of fire take time to make notes and then relax down again as you prepare to reflect upon the element of water.

- Our bodies are said to consist of 80–90 percent **water**. Imagine the water and fluids in your body. Water works to cleanse, to digest, to metabolize, to eliminate. Consider your urinary system and the processes of bodily elimination via the water element.

- Blood nourishes and circulates, bringing life to every bodily area: if we are wounded and lose too much blood we cannot survive; if we suffer from anaemia our energies become severely depleted. If you are a woman, ponder your menstrual cycle and the part which blood plays in gestation and birth.

- After five minutes reflection on the water element, take time to make notes and then relax down again as you prepare to consider the element of earth.

- **Earth** in the body is bone, muscle, flesh and physical substance. What kind of body do you have? Tall? Short? Lean? Well-covered? Stocky? Strong? Athletic? Healthy? Delicate? Fragile? Energetic? Lethargic?

- Consider the texture of your skin and hair; be aware of

your bones. What do you feel about your body? Does it carry you easily through life? Are you reasonably content with it? Are there improvements you long for? Can you think of your body as a friend or do you need to work on this?

- After five minutes contemplation write down the things you like and the things you dislike about your body. Which list is longer? How easy or difficult is it to admit to the things you like or the things you dislike?

- Having become aware of your body and its elements, reflect on its strengths and imbalances. Make any decisions you feel able to make at this point, as to how you might help to balance the elements in your body. In chakra terms, working with the root chakra helps the earth element; working with the sacral chakra balances the water element; working with the solar plexus aids the fire energy and working with the heart stabilizes the element of air.

- Reflect on the things your body does easily and the things it finds difficult. Ponder on the ways in which your body may be guiding you towards, or away from, certain occupations and interests and how this may reflect guidance or choice from your higher self (see also pages 25–6).

Exercise 4
Contacting Your Overlighting Angel

Make sure that you will be undisturbed, and that you have writing and drawing materials at hand. Sit or lie down for this exercise. Arrange your body symmetrically. Sit cross-legged or in a lotus position if you wish, but otherwise, whether seated on a chair or lying down, do not cross your legs at the knees or ankles. Your head should be in alignment with your spine and well balanced or supported if you are in a sitting position.

- Do the central column breathing exercise
- When are ready to do so, bring your attention into your crown chakra and sense its quality and movement. Imagine, see or visualize the constantly moving thousand-petalled lotus, reflecting the main colours of violet, gold and white. Sense a stream of golden light coming into the centre of the crown lotus from above. This light runs right through this chakra, down the central column and out through the root.
- Endeavour to sense an angelic being from which some of this golden light is streaming. Feel the light expanding around you like a cloak of golden light ... Let the light penetrate each part, each cell of your body, bringing you warmth, light and healing ... Ask to be made aware of the important key words for your life and purpose (see pages 25 and 29). Get a feeling of the things in life which feed your creativity and sense of fulfilment ... Ask for words or symbols which will enable you to be clearer about your sense of purpose in this lifetime ...
- After five to ten minutes, gradually let the light fade; be fully aware, once more, of your crown chakra; and visualize a cross of light in a circle of light above it as a blessing ... Thank your overlighting angel and your higher self for their light and wisdom ... Become aware of your body on the chair or the floor; feel your connection with the earth; and put a cloak of light with a hood around you, thus holding yourself in light so that you are not vulnerable, but also having light to take with you wherever you go.
- Make any notes or drawings which will help you remember anything which you experienced during this meditation. You may need to repeat it several times on different occasions before you get the answers or certainties you are looking for.

Exercise 5
The Archetype of the Sun

Follow the instructions given for Exercise 3 (page 35) about body position and making sure you will be undisturbed. Have drawing and writing materials to hand.

- Be in touch with the rhythm of your breathing, watching each in-breath and each out-breath. Allow yourself to enter a quiet, meditative, inner space.
- Reflect upon the journey of the sun throughout the day and throughout the year. Consider your favourite time of day and your best-loved season of the year. What is the position of the sun at these times?
- A day is born, a day dies, to be followed by a new day . . . Ponder the phases of your life . . . Where are you at present? Have you just made a new start? Is it a flourishing time, with the sun at its zenith? Or are you beginning to feel ready for a rest, a holiday or a rethink? Has something just ended and are you unsure of the rebirth or new beginning? Match where you are in your life to a time of day and reflect on the qualities of this time of day and what it has to offer . . .
- By knowing which season you prefer and matching a season to where you are now symbolically, in your life, you can gain a better understanding of what needs to be done or accepted before your favourite season begins once more.
- When you have finished these considerations, draw the sun meditatively, feeling as deeply as possible what it means to you and to life in general.

Exercise 6
The Archetype of the Moon

Make similar preparations to those suggested for Exercise 3 (page 35).

- Use the rhythm of your breathing to help you enter a meditative inner space ... In your mind's eye see the moon, shining brightly over the countryside, and surrounded by stars, on a clear night ... Note what season of the year it may be ... This is the full moon. As you absorb its silvery light, reflect on the other cycles of the moon: the waning; the dark of the moon; the new crescent and waxing moon; the full moon once more ...
- Ponder on how events and memories in life are sometimes in full consciousness and later become less conscious or forgotten, as in the waning and dark phases of the moon ... Remember the joy of a new idea or a new passion, at first, like the new moon, growing into its full strength, and then waning again ... Consider how your conscious and unconscious minds interact, and how dreams and meditations may sometimes bring useful material from the unconscious into form, memory or inspiration, feeding creativity and reminding you of the richness you carry within ...
- As you meditatively draw a picture of the moon, ask yourself whether you need to attend more to your dreams? Do you need more time for yourself, for withdrawal or meditation?
- Reflect on the cycles of the moon as phases of incarnation, reincarnation and evolution ... Endeavour to get a sense of what might have gone before, to place you where you are now in the evolutionary and karmic cycle ...

Exercise 7
The Archetype of the Stars

Make initial preparations as for Exercise 3 (page 35).

- Use the rhythm of your breath to help you enter your quiet, inner, meditative space . . . Find yourself, once more, contemplating a night-time scene, with the stars shining very clearly in the sky . . . Pick out the north, or pole star . . . Imagine yourself travelling to that star on a beam of light . . . When you have reached the star, look down upon the earth and get a sense of the direction you are at present facing and the direction in which you perhaps need to travel . . . Is the same path illuminated by your star? Is a slight change of direction indicated? Does the light of the star show a complete change of direction as being possible or viable for you?
- Reflect on how it feels to be a star in the ascendant, knowing your course and place in the universe . . .
- As you draw the stars in the sky, and the north star shining on your direction, consider the times in your life when you have really felt yourself to be on course, like a star in the sky. What are the ingredients you need to have around you in order to feel fulfilled? Which of these ingredients are significantly present or missing now?

THE COLOURS

The main colours for the root chakra are red, brown and mauve.

On the positive side, red is a colour associated with warmth, action and growth. On the negative side, it can be associated with anger, danger or emergency.

Red is a good healing colour for bones, muscles and the tissues of the body, though it is wise to modify it from a bright or cardinal red to a more gentle, rich, rosy red for healing.

Positively, brown is an earthy colour: fertile, fecund and gestating. Negatively, it can be depressive, static or limiting.

The positive attributes of mauve are coolness, peacefulness and purification. On its negative side it can be too cold, indefinite, sterile and disturbing.

Mauve is the colour from the root which most links with the crown centre, since violet is a deeper and higher vibrational development of mauve.

The main colours for the crown are violet, white and gold.

On the positive side, violet is warm, stimulating, regal, majestic, awakening of dormant spirituality and inspiring of vision. On the negative side, it can be distancing, negatively superior, antagonistic and over-stimulating.

Positively, white is pure, reflective, symbolic of both innocence and perfection, yang, or of the masculine principle. Negatively, it can signify cowardice, incomprehension, lack of depth and blankness.

In the technical sense white and black are not colours at all. White reflects all colours and black absorbs them all.

Gold, at the crown, is pure metallic gold. Positively, it is attainment, perfection, the sun, purity, value, integrity. Negatively, it may be seen as signifying false attachment, worldliness, false values, seduction and being dazzled or confused.

Exercise 8
Using the Colours

It would help to have a box of bright pastels for this and other exercises in this book. The ability of pastels to blend enables the greatest range of colours to be explored.

The colours as seen in the chakras are full of light and

vitality. They appear as stained glass does when sunlight passes through it.

- Consider these colours and meditatively draw their many shades and tones. As you draw, sense the tones or shades which are most attractive to you.
- Linking the root and crown chakras is particularly helped by drawing the tone scale from brightest cardinal red through to the bright violet of an African violet blossom.
- Use these colours to heal your root and crown chakras by breathing them in through the petals and out through the stems. Breathe each colour of your choice into the appropriate chakra for five breath sequences as follows. Draw the colour in through the petals on the in-breath, hold the colour in the centre of the chakra (where it interpenetrates with the physical body) for a count of three, and then breathe it out through the stem. (This equals one breath sequence.)

THE FRAGRANCES

If you are anxious about your purpose in life and about incarnation itself, if you find difficulty in putting down roots and dealing with the practical issues of life, if you often feel angry at the circumstances of your incarnation or about your body, then your root and crown chakras need the stimulating fragrances of musk, lavender or hyacinth for the root and violet and amber for the crown.

If you are over-diligent about your purpose in life and continually give yourself to others, if you find it difficult to allow yourself comfort and nurturing, then your crown chakra needs the quietening fragrances of rosemary and bergamot and your root needs the stimulating ones of musk, lavender and hyacinth.

If you are over-concerned about your earthly surroundings, always cleaning things which are already spotless, concerned with over-orderliness, living an immaculate life but often feeling uncomfortable with the demands it makes, then your root chakra needs the quietening fragrances of cedarwood and patchouli.

These quietening fragrances for the root chakra can also help anorexia and compulsive eating if used together with the quietening fragrances, for the solar plexus, of vetivert and rose. Quietening fragrances for the root can ease obsessional or compulsive behaviour patterns when used together with the quietening fragrances for the sacral chakra which are musk and amber.

You do not have to use all the fragrances for any one chakra or intention. You can choose the most compatible for you. Blend them together or use them alternately (see page 43 for more instructions and suggestions on how to work with fragrances).

THE CRYSTALS

The Glossary suggests methods for the full cleaning of crystals, but before you use a crystal for an exercise hold it under cold running water for a few moments and then dry it on a natural fibre cloth.

You do not need to do anything elaborate with a crystal in order to obtain its benefits. Just hold or examine it, have it in your environment where you can readily see it, put it near your bed, hold it during meditation, have it with you in your car, or wrap it in silk and take it with you in your pocket wherever you go. Use only one or two crystals at a time as you focus on a particular life improvement or enhancement you wish to make.

To strengthen your sense of contentment or acceptance at

being incarnate, and to link your root and crown chakras, select from the following crystals:

Onyx To bring strength and stamina and to heal the stresses which come from worldly responsibilities.

Tiger's Eye To encourage the making of creative choices. To create unity between your higher and lower selves. To bring strength for meeting life challenges.

Snowy Quartz To heal any sense of reluctance about being incarnate and to strengthen your relationship with your higher self.

Celestite For help with meditation in general and for making contact with your overlighting angel in particular.

PRAYERS OR AFFIRMATIONS

A prayer or affirmation for the root chakra is given on page 20 and for the crown on page 21.

To use the words given as an affirmation, say or read them through three times in succession two or three times daily.

To use the words as a prayer, read them through slowly, meditating a little after each phrase. Ask the angels of virtue, who deal with the energy of prayer, to take your prayer to the Divine Source and to bring an answering flow from the Source into your life. (For more on angels, see *The River of Life* and *Working With Guides and Angels* in the Bibliography.)

Chapter 3

Body of Evidence:
Healing Physical Ailments

Key Issues: The Body and its Healing Needs

Chakra Pair: Root and Crown

Archetype: Healing

This chapter will help you to:
- better understand and accept your body and your gender
- know that your body helps you to find your purpose and destiny in life
- understand something of the wisdom of dis-ease and work with symbols for self-healing

---

AREAS OF INFLUENCE

For lists of the areas of influence of the root and crown chakras see pages 19–21.

THE ROOT CHAKRA AND THE PHYSICAL BODY

Our auras, or subtle energy fields, surround and interpenetrate our physical bodies. Each chakra, in relation to the aura, enables us to connect with a particular energy level, layer, plane, vibration or body. The six energy planes or bodies which exist beyond the material and physical are termed 'subtle'. Clairvoyants, sensitives, healers, and those who work to develop greater spiritual awareness become more and more alert to the subtle fields and the way they reflect what may be happening, or what is about to happen, at the physical and emotional levels. Healing often has to come through the subtle bodies before it can manifest in the physical, which is why many healers work, at least partly, in the aura, without laying their hands directly on the physical body.

The root chakra connects directly to the physical body and the material plane. As we saw in Chapter 2 (pages 21–22), there is a strong interaction between the crown chakra (seat of the higher self) and the root chakra (seat of the energies of embodiment). Choices made by the higher self manifest in the physical body, giving it aptitudes, gifts and limitations. The other chakras have connections to the emotional, glandular and biochemic systems of the physical body but it is the link between crown and root chakras which most fully determines basic physical endowment (see also page 25).

THE COMPULSION TO CONFORM

We can be healed 'into' ourselves and our highest physical functioning but many basic strengths or inherent weaknesses have, to a large extent, to be accepted, understood and used in the shaping of our lives. Our mental and intellectual faculties play a strong part in determining the scope of outlets for us within our civilization but the body we inhabit, the outer shell, is immediately visible. First impressions can be very powerful and the way we appear can determine many implicit, as well as explicit, factors in the ever-important business of acceptance or rejection by our own kind.

Our society has a puzzling tendency to seek conformity and to set standards of beauty and excellence whilst affirming that each human being is unique. The seeking and upholding of a norm is also largely in direct opposition to theories of karmic learning and evolution through many lifetimes. Having the perfect body can seem to be more important than the quality of one's spirit. Human beings can be very cruel to those who deviate from the physical or mental norm, though in some instances they may assume that such individuals are endowed with special powers.

In some societies or historical eras – especially the Middle Ages in Europe – people have seen 'handicapped', 'mis-shapen' or mentally 'impaired' humans as objects of fear. They were often thought to have been touched by the devil (potentially inhabited by, and capable of, evil). In societies with a shamanic tradition (see Glossary), those who are born with, or develop some 'abnormality', may be chosen as potential healers, spiritual workers, or dreamers for the tribe.

Handicapped, disabled, or, in the now politically correct terminology, 'challenged', individuals can be set apart, pre-judged and condemned to loneliness or self-doubt which goes far beyond the physical. Even being regarded as 'special' can be a burden and limitation.

As teenagers, most of us, though roughly conforming to the 'norm', go through excruciatingly painful doubts about our physical endowments and attributes. We agonize over details such as the length and width of our trousers or skirts, and are desperate to be part of the 'in' group.

Are physical characteristics unfair accidents of genetics and birth? Is 'God' an unfairly selective Creator? Or do our bodies carry some more refined message and meaning?

When we come to believe in karma and evolution through

many lifetimes, these vagaries and apparent shifts of fortune no longer need to be seen as 'unfair' or as meted out by a judgmental and selective Creator. Existential diversity is central to the laws of cause and effect. In our higher selves we actively choose a pre-incarnational focus towards specific areas of learning experience intended to allow us to redress imbalances from other lifetimes.

GENDER

Below, Gildas states that the basic starting consciousness of your individual soul at the commencement of evolution is either yin (feminine principle) or yang (masculine principle). Yet a yin spark can, and, according to esoteric theory, must, also have incarnations as a man, and a yang spark as a woman. This is so that we can encompass the whole spectrum of experience and to enable us to learn about the nature of the divine principles from the joining of which all creativity must proceed.

It follows that one of the major decisions for each incarnation is our choice of gender. In different historical times or cultures, and often according to social milieu, the advantages and disadvantages of being born male or female may change and assume varying significance. At the immediate family level, many of my clients have found their self-worth and even sexual identity has been affected because their parents would have preferred a child of the opposite sex.

As the dysfunctional family of humanity struggles towards mindfulness and integration, the high-profile issues of our times are those of gender, race, colour and creed. Our personal, soul level, choice of gender and the issues which it arouses, relates to life purpose, karma and evolution (see pages 22–6).

We can learn much from reflecting on how we feel about being male/female; how at home we find ourselves to be in a male/female body; how we respond to the demands,

expectations or prejudices of society towards those who are
male/female; how we respond to, or feel about, the opposite
sex, both on an individual basis and as a role model; how
comfortable we feel with our sexuality; how we choose to
express ourselves sexually; our predisposition or bias towards
issues or practice of homosexuality – and many more questions.

Gildas, speaking in similar terms to many other guides, tells
us:

A human soul is a spark which splits off from the Source
and chooses human incarnation as its destiny. As it begins
its journey of evolution, which will, eventually, lead it back
to the Source, the spark partially splits once more. The
yin, or feminine of its essence, splits from the yang or
masculine. These two essences will take different but
complementary and inter-dependent journeys. Each part is
like a stem joined at the root or like two strands on a
necklace joined at the fastening. Each flower which each
stem produces will represent an incarnation. The beads
on each strand of the necklace represent opportunities for
incarnation. Although, basically, one stem or strand is yin
and the other yang, this does not mean that the flowers
from the yin stem or beads from the yin strand will always
undergo or choose feminine incarnation, nor will those
from the yang essence always take on a masculine body –
but, at the deepest level, they will carry either a stronger
yin or stronger yang, imprint.

The main divine principle is that of creation. Yin and
yang energies interacting together bring about the birth
of the new. Part of the purpose of evolution for human
beings is to understand, experience, and therefore use in
a balanced way, these sacred and divine energies. The
taking on of a gender is one of the ways in which this
learning happens. Since each stem or strand is slanted
towards one principle or the other, and since it is possible
for twin souls and soul aspects to meet in incarnation

bearing the same gender, homosexuality takes on a different connotation. These things are part of experience, part of exploration, not manifestations which need to be judged or categorically ruled as abnormal, unnatural or dangerous. When a person, on their journey through life, understands that they and others need all kinds of experience, then a broad-based compassion and tolerance develops more easily [see Chapter 6, page 132, for more on twin souls].

The overall purpose of evolution is for the soul to reunite in full consciousness with the Source of All Being. Humanity has chosen the path of knowledge. Unless all experience has been explored and understood, the journey back to the Source cannot be complete. As experience builds, clearer choices can be made. The love impulse which fundamentally governs the universal patterns does not allow the untried and untested to plunge into incarnations which are full of complex difficulties and horrors. Gradually the strand on which the beads are threaded, or the stem which nurtures the flowers, will take a more efficient part in choosing those incarnations most valuable to its continued evolution. The force which is known as karma or 'cause and effect' becomes active.

A personality bead or flower goes into incarnation, lives out its lifespan and dies. In the between-life state which takes place on the astral plane, personality bead and soul thread consider the scope of experience gained and assess all aspects of the harvest which has been reaped. It is on the basis of this assessment that the next life is chosen. A new personality bead prepares to incarnate. Its first brief will be to continue to broaden the scope of experience but it will also carry the knowledge that certain things which may have been out of balance because of choices made during incarnation by the previous bead, need to be rectified or redeemed. The incarnating being, then, will carry a motivation to avoid some types of experience, to embrace others and to confront others.

The choice of historical time, social standing, type of body, parents and siblings will have been made by the higher self to expedite the purposes and tasks of the incarnating being. This includes awareness of other higher selves sending personality beads or flowers into incarnation at a similar time. There may be agreement about helping each other with lessons to be learned or experience to be gained. Where there is a group soul purpose, this will be taken into account so that members of the same group or family can facilitate the group learning process by incarnating together [see also Chapter 4, page 84, for more about group and family karma].

The higher selves making these plans might be seen as actors in the wings of a stage considering the parts they will play, and the interaction they will have, when they actually walk on to the stage. As well as being a personal endeavour and responsibility, evolution is a collective journey.

DISABILITY

We may still ask: 'Why does anyone *choose* to incarnate with a less than perfect, less than optimally functioning physical body?'

Guides and spiritual teachers tend to give the following answers: 'In order to experience and redeem the sort of suffering which has been meted out to others by another personality bead in a previous lifetime'; 'To teach others the compassion a previous bead on your stem lacked'; To make your soul stem more aware and respectful of the physical body rather than taking it for granted'; 'In order to learn the lesson of humility'; 'To compensate for the hedonism or false vanity of another lifetime'; or 'To focus this present lifetime more specifically towards the lessons to be learned and the tasks to be fulfilled'.

If we over-identify with previous lifetimes we can either carry a heavy burden of guilt or suffer from hubris. It is important to remember that it was not I, as I am now, who was physically violent to others in the Middle Ages. Neither was it I, as I am now, who was a wise alchemist in ancient Persia. These were other flowers or beads on the soul stem or thread. I may have access to some of the wisdom gained by that alchemist, but the journey of evolution is not linear and hierarchical. As each personality bead manifests, it may or may not consciously carry past attributes. Sometimes, if we have experienced what it is to be wise, we may need to balance up by experiencing what it is to be foolish. Since *all* experience is necessary to evolution, a gentle incarnation followed by a more violent one can also have a place in the rich tapestry which we can only ever partially comprehend with the finite mind.

The crown chakra helps us to be more in touch with the higher self (see also Glossary) and its intentions and support for the present incarnation. The root chakra gives us the strength to be fully in our physical bodies, to love them for their gifts *and* their limitations, to love the earth and to be fully embodied and present on it. These are among the most important lessons of any incarnation. Understanding and accepting the body we have incarnated into is essential. The following personal story may help to make some of these points clearer and more tangible.

Case Study: Accepting and Loving Your Body

I was born with very limited sight in my right eye but this was not fully diagnosed until I was twelve, by which time I was also very short-sighted in my left eye. In my early years at school my right eye was thought to be 'lazy' and my left, seeing, eye was patched in order to make the right one work. I identified with my right eye and thought that *I* must be lazy or wrong in some way when the patching treatment did not work. With my seeing eye patched, I was virtually blind and so retreated more and more into my own inner world which was already very clear, rich and satisfying.

Partly because of my sight, my body movements were never well synchronized. I longed to be good at sports, gym, ball games and physical feats. I was puzzled that I was unable to achieve the bodily and hand/eye coordination required. I loved animals and yearned to ride horses well but had no natural aptitude. I persisted with trying to fulfil this dream until my late thirties and now carry the scars of dangerous falls. In my dreams I could compete with the most lithe of athletes and ride the wildest of horses.

I have never had any difficulty in meditating or with subtle vision. In this sense I sit lightly upon the earth, yet my physical body is heavy. Carrying too much weight is a constant problem. Although I have often found it difficult to understand why my higher self chose this body, I have gradually accepted that the vivid scenery of some of my dreams of physical prowess belongs to past lives of other beads on my soul stem. My soul stem has already stored this experience. In this lifetime I have needed to look within and develop my inner vision. If I had the body and physical skills of my dreams, I would be riding wild horses, climbing mountains, running races and canoeing down rivers. My life task for this incarnation does not include these things.

I have not found it easy to be on earth. Putting down roots and committing to staying in one place for a lengthy period of time is difficult. I now understand that part of the heaviness of my body is to hold me down and to help me to know earth and substance by having it to deal with in my embodiment.

I have interpreted the lessons for this incarnation which are governed by my body to be:

– Developing a vivid inner world.

- Having clearer subtle sight than outer sight.
- Using these gifts as part of my service to others and teaching others how to develop them.
- Remaining earthed and grounded, so that spirituality is not experienced as something apart from, or rejecting of earth but as an instrument to enhance life on earth and the love of it.
- Not getting diverted from the particular experience which it is my task to take back to my soul thread.

Learning to accept without harbouring resentment is a prime factor in the self-healing process. At fourteen, I was in turmoil about my inner life and my experience of Gildas which had been there as far back as I could remember. Eye specialists feared I might go blind. At nineteen I met Dr Mary Swainson, a Jungian therapist with esoteric and spiritual training. She helped me to see my subtle abilities as a gift. As I did so, my eyesight stabilized and, though I shall always wear spectacles or contact lenses, has never again been the subject of over-concern. My greatest physical weakness or abnormality thus revealed to me my richest gifts, and enabled me to find my greatest strength.

Some lessons take longer! Now, in my sixtieth year, I think and hope that I am coming to terms with my rooting problem. I have also learned to respect and love my body as it is and to appreciate the quality of stamina it has always given me. As this happens, my sense is that some of my body weight may drop away, whereas before, it has always persisted. Strangely, at this point, it is no longer of great importance to me whether the weight shifts or not – but this recognition or acceptance is also one of the intrinsic lessons my body has been able to teach me.

ACCEPTANCE

It is often so! When we stop fighting and the personality or 'little ego' ceases rebelling, physical healing miracles are no longer required or may spontaneously happen where there seemed to be no hope before.

Beyond the size, nature, shape, limitations and gifts of our physical bodies, lie strengths or weaknesses in particular bodily systems. Though other chakras are linked to the body's biochemic constitution, the crown remains the place of choice and the root the place of manifestation and embodiment. When crown and root chakras work in harmony together there is a strong foundation from which understanding and healing can flow.

Gildas gives us 'Acceptance' as one of the key words for spiritual growth. He does not mean that our attitude should be passive. This key word can teach us that graceful acceptance of a status quo will release blockages and enable creativity. Through active acceptance we learn to work more skilfully with the basic materials and gifts that are to hand instead of yearning for something other. In short, we learn to accept and value ourselves.

Acceptance must never mean that we lose faith in healing. But healing cannot properly start until some acceptance of the imbalance and its process has been attained. Complete healing can only take place when the nature of our imbalance or illness has been understood. Imbalance and disease carry a wisdom and guidance within them. In order to receive this wisdom and unlock the full power of the body to heal itself, we need to explore the symbolic nature of our ills.

UNDERSTANDING THE WISDOM WITHIN IMBALANCE AND DIS-EASE

Finding the wisdom within dis-ease or imbalance involves interpreting symptoms as symbols. Our bodies speak a very simple, even primitive, language. Attunement to the root chakra enables us to be more in touch with our bodies and the language they speak. We get most from symbols when we seek to live alongside them for a while, rather than rushing to interpret them intellectually. Symbols are rich and many-faceted, yet in another sense economical, since out of apparent simplicity comes so much. Recognizing that a symbol exists starts a communication process with it, and within ourselves.

When we experience difficulties and oppositions which we cannot immediately deal with, or choose to ignore, our bodies tend to produce symptoms. In areas where we have been heavily conditioned by parents or society to live a certain lifestyle or achieve certain standards, the mind tries to exert willpower over emotion and even over matter. Our emotions help us to question the old order and encourage us to find and live our own personal truths and values. The body interacts and colludes with the emotions. Eventually, if the bodily symptoms are pressing enough, we *have* to change our lifestyle, even if only to take a few days' sick leave.

The body does not become ill without reason. Some bodily weak spots may be karmic and need to be interpreted mainly in the light of what has gone before in this chapter. Most of us have constitutionally vulnerable areas and, when we are stressed by life or relationships, tend to produce a certain type of symptom. An initial look at the language of the symptoms may help us to understand the symbolic message they are giving.

My back and neck are my most vulnerable areas. When I get neck pain I have learned to ask the following questions:

- Am I being stiff-necked about something?
- Could I gain from being *more* stiff-necked about something?
- Is something (or someone!) being a 'pain in the neck' to me?
- Am I being a 'pain in the neck' to myself or someone else?

- Am I 'sticking my neck out' unnecessarily about some matter?
- Ought I to 'stick my neck out' more in the present situation?

Each question must always be reversed – and in the end I am the only one who can answer it!

Similarly, with my back, I need to ask:

- Am I being too rigid?
- Am I being too flexible?
- Is someone 'on my back'?
- Am I on someone else's back?
- Am I carrying too much, for myself or others?
- Am I carrying enough? Taking enough responsibility?

Recently I caught a virus, which left my body, particularly my legs, full of aches and pains. I lost any ease of movement and had to do everything much more slowly. I had known for some time that I was living at a very hectic pace and sometimes forcing myself to keep it up. My body was asking me to slow down. I interpreted this as quite a serious warning and have since tried to rest more, to look after my body, to take some more space for myself and to get some of my commitments into proportion.

The symbolic language of symptoms helps us to begin our understanding of bodily messages but, at a deeper level, it can also lead us to explore bodily *memory* and its links with our emotions.

The following case illustrates and amplifies some of these issues.

Case Study: Bodily Memory

Chloe, a West Indian client, whose family came to live in Southern England before she was one year old, wanted to explore the symbolism of a pulled ankle tendon.

The original injury had occurred two years previously

whilst she and her partner were leading a group into a dance at a social gathering. The continuing pain, stiffness and weakness in her ankle were still resistant to improvement. She had explored the possibilities that she was carrying too much on behalf of others, or not being true to herself (following her own path). These were true insights and she had taken steps to redress some balances, yet her ankle still did not heal. Medical investigation simply confirmed that the tendons had been sprained and were still weak. There was no other physical injury or contributory cause.

Chloe's *right* ankle was affected. The right side of the body is symbolically associated with the aspects of life which demand focus, direction, thrust, active masculine principle (yang), energy. The left side connects with the areas of life which need diffuse awareness, subtlety, yielding, receptive, receding, feminine principle (yin) energy.

Bearing this in mind, I asked Chloe whether she most often put her right, masculine, yang, leadership side forward in life, or whether she tended to function more from her feminine, yielding, receptive side?

Chloe felt that life itself had pushed her towards being 'up front', 'in the lead' and 'visible'. She was an attractive woman, in a good partnership, but felt that in many ways the development of her truly feminine side had taken a back seat. Her family had always pushed her to do well at school. In art classes she had discovered a talent for design but had never been allowed to enjoy it in a relaxed way. Any gift had to be seriously fostered, and she had been expected to work hard, get top grades and go on to get a degree. She thoroughly enjoyed her present job, working with a design and display team for a large organization, yet she often had a sense of frustration and felt that her talent had always been too developed and focused. She had never been able to enjoy it for its own sake or to 'dabble' with all the potentials which might have been open to her.

Remarking that the injury to her ankle had occurred when

she was leading others into a dance, I asked her to consider whether her right ankle might be telling her that the masculine side needed a rest, and that it could be time to give the left, feminine, side more chance to develop. She felt that this explanation was too simplistic and that there was something deeper and more complex involved.

I asked Chloe to close her eyes and see what image came to mind when she considered her right ankle and its injury. After a while she said she could see herself, aged about seven years old, in a Brownie uniform. The word 'tenderfoot' accompanied this image.

I asked Chloe to associate to the word and the image and she began to talk about a phase in her life which had never clearly come into her memory before.

As a tenderfoot Brownie, working towards full enrolment, which would mean receiving her Brownie badge, and becoming a full Brownie member, Chloe was required to do at least one good turn every day. In order to keep a check on this, and literally, to gain 'Brownie points', Brown Owl had given each of the tenderfoot Brownies a card and some 'stick-on' stars. As good turns were done, so a star could be stuck onto the card. At the end of each week, before the Brownie meeting, Chloe had to get one of her parents to sign the card and verify the number of good turns completed that week.

Chloe's parents had required her, from a very young age, to share tasks in the household. They told her that any good turn for her Brownie membership had to be something over and above the things she was normally expected to do. Since, as a seven-year-old, quite a lot was already demanded of her, she had difficulty in finding something extra each day which her parents would agree to mark on her card as her good turn. Indeed, if she had not done one of her usual chores to perfection even the extra 'good turn' was not considered worthy of a star. At the next Brownie meeting Chloe had the least number of good turns on her record. She knew that her friends did not help in the home nearly as much as she did and was desperately upset when the Brown Owl told her that she obviously needed to try harder if she truly wanted to be an enrolled Brownie. She was unable to explain to her parents what was happening. They consistently refused to consider anything which was within their normal high demands on her as a good turn. Eventually, in desperation and though it cut her off from many of her friends, Chloe gave up Brownies and the tenderfoot requirements. She was then criticized by her parents for lack of commitment.

As this memory surfaced, Chloe realized that there were similar factors operating in her current situation. Although she loved her work, knew she was good at it and often willingly worked unpaid overtime, she was continually being overlooked or under-rewarded when it came to promotions and salary rises. She recognized that she tended not to fight this particular corner. Although, as a black woman in a white culture, she had learned the value of self-assertion, she now saw that she did not expect to be paid or rewarded for her dedication. She felt she had to be more than exceptional before recognition could come her way. She was doing more than others in the team but not getting her 'brownie points'.

In relation to her foot, Chloe now realized that she was often putting her 'best foot forward' to the point of stress and without receiving her just reward or support. Her physical foot had been showing her that something was lacking and that an old pattern needed to be recognized and dealt with. She needed more balance between right and left, yin and yang, and also to make sure she used her yang side to see that she was fairly treated. An underlying resentment was beginning to surface which might affect her decisions about, and attitudes to, her work.

A few weeks later she reported that she had requested, and been awarded, a long overdue promotion and pay award. Her right foot was much less painful and she felt that it was healing successfully at last. We had got to the root cause of the continuing tender foot.

THE DIMENSION ADDED BY THE CROWN CHAKRA

When seeking this kind of insight, working with the root chakra, (as suggested on pages 41–45 and in Exercise 3, page 35) helps the body and the unconscious mind to explore symptoms and symbols more deeply. The dimension added by the crown chakra is that when we stimulate and feed it, as suggested on pages 41–45, a wider facility for understanding our life lessons will be activated.

Chloe was interested in knowing more about her spiritual path, and had been working with her chakras in order to access extra dimensions of information about her ankle. As her ankle healed she became aware that all her life she had been pushed to excel and to have high standards in worldly and mundane spheres. She surmised that she must be balancing a lifetime in which another personality bead had perhaps been lax and uncaring about these, or other areas. She also understood that high standards and self-discipline could be very positive tools to help her live efficiently in the world and learned to let spiritual meaning blend with, and enhance, the task of living to the full. Chloe felt a deeper connection with her higher self and its intentions in choosing her parents, early environment and even her colour, as she got a clearer insight into, and acceptance of, these aspects of her life task.

Case studies are chosen because they are as close as possible to 'textbook' illustrations of points under discussion. You may find that, for you, the issues are not always as clear as mine or Chloe's in their final revelation. Sometimes it is necessary to persevere and wait for insight, but refusing to accept that we are all subject to 'accidents of birth' will help you to open up to fuller self-knowledge at the psychological *and* spiritual levels.

ARCHETYPE: HEALING

Healing should not be seen only in terms of the physical body or the removal of symptoms. It can be described as an archetype since most of us have a drive to perfection or wholeness of body, mind or spirit. As we become conscious of ourselves as individuals and also as part of the human race, we realize that one of our greatest needs is healing. We are all wounded in some aspect of our beings or experience dis-ease within our lives.

Over recent decades we have seen the personal growth movement emerge and flourish. Healing and growth can be synonymous. Gildas has told us not to see healing as an attempt to return to a previously known standard of health but as helping us move on to a new and positive level of health not previously experienced. This enhancement of our health will not occur if healing is merely directed to the removal of symptoms. As we have seen, particularly in the case history of Chloe (see page 58), understanding the language of symptoms leads us to causes of continuing pain or dis-ease which go far deeper than the physical. The body is our evidence for many levels of emotional and spiritual investigation and understanding.

When healing concentrates only on symptoms, or at best, purely physical causes, disease may become chronic or one ailment may be 'cured' only to give way to another. Before true healing can take place, there are messages to comprehend which speak also from the soul. Assimilating these is vital. When we appreciate this, then physical healing as a totality becomes less important. We learn that a state of true health emanates from within our beings and, though we may become physically 'sick unto death', our incarnate spirit can attain a wholeness, or degree of perfection, which shines through and brings blessing and inspiration to others.

Seeing health or beauty as totally body-orientated is narcissistic. To be stuck in narcissism is to remain ignorant both of the greater depths and purposes which life can reveal and of the complex interactions of body, mind, spirit and emotions. Healing is balance and balance is healing.

Of course healing should concern itself with the relief of distressing symptoms and the trials of pain. Yet removing a headache, without addressing the stress which caused it, might eventually lead to physical breakdown. Minor symptoms are an early warning system and should never be ignored or masked by taking a medicament – whether it be from the allopathic *or* complementary range. Healing into ourselves is attained when there is alignment between crown and root chakras and when we take the serious steps towards true self-expression which this alignment may demand. Spirit and soul speak through our emotions. When we neglect the emotions they speak through our bodies; and our bodies give us evidence of our karma and spiritual tasks. The revelation of these will enable true purpose to be released and deep healing to take place. When we widen our paradigms so that it is the essence of a person, not the physical vehicle, which determines our standards, even the most 'imperfect' body, with the spirit shining through, becomes beautiful.

Death itself can be seen as a healing when we consider a greater life cycle than the relatively brief span of one earth life. It is not futile to hope for eventual total healing for all if we believe in the immortality of the life-spark and the eternity of being. Healing, as a process of entering a previously unknown state of health, then becomes synchronous with spiritual evolution.

EXERCISES

The more direct work with crown and root chakras and their colours and archetypes given in Chapters 1 and 2 forms a background to the exercises given here. The more your crown and root chakras are in alignment, the more the information you are seeking will be assisted into your consciousness.

As you have been reading this chapter, you have probably begun to reflect on your own body: its weaknesses, strengths, symptoms and symbols. This exercise is designed to take you, step by step, through the exploration of symptom as symbol. It can be helpful to share an exercise such as this with a partner, or with a group of friends. Suggestions from others and pooling of resources for interpreting symbolism can be very helpful. If you decide to do this, or to discuss your own material with a friend, it is important to remember that:

- There are no categorical meanings.
- There are no quickly accessible 'neat' solutions.
- One person's view, insight or intuition should always be offered as a suggestion and never forced on to the one who is exploring symptoms or symbols. It is essential that the 'protagonist' should come to their own acceptable insights at their own pace and in their own time.
- Unconscious and newly surfacing material is sometimes highly defended. Unless it is very gently encouraged, or given 'permission' to emerge with patience and support, the defences may grow stronger rather than opening up.
- Battering away too strongly at your own or another's defence system may amount to self-abuse or 'psychological rape'.
- When the psyche is unhurried, with its insights gently sought and respected, it will give of its wisdom.
- Symbols which have many layers to be understood are the language and wisdom of the psyche (see Glossary).

Exercise 9
Symptom as Symbol

Before you begin this exercise, know which bodily symptom you wish to explore. Only attempt to explore one symptom at a time. You can repeat the exercise for other symptoms, or to gain a deeper insight into the same symptom, at frequent,

regular, or irregular intervals. (I would suggest that
'frequent' is no more than twice a week.)

Have crayons, paper and writing materials to hand.

The exercise is in three parts. *Leave at least two days between
each part.*

Part 1: Some Important Questions and Reflections

Making sure that you will be undisturbed, sit or lie
comfortably so that your body is symmetrically arranged and
can relax. Be in touch with the rhythm of your breathing
and practise the 'central column breathing', running from
crown to root and root to crown (see page 17). Gradually let
your breath rhythm return to normal.

- Focus your attention on the area, organ or function of your
  body affected by the symptom. Internally ponder the
  following questions:
  a) What is the name of this area, organ or function of your
     body?
  b) Do you, or your family have a 'pet name' or non-
     anatomical name for this area, organ or function?
  c) What is the natural function of this organ or area of
     your body?
  d) How is that natural function being inhibited at present?
  e) Is the symptom affecting your right or left side?
  f) How do you, or would you, describe your symptom/
     disease to another person?
  g) If you have pain, what are the words you would use to
     describe it?
  For (f) and (g) above, give your imagination full rein. See
  whether there are emotive words which come naturally,
  e.g. 'I feel as if I am on the rack'; 'I am being dragged
  down'; 'I am being stabbed'; 'It is a shooting pain'; 'I feel
  sick [nauseous, want to vomit, sick at heart]'; 'It grips me
  like a vice'; 'It takes all my energy away'; 'It diminishes

me'; 'It makes me helpless [dependent, despairing]'; 'It
gets me down'. There are any number of possibilities. The
words which come most naturally to you could be full of
symbolic meaning.
• Now write down all your thoughts. Reflect on the symbolic
  content of what you have written and felt. Ponder the
  symbolic function of the affected area of your body or
  bodily function. Consider the symbolic significance of any
  pet or family names you use for the affected area or
  function. As you contemplate the significance of left- and
  right-sided symptoms look again at page 59.
• Now ask yourself: 'Are there situations or people in your
  life which could be described similarly to the way in which
  you describe your symptom or pain?'
• Begin to consider ways in which you could help yourself:
  – Do you need some kind of break?
  – Do you need to ask for more help and support in your
    life, or with your work?
  – Are you nurturing yourself sufficiently?
  – Are you being too receptive or passive? Do you need to
    change or modify this?
  – Are you being too assertive or aggressive? Do you need
    to change or modify this?
  – Are you turning anger inwards? Could you express it
    differently or explore its origins more?
  – Do you need to consider or set in motion a significant
    life change?
  – Do you need to meditate on 'acceptance'? (see page 56)

*Remember that you can separate the parts of this exercise by days or
weeks but leave at least two days before attempting Part 2. Do not
attempt too much insight too soon or be tempted to try to force or
create a flood of insights.*

The psyche (see Glossary) has its own wisdom and timing. It
responds best when you respect these and gently encourage

its revelations. Hidden or symbolic meanings and unsuspected inner dynamics have usually developed as survival mechanisms or valuable defences when life was threatening. If you approach with care and respect for yourself and your inner processes, the defences will gradually melt and allow you access to the treasures of insight. If, as you meet obstacles within yourself, you try to tear them down or blow them apart they will tend to get stronger, for they are like scar tissue round a wound.

A gentle approach allows the scar tissue to soften so that deep healing can happen and the nature of the wound be fully known. Impatience creates new scarring, underneath which the wound may continue to suppurate. Remember that visualizations often present you with well-known material, which the psyche, in its wisdom, may be asking you to look at from a new angle. When you are ready to hear your own story, with wonder, empathy and without judgement, it will unfold, episode by episode.

A client of mine who was very impatient and judgemental with herself longed for her inner journeys and visualizations to be rich and revelatory. Even when they were, she had difficulty acknowledging their significance – she was always pushing for more. Gradually she realized that she must first learn to be a less stern self-critic in order to hear and see herself more clearly. She worked to become less of a perfectionist in her expectations and eventually had a beautiful dream in which a forest which had been totally ravaged by fire was to be carefully excavated by experts who had the secret of nurturing new growth. This dream presaged the release of her long-blocked creativity and the relaxing of her deep defences.

If you are ever in doubt about self-exploration it is wise to seek advice from a counsellor or therapist. Transpersonally trained counsellors and therapists will usually be most helpful with visualization techniques (see Glossary).

Part 2 Image or Symbol

You will need crayons or pastels and paper for this second part of the exercise.

Make the same initial preparations as for Part 1. Practise central column breathing (see page 17). Then let your breathing find its normal rhythm.

- With your eyes closed, and with the same symptom in mind that you used for Part 1 of this exercise, imagine that you are looking at an inner screen. Mentally ask for a symbol, or an image representing your symptom, to appear on your screen.
- After five minutes, take your paper and colours and draw this image meditatively, letting it develop more fully as you draw. Take as long as you need to complete the drawing to your satisfaction.
- Even if no image or symbol appeared on your inner screen, try to let something emerge freely on paper as you doodle or draw. Do not be concerned about your drawing ability or the quality of your drawing. You are seeking to bring information from the inner world to the outer and drawing is one of the ways in which this can be accomplished. Only if you are really inhibited about drawing should you use words as a description instead.

Wait at least two days before attempting Part 3 of this exercise. In the intervening time look often at your drawing without trying to interpret the image or symbol intellectually.

Part 3 Bodily Memory

Making sure that you will be undisturbed, read over the notes you made for Part 1 of this exercise and consider again your drawing of your image or symbol from Part 2.

Sitting, or lying down, practise central column breathing (see page 17). Gradually let your breathing return to its normal rhythm.

- Using the same symptom as for Parts 1 and 2 of this exercise, focus your attention on the relevant part of your body or bodily function. Look back over your life, mentally asking your memory to bring to mind anything which could be associated with the symptoms you are now experiencing. Do not judge or criticize what your memory finds. At this point it is particularly important not to examine the relevance of what your psyche is offering you. Do not strive to get memories from childhood. Something which happened to you more recently could be significant in opening up further or deeper insights. When you feel ready to do so, write up, as fully as possible, the memory which is coming most insistently to the surface.
- When you have finished writing, read again the passage from Chloe's case study relating to her Brownie tenderfoot (page 60).
- Only now, begin to muse upon what the memory your psyche has given you could mean in relationship to the symbolism of your symptom. Do not reflect too intently. Let the memory remain with you over a period of time and read your write-up of it once a day. Gradually the key words and insights will emerge. They may easily vanish if you do not record them, so write things down immediately as they surface.

Exercise 10
Guided Journey to the Healing Archetype

It can be helpful to speak the words of an inner journey, with appropriate periods of silence, onto a cassette, so that you can listen as you go, rather than trying to remember or follow the instructions from merely reading them through.

If you are unfamiliar with inner journeying you may want to refer to the 'Inner Journeying' entry in the Glossary or one of my previous books, such as *The River of Life* (see Bibliography), before embarking on this exercise.

Making sure that you will be undisturbed and with colours and writing materials to hand, sit or lie in a relaxed position, where your spine can be straight and supported, if necessary, in comfort. Your head should be well-balanced on your neck. Do not cross your legs at the knees or ankles, though a cross-legged or lotus position is favourable, if comfortable for you.

Practise central column breathing (see page 17) until you feel the two-way flow between your crown and root chakras, then gradually let your breathing find its normal rhythm.

- When you are ready, move into your inner space or landscape and find yourself in a meadow. (This may be modelled on an outer meadow you know or remember, or be a meadow which purely exists within.)
- Take the opportunity of being in the meadow to activate all your inner senses . . . See the colours and the objects . . . Hear the sounds . . . Smell the fragrances . . . Touch the textures . . . Taste the tastes . . .
- Beyond the meadow there is undulating countryside leading into steeper hills and mountains . . . As you look out over the landscape, a part of you knows where you need to go in order to meet the archetype of healing . . . (You may travel to water; to a cave; to a hill or mountain top; into a special valley; to a special tree; to a sanctuary;

to a place where there is fire. There are many possibilities
which your psyche can open up for you.)

- Once you know in which direction you need to travel you
  may wish to take companions with you. You can invite
  your inner wise presence (which may be personified, or
  could be a light, colour or essence), and a power animal
  to go with you. Your inner power animals are protectors,
  guardians and guides. They may be very fierce in the outer
  wild state, but in your inner world they are your friends
  and you can communicate with them. You may also wish
  to take a talisman or amulet (a special object which helps
  you to centre and be empowered – see Glossary).
- When you are totally ready, begin your journey to the place
  where you know you will be able to meet your archetype
  of healing . . . (Five minutes silence.)
- When you arrive at the right place, if your archetype is not
  immediately there to meet you, look around and explore
  the area a little and then settle yourself comfortably with
  your wise presence and your power animal near you and
  invite your archetype of healing to appear . . . (Two minutes
  of silence.)
- Greet your archetype of healing . . . Ask if you might be
  shown a healing sanctuary or temple of colour healing to
  which you can go now, or on any other occasion when you
  are in need of healing . . . Your healing archetype will
  accompany you to this place and see that you receive
  healing and refreshment . . . (Ten minutes of silence.)
- Before you leave the healing temple or sanctuary and your
  archetype of healing, ask whether there is any message or
  symbolic gift to help forward your inner and outer
  processes of healing and growth . . . Thank your healing
  archetype and prepare for the journey back to the
  meadow . . .
- Your healing archetype may accompany you back to your
  meadow, or may stay in the area around the sanctuary or
  temple . . . Certainly your inner wise presence and your

power animal will travel back with you . . . Make the
journey in your own time . . . and then move from the
meadow to an awareness of the rhythm of your
breathing . . . Be aware of your body on the floor, couch or
chair . . . Breathe the central column breath . . . Imagine
that you are surrounded by a cloak of light with a hood,
and then return fully to your outer surroundings to
draw and record your journey.

Exercise 11
Considering Gender

Gender and its inevitable outcome of sexuality are major
themes in our lives. This exercise is based on the introductory
questions on page 48. Another exercise relating to issues of
sexuality is Exercise 23, page 150.

Making sure that you will be undisturbed and that you have
pen or pencil, coloured crayons and paper to hand, read
again the section on gender on page 49.

- Now practise central column breathing until you feel
  centred and relaxed. Take a sheet of paper and, if you are
  female, write the heading: 'I am a woman'. If you are male
  write the heading 'I am a man'. Use colour for the heading
  if you wish.
- Reflect on this heading for a few moments and then write
  the sub-heading: 'This means that: . . .'
- Now take twenty minutes to half an hour, to reflect on what
  your gender means to you, how you feel about it and the
  messages which society gives about it. As you write your lists
  and comments be aware of any tensions in your body and
  the areas in which you are holding them. Do not analyse
  what you have written too strongly at this moment; just
  let what has come rest in your consciousness. When you
  feel ready to do so, it could be helpful to share your

reflections and comments with a friend or partner if that is possible.

THE COLOURS

The colours for the root chakra are red, brown and mauve; and, for the crown chakra, violet, white and gold. To strengthen the colours in your crown and root chakras refer to Exercise 8 (page 42).

THE FRAGRANCES

For the root chakra the quietening fragrances are cedarwood and patchouli, and the stimulating ones are musk, lavender and hyacinth. For the crown chakra the quietening fragrances are rosemary and bergamot, and the stimulating ones are violet and amber. Refer to page 43 for notes on the use of the fragrances for these chakras.

THE CRYSTALS

Refer to page 44 and the Glossary for general guidance on using crystals. The crystals which will best help the issues considered in this chapter are:

White Tourmaline To encourage integrity and facilitate the deeper understanding of spiritual surrender and obedience. This is a spiritually purifying stone which promotes inner honesty and insight.

Smoky Quartz To promote calmness, centring and grounding. It helps to calm fear and panic and minimizes shock.

Garnet This crystal aids tissue healing and regeneration and so speeds the healing of actual physical wounds to the body, including those made through surgery. It also brings comfort for loss or bereavement and during all times of life change.

PRAYERS OF AFFIRMATIONS

The root chakra prayer or affirmation is:

> Through incarnation may spirit be brought into matter. Through rootedness may life-force be recharged and exchanged. We acknowledge wholeness and seek to gain and to reflect acceptance.

The crown chakra prayer or affirmation is:

> Through surrender and release let the incoming will be truly the will of God working within us and through us, leading us increasingly to knowledge of mystical union and mystical marriage.

For suggestions on using the prayers or affirmations, see page 45.

Chapter 4

The Tentacles of the Octopus:
Improving Family Relationships

Key Issues: Healing the Family of Origin, Improving Family
Relationships, the Inner Child
Chakra Triad: Root, Heart and Crown
Archetypes: Great Mother and Great Father

This chapter will help you gain:
- insight into the karmic reasons for your choice of parents
- information about spiritual and genetic families
- an understanding of the needs of the inner child
- knowledge of how to heal family pains and wounds
- insight into what may go wrong in relationships with friends, colleagues and lovers

---

AREAS OF INFLUENCE

For lists of the areas of influence of the root and crown chakras
see pages 19–21.

The Heart Chakra:

Location On the same level as the physical heart, but in the centre of the body (stem at back).
Key Words Compassion, Feeling, Tenderness, Love of God, Love of Others, Detachment
Developmental Age 12–15 years
Colours Spring Green, Rose, Rose Amethyst
Element Air
Sense Touch
Body Feeling
Glandular Connection Thymus
Quietening Fragrances Sandalwood, Rose
Stimulating Fragrances Pine, Honeysuckle
Crystals and Gemstones Emerald, Green Calcite, Amber, Azurite, Chrysoberyl, Jade, Rose, Watermelon Tourmaline

Prayer or Affirmation

In the golden centre of the rose of the heart may tender compassion be linked to unconditional love. May true detachment enable growth and continuity. Through the understanding of birth within death and death within birth may there be transformation.

THE HEART CHAKRA AND LIFE

When the heart chakra is healthy and flexible the link between the concerns of root and crown becomes alive and less clinical or esoteric. The sense for the heart chakra is that of touch. As we come into incarnation we touch the earth and are touched by it physically, emotionally and symbolically. A native American Indian saying states that nothing exists except in relationship to something else. Thus, through touch we form relationships and create our existence.

The science of human behaviour has clearly established that

living creatures need to be touched in order to thrive. Yet European cultures, in particular, often have difficulties with touch. A tendency to want to be told how to, rather than relying on our instincts, about the bearing and nurturing of our babies and children, leads to confusion. So-called child experts have, in the past, advised over-strict routines. Before the definitive scientific experiments with touch, almost a whole generation of babies was deprived of natural fondling and caressing on the advice of Truby King, an influential American paediatrician.

Left untouched in their cots for the recommended four hours between feeds, crying babies could be checked for wind or protruding nappy pins but were trained to express hunger only by the clock. The thought that small babies might need loving touch, comfort and stimulation, as well as warmth and food, was denied. Mothers who obeyed their instincts and enjoyed interim cuddles with their babies were told that they were being 'conditioned' by the child and storing up discipline problems for later. A generation of touch-deprived babies, and of parents denied a natural instinctive pleasure in their children, makes a big impact on society, dampening qualities of the heart and suppressing creativity.

The connection of the heart chakra to the sense of touch, gives us the central issue for heart chakra functioning. The word 'touch' must be understood in its full meaning. We touch each other physically but we are also touched by each other emotionally. The symbolism of touch comes into our language when we use such phrases as 'keep in touch' or 'I'll be in touch'.

The other heart chakra key words arise mainly from the wider meanings and applications of touch. These are: compassion, feeling, tenderness, love of God, and love of others. In considering these key words, and what they may say to you about the condition of your own heart chakra, it is essential to ask yourself whether you are able to *receive* these qualities from others as well as *give* them. Perhaps most difficult of all, you should also consider whether you have a healthy love for yourself as well as for others.

The key word of 'detachment' may seem a strange one to apply to the heart chakra, yet it is crucial in enabling us to differentiate between basic emotion and the true feeling quality of the heart. Traditionally the symbol of the heart, as seen on Valentine's Day cards, is associated with emotion and romantic love; it is also considerably overworked in terms of love of places, food, or makes of car.

True heart love is constant, warm and goes beyond the fires of passion. Of course we need romance and burning ardour, but in true chakra terms these belong more to the sacral and solar plexus than to the heart (see page 132). The heart *chakra* is not the seat of the emotions but of feeling. The subtle body connection for the heart is the 'feeling body'. When the heart chakra unfolds there is a progression from the gut-level emotions of the sacral centre, through self-awareness at the solar plexus, to a shining quality of feeling, tempered with wisdom.

The truly heart-centred individual brings a feeling quality to life without being governed by raw emotion. It is possible to have, acknowledge and use feeling without it controlling our lives in a way which evades rationality and responsibility. These emotions can be harnessed without being denied. Their energies can be used advisedly, enhancing empowerment of self and others. Thus, *detachment* does not mean cold or uncaring withdrawal but the discipline which enables us to see an emotive situation with clarity and make a dispassionate appraisal of problems in order to act with the love which is both enhanced and tempered by wisdom. Understood in this way, detachment can be the midwife who brings love and wisdom to birth.

As you look into your own heart chakra, a question to ask is: 'How do I touch the world and how does the world touch me?' If, as is likely, your considered responses to this question

indicate blockages, then working with the root/heart/crown
chakra combination will be of particular value.

ROOT, HEART AND CROWN AS A CHAKRA TRIAD

Chapters 2 and 3 examined the relationship and interactions
between the root and crown chakras, emphasizing the part
they play in helping us to understand our major incarnational
choices as well as the way in which our selection of physical
body and constitution is related to issues of purpose and evolution.

The heart enables relationship. The interaction of crown
and root in manifesting the purposes of the higher self can
seem cold, clinical or even calculating without the heart
element. Less the qualities of heart, the whole plan of incarnation and evolution on earth could be seen as something of
a life sentence – to be endured until we can return to softer
realms.

Because the heart chakra plays a major part in enabling us
to feel love, it also puts us in touch with our pain. As human
beings, we know and identify our feelings by contrast or
because of polarities. In experiencing the lighter side of life
and tender feelings, such as love, joy, fulfilment, security and
passion, we also open ourselves to the *heartache* conditions
of loneliness, lack of love, sadness, frustration, insecurity and
boredom. Often it is the negative experience which spurs us
on to transformation, to seek higher ideals, to serve each other
and society and aspire to a higher potential for humankind.
In a more perfect society we would hope for love, rather than
the lack of it, to be the major catalyst.

The heart chakra gives us a more direct and personal
relationship with our tasks. In engendering in us 'a love of
God' or, more widely interpreted, a search for positive meaning
and pattern, it helps us to place ourselves within the greater

plan of the universe and to understand the function of the
microcosm within the macrocosm. Using Exercise 12 on page
97 will help you to be more in touch with your heart chakra
energy and to strengthen the important flow between root,
heart and crown chakras.

THE FAMILY OF ORIGIN

In terms of life choices the heart chakra is most linked to
family affiliations and the learning and growth which come
from them. At soul level, a careful overview is made as to our
choice of parents and the experiences which being brought
into incarnation and reared by them will give us.

Gildas explains that at the higher levels of our existence we
all belong to soul groups or families. He asks us to:

Imagine a tree, then the forest in which it stands, then
many other forests of trees. Twigs, leaves, fruits and flowers
which spring from the same branch are soul families.
Branches on the same tree, or the tree seen as a whole,
are soul groups. Forests are wider soul groups. In life you
meet those who are from the same branch as yourself and
will often recognize them joyfully as your true 'spiritual
family'. This means that genetic family is not necessarily
spiritual family, and recognition of this can often ease the
build-up of expectations within the genetic family.

You will also meet with those who are from your own tree
and those who are of your wider group soul. Often so-
called 'difficult karma' comes from the efforts of soul family
and group to mirror lessons for each other. The impulse
of this mirroring comes from love and understanding and
will have relevance to the joint evolution of the group.

You are never alone. You always have soul family and soul
group contacts around you and joint work to be
recognized and carried out. Sometimes you may seem to

be living in conditions of isolation, or in alien territory.
Even when the direct contacts are not there, try to sense
all the subtle energetic forces of love and acceptance
surrounding you.

Choice of Parents

Our acceptance and comprehension of our choice of parents
and families will depend initially on the nature of our
encounter with them. If our parents have been welcoming,
loving, supportive, communicative, united, understanding,
generous and just, then putting down roots, finding our true
identity and being content to be human can be a natural,
joyful progression. Our entry into incarnation is eased, allowing
the heart chakra to open naturally and function strongly.

It is, however, in the nature of parents to be less than perfect.
Psychologically it has been suggested that they can, at best, be
only 'good enough'. It may be problematic for us to accept
that we have 'chosen' parents who have been less than welcoming, loving and supportive, and the thought of choosing a
hostile or even rejecting early environment may be incompre-
hensible. Our reactions to our initial surroundings affect the
relationship between root and crown as well as the development of a fully functioning heart chakra.

The physical family of origin into which we incarnate will
reflect and be the means of implementing some of the purposes of soul family evolution. As part of this implementation
we may either choose to be born into a family where we know
and subtly recognize our parents and siblings or into a family
which has been chosen for other reasons, such as genetic,
cultural or social inheritance. It is also possible that the choice
of family may be connected to the balancing and reparation of
direct karma, providing an opportunity to meet our most
challenging lessons and teachers.

When we are among those we love and remember, making
the transition from the other worlds to the material plane is
very easy, and the problems of rooting, grounding and being

incarnate are lessened. This option may be taken perhaps as a contrast to a previous lonely or traumatic incarnation, or when our main incarnational focus is the development of a special gift. In such a case we may choose to incarnate to those who will nurture us in every way and protect us from having to give energy to the overcoming of serious life obstacles.

When we select a more hostile or difficult early environment, with parents and siblings who are not of our soul wavelength or group, then much of our learning will be centred around the obstacles we encounter and the consciousness dealing with these will engender. Some difficulties are chosen in order to help us understand the effects of causes we set in motion in another lifetime, others simply to provide a challenge and hone our strengths. Having to fight for one's identity is not easy, but it leads towards greater self-knowledge and self-appreciation of a healthy kind.

Dodi Smith wrote a well-known play, entitled *Dear Octopus*, about the family, its powers, strengths, influences and weaknesses. The octopus is known, and feared, for its ability to stretch out its long tentacles, grip hard and squeeze the life-force from its victim. It also squirts a dark ink, when being pursued, in order to confuse its predators. According to myth, if one tentacle of the octopus is cut off, another will immediately grow. It can be a hero's task to escape its grip and slay the life-threatening monster. The last line of Dodi Smith's play is: 'Whose tentacles we never quite forget'.

Even in the most positive sense, families make demands and their influence shapes our lives. We all need to 'belong' and this need gives great power to families of all kinds. Family strength and sustenance may be our mainstay; unconditional family love our solace. Pride in our kith and kin can be an inspiration. Genetically, we carry the family within us and our genealogical heredity forms an important part of our identity. When loyalties are under duress the well-known saying 'blood is thicker than water' is often proved true.

Conversely, family commitments may be limitations. Issues

of personal freedom and the process of finding our true selves can be aided or impeded by family dynamics. Grandparents, parents and siblings are strong forces, affecting the psychological formation of the individual psyche. Negative family currents, such as jealousies, enmities and the negative power of possessive love, may seem to sap our spirit. The themes of the perils of divided loyalties, rigid expectations and lack of permission are constantly reflected back to us by writers of potent novels and dramas. Yet psychological struggles, vitality-sapping as they may be, have a wider scale of reference when given a spiritual dimension and seen against the continuum of more than one lifetime. The concept of the evolution of the soul can inspire us through the bitterest struggles and ensure that we do not fall victim to a sense of meaninglessness.

Karmically, the family is our nurturer, teacher and the backdrop against which we learn about life. The greater families of society, nation or race also influence and condition us powerfully. The expectations of our society affect those of our family of origin. Certain moral and ethical requirements and conformities are part of the search for justice and help to oil the wheels of life. Within the different strata of society, there are social mores, fashions, and power games which influence families and their vision. Parents largely condition children to conform to the models that society or a particular culture find acceptable or desirable at any given time. When individuals are seen as clay to be moulded or forced into a convenient shape, rather than seeds with an inbuilt potential to blossom, the negative pressures of family dynamics can seriously affect the individual search for identity and self-worth.

At the more subtle level of the spiritual family or soul group, our inbuilt potential is fully known. Yet, even here, the conditions of our incarnation will be affected by the need to work not only for our own evolution but also for that of the group. Evolution is something which the individual achieves as part of a soul family and aspects of the 'brief' we bring with us into incarnation will go beyond our personal needs to reflect the higher-level family task.

The process of incarnation, being present on earth, and being born into a specific family of origin, in order to further our personal evolution as well as that of our soul family and group is thus immensely complex. Gildas tells us that, from the level of the higher selves of the soul family group, we contemplate the interweaving threads of incarnations as might a group of actors standing in the wings of a stage and planning the moves for the enactment of a drama. Those who, on earth, seem to be our harshest taskmasters, may be very close to us in our soul group. When there is an important lesson to be learned, we play confrontational roles for each other if this will enable the learning to take place sooner rather than later. It can take deep love to face the pain of being the catalyst for another's learning if any degree of suffering is involved.

Our evolutionary learning, derived from many lifetimes, is recorded and stored within our chakras. As more experience is recorded, so the chakras themselves mature and evolve. Family dynamics, from the soul level, through the total family of humanity, to our immediate incarnate family of origin, are intricately connected to the heart chakra. The developed heart chakra causes us to turn living into an art. It demands that we relate to the wider, as well as the immediate family, as part of our search for meaning and purpose in life. The heart chakra is unfolding and engaging when we feel that it is no longer enough to accept the conditions of life on earth as unalterable or merely to identify a task and get on with it.

The interaction between root, heart and crown chakras leads to a more passionate reality. Families form the arena within which our feelings are played out. Strong families, where relationship skills are inherent or have been worked for, sustain intensity well and become even stronger when faced with the inevitable challenges and woundings of growth. A self-healing mechanism may seem to operate. Less close-knit families, when under stress, can be so wounded as to become dysfunctional.

A vicious circle of wounding and re-wounding may occur and active healing intervention may be required. The following case study reflects some of these issues.

Case Study: Family Dynamics

Thomas, in his early sixties, married to Joyce, had recently been diagnosed as having Parkinson's disease. Hoping to gain perspective for the current and future challenges of his difficult, degenerative and incurable condition, he had decided to look back over his life. By so doing he had hoped to form a plan for the future and the management of his illness. Instead, what he saw and the value judgments he had brought to his review had made him extremely depressed. Joyce had recently read one of my books and managed to persuade Thomas to book a personal appointment. They came to talk to me together.

He told me that he felt a failure, and could see little meaning or purpose either in his own life or in life as a whole. He came from what he described as 'humble origins'. His father had been a farm labourer but had voluntarily 'joined up' as soon as the war began. He was killed in action whilst Thomas was still a young child. Thomas left school as soon as possible, feeling that he was the man of the house and responsible for helping his mother. He trained in carpentry but as he was becoming established in his work he suffered greatly when his mother, still relatively young, met and married another man. Although they offered him a home he preferred to find lodgings. He harboured a deep resentment towards his mother for having, as he felt, betrayed the memory of his father.

Although Thomas enjoyed carpentry and was good at it, he had artistic skills which did not find expression in the straightforward work he was required to do. He met Joyce, a nurse at the local cottage hospital, when he had to attend for regular dressings on an infected wound originally caused by the slip of a chisel. Though Thomas would occasionally use the lathe to make a beautiful bowl or other wooden objects, he continued as a regular carpenter until retirement.

Joyce gave up nursing when their two children, Frances and Gary, were born with barely eighteen months between them. Thomas loved his children dearly but, as they grew older, determined that they should pursue careers which would give them a different lifestyle to any he had known. His vision for Frances was that she should work in an environment where she might meet a husband who would lift her from the social level in which he felt himself to be stuck. For Gary, his vision was of the banking world, with eventual progression to bank manager.

Joyce confirmed that he had put a lot of pressure on the children as they neared school-leaving age to enter careers that he, rather than they, had chosen. Frances became an air hostess and Gary began his career in banking. Both had indicated that there were other choices they would prefer, since both had inherited their father's latent artistic gifts. Gary had begged to be trained in carpentry and Frances longed for drama school but their objections had been over-ruled.

When Frances saved all her wages from the airline and eventually worked her way through drama school and into repertory work, Thomas had been devastated. When Gary left banking to learn wood-turning he was distraught. His relationship with his children had broken down. Frances's artistic and creatively dressed friends and boyfriends horrified him and, as Gary began to be successful in his chosen career, he would hardly speak to him when he came to visit.

Joyce loved Thomas very much, but she too had suffered from his narrow views and frustrations about their social standing in life. She had been very angry when he had thwarted her desire to return to her career. She had resolved her dilemma by taking an interest in counselling and eventually in spiritual subjects. She had pointed out to Thomas that he was jealous of Gary who was doing something which really lay close to Thomas's own heart, and she had supported her daughter in her determination to follow her own way rather than act out her pre-planned destiny. Joyce said that both children understood that their father had always only wanted the best for them but, since they had both made their life changes, they found it difficult to cope with Thomas's open antagonism and barely suppressed rage.

Both Frances and Gary were living with partners, but there were no plans yet, it seemed, for grandchildren. Thomas also had difficulty accepting the trend for living together without marriage. The family dynamic had broken down.

As Thomas reviewed all this, he was full of regrets and frustrations. At first these were directed towards others: he felt that what he saw as his care for others had been rejected. His rage at this was considerable. He accused his children of spoiling his life. As we worked together, though, he gradually began to see that he was also angry and frustrated with himself and there was a big breakthrough point when he felt able to express the distressing but insightful thought that it was perhaps not his children who had spoiled his life, but he who had made big difficulties for Frances and Gary. Gradually he began to admire the spirit and determination they had both shown in finding their own way through life.

Big changes in thinking and expectations, like these, do not come quickly or easily. Whatever insights Thomas had, there was still no cure for his Parkinsonism. Nor could he fulfil his frustrated artistic talent, since the tremor and rigidity of Parkinsons now made working with tools dangerous. Aided and encouraged by Joyce, Thomas did change greatly. Eventually he began to explore the spiritual approach to meaning in life and found solace in the thought that Frances and Gary had chosen himself and Joyce as parents. They had given their children a lot of early love and security, but he could see that maybe they needed to have obstacles in their way to make them more appreciative and conscious about the finding of their true identities. He could also accept that in this present lifetime he had, in himself, to learn about rigidity and to come through it to greater tolerance. He also recognized the rigidity of his concept of masculine and feminine roles. He began to join Joyce in some of her chakra exercises and meditations.

Eventually Thomas's change of heart brought healing to the family dynamic. He became much more tolerant of his children's lifestyles and genuinely interested in their achievements. Joyce still keeps in touch from time to time and in a recent letter told me that Thomas had invested some money, saved over the years, in helping Gary to open his own workshop and small gallery for the production and display of his work. He was able to work in the gallery himself, on a part-time basis, discussing and marketing the lovely objects. Gary often sought his advice about different woods and tools, and father and son had grown much closer. Joyce also told me that Frances was expecting their first grandchild, was shortly to be married and had delighted Thomas by being traditional enough to ask him to 'give her away'.

Had Thomas not come for help and the above story been told by Frances or Gary, there would have been a great deal of emphasis on their frustrations. They might have expressed distress about the role their mother was forced to play. If Thomas had been unable to change, strands of guilt about not fulfilling parental expectations might have affected all their life decisions. If and when they had created their own families the breakdown in communication with their parents could have become more and more painful. The tentacles of the family octopus, so out of touch or cut off in one sense, would have become more complex and powerful.

One of Thomas's greatest original wounds came from the wartime death of his father. As a boy he felt thrust into premature responsibility for his mother. This sense became so strong that, even as a young man, he felt rejected, estranged and undermined when she decided to remarry. A part of him always wanted to regain masculine control, and Joyce and his children suffered because of this. If the eventual family rift had not been healed, the spirit of rebellion could have turned negative in its effect on the future development of Frances and Gary. Frances's decision to have a church wedding and to be 'given away' by her father was a very healing choice. In families, when one healing move or creative compromise is made, others often follow.

The heart chakra, linked to crown and root enables us to relate to the meaning of life. Once meaning dawns, healing, understanding and forgiveness come more easily. Knowing that we are working out an intricate evolutionary plan, as instruments of growth for each other, lifts frustrations and puts anger into perspective. We understand the drama of life as clearly as we might understand a complex play in a theatre.

We need to remember, though, that spiritual, emotional and psychological worlds intermingle just as the spiritual and physical do (see Chapter 3). Finding that detachment from the heart which enables us to take an overview of life's challenges and pains does not of itself heal all the vulnerability within. Frustrations, deprivations, neglect, and the hurt of being unseen and unheard in childhood, go deep. As a preparation for all family healing, the child within must be considered and helped. Without healing, the inner child retains a negative autonomy which often perpetuates a negative influence within the family. As we attempt to make modifications in our lives, all sorts of obstacles may unexpectedly appear. We try to alter the patterns, but they reassert themselves. Usually, at the heart of resistance to change, lies the fear, neediness, uncertainty and suffering of the inner child.

THE INNER CHILD

During childhood it is almost inevitable that parents and teachers will misunderstand or misinterpret our behaviour and needs from time to time. If, for instance, a child is constantly deprived of the right kind of attention, it may discover that being 'naughty' wins notice, and conclude that a negative response, or even punishment, is better than no attention at all. In such a case the true needs of the child are not met. With growth into adulthood, an immature, unsatisfied inner part will live on as a needy and perhaps naughty, neglected and angry inner child. The adult's life and behaviour will be marked, at moments which may come as a surprise or embarrassment, by this autonomous aspect making itself known and felt. (See also Chapter 7, page 165).

The needy aspects of the child within lead us to seek parenting and permission from others, often for much of our lives. We cannot truly empower ourselves to make free choices until we recognize our inner child's needs and take responsibility for healing these parts within ourselves. To make the process more complicated, until we gain fuller insights our own inner censor may reflect our parents' attitudes. Thus we may continue to punish and oppress the fearful, over-indulge the spoiled, and undernourish the hungry children within. Such mechanisms are all part of the complexities of conditioning and can present huge obstacles to family healing unless they are seen as intrinsic to it.

When, as adults, we create our own good inner parent, we take pressure from the family of origin and change the expectations which may still be bound up within it. Self-help for the inner child is very effective. One of the tools for healing is the heart chakra (see Exercise 13, page 98). It should be noted, however, that if the childhood difficulties were severe or overwhelming the help of a trained therapist could be needed.

CUTTING THE TIES THAT BIND

The symbolic image of the octopus is of a creature which holds its victim in a crushing grip which drains life-force away. It binds the victim with its sucker-encrusted tentacles and will not let go. When family relationships become difficult or blocked, before true healing can take place, it may be necessary to cut negative ties. Clairvoyantly, these ties can often be seen as grey pulsating cords which carry a two-way flow of energy, keeping grievances alive, preventing the healing of old patterns and the emergence of the new.

There are ties created by conditioning, emotional blackmail, false or divided loyalties, and unreasonable expectations of, or from, ourselves and others. These affect every aspect of interpersonal and intrapersonal relationships. Once their existence is recognized, their effective cutting or dissolving is aided by visualization and prayer, since, in addition to being psychological mechanisms, they actually exist energetically on the psychic and subtle planes.

You may only have considered ties to be of a valuable and positive nature. The prospect of cutting even those which are subtly destructive can be daunting. Though we crave freedom to be ourselves, we may also fear it. We have negative investments in the things which prevent or hold back our forward progress. Negative patterns have hidden 'benefits' which we should endeavour to understand before attempting to cut the ties and bring ourselves the challenge of freedom.

The ties that bind can give us excuses for not facing the challenges of life. Nelson Mandela reminded us in his famous inaugural speech:

Our deepest fear is not that we are inadequate. Our deepest
fear is that we are powerful beyond measure. It is our
light, not our darkness, that most frightens us. We ask
ourselves, who am I to be brilliant, gorgeous, talented and
fabulous? Actually, who are you not to be? You are a child

of God – your playing small doesn't serve the world. There is nothing enlightened about shrinking so that other people will not feel insecure around you. We were born to make manifest the glory of God that is within us. It is not in just some of us; it is in everyone. And as we let our own light shine, we unconsciously give people permission to do the same. As we are liberated from our own fear, our presence automatically liberates others.

Positive cutting of the ties that bind means that we release more energy into our lives, cut out negative collusions, provide opportunity for emotional climates to change and leave space for the true, higher nature of our relationships to become clear. True tie-cutting needs the detachment and wisdom of the heart chakra to make it successful. The heart chakra may need negative emotional ties to be cut before it can function at its highest level and help us to stay in positive relationship to others. Far from driving us apart from others, tie-cutting sets us free to love without encumbrance. Two visualizations for tie-cutting, designed by Gildas, are given in Exercise 14 on page 99.

PERSONIFIED ARCHETYPES: THE GREAT MOTHER AND GREAT FATHER

These archetypes have been chosen for this chapter because they lead on from the Sun, Moon and Stars archetypes chosen for Chapter 2 (see page 32). As the heart chakra forms a trio with the root and crown, the qualities of the sun, moon and stars become less remote. The mother/father archetypes can be used for healing the inner child and the family of origin (see Exercise 13, page 98).

An extract from J.C. Cooper, writing of the Great Mother in *An Illustrated Encyclopaedia of Traditional Symbols*, shows something of the complexity and all-embracing nature of this archetype:

> She is the archetypal feminine, the origin of all life; the containing principle; she symbolizes all phases of cosmic life, uniting all the elements, both celestial and chthonic [relating to, or inhabiting the underworld]. She is the Queen of Heaven, Mother of God, 'opener of the way'; the keeper of the keys of fertility and the gates of birth, death and rebirth. As the Moon Goddess she is perpetual renewal, the bringer of the seasons, the controller of the life-giving waters. She is the measurer of time, the weaver of fate, weaving the web and pattern of life with the thread of destiny, symbolic of her power of ensnaring and binding, but also of loosing and freeing. She has the dual nature of creator and destroyer and is both nourisher, protector, provider of warmth and shelter, and the terrible forces of dissolution, devouring and death-dealing; she is the creator and nourisher of all life and its grave.

The Great Father is also known as the All Father or simply, The Father. Though also complex, J.C. Cooper's description is relatively succinct: He is:

> The sun; the Spirit; the masculine principle; conventional forces of law and order as opposed to the feminine and intuitive instinctual powers. The sky god is the All-Father. In myth and legend the figure of the father symbolizes physical, mental and spiritual superiority. Father Time, identified with Cronos/Saturn, holds a scythe or sickle as god of agriculture and as the Reaper, Time. An hourglass is also his attribute.

The Great Mother archetype has more negative symbolism than the Great Father. This is because these archetypes also largely personify the feminine and masculine principles. The masculine principle, being more direct, focused and less absorbent, acquires fewer trappings. The feminine principle, in its diffuseness, ability to gestate, give birth and embody the chthonic, encompasses the depths as well as the heights. The Great Mother teaches us more about the shadow side of life than does the Great Father. Yet the Great Father has a major part in creating shadow, since the focused awareness of the masculine principle can lead to a denial of unconscious forces, causing them to gain autonomy.

The Great Mother and Great Father as Healers

In concentrating on the Great Mother and Great Father for individual and family healing, we need to use the highest principles held by these archetypes.

We have expectations of how good mothers and good fathers should be. When our family-of-origin parents are less than exemplary, something within us is dissatisfied. Often long into adult life, even when we have children of our own, an aspect of the inner child may hold the belief that our parents will change overnight and satisfy its outstanding needs. Of course, the adult knows that our parents are as they are. Probably they have done the best they can for us. If they have been totally inadequate, then the adult can see that they were a product of their own environment, and even where conditions have been very traumatic, some compassion may be felt and forgiveness possible. This process of acceptance (see also page 56) is greatly helped by taking a spiritual view of evolution.

The inner child, though, does not accept so easily. Its needs live on, and, for full healing to take place, must be met. If the parents of origin are unlikely to provide for the inner child within the adult, we need to strengthen the ability to parent ourselves. We need to envision inner parents who carry the qualities of parenting we need and can therefore help the inner child from within. This process can be lonely. The fortunate minority can have long-term therapy where the therapist witnesses and accompanies this important development. Where initial parenting has been inadequate, we may need to call on the positive qualities of the parent archetypes to strengthen our inner self-nurturing abilities. We can use the combination of crown/root/heart chakra energies to link with the archetypes and to bring the healing parent flow into our natural energy system.

Cooperative family healing, such as that which eventually took place in Thomas's family (see case study, page 86), is not always possible. No matter what overtures we make, they may be rejected, misunderstood or simply not recognized. Before it can be worked on cooperatively, all parties have to acknowledge that a problem exists. Sometimes, all we can do as individuals is to change our attitude or perspective and heal ourselves inwardly. When we do this, we gradually become free of the power of the octopus to hold us in negative patterns and free of the model of negative, self-fulfilling prophecies.

FRIENDS, LOVERS AND COLLEAGUES

Blending the energies of crown, heart and root chakras lays a foundation for inner freedom and empowerment. This will not only affect our relationship with our family of origin, but will flood over into all our relationships. When we speak of a persons' heart being 'in the right place' in chakra terms, it means that it is well connected to the root/crown flow. Such people make deep and lasting friendships and relationships. They are reliable colleagues and often, in a subtle way, positively affect relationships in the workplace.

The chakras are more than a system. They are a family in their own right. Practising chakra exercises means that your chakra family begins to work in cooperative harmony. The particular work specified in this chapter, and in Chapters 5 and 7, will help you to become a warm, empowered and heart-centred person who finds fewer complications in relationships and has deeper resources with which to heal or review difficulties. The combined work on self will mean that unreal expectations, and the tendency to seek partnerships or love for the wrong reasons, will recede as your body, emotions and spirit achieve a stronger alignment.

The tie-cutting exercise on page 99 can be used to heal your friendships, your love life and work life as well as your immediate family relationships.

EXERCISES

Exercise 12
Energetically Connecting the Crown/Root/Heart Trio

For this exercise it is better to sit in an upright chair, adopt a cross-legged or lotus position, or to stand.

- Begin by practising central column breathing (see page 17). When you feel that you have become focused and in alignment, direct your attention towards your heart chakra.
- Breathe into the petals of your heart chakra and out through the stem for four or five in/out breath sequences.
- Breathe into your heart chakra, holding the breath in its centre, then breathe up and out through the crown chakra. Breathe in at the crown chakra, bring the breath down to the heart chakra and breathe out through the petals of the heart. Repeat this sequence for four or five in/out breath sequences.
- Breathe into your heart chakra, holding the breath in its centre, then breathe down and out through the root chakra. Breathe in at the root chakra, bring the breath up to the heart chakra and breathe out though the petals of the heart. Repeat this sequence for four or five in/out breath sequences.
- Breathe into your heart chakra, holding the breath in its

centre, then imagine the breath energy going both down
to the root and up to the crown as you breathe out through
your nose. Repeat this sequence for four or five in/out
breath sequences.

Exercise 13
Healing the Inner Child

Before you begin this exercise, consider which aspect of
parenting you most lacked as a child. What did you require
from your father which he was unable to give? What did you
require from your mother which she was unable to give? If
you identify many aspects, work with one at a time. Therefore
use this exercise progressively as you feel healing taking
place.

- Making sure that you will be undisturbed, practise central
  column breathing (see page 17). Bring the breath rhythm
  into your heart chakra . . . As you breathe in and out
  through the petals of your heart, imagine a warm, rose-
  pink colour permeating your heart chakra . . .
- Now imagine your inner child, in your heart chakra,
  surrounded by this warm, rose-pink colour . . . Be aware
  of the needs of your inner child . . .
- If your inner child lacked father qualities, whilst still
  holding the child in the rose-pink of your heart centre,
  imagine a flow of energy, carrying the lacking qualities,
  coming into your heart from your crown chakra . . . This
  flow is coming from the Great Father towards your inner
  child with tenderness and healing . . . Let the rose-pink
  colour of your heart and your tender holding of your inner
  child in your heart chakra enable the healing energy from
  the Great Father to be received . . .
- If your inner child lacked mother qualities, whilst still
  holding the child in the rose-pink of your heart centre,

imagine a flow of energy, carrying the lacking qualities, coming into your heart from your root chakra . . . This flow of energy is coming from the Great Mother towards your inner child, with tenderness and healing . . . Let the rose-pink colour of your heart and your tender holding of your inner child in your heart chakra enable the healing energy from the Great Mother to be received . . .

Exercise 14
Cutting the Ties that Bind

This exercise will help to heal any negative links to your family of origin, friends, lovers or colleagues, and enable the purer energy of the acceptance of karmic purpose and true heart love to bring about healing on an energetic level.

To be effective, tie-cutting visualizations need to be repeated frequently (daily or every other day) for about a month. They should then be repeated about once a week until a difference is noticed, and thereafter used from time to time as reinforcement or if similar situations or old-style reactions recur. Getting a friend, partner or counsellor to 'witness' your intention in cutting the ties can be a great help. If you want to cut the ties with more than one person, make a separate visualization for each. If there are more than two people or situations to deal with, first select the two most vital ones to work on. Start new visualizations only after you have worked for approximately two months with the original ones.

Either select one of the following methods for use, or use each of them alternately.

Method 1

- Begin with central column breathing (see page 17) and then breathe in and out through your heart chakra.
- Visualize yourself standing in a circle of light. The person with whom you wish to cut the ties is also standing in a circle of light, facing you. Your circles of light are touching each other or even slightly overlapping. There are greyish pulsating cords running from some of your vital centres or chakras to the corresponding centres in the other person. (These most commonly run from root chakra to root chakra, sacral to sacral, solar plexus to solar plexus.)
- In your visualization move back so that your circles no longer overlap; now put an extra circle of violet light around your existing circle and then a fine circle of silver light around that. Do the same for the person with whom you are intending to cut the ties. Emphasize the space between your circles.
- Now visualize the grey cords withering and dropping away into the space between you. Let the space between you become a river of light. The river of light takes the cords into its flow, filling them with light and washing them away to the sea.
- Ask your guardian angel for a blessing, and ask the other person's guardian angel to do the same for them. As you bask in the light of blessing, try to become aware of the lessons that you and the other person have taught or mirrored to each other and be thankful for those lessons.
- Feel your own space firmly around you as you let the visualization fade.

Method 2

- Begin with central column breathing (see page 17) and then breathe in and out through your heart chakra.
- Visualize yourself standing opposite the person with whom you wish to cut the ties. Visualize a symbol of peace

which you would wish to offer to this person, and see them
holding it. See yourself holding a replica of this symbol.
As you hold the symbols, be aware of the lessons you have
reflected for each other.

- As in Method 1, see the grey and pulsating cords which
bind, running between your vital areas or chakras.
Visualize a shaft of silver light, which flashes three times
between you, melting away the cords and leaving you free.

- See a pathway of light behind you and behind the person
with whom you are cutting the ties. See each of you
turn, with your symbol of peace, to follow your own
distinctive path. As you walk away, the shaft of light
appears to define a boundary. In future neither of you can
cross that boundary except at the other's invitation. (This
method is particularly good where there has been a sense
of 'invasion' by another person.)

THE COLOURS

The main colours for the heart chakra are spring green, rose
and rose amethyst.

Spring green is the colour of young beech leaves in early
spring. It is a delicate colour linking to the key word of tenderness.

Positively, green is the colour of spring, growth, opening and
permission to move forward. It helps to heal the pain which
comes from being over-vulnerable to life and to open the heart
when it has 'hardened' as a result of opposition or devastating
emotional experiences.

Negatively, it may be considered to be unlucky. (Older types
of green paint contained lead and led to ill-health and
poisoning.) It is also the colour of jealousy – 'green with envy'.

Rose is a gentle rose-pink; rose quartz crystals give the right
depth and quality for this heart colour.

Positively, rose is a warm colour, also indicating tenderness and delicacy of approach. It brings warmth and softness and is comforting to the bereaved.

Negatively, it may be rather sickly-sweet and produce a vibration of discord.

Rose amethyst is a deeper rose colour, with a touch of mauve or amethyst in it, making it a bluer pink. It is linked to the key word of detachment in the heart chakra.

Positively, rose amethyst helps to lead us towards wisdom and is strengthening to the heart after debilitating illnesses or in stress conditions. It balances blood pressure.

Negatively, it can become the colour of too cold, over-clinical detachment.

Follow the directions for Exercise 8, page 42, for breathing these colours into your heart chakra to develop and strengthen it.

THE FRAGRANCES

Sandalwood and rose quieten the heart chakra, while pine and honeysuckle stimulate it. If you sense that your heart is too open and that you tend to put other people's needs before your own, then use sandalwood and rose. If you find it difficult to express your feelings, or are hesitant about touching and being touched, you will benefit from using pine and honeysuckle. Look back to your reflections on the heart chakra question on page 80 to get a sense of which of these fragrances will benefit you most.

See page 43 for suggestions for using the fragrances. Also consider making a balancing blend of one stimulating and one quietening fragrance from each of the root, crown and heart chakras. This will help to establish and energize the root/crown/heart trio.

THE CRYSTALS

Refer to page 44 and the Glossary for general guidance on using crystals. The crystals which will best help the issues considered in this chapter are:

Ruby To vitalize, nourish and warm. This is the stone to use for healing when there has been a difficult birth or where bonding of the baby to the mother has been delayed for some reason.

Rose Quartz To encourage self-nurturing and bring the quality of warm, unconditional, motherly love to heal all who have had too little of this in their lives.

Green Calcite To vitalize all our subtle bodies, but particularly the feeling body. This helps the communication between head and heart, brings strength during periods of change and transition, heals the wounds of the heart and encourages the development of positive tenderness.

Amber All shades of amber resonate with the heart chakra. It purifies and helps to develop balance and love.

PRAYERS OR AFFIRMATIONS

The root chakra prayer or affirmation is:

> Through incarnation may spirit be brought into matter.
> Through rootedness may life-force be recharged and
> exchanged. We acknowledge wholeness and seek to gain
> and to reflect acceptance.

The crown chakra prayer or affirmation is:

> Through surrender and release let the incoming will be
> truly the will of God working within us and through us,
> leading us increasingly to knowledge of mystical union and
> mystical marriage.

The heart chakra prayer or affirmation is:

> In the golden centre of the rose of the heart may tender
> compassion be linked to unconditional love. May true
> detachment enable growth and continuity. Through the
> understanding of birth within death and death within
> birth may there be transformation.

For suggestions on using prayers or affirmations, see page 45.

Chapter 5

Affairs of the Heart:
Love and Passion

Key Issues: Passion, Tenderness

Chakra Pair: Root and Heart

Archetype: Love

This chapter will help you to:
- love life on earth
- understand and combine the qualities of passion and tenderness
- have a fuller appreciation of natural beauty
- understand better and live more effectively with the law of love within the universe

---

For lists of the areas of influence see page 19 for the root chakra and page 77 for the heart chakra.

THE ROOT AND HEART AS A CHAKRA PAIR

In Chapter 4 we looked at the root, heart and crown chakras as a trio but the energy link between the root and heart as a pair is also significant. We have seen how the heart chakra brings in the dimension of relationship. In the trio with root and crown, its main influence is on our relationship to our karmic task and our family of origin. When *paired* with the root it enables us fully to relate to the earth and to feel the passions which are one of the gifts of human experience. The sacral/heart link (to be explored in Chapter 6) is also connected with passion, but more directly to sexual passion and the passions of power and empowerment.

The root/heart connection gives us a love of beauty, harmony and comfort and inspires us to high ideals in these areas. When the link between root and heart chakras is clear, our living on earth, our use of its resources and our relationships with each other are as though blessed by the goddess. If the collective root/heart connection were in order we would be unable to:

- blot the landscape with ugly buildings
- pollute the rivers and the soil
- use negative, violence-generating, sounds or rhythms in our music
- feel violence or hatred towards each other
- misuse the world's resources
- be motivated by greed and envy
- be unconscious of our natural responsibilities
- see our times of incarnation on earth as some kind of exile
- sow the seeds of discontent
- suffer from loss of meaning
- be without love

In short, we would all be united in working towards a utopian society. Yet, moving away from idealism, if we look at the above list on an individual basis, it can be seen that the root/heart connection has the potential to heal many of the areas of unease and discontent to which most of us fall victim from time to time.

Because a major part of our evolution is worked out through earth incarnation, we need the root chakra. It enables us to be in our bodies, to adapt to the vibrations of matter, to have the instinct to fulfil our basic needs, and to deal with the material world. On its own, it merely enables us to live and to be aware of our physiological needs. In its links to other chakras it plays its part in enabling us to be healthy, wealthy and wise.

PASSION

When root is linked to heart, we can feel a passion for life which motivates us to deepen our experiences. Rather than having the feeling of just 'passing through', we become, not only voluntarily, but passionately, resident here. We begin to care, not only for ourselves, our immediate families or our race, but for each other as members of the total family of humanity. We not only conceive visions of higher ideals and values but we work towards them. We do not sit back and moan whilst others govern and make decisions – instead we insist on becoming a part of the decision-making mechanisms. We become witnesses for each other, in the sense of being mutual reminders that we should refuse to accept less than the best, not from vanity, but from a healthy sense of self-worth and because we believe in a high potential for humanity.

Gildas, along with many other guides, has long assured us that we are on the brink of entering a new and golden age. One of the most potent things we can do, to help us more towards this state of new awareness, is to work on connecting the heart and root chakras. When the connection is made we do not have to *try* to be better human beings than we are; the energy which prevents us being anything other than a true and passionate world citizen actually flows through our subtle energy systems, positively affecting our beliefs and actions.

TENDERNESS

In Chapter 4 we also saw that the capacity of the heart for tenderness is a major factor in bringing about relationship. Tenderness can also mean vulnerability. The root chakra gives us instinctual, survival strengths but, without moderating factors, these would remain at a rather primitive, neanderthal level. To the neanderthal human, tenderness could have been a threat to survival. Yet because, as a species, we have evolved into greater consciousness, we are now in a position where we may need tenderness and vulnerability to help keep the wisdom of our instincts alive. The development of the mind and our ability to find mechanical solutions to most material problems can mask a necessary awareness of vulnerability. There is, of course, a vicious circle, since our initial vulnerability stimulated the mechanical creativity which is now in danger of masking our natural instincts. Tenderness, which is an antidote to force, can help us preserve our instincts without denying our powers of mind and creativity.

When we have a more tender relationship with earth we respect its life-force and release the nurturer or the mother goddess within it (see also pages 94, 95 and 98) without setting ourselves up in opposition or conflict with that which is natural. With tenderness we can be responsive without becoming negatively vulnerable. The art of linking and exchanging energies between root and heart chakras can enable this shift and resolution.

Case Study: Affairs of the Heart

Sharon could not form lasting relationships, yet her main passion in life, as a successful journalist, was an interest in people. An only child, she described her childhood as one where she was technically well-provided for and loved. Her father worked as a freelance radio broadcaster and journalist. When he had fulfilled a good contract or been well paid for an article, he and her mother would 'get on a high' and take sudden trips by car to France, a country they both loved. Within hours they would be ready to depart. Sharon found that she let friends down, when plans had been made, or missed things she had been looking forward to at school. She felt temperamentally different from her parents and their mood swings but learned not to make commitments in case they could not be honoured. When her father was not doing well he would become withdrawn, depressed and prone to drown his sorrows in drink. As a situation developed which made Sharon feel she could never invite anyone home, she increasingly held people at arm's length.

When Sharon was fourteen her mother contracted a long-term degenerative illness. On the surface her father dealt with this well and, as the illness got worse, was an attentive carer and nurse. But at an emotional level Sharon felt that her father did not cope at all. Later she had understood that the only way he could deal with his feelings was to deny them.

His drinking became heavier and he encouraged his sick wife to drink with him whenever she became depressed about her condition. Few outsiders or relatives realized it, since most of the drinking was in private, but eventually Sharon was living with two alcoholics. There was no violence. Her father became maudlin when drunk and her mother would just withdraw and sleep, but everything in the household was unpredictable and disorganized. She learned not to ask for help, understanding that the family secret must be kept. Sharon was eighteen when, at last, her father faced some of his need and vulnerability and asked his unmarried sister to move in. Sharon had just been accepted as a cub reporter on a local newspaper. She moved into a flat of her own so that she could live a more ordered life.

The insecure, Bohemian existence with strong emotional undercurrents denied at surface level, and the pathos of her parents' dilemma, together with her mother's early death, had caused Sharon to withdraw into herself. She felt cold and clinical inside. Some of her journalistic writing showed passion but she was concerned that, often, when other reporters were moved by the life situations they had to confront, she stayed not only detached but unaffected.

In many ways Sharon was an attractive woman of the world. She was not short of male escorts but somehow nothing ever seemed to develop into the loving relationship she longed for. She was seeking help now, because her latest boyfriend, in parting from her, had described her as a 'cold, calculating, ice-maiden'.

At a psychological level there was relatively long-term work to be done on resurrecting and understanding the feelings from Sharon's childhood. Through an 'alternative therapies' page in the newspaper for which she worked, Sharon had become interested in chakras and the spiritual approach. She wanted self-help tools.

Soon Sharon understood that the connection between her heart and root chakras had had little chance of forming. She began to work with these chakras separately and also with the breathing exercise for the transformative link. She felt that this energetic work enabled her to change some things quite quickly and also that it sustained her during the painful process of finding the feelings she had needed to deny in order to survive. Before her therapy was finished she had found a new male partner and was contemplating the big step, especially for her, of moving in with him.

THE ARCHETYPE: LOVE

This archetype has been chosen for this chapter because I believe it to be the basic law on which the universe is founded. Establishing the flow between the root and heart chakras brings love in its highest forms into manifestation.

In the English language we have only one word for love and it has become very overworked. Other languages, particularly ancient Greek, provide words for gradations of love. *Filios* is family love; *Eros* is erotic or romantic love; *Agape* (literally translated as 'the love feast') is the love which comes from mutuality and spiritual communion. This last probably comes closest to that which Gildas describes as an archetype in process of being born: the archetype of unconditional love. He names one of the 'new' chakras as The Unconditional Love Centre (see page 243), and describes it as a deeper opening of the heart. To enable that deeper opening and the connection to the chakra and archetype of unconditional love the root/heart links first need to be strengthened. Gildas sees trust as essential to the flow of love:

Trust that 'all is well, all manner of things are well and all shall be very well indeed'. Such trust casts out fear and allows love to flow in. Love enables, creates and transforms. Even, and especially in the face of all your current difficulties on earth, practise love more consistently in your inner and outer lives. Give it out and allow it to flow in. It is the life-force of change.

EXERCISES

Exercise 15
Linking Root and Heart Energies

This is the basic exercise for making a connection between your root and heart chakras. Besides strengthening and harmonizing your energy body, it will help you to be more positive in your approach to life; to heal or balance any negative feelings you have towards yourself or others; strengthen your resistance to atmospheric pollution of all kinds, including noise pollution; give you a clearer sense of responsibility; link you to the Source of All Life; improve your access to contentment; aid your search for meaning; enable you to be more loving to others and to be more receptive to love from others.

- Begin with central column breathing (see page 17). When you feel ready to do so, breathe in and out at your heart centre, keeping a natural breath rhythm.
- Now breathe in through the petals of the heart chakra, hold the breath in its centre for a count of three, then breathe down into the root chakra and out deeply into the earth. (Practise this for ten in-out breath sequences.)
- Change to breathing in from the earth, into the root chakra, holding the breath in the centre of the root chakra for a count of three, then breathe on up into the centre of the heart chakra and out through the heart petals. (Practise this for ten in-out breaths.)
- Re-establish your own normal, relaxed, breathing pattern.

Exercise 16
A Love Meditation

- Make sure that you will be undisturbed and begin with the usual practice of central column breathing (see page 17), gradually focusing into finding a natural rhythm of breathing in and out through your heart chakra.
- Imagine a cosmic source of love-light just above the crown of your head . . . As you breathe in, draw love into your body from this source. . . Imagine it permeating each bodily area . . . Imagine it flowing through your blood vessels and vitalizing your cells . . . Imagine your whole body glowing with the light of love . . . Continue to breathe love-light into your own body and being on each in-breath,

and on each out-breath breathe it into the atmosphere
around you . . . Breathe it into the earth, the furniture,
the walls and ceilings and all the physical substance of your
home . . . Send it out to loved ones and to your pets . . .
Breathe it into your plants, your garden, the substance of
earth itself . . . Sense that each particle which begins to
glow with this love-light passes its luminosity on to whatever
is next to it . . . The glow of love in the earth goes deeper
and deeper . . . The love-light in each person touches that
in another . . . Imagine the whole planet and all its peoples
bathed in the light of love, causing everything to flourish
in peak health and vitality . . .

- When you are ready to do so, come back gently to your
everyday surroundings. As you go about your tasks,
continue to carry a sense of the love-light with you . . . Let
it be there, subtly, to touch all whom you meet.

THE COLOURS

The colours for the root chakra are red, brown and mauve;
and, for the heart chakra, spring green, rose and rose amethyst.
To strengthen the colours in your root and heart chakras, refer
to Exercise 8 (page 42).

THE FRAGRANCES

For the root chakra the quietening fragrances are cedarwood
and patchouli, and the stimulating ones are musk, lavender and
hyacinth. For the heart chakra the quietening fragrances are
sandalwood and rose, and the stimulating ones are pine and
honeysuckle. See page 43 for suggestions for using the fragrances.

For strengthening and balancing the root/heart connection choose one stimulating and one quietening fragrance for each chakra, then blend the oils together to make a balancing essence.

THE CRYSTALS

Refer to page 44 and the Glossary for general guidance on using crystals. The crystals which will best help the issues considered in this chapter are:

Watermelon Tourmaline. To aid tolerance, flexibility, compassion and transformation. Watermelon tourmaline helps the heart chakra to open and to maintain the sort of flexibility which keeps it healthy.

Apache Tears. These are small, tear-shaped pieces of black obsidian. They promote tenderness but also help us to link to the natural cycles of the earth. They strengthen our ability to link instinct with creativity.

PRAYERS OR AFFIRMATIONS

The root chakra prayer or affirmation is:

> Through incarnation may spirit be brought into matter.
> Through rootedness may life-force be recharged and
> exchanged. We acknowledge wholeness and seek to gain
> and to reflect acceptance.

The heart chakra prayer or affirmation is:

> In the golden centre of the rose of the heart may tender
> compassion be linked to unconditional love. May true
> detachment enable growth and continuity. Through the

understanding of birth within death and death within birth may there be transformation.

For suggestions on using prayers or affirmations, see page 45.

Chapter 6

The Life-Force:
Sex, Power and Creativity

Key Issues: Sex, Violence, Creativity, Romance, Enduring Love,
Power Games, Empowerment, Power, Abundance
Chakra Pairs: Sacral and Root, Sacral and Heart
Chakra Triad: Sacral, Root and Heart
Archetypes: Creativity, Peace, Sexuality, Power and Abundance

---

This chapter will help you to:
- release blockages around sex, money and authority
- understand more about violence and its relationship to creativity
- take another step towards owning your own power
- learn more about the nature of abundance

AREAS OF INFLUENCE

For lists of the areas of influence see page 19 for the root chakra and page 77 for the heart chakra.

The Sacral Chakra:

Location The petals are approximately two fingers below the navel. The stem corresponds to the sacrum area of the spine.
Key Words Security, Sense of Others, Sexuality, Creativity, Empowerment, Co-creativity, Sincerity
Developmental Age 3/5–8yrs
Colours Orange, Amber, Gold (non-metallic)
Element Water
Sense Taste
Body Etheric
Glandular Connection Lymphatics
Quietening Fragrances Musk, Amber
Stimulating Fragrances Rosemary, Rose Geranium
Crystals and Gemstones Amber, Citrine, Topaz, Aventurine, Moonstone, Jasper

Prayer or Affirmation

May the unity of humanity with each other and the earth enable true creativity. May release from a sense of sin and unworthiness lead us into the full knowledge of our empowerment as co-creators, at one with, and a part of the Divine.

SACRAL AND ROOT AS A CHAKRA PAIR

The developmental stage for the sacral chakra is 3/5–8yrs. The variation in the lower age as a starting point for the age most developmentally linked to this chakra is partly generational. The modern baby develops much faster than a baby of thirty years or more ago was encouraged to do. Thus wider issues become important at an earlier age. It will always, whatever the generation, depend to a large extent on individual development, but if you are over thirty it is likely that your sacral chakra stage would have started at around the age of five. If you are younger than twenty then it will more probably have started at around three. Looking back to these ages will give you a fuller insight into the emotional and physical factors affecting your chakra's development.

Linked to the sense of taste, the element of water and the lymphatic glands, the sacral chakra in its own right affects, and is affected by, our emotional mood swings, our preferences (not only in foods but in the broad sense of the tastes and fashions of life), our symbolic relationship to flow and fluidity, our fertility or fecundity and the surges of our sexual awareness and desires. The question to ask yourself at the sacral chakra is: 'How do I taste the world and how does the world taste me?'

When a chakra is studied in isolation or as an individual member of the full team, then understanding its full range of areas of influence is the primary aim. In considering the energetic links formed by pairs and trios of chakras, the intensity of relationship between the centres affects the original key words by creating key *issues*. In viewing the sacral chakra in conjunction with the root and heart, the key issues become: sexuality, creativity, co-creativity, violence, power, empowerment, romantic and enduring love, wealth, abundance and poverty. The issues most linked to the root/sacral pair are sexuality, creativity, co-creativity, violence, power, empowerment, wealth, abundance and poverty.

We have seen that the root chakra, with its element of earth, supplies the energetic force which enables us to live on earth and to deal with our bodies and the material world. The sacral chakra also, through the etheric body and the element of water, closely interacts with the material plane. Earth, at the root chakra, gives fixity and stability. Water, at the sacral, brings a sense of movement. Water is linked to the moon. Symbolically it is often interpreted as governing the emotions. Inevitably it connects with time and tide, to fertility cycles, to the patterns of menstruation and ovulation in women and the production of seminal fluid in men.

Earth and water define each other. Watercourses cut their way even through the bed-rock of earth but the earth contains them. Without water, earth is infertile and inert. With it, earth becomes alive and productive. The element of water at the sacral chakra also means that it is linked to bodily fluids such as the life-force of blood, the hydration of the body, and the fluid processes of cleansing and elimination.

Symbolically, this consideration of the interaction of the elements of water and earth teaches us a great deal about the relationship between the sacral and the root. Water needs the containment of earth, but without water earth becomes infertile and inert. Blood is life-force and the blood is fluid. The sacral chakra, then, imbues our incarnation and evolution with life-force. Apart from the general vitality which flows through us, our most potent connection to life-force is our ability to procreate and reproduce the species. Around our consciousness of this ability many powerful issues arise. They mostly accumulate around the emotive subject of sex.

Sex and Sexuality

Sex, as an instinctual drive for the furtherance of the species, belongs to the root chakra. Sexuality covers a much wider field. If earth is the containing substance for watercourses, then sex alone is the coursing of the waters, whilst sexuality is the interaction between the earth and the flowing water. It is a term which covers all aspects of gender, sexual awareness and procreation.

As the family of humanity has increased and communications have become more sophisticated, we have studied ourselves and our behaviour patterns. We are aware of concerns such as world population and its increases, decreases and distribution in relationship to world resources. We study matters of sexual potency, fertility and contraception. Using the latter, we endeavour to control patterns of population and their relationship to national or world economy. Fashions and expectations, as to the accepted size of a family, keep changing. We develop social mores and, as individuals, demand the right to make decisions about our sexual behaviours and orientation. We practise sexual intercourse and the stimulation of orgasm as an art, seeing it not only as signifying a special relationship with another human being but as a deep and intimate expression of love.

From this consciousness of sexual power and the strong motivating instinct within it, much confusion and many double standards have arisen. For Western cultures the strict morality of Victorian times actually and figuratively pushed sex into the closet. Although today there is a comparative openness about sexual behaviour and desires, it can be very difficult for a young person reaching puberty to obtain good sexual teaching and information. Often the family, which would seem the best environment in which to learn and be guided about intimate matters, is a place where sexual matters are avoided or approached with such embarrassment that only minimal knowledge is given. Information given in the school classroom may prepare young people for puberty, explain the mysteries of wet dreams, voice changes and shaving for boys, the management of menstruation for girls, the facts of sexual intercourse and the making of babies for both, but all too often this is where it stops. Full discussion of sex as an art, or of the force of bodily and emotional feelings which sexual awakening engenders, is rare. Unprejudiced, supervised opportunities for openness about homosexuality and sexual orientation are even rarer.

Despite all our knowledge, and our desire to shape and control ourselves and our world, we plunge, or are plunged, into our sexual lives, either to learn from painful experience or to acquire inhibitions which last for the rest of our lives. It is sad that such a situation exists when this is the very area of life in which we can find and acknowledge our most potent sense of co-creatorship. With feelings of passion, tenderness and orgasmic experience, we can reproduce ourselves and experience the joy of giving birth to, and nurturing, another being.

Since we have gained knowledge about fertility cycles and mechanical means of contraception it has also been more possible, within relationships, to explore sex as a celebration of our existence and as an expression of mutual love. Gildas teaches that sex which is deliberately 'not an invitation to another soul to incarnate' can channel our passions to enhance and feed our joy in life and our natural creativity for other projects. When we do not understand this more subtle fertility which we can give each other, and feel that continence or abstinence are virtues in themselves, then full understanding of ourselves as co-creators within the universe is clouded.

Lack of sexual knowledge, together with shame and inhibition about our sexuality, lead to the growth of the shadow side of sex. Promiscuity, rape, pornography, power issues and true sexual perversions become rabid social problems. In our intimate areas we feel ourselves to be most piteously at risk. We carry a corporate wound. It is not difficult to account, symbolically, for the current prevalence of AIDS, the sexually transmitted auto-immune disease.

We can help our bodies and our emotions to achieve greater harmony with our sexual drives and practices by working with the sacral and root chakras as an energy pair. When the energy flow between these two chakras is fully connected and freely flowing we can become guilt-free about our sexuality and in the control or focus of powerful urges. Thus it becomes easier for us to happily practise self-release (masturbation), continence or abstinence when necessary, learn to better respect sexual drives and orientation in ourselves and others, celebrate our sexuality as a co-creative power and exciting expression of our love for a partner, consciously rejoice in the joy of procreation and physicality, and aid the healing of any sexual, or sexually linked, physical or emotional dysfunction (see page 143 for Exercise 17, Linking Root and Sacral Energies).

Co-creativity, Empowerment, Creativity and Violence

Procreation is our primary area of co-creativity. Whatever our spiritual or metaphysical beliefs, the mystery of the creation of humanity is central and enduring. If we and other living species in the universe have been created by some divine power or explosive creative force, then embodied within us is the ability to reproduce ourselves. This must be seen as a reflection of a universe which is continually in the process of 'becoming'.

If we can reproduce ourselves, then we also create, mould or condition ourselves and the world in which we live. Currently we are experiencing the flip-side of much of what we have brought into being. As we learn from this, and reap the harvest which tells us that we need to do better, the Divine Principles or higher archetypes constantly reassert themselves (see Chapter 2, page 23). As we give attention to this reassertion, so our awareness of the privilege and empowerment of co-creativity within the universe also impinges strongly upon us. We see the laws of cause and effect fully enacted within and around us. An awesome responsibility dawns and we are required to grow beyond power, into empowerment.

Power is a *principle* and empowerment is the *process* of making use of that principle. Psychological empowerment is about having access to all our capabilities and not waiting for permission or approval from others in order to use them. The truly empowered person has overcome negative conditioning and authority issues, is free to be creative, and uses his or her creativity to empower others.

A phrase often used in groups dedicated to self-help or self-growth is 'giving away your power'. When other people, parents, teachers, society or outer authorities are seen as manipulative, judgmental or limiting, it is possible that we are *giving* them this power. We may be *allowing* them unreasonably to influence our adult choices and make unjustified demands on our time and resources. When others are set on a pedestal and made into gurus or invincible leaders, our own roles are limited to those of disciples or followers. If the idol is discovered to have feet of clay, distress can be great and the recovery period long. The empowered person respects the authority, wisdom or expertise of another without self-belittlement and becomes more empowered by the contact. True teachers and leaders seek to empower others and to work towards their own redundancy. They do not seek glamour or applause for its own sake. When we respect multiplicity of talents and celebrate each other's gifts, rather than feeling jealous or devalued by what others have, we can work towards mutual empowerment in every human relationship and contact.

Creativity is not simply about being artistic or able to make beautiful objects, but about living creatively. We may be totally unable to wield a paintbrush, use colour well, write poetry or prose, cook, sew or produce other handicrafts, yet be creative in living. We may be problem-solvers, good at relationships and mediation, inspired home-makers, appreciators of beauty or nature, in tune with incarnation, or skilled in the art of compromise and creative decision-making. The creative person maintains an ability to play, is not afraid to take risks, sustains a belief in magic, and delights in a sense of wonder. The golden child is alive and nurtured within. (For more on this, see *The River of Life*, details in the Bibliography.)

Violence often comes from frustrated sexuality and creativity. If we accept that sexual energies come from the urge to create and that violence often erupts when the creative force is unchannelled, we must look carefully at the relationship between these energies within ourselves as well as within society as a whole. Many of us turn anger or violence inwards. Rather than join the football hooligans or vandals, we inwardly destroy our own sense of worth.

When we have little sense of self-value we get stuck in dead-end situations, seeing no way out and entering the downward energy spiral of misery and depression (see page 144 for Exercise 18, Correcting the Downward Energy Spiral). This downward energy spiral is also a series of vicious circles. If our environment and circumstances are dreary we identify with them and so increasingly reflect back to ourselves that we are no good and unworthy. Anger can be a valuable catalyst in this situation. Becoming angry about our situation, the way others are treating us, or our lack of opportunity can signal the birth of self-value and respect.

If we can use the word 'outrageous' about the things which block us, then we are on our way to being able to convert our anger into creative action. We may also need to use much stronger language to express our anger and allow ourselves to stamp, scream, punch, thump and shout our rage, but within the word 'outrageous' there is the dawning of non-identification with those aspects of our lot in life which have made us feel so separated or underprivileged. 'Outrageous' says 'I am worth more'; 'Things can get better'; 'I am on the brink of change'; 'My potential to live creatively is awakening'. At a wider level it also says: 'The human condition can be improved'; 'If we work together, we can create a better society for the whole family of humanity'. The spiral exercise on page 144 may awaken any dormant sense of outrage within you. Remember that it is often the necessary prelude to the release of creative energy for life-change.

The following case study illustrates some of the ways in which frustrated creativity, sexuality and violence can interact in our lives.

Case Study: The Creative Life-Force

Living in a one-roomed flat in a near derelict house in a down-at-heel area of an inner city, Elizabeth had never really found her way in life. An only child, when she was five years old, her mother had left the marital home, taking Elizabeth with her. Shortly afterwards her parents divorced. Her father failed to make any regular arrangements to continue contact with her. His reluctance to put himself out to look after her as a child made Elizabeth conclude that she was of little interest or concern to him.

Her mother was a career woman and had a well-paid job. The financial aspects of being a single parent were not particularly pressing. Nevertheless Elizabeth was affected not only by the disruption and bewilderment of the divorce and separation from her father but by her mother's emotional turmoil and series of relationships with unsuitable men. From an early age Elizabeth began to think negatively about herself. Although she was extremely intelligent she had always under-achieved, usually joining the trouble-makers and drop-outs within the school system. Not knowing what she really wanted to do with her life, she acquired a few secretarial skills, left school and home early, lived in a bedsit, and had a series of low-paid, unstimulating jobs.

She eventually drifted into a relationship with an unemployed man, and moved in with him, to a house shared with two other out-of-work couples. Her partner and the others in the house were all musical and artistic. Elizabeth felt that she was moving into an environment where she might develop a talent she knew she had for poetry and artistic illustration. She, too, gave up work and began claiming benefits.

Elizabeth had a passionate nature and had had previous sexual experience. Initially, making love with her first live-in partner was exciting and fulfilling. In the Bohemian environment she had moved into, she felt that her artistic side was being brought out and inspired. Yet, gradually, things began to go wrong. Elizabeth discovered that she could not maintain her own space in a full-time relationship. A naturally fastidious person, the condition of the shared living conditions, especially the bathroom, became daunting. No one except herself seemed to care about cleanliness or order. Because they were all unemployed they were always in each other's way. Even the room she shared with her partner became claustrophobic. Although those around her were certainly artistically and musically gifted, they were unmotivated when it came to thoroughly practising or channelling their gifts. The vision she had glimpsed of developing her own talent in a supportive community situation shifted and died.

In these conditions Elizabeth's sense of self, already fragile, plunged to a new low. She became despondent and lethargic. Her partner, basically creatively frustrated, wanted her to experiment with some sexual variations which she found distasteful. He became sexually importunate and eventually violent towards her, destroying the last vestiges of passion and joy in the relationship. At this point Elizabeth found enough energy and sense of self-preservation to move out into a small flat lent to her by a friend who had gone abroad. She was still living there when she came to me and had been through a period of overwhelming loneliness, suicidal depression and despair. She had eventually glimpsed a chink of light at the end of the tunnel when, visiting a local market, she had bumped into one of her former dropout/troublemaker friends from her schooldays. The friend was now happily married. She had taken a silver-smithing course and produced her own jewellery which she sold at various markets and craft fairs.

The friend saw Elizabeth's dilemma and, concerned for her, invited her to come to her home. Eventually Elizabeth began to help on her friend's market stall. The friend had also become interested in yoga and, from that, in chakras and the spiritual approach to life. She lent Elizabeth one of my books and eventually they came to a workshop when I was visiting their part of the country. After the workshop Elizabeth asked me for some personal help with working with her chakras. She also realized that she needed some long-term counselling to help her deal with the enormous rages she had begun to experience and which often frightened her with their intensity.

She worked with a local counsellor and visited me from

time to time. It took a while for Elizabeth's rage to turn to outrage at what life had done to her, but when it did she quickly realized how to channel the energy of the anger into initiating changes for herself. She continued to help with her friend's jewellery marketing, which was now becoming so successful that she could be paid for what she did and gradually come off state benefits. She took a part-time art course to build up a portfolio and was eventually successful in getting a place on a foundation year and then an art degree course.

Although her relationship with her parents had been very tenuous for some years, both her father and her mother rallied round when she approached them, and supported her financially so that she could do the training of her choice.

Elizabeth valued the way in which her long-term counselling helped her to have insights and to find her inner strength, but she always maintained that the work with her chakras was a vital force in enabling her to pull back from her lowest points. She found the spiral exercise (page 144) particularly valuable in balancing her sexual and creative energies and combating depression.

SACRAL AND HEART AS A CHAKRA PAIR

The flow from the physiological and primal needs of the root chakra, into power, empowerment, sexuality, passion, creativity and greater consciousness, at the sacral, means that the sacral is the main energetic seat of the emotions. Given a reasonably free and encouraging environment, the young child is a passionate being. The developmental age for the sacral chakra covers the time in which we struggle with aspects of power, authority and dominance. To handle the temper tantrums of the three-year-old, give the necessary boundaries and yet leave the child with a sense of empowerment is a difficult task indeed. The young child *becomes* its rage. Children's emotions are often bigger than the small being can contain.

The art of emotional maturity is not as simple as learning self-control and the ability to behave appropriately to the occasion or to society's expectations. If the child experiences an emotionally wounding environment, or is disempowered or controlled through over-harsh discipline, the inner child within the adult may be seething with resentment, hostility and rage. Continued attempts by the growing adult to contain, control or repress this aspect of themselves will lead to its gaining ever greater autonomy. That which is pushed down too strenuously into unconsciousness eventually becomes more powerful than, and directly opposes, that which is seemingly determinedly held at the zenith of consciousness. The repressed, passionate child self will eventually and unexpectedly erupt in the most inappropriate situations.

Since, in a sense, the child *is* the emotion, the experience of being 'had' and controlled by emotion will continue into adult experience. The violent action immediately regretted, the words said which we wish unsaid, the bewildered question 'Whatever came over me?' are all indications that true emotional maturity has eluded us in some area of life. In chakra terms such reactions mean that the link between the sacral and the heart needs attention, since the heart is the seat of feeling which is the second, or higher level of emotion (see also Chapters 4 and 9).

If, at the developmental stage of the sacral chakra, all has been reasonably well and conditions have been 'good enough' for the child, then a certain amount of emotional control without repression will have been gained. The child will be in touch with emotion without being overwhelmed by it, but the true conversion of that emotion into the ability to *feel* without being inappropriately *emotional* happens at the heart chakra stage for which the developmental age is 12–15 years (see also page 79).

Entry into adolescence is also a time when we are in touch

with deep emotions, feelings, passions, romantic ideals and the need to 'act out' our fervours. Once again sexuality is at the forefront of life. Our physical bodies change and mature; our hormones become active; drives which may bewilder us assert themselves; and being accepted by our peer group is all-important.

If parents, teachers, the climate in which we live and the primary foundations laid at the sacral chakra are all 'good enough', we come through this period positively with our feeling selves active. We are well on our way to developing tenderness, compassion, and the ability to touch and be touched by the world around us. Our emotions become mellowed by wisdom. 'Acting out' ripens into knowing what we feel but also knowing where and how to channel that feeling without repressing it. We are fully capable of having emotions without being governed and driven by them. A seasoned quality of true feeling emerges which enables us to appreciate the higher principles of life, feel passionate about them and express them wisely in our lives.

Where there are difficulties in the natural development of this most significant link between the sacral and heart chakras, there may be much work for us to do in order to be content with our emotional and feeling lives. Working with the inner child and/or inner adolescent can help the psychological healing process (see also page 91 and Exercises 13 and 28). Energetically, this growth can be initiated, aided and supported by working with the sacral/heart chakra connection (see Exercise 19, page 146).

The Emotional Body

The relationship between sacral and heart chakras introduces another subtle body into the energetic system. This is the emotional body which carries the record of all our emotional development. When the heart chakra is balanced and a sound feeling body is developed, then there is the potential for a good relationship between the emotional and feeling bodies. A balanced emotional body, resulting from working energetically with the sacral/heart connection, lays a strong foundation for healing within the psyche and energy systems.

In recent years the 'stiff upper lip' characteristic of the British has been much criticized. This has led to psychological encouragement for repressed emotions from the past (that which is stored in the emotional body) to be contacted and acted out as an essential part of any full healing or growth process. To some extent this is correct but sometimes it can go too far.

Our lives are difficult when our emotional bodies 'lead' us. Through the mechanism of repression and the formation of the shadow side of our natures (see the entry for Shadow in the Glossary), the emotional body can be in the lead without us being fully aware of it. By placing *too much* emphasis on emotional ventilation, the emotional body can also become the leading aspect. This makes it more, rather than less, difficult for us to leave past hurts behind. It affects the present by producing irrational behaviour patterns and inhibiting the ability to make considered choices. Acting out can become addictive. Too much control can lead to bizarre and dissociated emotional eruptions. A strong energetic connection between root and sacral chakras (as encouraged by Exercise 17, page 143.) brings the necessary balance and interaction between the emotional and feeling bodies.

Romantic and Enduring Love

Let me make it clear that I consider romance to be one of the ingredients of magic. It is, therefore, of great importance among the delights and experiences of life. When there is imbalance, however, in the sacral/heart connection, and between the emotional and feeling bodies, romance can become an obstacle to enduring love.

The stylized illustration of the heart has become a symbol or sign for romantic love. We all hope to enter into the spirit of St Valentine's Day and the reminders it can bring of love's young dream. When used to keep that aspect of love alive within a relationship, it can be very positive.

It is the expectation within the dream of romantic love which can be at fault. Inevitably, in lasting relationships the mundane has to be faced and many relationships have failed because the Prince and his Princess no longer recognize each other behind the frowns over bills or after suffering sleepless nights and dealing with soggy, smelly nappies. We are often conditioned by popular fiction and magazines to expect that romance will continue without us having to work at it. In such cases, when the expectation proves false, the ability to develop enduring love founders.

Another aspect of romantic love which can prevent the growth of the emotional maturity on which enduring love is based is that of possessiveness and jealousy. These emotions cause agonies for the adolescent as first passions and loves develop. Where they exist too strongly in a relationship they are a sign that the link between the emotional and feeling bodies is insufficiently activated. Rather than ensuring constancy of affection, the possessiveness, insecurities, control mechanisms and hurts (real or imagined) which come from jealousy, can drive relationships apart and block the growth of the natural fidelity which is based on mutual respect.

When love is unable to mature, then, once again, the emotional and feeling bodies will usually be out of balance, and Exercise 17 (page 143) can be invaluable when a relationship is going through a difficult patch. When these energetic connections are sound, decisions about the potential in relationships also become clearer. There is less likelihood of 'hanging in there' for the wrong reasons, more strength to weather the mundane, and also, perhaps paradoxically, more likelihood of being able to keep true romance alive despite the obstacles to it.

Twin Souls

Our expectations of love and partnership are also coloured by our desire or drive to find our twin souls. On page 50 Gildas describes the start of the evolutionary journey. The original spark from the Source splits into yin and yang and these become complementary soul threads or stems, each carrying the beads or flowers of potential incarnations.

Gildas goes on to say:

> The longing for the twin soul is well known. When evolution is complete, which means that all the beads on the thread have incarnated and returned, the two strands or stems will become one again. During incarnation, until that is possible, a flower from one stem or a bead from one strand may meet with a flower or bead from its twin essence, but twin souls do not always incarnate at the same time.
>
> The complete being does not incarnate. The flowers from the stems or the beads from the threads are aspects of the essential soul. As many as seven aspects from each stem or strand may be incarnate at any one time and, if they meet, will have a very close relationship. Again, this meeting is rare, since the purpose of incarnation is to gain experience. The impulse behind putting out more than one aspect at a particular period is to ensure as broad a knowledge of that historical earth era as possible. The number of beads on a thread or flowers on a stem varies from soul to soul.
>
> There have been periods in your history where it was more common for twin souls to meet, such as in Atlantean, Egyptian, Grecian or Native American Indian incarnations. In the present time an extraordinary amount of work is often taken on during the course of one incarnation and this means that meeting with twin souls is discouraged by the karmic advisers and helpers. The danger is that the two

beings may be so absorbed in each other that the degree to which they move forward their learning process is lessened. With the dawning of the Golden Age it will be *usual* for twin souls to be working together in incarnation once more. Now, the range of available experience is very great and twin souls must tend to live separately in order to cover as much evolutionary ground as possible.

It may be both disconcerting and disappointing to realize that we are unlikely to meet our perfect mate, or other half, in this present incarnation. Yet, once we know and understand this, a certain discontent and longing in us may be put to rest, as our expectations of the partners we do meet become more realistic. When this particular spiritual perspective is taken, we can see life as an evolutionary workplace and understand more about the overall organization and intent behind the system in which we operate.

The unlikelihood of meeting with our twin souls does not rule out the many possibilities of meeting members of our soul family or wider soul group. These meetings can bring great joy and a great sense of companionship, as well as giving opportunities to be each other's teachers and supporters (see also page 82).

ROOT, SACRAL AND HEART AS A CHAKRA TRIAD

We have so far considered the root/sacral and sacral/heart chakras as separate pairs. Yet these three centres also form an important energetic triad.

Working with the root and sacral chakras helps to stop upsurges of greed and imbalances of power which affect us both personally and collectively. Yet when there is a full, vigorous interaction and balance between the triad now under discussion an important humanizing and tenderizing factor is added. If this particular equilibrium is present, we can rule and shape our microcosmic worlds in a positive way which reflects out into the macrocosm. When the heart link in the triad has yet to be made, we find it harder to throw off conditioning or expectations from the macrocosm, are over-affected by the negativity 'out there', and tend to lose touch with our potential for co-creativity.

Power Games

If the root and sacral pair are insufficiently in communication we tend to get caught up in the playing of power games and the creation of false hierarchies. We can become obsessed with material and worldly power, seemingly blind to any sense of spiritual purpose. Though we may work with the root/sacral pair because we recognize, even minimally, such tendencies within ourselves and want to bring them into harmony as part of our spiritual journey, it is at the collective level that we can see the fullest effects of what can happen when root and sacral are imperfectly connected.

In an era where power, greed and materialism have become false gods, it is important to work with the chakra triad as well as the pairs under discussion. The triadic energy connection complements and enhances the work already done with the pairs. The qualities of touch and tenderness from the heart temper our ability to handle power and to produce good leaders.

Throughout spiritual and religious history, leadership has often been used negatively. The heart dimension frequently gets lost when there is an over-emphasis on dogma and where religious and spiritual practice is based on the enlisting of an elitist few. Belief in a jealous god who breeds fear in would-be followers or devotees is dangerous. Spiritual practice should empower, not disempower and render vulnerable.

Equally, in more worldly terms, leaders who have no true root/sacral/heart triadic connection may be intent on personal gain and power over others. Where there are also imbalances in the relevant single chakras or chakric pairs, only dictatorship – with all its potential for engendering negative anarchy – can result.

When leaders have more of the triadic energy flowing they become more positively and spiritually aligned with the positive potential of leadership for shaping a harmonious world for all. They are more likely to work for the fulfilment of human potential and the empowerment of the individual for the good of the whole. In *The Tao of Leadership* (see Bibliography), John Heider describes the qualities cultivated by leaders with the root/sacral/heart triad in alignment. He says:

The greatest administrators do not achieve production through constraints and limitations. They provide opportunities.

Good leadership consists of motivating people to their highest levels by offering them opportunities, not obligations.

That is how things happen naturally. Life is an opportunity and not an obligation . . .

The group will not prosper if the leader grabs the lion's share of the credit for the good work that has been done.

The group will rebel and resist if the leader relies on strict controls in an effort to make things come out a certain way.

The group members will become deadened and unresponsive if the leader is critical and harsh.

The wise leader is not greedy, selfish, defensive or demanding. That is why the leader can be trusted to allow any event to unfold naturally . . .

Natural events are cyclical, always changing from one extreme toward an opposite . . .

. . . That is the way of nature: to relax what is tense, to fill what is empty, to reduce what is overflowing.

But a society based on materialism and the conquest of nature works to overcome these cycles. If some is good,

more must be better and an absolute glut seems best. At
the same time, those who have little get even less. By
serving others and being generous, the leader knows
abundance. By being selfless, the leader helps others
realize themselves. By being a disinterested facilitator,
unconcerned with praise or pay, the leader becomes
potent and successful.

When we are insecure in ourselves we seek aggressive power
over others, or become victims, so colluding with patterns of
tyranny and oppression. If we seek control of others (because
we fear that if they were free they might destroy us) we cannot
move to the vision of empowered individuals who mutually
empower. If we fear the breakdown of the old order, we can
only become prisoners of its structure.

Feelings of insecurity can also make us both greedy and
miserly. We stockpile in order to be certain of supplies, but
fear to use them in case they should be impossible to replenish.
From our greed eventually come waste *and* scarcity, evidenced
by such contemporary scandals as the 'butter mountain' and
the destruction of surplus harvests in times of glut or abundance, whilst some of our fellow human beings in the Third
World are starving.

Lack of self-worth underlies much of the materialistic ethos.
Uncertain of our own inner empowerment, we need to make
ourselves important or notable by what we possess. Once again,
we create waste by discarding the old in order to be in the
vanguard of fashion. We become a ravening consumer society
by building a calculated obsolescence into that which we manu-
facture.

Even when we have worked with root/sacral and sacral/
heart connections, until the triadic energy is also flourishing
we can remain stuck in the pursuit of material objectives. We
can lose, or fail to develop, vision or imagination and continue
to live in a world where dictatorships, tyrants, victims, and false
hierarchies show us to be driven by frustrated and unresolved

power and emotional issues. Working with the chakra pairs of this chapter lays down the foundation on which the triadic (root/sacral/heart) connection can be built. The activation of the pairs (root/sacral; sacral/heart) will help us to heal ourselves as individuals, but the healing which permeates out into society does not proceed until an optimum number of us have perceived the different, richer, harmonies which are made possible by activating the root/sacral/heart triad.

When this triad is positively functioning, we become:

- more aware of inner wealth
- more creative in shaping our world
- more discerning in our choice of leaders
- more conscious of the part we, as individuals, may play in creating the poverty or deprivation of others
- more trusting in an abundant universe and therefore more able to link a respect for natural growth patterns and fertility to a true sharing of resources
- more in touch with our self-empowerment and therefore able to be more generous-hearted and empowering towards others
- less motivated by jealousies and envies
- less authoritarian
- less subject to, or enslaved by, swings of fashion.

Diana, Princess of Wales

Much of this book is being written in the aftermath of the sudden death of Diana, Princess of Wales. Reflection on Princess Diana's life and the outcome of her death will bring a deeper understanding of the effect which a person with a strongly functioning root/sacral/heart triad can have on the shaping of collective and individual worlds.

Princess Diana became a popular and compassionate woman who, in addition to her capacity for unconditional love (see also page 243), fully demonstrated in her life the need to link power issues to the heart chakra.

She saw the human being behind each dilemma and the human suffering which continues whilst protocol procrastinates and red tape proliferates. She constantly overcame the divide between the falsely elevated and the ordinary. She knew that she had the human power to make ripples on stagnant ponds and did not shrink from making them. She campaigned for social justice and effectively used her outrage at some aspects of the common human lot.

Despite a tremendous and often desperate struggle, in the face of unmitigating odds, she attained that self-worth which is free from overweening pride and therefore also empowers others to a better vision of self and to hope for the future. Notwithstanding her experience of personal tragedy she maintained an infectious sense of joy, light and healing, which touched, lifted and blessed many, even in the midst of their own harsh encounters with life, sickness, disability, or certain death.

THE ARCHETYPES: CREATIVITY, PEACE, SEXUALITY, POWER AND ABUNDANCE

Creativity

A useful definition of creativity on which to reflect is: 'The coming together of two known but separate forces to produce a new, previously unknown or unmanifest force.'

When we take a spiritual overview of many lifetimes and believe in the interaction of our souls in making incarnational choices, we can see that we do indeed create our own world in the widest sense. Learning to go on co-creating our personal world by linking personality development to the evolution of the soul is a prime objective of spiritual growth. Thus creativity, with its closely connected partner, co-creativity, becomes a driving force by which we live. As such, it is an archetype.

As an archetype, creativity signifies the powerful intercourse between those most basic principles of the universe, yin and yang. Creativity thus incorporates many aspects of sexuality and of our relationships with each other and the universe.

The connections between the root and sacral, and the sacral and heart chakras, are essential to generating spiritual creativity (see Exercise 17, page 143). There is also more about creativity on page 122.

Peace

When there are positive energetic links between the root and sacral, and the sacral and heart chakras, a sense of peace is generated. This background of energetic peace within ourselves can enable us to work out our difficulties even in the emotionally loaded areas of sexuality and violence.

Sometimes we may see peace as a very passive quality, but in reality it is close to harmony which is active and interactive. When a musical note is sounded it reverberates and resonates and causes other notes, with which it is in harmony or relationship, to reverberate back. Peace is a note. When it sounds within us and from us it produces other resonating sounds which positively affect our lives and relationships. The energy balances and movements brought about by practising the exercises on pages 143–7 will help to harmonize your energy system and generate your own personal peace notes. When we sound peace notes in our personal energy fields they reverberate out into the atmosphere, finding and creating resonances in others. When we are considering peace it is particularly true that, if we want to create change around us, we do well to start with ourselves (see Exercise 22, page 149).

Sexuality

A guided journey in a workshop on sexuality and spirituality involved a meeting with the archetype of sexuality. When the archetype was asked to speak, and show some of its many facets, several of the group members had an experience in which the archetype expressed distress at the way in which it had become laden with heavy and negative baggage from humanity. The positive side of the archetype is full of joy, spontaneity, fun, laughter and creativity. It is about celebration of womanhood and manhood and the tremendous potential which exists between the sexes and between the yin/yang principles within each one of us and the universe (see also 'creativity', page 138).

In the area of sexuality we have been given many prohibitions and inhibitions. The dark side of sexuality (rape, sexual abuse, violence, repression and pornography) is very prevalent in our world today. It is very sobering to reflect on what has happened to an archetype which is at the source of the life-force.

As we consider the archetype as an aid to personal healing, we need to look at what we personally have placed upon its shoulders. Seeing what we have to release, and the bright side which the archetype has to offer, can help to shape, activate and direct any healing we need in the areas of sex and sexuality (see Exercise 23, page 150).

Power

Power is an energy. In itself it is neither bad nor good, merely a force to be reckoned with. If we think in terms of 'power to' and 'power of' we are likely to complete the phrase with more positive words and sentiments than if we think in terms of 'power over'. In the spiritual sense we may refer to the 'power to heal', the 'power of healing' or 'the power of prayer'.

Part of the *Chambers' English Dictionary*'s definition of power reads:

ability to do anything – physical, mental, spiritual, legal, etc; capacity for producing an effect; strength; energy; faculty of the mind; moving force of anything; right to command; authority; rule; influence; control; governing office; permission to act; potentiality; strong influence or rule

Power is almost synonymous with life-force. Without it, life goes into stasis. It is an energy which powers the creation and continuity of the universe and at the same time a force which can be used for physical, mental, emotional or spiritual destruction. It is an intensity within us which demands that we come to terms with it. Without power we cannot function. If it is wrongly distributed or managed it can lead to great suffering. The power of the Divine is 'aweful'; the consequences of temporal power can be both 'aweful' *and* 'awful'!

As an archetype, power includes authority and leadership. Our personal power or empowerment is affected by our interaction with, and our relationship to, these factors of society.

Power is often automatically seen as something rigid, negative or destructive. This interpretation of the archetype says much about our frequent inability to come to terms with it. Religious and spiritual teachings tend to leave us confused about our inner power/divinity by facing us with unresolved and paradoxical questions: 'Are we created in the image of God, maintaining an essence or spark of the Divine within? or 'Are we outcast, miserable sinners, unworthy of the Divine, and with the inner spark either non-existent or extinguished by our misdemeanours?'

Contemplating power as an archetype means being aware of its potential for misuse and yet also learning to come to terms with it as a pure and vital force of divine origin. It means learning to use this force for inner change and attaining the belief that all obstacles can be either overcome or transformed.

Abundance

We can see abundance as an archetype only if we hold the belief that it is a Divine Principle. Religious teachings, together with spiritual paths and disciplines, have tended to lead us to regard self-deprivation and the practice of abstinence as virtues. Hedonism is often seen as the ultimate obstacle to spirituality. Paradoxically, religious thinkers have sometimes seen the rich man as divinely blessed or favoured and the poor man as having smaller hope of, or right to, divine favour. Though the hymn 'All Things Bright and Beautiful' has been many people's favourite, and speaks of abundance, it used to contain the controversial verse:

> The rich man in his castle,
> The poor man at his gate,
> The Lord God made them all
> And ordered their estate.

Perhaps another lesson which Diana, Princess of Wales, had to teach us, was that of living abundantly. Worldly wealth apart, she threw herself into life and drew an abundance of experience towards her. By so-doing she rendered herself vulnerable. She even suffered from, but overcame, anorexia and bulimia, those disorders of our times which symbolically say so much about our abundance/scarcity confusions.

Fear of life, and fear of scarcity, create not only greed, but transgressions against the archetype of abundance. We tend to believe that things are rationed and will run out; then transfer this belief to things emotional – particularly love. In this way we become comparative and competitive. 'Who do you love best?', 'Who do you love most?', 'Do you love me as much as him?', are questions many of us ask of parents during childhood, or of lovers during adolescence. It seems that we go on asking those questions of gods, goddesses or the universe, for most of our lives.

We tend to divide people around us into those we love and those we don't. Of course there will always be natural affinities and attractions (see page 132) but over-quantifying and thinking in polarities makes it difficult for us to get to that place of feeling and acceptance where we cherish the whole underlying essence of humanity and are both moved and inspired by the human condition. Before we can truly open to abundance we must recognize that we, personally, are cherishable and that the universe has the potential to cherish us.

There is nothing wrong with material abundance and we do not have to misuse resources in order to create it. In every field of our endeavours it is not what we possess which is wrong, but our attitude to it. Non-attachment, an oft-quoted and oft-misinterpreted key word for the spiritual path, does not mean that we cannot possess – only that we should not hoard and use possessions as a means of acquiring power. Abundance is a flow. *Over-attachment* to what we possess creates unlawful dams in the river. If we wish to create material abundance in our lives and release hang-ups about money we must come to terms with the archetype of abundance and see ourselves as worthy of, and having full permission to, receive and possess.

Being taught to hold something back and never to go 'over the top' are contradictions to, and denials of, abundance as an archetype. Setting norms puts those who do not conform 'beyond the fringe' and can be a denial of creativity (which is closely related to, and inspired by, abundance). If we can create and therefore live creatively, abundance will never fail. Linking the root, sacral and heart chakra triad will help us identify any personal blockages, insecurities and 'hang-ups' which may be preventing the manifestation of abundance in our lives. It will also activate and heal energy patterns within us which attract the abundance flow.

EXERCISES

Exercise 17
Connecting the Sacral and Root Chakras

For this exercise you should sit or stand with your spine straight and supported if necessary. Your legs should be uncrossed, unless sitting in a full cross-legged, semi-lotus or lotus position.

- Begin with central column breathing (see page 17).
- When you feel centred, let your breathing rhythm help you to focus your attention into your sacral chakra. Breathe in and out through your sacral chakra, taking the breath in through the petals and breathing it out through the stem. You can either concentrate solely on the breath rhythm or, if you wish, you can also visualize an amber or orange colour, thus combining two exercises for activating your sacral chakra (see page 156 for more description and explanation of these colours).
- After five to ten in/out breaths through your sacral chakra, change the pattern by breathing into the centre of the chakra, holding the breath for a count of three, and then breathing down into your root chakra and out deeply into the earth for a further five to ten in/out breaths. (If using colour visualization at the same time, you should still be working with amber or orange.)
- If you are using colour as well as breath, change the colour now to either a deep rosy red, or to mauve (see page 41). Breathe up from the earth into the centre of your root chakra, hold the breath there for a count of three, then breathe up into the centre of your sacral chakra and out through its petals (five to ten in/out breaths).
- Finish this linking exercise by using again the sacral–root–earth breath sequence described above (last step but one).

Exercise 18
Correcting the Downward Energy Spiral

Sit or stand with your spine straight for this exercise (as for Exercise 17, above).

- Begin with central column breathing (see page 17).
- When you feel centred, breathe in and out through the

petals of your sacral chakra. Visualize a spiral of energy
which flows down from the centre of your sacral chakra
through the downward-pointing petals of your root
chakra and into the earth. (*When this spiral is out of balance,
as described on pages 171–72, the energy dissipates, either in the
root chakra itself, or as it reaches the earth, without becoming
engaged in an essential, complementary, upward flow.*) To
correct or strengthen the complementary flow, imagine a
huge diamond lying deep within the earth. Visualize the
downward energy spiral from the sacral chakra going
deeply and strongly down through the earth into this
diamond crystal. Use your breath to help you to breathe
the spiral strongly downwards and into the diamond (five
to ten in/out breaths).

• Now visualize a strong upward-flowing energy spiral,
coming from the diamond crystal in the earth, up through
your root chakra, through your sacral chakra, on up via the
central column, through your solar plexus chakra, to
the centre of your heart chakra. Assist this energy spiral on
its journey by breathing it up. When it reaches the centre
of your heart chakra breathe it out through the petals of
your heart, keeping the sense of the spiral strongly in
mind (five to ten in/out breaths).

This exercise is similar to the central column breathing
described in Exercise 1 (page 17). But here the emphasis is
on correcting the energy spiral so that there are no power
loop backs between the sacral and root chakras (see also
page 171).

Exercise 19
Connecting the Sacral and Heart Chakras

Position yourself as for Exercise 17 (see page 143).

- Begin with central column breathing (see page 17).
- Breathe in through the petals of your sacral chakra and out through its stem. If you wish to visualize colour at the same time as focusing on the breath, use amber or gold (see page 156) (five to ten in/out breath sequences).
- Breathe in through the petals of your sacral chakra (still using amber or gold if you wish). Hold the breath in the centre of the sacral chakra to a count of three, then breathe up through the central column into the centre of your heart chakra, and out through the petals of your heart (five to ten in/out breath sequences).
- Breathe in through the petals of your heart and out through its stem. If you wish to use colour at the same time work with spring green (see page 101) (five to ten in/ out breath sequences).
- Breathe in through the petals of your heart chakra, still using the spring green visualization if you wish. Hold the breath in the centre of the heart for a count of three. Breathe down through the central column into the centre of your sacral chakra and out through its petals (five to ten in/out breath sequences).

Exercise 20
Connecting the Root/Sacral/Heart triad

Position yourself as for Exercise 17 (see page 143).

- Begin with central column breathing (see page 17).
- When you feel centred, begin to breathe in and out

through the petals of your heart chakra (five to ten in/ out breath sequences).

- Now breathe in to the centre of your heart chakra, hold your breath for a count of three, and then breathe down through the central column into the centre of your sacral chakra. Breathe out through the petals of your sacral chakra (five to ten in/out breath sequences).
- Breathe in through the petals of your sacral chakra, hold the breath in the centre of your sacral chakra for a count of three, and then breathe down into the centre of your root chakra and out through its petals into the earth (five to ten in/out breath sequences).
- Breathe in through the petals of your root chakra, hold the breath in its centre for a count of three, breathe up through your central column into your heart chakra and out through the petals of your heart (five to ten in/out breath sequences).
- Now take a deep breath in through the petals of your heart chakra, visualizing it as an energy stream which travels out through the stem of your heart chakra, down your spine and in through the stem of your sacral chakra to its centre, and then down, through your central column to your root chakra, and out into the earth (five to ten in/ out breath sequences).
- Breathe in through the downward-facing petals of your root chakra, and visualize your breath as a stream of energy which comes into the centre of your sacral chakra, out through its stem, up your spine, in through the stem of your heart and out through your heart chakra petals (five to ten in/out breath sequences).
- Conclude this exercise with central column breathing for a further five to ten in/out breath sequences.

Exercise 21
*Guided Visualization for Contacting the Archetype of
Creativity*

Making sure that you will be undisturbed and that you have
paper, writing and drawing materials to hand, sit or lie down
in a comfortable position, with a blanket for warmth if
necessary. Your body should be symmetrically arranged and
your legs should not be crossed at the knees or ankles.

• Begin with central column breathing (see page 17). When
  you feel centred, let your breath rhythm help you to focus
  on, and thus activate, your root chakra and your sacral
  chakra.
• Now bring the breath rhythm into your heart chakra so
  that each in-breath and out-breath activates your heart
  energy . . . Travel on the heart breath into your inner world
  or landscape and find yourself in a meadow . . . As you
  experience your meadow, activate all your inner senses so
  that you see the objects and colours . . . hear the
  sounds . . . touch the textures . . . smell the fragrances . . .
  and taste the tastes . . .
• As you look out into the landscape from your meadow, you
  can see a beautiful rainbow . . . The spot where the
  rainbow begins (or ends), rising up powerfully from the
  earth, is very clear . . . You know that in your inner world
  you can do that which is improbable in the outer . . . You
  can travel to the spot where the rainbow has its source . . .
  When you arrive at this magical place the colours are very
  clear . . . They are so tangible as to be almost touchable . . .
  They seem to have a fragrance and a sound . . . Within this
  rainbow of light, if you invite it to do so, the archetype of
  creativity will appear, and as you watch, will blend these
  wondrous colours for your entertainment . . . They will be
  mixed, matched, blended, until new colours of every shade,

depth and texture appear for you . . . Note how two known colours, blended together in different ways, can produce new colour ranges and tones . . . In observing this, you are observing the basic interaction of the force which is creativity . . .

- As you watch, if you have any pressing life problem or question which needs an answer or solution, become aware of it and ask that it may receive a blessing from the archetype of creativity . . . If there is no particular problem you want to bring here, then ask that your own inner creativity be blessed and inspired . . .
- When you have been with the archetype of creativity for not more than fifteen minutes, thank the archetype for its presence, and leave the rainbow source . . . Come back to the meadow where you began this visualization . . . Gradually become aware of the rhythm of your breathing in your heart centre . . . Feel your body in touch with your chair or the floor . . . Come fully back into the outer world . . . Visualize a cloak of light with a hood right around you . . .
- Take time to draw and record your journey.

Exercise 22
Reflection for Contacting the Archetype of Peace

Making sure that you will be undisturbed, sit or lie in a comfortable position, with your body symmetrically arranged. Unless sitting in a cross-legged or lotus posture do not cross your legs at the knees or ankles. Support your spine if necessary and have a rug for warmth if you wish.

- Begin with central column breathing (see page 17).
- When you feel centred, breathe in through the petals of your sacral chakra, into its centre, and then down through

the root chakra and out into the earth . . . (five to ten in/ out breath sequences).

- Now breathe in through the petals of your heart chakra, into its centre and then down through the central column, through the centre of the sacral chakra, through the root and out into the earth . . . (five to ten in/out breath sequences).
- Continue breathing from your heart chakra down into the earth and begin to recite, mentally, the mantram 'At peace', repeating the two words over and over again, and letting any thoughts or images which come to you during this process pass by as though on a television screen in front of you, so that you are noting them without engaging with them . . . (ten to fifteen minutes).
- Visualize a cloak of light with a hood around you and then write down or draw any impressions about peace which came to you during this reflection.

Exercise 23
Guided Visualization for Contacting the Archetype of Sexuality

There are two possible stages in this visualization. The first takes you to the archetype of sexuality in its most positive form. The second gives you the opportunity to ask the archetype to show you any negativity it is carrying for you. You can do both parts of the visualization on the same occasion if you wish, separate them by a period of time or, if your sexuality needs a lot of healing, make sure you only do the second part when you are completely ready or can be supported by a trusted friend, partner or counsellor.

Making sure that you will be undisturbed, and that you have paper, writing and drawing materials to hand, sit or lie down in a comfortable position, with a blanket for warmth if necessary. Your body should be symmetrically arranged and, unless sitting in a cross-legged or lotus position, your legs should not be crossed at the knees or ankles.

- Begin with central column breathing (see page 17). When you feel centred, let your breath rhythm help you to focus on, and thus activate, your root chakra and your sacral chakra.
- Now bring the breath rhythm into your heart chakra so that each in-breath and out-breath activates your heart energy . . . Travel on the heart breath into your inner world or landscape and find yourself in a meadow . . . As you experience your meadow, activate all your inner senses so that you see the objects and colours . . . hear the sounds . . . touch the textures . . . smell the fragrances . . . and taste the tastes . . .
- Find a quiet, sunny spot in the meadow where you can sit and reflect for a while . . . It is good to sit with your back against a tree or a rock . . . As you reflect, in preparation for your journey to meet the archetype of sexuality, consider any questions you would like to ask and be aware of any aspects of your sexuality which need healing . . . (five minutes).
- From the meadow you can view your landscape. . . Begin now to look around and as you do so, express the wish to meet with the archetype of sexuality. . . Somewhere on higher ground in your landscape you can see an area of light and you know that this is the place where you can meet safely with the archetype. . . In the next three minutes travel to this place of light and once again find somewhere where you can sit comfortably and ask the archetype to appear. . . Remember that you are meeting the clear archetype of sexuality, in its most positive form. . .

The two stages for working with the archetype are now given. You may wish to read again the suggestions given above, at the start of this exercise.

Stage 1

- When the archetype appears to you, ask it any question you have or tell it about any healing you need for your sexuality . . . The archetype may speak to you, you may get an inner knowing, or you may see a symbol or be given a symbolic gift . . . (five to ten minutes).

If you are not proceeding to Stage 2, return now to your meadow, to your awareness of your breathing and of your body in contact with the chair or floor. Put a cloak of light with a hood around you and take time to draw and record your journey.

Stage 2

- You may now ask the archetype of sexuality to show you anything of a more negative nature which it is carrying for you and ask it for help in releasing any fears, inhibitions or negative beliefs which may prevent you from owning your true sexual nature and orientation . . . (five minutes).
- Ask the archetype of sexuality how you can help to relieve it, and yourself, of these particular burdens . . . Again, you may inwardly hear the archetype speak, experience an inner knowing, see a symbol, or be given a symbolic gift . . . (five minutes).
- Knowing that, once you have used an area of your inner landscape, you can always return, thank and take leave of the archetype of sexuality, and return to your meadow . . . From your meadow become aware of your breathing and of your body in contact with the chair or floor . . . Visualize a cloak of light with a hood right around you . . . Come fully back into the outer world and take time to draw and record your journey.

Exercise 24
Reflection on Your Connection with the Archetype of Power

Making sure that you will be undisturbed and with paper, drawing and writing materials to hand, sit or lie down in a comfortable position, with your spine straight, your body symmetrical and your legs uncrossed at the knees or ankles. Have a rug for warmth if you wish.

- Begin with central column breathing (see page 17).
- When you feel centred, begin to write a letter to the archetype of power. Make the theme of this letter a review of your life, starting from the present and going back as far as you wish, in seven-year stages, recalling all the life events which have affected your relationship with power.
- You might begin, for instance, with today's date and then:

> Dear Archetype of Power,
>   At the present moment I feel in charge of my life in the following areas . . .
>   I feel less in charge when I am put into a difficult position by . . .
>   Seven years ago, the things in my life connected with power were . . .
>   Seven years before that you were helping me to . . .

- Go back to around the time of your birth if you can. Although you will not remember this time, you will have been told things about your birth and the circumstances in which it took place. Reflect on, and write or draw about the balance of power in the family at the time that you were born.
- If you do not wish to write in full, you can make key word notes of your life-review or make a series of drawings.

• If you do not want to do your whole life at one sitting, you can spread this exercise over a period of time.

Exercise 25
Inner Abundance (A Guided Journey)

Making sure that you will be undisturbed and with pens, drawing materials and paper to hand, sit or lie down in a comfortable position with your spine straight, your body symmetrically arranged and, unless sitting in a cross-legged or lotus position, have your legs uncrossed at the knees or ankles. Have a rug for warmth if you wish.

• Begin with central column breathing (see page 17).
• When you feel centred, begin to breathe in and out through the petals of your heart chakra . . . Travel on your heart breath, into your inner landscape and find yourself in a meadow . . .
• Take the opportunity of being in the meadow, to activate your inner senses . . . See the objects and the colours . . . Hear the sounds . . . Small the fragrances . . . Touch the textures . . . Taste the tastes . . .
• You are going to take an overview of your inner landscape and you can choose how you wish accomplish this:
  – You might travel to a high point in your landscape.
  – You might fly on a magic carpet, which you can call to you and which is totally in your control.
  – You might ride on a horse, a unicorn, a winged horse or winged unicorn, on a large bird, or on the back of some other inner animal.
  – You might ascend on a rainbow, a single colour, a sunbeam or moonbeam.
  – You might fly, hand in hand, with an inner wise figure, guardian or angel.
• You may make a conscious choice of your mode of

transport, or it may appear naturally, in your
visualization . . . When you are ready to travel, set out to
survey your landscape, taking the key word 'Abundance'
with you . . .

• As you travel, become aware of all the areas of your
  landscape which are lush, fruitful and beautiful . . .
  Anything representing abundance can be present in your
  landscape:
  – Fields of ripe corn
  – Orchards full of blossoms or fruits
  – Full-flowing rivers or waterfalls
  – Lush water meadows
  – Tree-covered mountain slopes with alpine meadows,
    where cows graze
  – Blue seas, with sandy shores
  – Beautiful lakes
  – Thick, fertile forests
  – Places warmed but not burned by the sun
  – Areas abundant with flowers
  – Crystal and jewelled caves
  – Gold or silver mines, well looked after and not blotting
    the landscape
  – Places of abundant peace
  – Ever-burning, but non-consuming, fires or flames
  – Deep, fish-filled oceans
  – Places of abundant wildlife
  These are suggestions, you may find any or all of these or
  other different areas which represent abundance for you . . .

• Take about ten minutes for this overview of your inner
  abundance and then return to your meadow . . .

• Spend a few moments in your meadow, before you return
  to the outer world, to reflect on the abundance within, its
  distribution and the ease with which you found it . . .

• Ask yourself how you feel about this inner abundance . . .

• Thank any companions you had for this journey, return
  from your meadow, to the consciousness of your breathing

in your heart centre . . . your awareness of your body and your outer surroundings . . . Visualize a cloak of light, with a hood of light right around you . . .

- Take time to draw or record your journey and to reflect on anything it may teach you about your inner relationship with abundance.

THE COLOURS

The colours for the sacral chakra are: orange, amber and gold (non-metallic). They are colours of vitality.

Positively, orange is warming and energizing. To some people, in its more vivid forms it can be experienced as enervating or confrontational. If this is your personal reaction to orange, focus more on amber and gold shades.

When convalescing from illness, feeling tired or just needing an energy boost, visualizing orange light flowing into your sacral chakra will be effective. A bowl of oranges in a room, or some orange or amber glass hanging in a window where sunlight can pass through it also helps general vitality and the development of the sacral chakra.

Negative tones of orange are disharmonizing and can generate unrest or even violence.

Amber is a colour which we use in everyday life to indicate caution – or proceed with caution. In other words it is used to remind us to be aware. One of the most basic and effective spiritual lessons is to learn to 'be present' at all times and in all situations. Being present also helps us protect ourselves from the unexpected or negative sides of life. When our presence is finely attuned we automatically pre-empt situations. We are 'on the ball' and can therefore prepare ourselves for action, whether it be for avoidance, confrontation or participation.

On the negative side, amber may make us over-cautious or generate non-specific fears and anxieties.

Non-metallic gold is a warm, glowing colour which generates creativity, especially in human relationships.

Negative or murky tones of gold can cause depression or lethargy.

Use these colours as suggested in Exercise 8 (page 42) to develop, awaken and heal your sacral chakra.

The colours for the root chakra are red, brown and mauve; and, for the heart chakra, spring green, rose and rose amethyst. To strengthen the colours in your root and heart chakras, refer to Exercise 8 (page 42).

THE FRAGRANCES

Musk and amber stimulate the sacral centre, while rosemary and rose-geranium quieten it. Musk oil is a plant product, as is amber, and these fragrances should not be confused with the animal extracts often used in the perfume industry. Use the stimulating fragrances if you have a tendency to be rather passive, lacking in vitality, have difficulty in making choices or need more sexual vitality. Use the quietening fragrances if you are over-active, fear loss of control or find it difficult to 'play', relax or sleep.

For the root chakra the quietening fragrances are cedarwood and patchouli, and the stimulating ones are musk, lavender and hyacinth. For the heart chakra the quietening fragrances are sandalwood and rose, and the stimulating ones are pine and honeysuckle. See page 43 for suggestions for using the fragrances.

You can experiment with blending fragrances for the sacral/ root and sacral/heart connections.

THE CRYSTALS

Refer to page 44 and the Glossary for general guidance on using crystals. The crystals which will best help the issues considered in this chapter are:

Agate To strengthen your relationship to life and bring a *joie de vivre*. It encourages abundance and helps to heal fears of, or wounds from, poverty and deprivation. It balances inner masculine and feminine energies. It helps us to be good parents to our children.

Aventurine To help release blocked creativity and activate the imagination.

Jasper This is a stone of power and empowerment. The water element is often interpreted as being unstable and over-sensitive but it can also be directed, active and full of power. Jasper encourages the blossoming of these latter qualities without loss of sensitivity.

Chrysoberyl This is a beautiful stone, having many different colours and forms, of which emerald is one. Chrysoberyls are comparatively rare and expensive but they attract and produce kindness and generosity. They revitalize all our energies and are sometimes called the 'stone of perpetual youth'.

Angelite A stone which, as its name suggests, helps to attract angelic blessings. It is a transformative stone which helps lift the burden of old patterns and blockages from us.

PRAYERS OR AFFIRMATIONS

The root chakra prayer or affirmation is:

Through incarnation may spirit be brought into matter.
Through rootedness may life-force be recharged and
exchanged. We acknowledge wholeness and seek to gain
and to reflect acceptance.

The sacral chakra prayer or affirmation is:

May the unity of humanity with each other and the earth enable true creativity. May release from a sense of sin and unworthiness lead us into the full knowledge of our empowerment as co-creators, at one with, and a part of the Divine.

The heart chakra prayer or affirmation is:

In the golden centre of the rose of the heart may tender compassion be linked to unconditional love. May true detachment enable growth and continuity. Through the understanding of birth within death and death within birth may there be transformation.

For suggestions on using prayers or affirmations, see page 45.

Chapter 7

Song of Myself:
The Individual in the World

Key Issues: The Jigsaw Puzzle of Self, Work and Expression in the World; Being Heard and Finding Your Voice

Chakra Pairs: Sacral and Solar Plexus; Sacral and Throat

Archetype: The World

This chapter will help you to:
- gain greater insight into the many aspects of your personality
- better understand the power of self-expression and gain easier access to it

---

AREAS OF INFLUENCE

For a list of the areas of influence for the sacral chakra see page 117.

The Solar Plexus Chakra

Location Just below the sternum, extending down to the navel (stem in corresponding position at the back)
Key Words Logic, Reason, Opinion, Assimilation, Psychic Intuition
Developmental Age 8–12 years
Colours Yellow, Gold, Rose
Element Fire
Sense Sight
Body Astral
Glandular Connection Adrenals
Quietening Fragrances Vetivert, Rose
Stimulating Fragrances Bergamot, Ylang-ylang
Crystals and Gemstones Yellow Citrine, Apatite, Calcite, Kunzite, Rose Quartz, Iron Pyrites (Fool's Gold), Topaz, Malachite

Prayer or Affirmation

Through the gift of fire, let reason, logic, opinion and assimilation become truly linked to inspiration that we are not bound within limitation and separation.

The Throat Chakra

Location The neck (petals at the front, stem at the back)
Key Words Expression, Responsibility, Communication, Universal Truth
Developmental Age 15–21 years
Colours Blue, Silver, Turquoise
Element Ether/Akasha
Sense Hearing
Body Mental
Glandular Connection Thyroid and Parathyroids
Quietening Fragrances Lavender, Hyacinth
Stimulating Fragrances Patchouli, White Musk

Crystals and Gemstones Lapis Lazuli, Aquamarine, Sodalite, Turquoise, Sapphire

Prayer or Affirmation

Help us to develop responsibility. May universal truth impregnate causal action so that the voice of humanity may find true harmony with the voice of the earth.

THE SACRAL AND SOLAR PLEXUS AS A CHAKRA PAIR

The solar plexus is a complex centre, as can be seen from the range of its key words. Perhaps most of its complexity comes from its connection to our lower will, personality and ego. When we are looking at living more spiritually and bringing meaning to life, the lower self or ego has to feel recognized and respected, before it can begin to cooperate with higher destiny.

Personality and Ego

There is a traditional spiritual injunction which instructs the follower of the path to 'lose the ego'. This is often wrongly understood and quoted out of context. My feeling is that it has even been mistranslated. Those three words, standing alone, as a key to spirituality, are suspect and dangerous and do not allow for the bridge which needs to be made between the psychological and the spiritual worlds.

Our ego is our identity. It must be strongly built before any wider explorations can take place with safety. Some psychotic conditions are linked to loss of identity. There are far too many instances of spiritual and religious travellers becoming lost and needing psychiatric treatment, simply because their ego structure was not strong enough for the intensity of the spiritual journey which they had undertaken.

Spirituality cannot *replace* psychological growth, without spirituality, does not necessarily answer all our questions. But when the two go hand in hand, human potential soars beyond expectations. Eventually, and perhaps somewhat paradoxically in view of the foregoing, the attainment of spiritual goals is dependent upon the *surrender* of the ego, with grace and joy, to the higher will and purpose. If that which is surrendered is a strong and well-honed tool, then it will potentially be a better instrument for that higher will.

The solar plexus, then, focuses us on personality development. Yet at the same time, with fire as its element, it is the seat of vision. When the solar plexus is functioning healthily our physical as well as our spiritual sight can improve. The question which the solar plexus prompts us to ask is: 'How do I see the world and how does the world see me?'.

Logic, Reason and Opinion

The key words of logic, reason and opinion belong strongly to the aspect of the solar plexus which is connected with our personality and our ability to manage the mundane well. In life we need a logical and reasonable approach. We need to be able to form and state personal opinions. An independent rationality is needed in order to make decisions about life which allow us to reach our personal and full potential. Intellect and mind have an important relationship with the solar plexus. The sacral centre and its connections to root and heart are concerned with empowerment, as we saw in Chapter 6. The solar plexus has its own input into a continued empowerment process. It is not possible to form and affirm our personal belief systems or to challenge any of society's without the qualities of logic, reason and opinion.

The Psychic Faculty

Though the solar plexus might be called the 'seat' of the lower will, with its connection to the sense of vision and to qualities of psychic intuition, it is also a centre of awareness of other worlds and the recognition that there is more than one reality.

Many people who come to esoteric spiritual study are confused by the difference between the psychic, the spiritual and the use of the word 'psyche' in psychology and psychotherapy.

Psychologically speaking, 'psychic' refers to that which is 'of the psyche' (see Glossary). It is used to describe the interacting personality and behaviour patterns which make each individual a unique and multi-faceted being.

In esoteric realms the word 'psychic' is used to denote a particular kind of sensitivity. The psychic individual may have premonitions, either in dreams or through 'hunches' or 'knowings'. Crystal ball gazers use the psychic faculty. Tarot card, palm and astrology readings are re-establishing themselves now as serious studies offering valuable spiritual guidance. They can also be practised specifically and solely from a psychic level.

The psychic faculty is an important ingredient in spiritual growth and practice. But it must be taken further and connected to the higher centres in the chakra system if it is to relate to more than our material world, the future, our love lives, 'luck' and all the areas generally associated with 'fortune-telling'.

Some people become so over-fascinated by phenomena linked to psychic energy that their pursuit of evidence of telekinesis, spoon-bending, clock-stopping, poltergeist hauntings and psychometry can become a serious obstacle on their spiritual path. Others, confusing the psychic with darker occult practices, become very afraid and often retreat behind the strong boundaries of a dogmatic and literal religion.

Indeed the psychic world can be both over-fascinating and very frightening, but psychic energy is a necessary ingredient in the vision and power which enable us to see, define, implement and change our spiritual direction where necessary.

The Element of Fire

Fire consumes but also sets processes in motion, changes things and enables assimilation. We may refer to ourselves as burning with desire, passion or purpose. Or we may say we are *fired* by imagination or the spirit.

When the solar plexus is under-functioning we tend to get stuck on an inappropriate treadmill, unable to see how to bring about creative change in our lives. Vision, as well as action, can be blocked. An active fire element, nourished by a well-functioning solar plexus, brings enjoyment and passion into our lives.

An over-active solar plexus or fire element can make us over-fiery, dry-skinned, irritable, uncomfortable, and prickly to ourselves and others. In our bodies food may be burned up too quickly and nutrients imperfectly absorbed.

Sub-Personalities

The solar plexus chakra is connected to the development and expression of the lower will and the personality or ego self. It needs the dynamic animation and attributes which come from the sacral centre in order to feed the development of this most basic part of ourselves. As we come to terms with our internal drives and conditioning, so the sacral and solar plexus chakras work powerfully together.

As the sacral energy blends with that of the solar plexus, we are led to the basic question: 'What/who do I mean when I say "I"?' In asking this, we become aware of our complexity and multiplicity. Somewhere there is a central integrating 'I', but it can seem elusive as we observe that 'a part of me feels this . . . but another part feels that . . .'. In matters of choice, how do we finally arrive at what 'I' as a central being wants, or become able to make a creative compromise which allows scope for all the rich, contributing parts?

These are the dilemmas of life. They underlie not only the
search for 'I' in a psychological and worldly sense, but also
the drive to search for spiritual meaning and purpose. Both the
dilemma and the solution are contained within the maturation
process of the sacral/solar plexus link. Exercise 26 (on page
175) is a balancing and connecting exercise for the sacral/
solar plexus chakras. Basic integrative psychological work is
supported when the energy connection is made, and the
energy connection becomes stronger when the psychological
work goes alongside.

The concept of the higher self and the 'beads on the thread'
(see page 50) may lead us to suppose that the higher self is in
charge and is the integrating force which we seek. Yet the
being which we are on earth, the personality from which we
function, fully exists in its own right. If we are too anxious to let
the higher self take over, we may give insufficient importance to
ego development. The tool which the higher self would use is
then insufficiently formed and could be subject to delusions
of grandeur, inability to make choices, slavishness to authority,
a sense of non-being, or psychosis. These are the dangers which
can exist when psychological understanding and spiritual
growth become divorced from each other.

When we are psychologically aware of our many parts and
work to understand them, we come to a place of integration
in which we appreciate our own richness and multi-faceted
potential. The voice which says 'I' is informed by that potential
and has a wisdom and maturity of its own. If it then chooses
to link with a higher self and pursue a deeper meaning and
purpose in life, a state called 'Individuation' by Jung and 'Self-
Actualization' by Maslow is attained (see C.G. Jung in the
Bibliography).

The Italian psychologist, Assagioli, who formulated the
system of self-analysis known as psychosynthesis (see Pierro
Ferrucci in the Bibliography), spoke of the many facets within
ourselves as sub-personalities. Earlier, Jung had spoken of the
persona or mask. Our working selves are usually very different

from our relaxed, private or holiday selves. We, and those with whom we live and work, need these masks, which help us to play the many different roles life demands of us. We even wear certain uniforms to help the persona to operate: the pin-striped suit for business, the apron for housework, the sporting gear for jogging, the T-shirt for relaxation, the formal or beautiful clothes for entertaining and party-going, are all supports for essential aspects of our day-to-day interactions.

The concept of the sub-personality goes further than that of the persona and refers to the deeper dynamics at work within the psyche. We use the persona more consciously. The sub-personalities develop as a result of conditioning and can be survival mechanisms. They are distinctive energies within the psyche. Ferrucci, a disciple of Assagioli, refers to them as 'degraded archetypes'.

Conditioning influences often derive from degraded or mis-interpreted archetypal forces. In order to deal with the growth difficulties inflicted in this way, we ingest or inwardly create the degraded archetypes which are our sub-personalities. They usually manifest as pairs of opposites.

People who have been required to be over-orderly in child-hood will probably have an obsessively tidy sub-personality but also one which is disordered and chaotic. People who have been subject to power and manipulation may have an inner tyrant but also an inner victim. People who have been required to be too 'good' may have an inner 'goody-goody' but also a naughty, devious, dishonest or sly sub-personality.

These polarized pairs perpetuate each other. We push away those parts of ourselves which we consider to be undesirable. Our success at this means that, until we begin to work with them, sub-personalities are relatively unconscious. Things which exist but are denied gain autonomy. Thus, autonomous sub-personalities may emerge to surprise and embarrass us in unexpected situations, particularly when we are under stress. The remark from friends 'I've never seen that side of you before', or your own self-criticism: 'I really don't know what got into me', are usually warnings that an autonomous or somewhat dissociated sub-personality has revealed itself.

Sub-personalities are rewarding to work with. They reveal themselves readily when we seek them out, telling their stories and helping us to understand what they seek and why they have developed. They will eventually become important allies on our journey to self-knowledge and integration. Knowing and working with them will eventually make our connection with our higher selves clearer and more productive.

Exercise 28 on page 177 will help you to get in touch with your sub-personalities. Use it alongside exercise linking the sacral and solar plexus energies on page 175.

THE SACRAL AND THROAT AS A CHAKRA PAIR

After the crown/root connection (see Chapter 2) that between sacral and throat is the strongest natural link within the chakra system. Weaknesses in this interaction can seriously affect our life and health, while strengthening the connection can help us to function more strongly in the world.

Since the sevenfold chakra system is sub-divided into two interacting groups and the throat chakra is a member of each, it is a gateway chakra. As one of the five lower chakras, it is related to an element, a developmental age and a sense. As the first of three upper chakras, it is concerned with transpersonal expression and connections to the higher self, spirit and soul.

The throat chakra is connected to the sense of hearing, but also to the voice. The question to ask at the throat chakra is: 'How do I hear the world and how does the world hear me?'

How we hear ourselves and how we 'sound ourselves' is also important. As always, the sense for this chakra needs to be interpreted symbolically as well as actually. When a note is sounded, it resonates and reverberates, attracting answering sounds in various harmonic forms or disharmonies. When we strike our true note, disharmonies are reduced and we draw positive synchronicities and compatibilities towards us. Thus life will flow more smoothly because we will recognize that we are always in the right place at the right time. If we have felt lonely in life, and our family of origin has been largely of genetic rather than spiritual derivation, learning to sound our true note attracts friends, companions and family from our soul group towards us and helps to heal our roots (see also Chapter 4).

Strengthening the throat chakra and its connections helps us to find our own note and to sound it with confidence.

The connection to voice and hearing means that the throat chakra is concerned with the actual and metaphoric aspects of finding one's voice and being heard – or the way in which one expresses oneself in the world. At a more spiritual level the throat enables us to connect to our higher selves and our spiritual qualities. Once this link is made, we become uncompromising in expressing our true selves.

During the developmental age of the throat chakra (15–21 years), we go through the rite of passage of 'coming of age', when we are legally adult and therefore held totally responsible for all our actions.

Spiritual coming of age is concerned with responding to, and interpreting the requirements of, a divine or higher purpose. Working with the throat chakra helps us to know and respond to our calling or vocation in life.

Communication

Communication is a complex subject. We develop language in order to communicate with each other, yet what we communicate goes far beyond the written word or the power of speech and hearing. Body language, the clothes we wear, the subtle smells we exude, and what is left unsaid as well as what is said, are all important factors.

Our bodies work for us because our organs are in communication with each other. Each body part is dependent upon another, though we may only become aware of the existence of this interdependent communication when there is a minor or major breakdown within the system. When our diet agrees with us, our digestive and eliminative processes work happily together and we do not need to think about them. But if we eat something disagreeable the system lets us know about it. If we develop a serious bout of flu we can no longer get our limbs to obey us. The internal communication knows that rest is required. In times of health and well-being the signallings of our miraculous and finely tuned inner communication system remain unconscious and are taken for granted. Working with the throat chakra enables us to listen better to our bodies and become more attuned to our health patterns.

With much communication linked to sound, it is interesting that some scientists believe that sound is the basic pattern which enabled the universe to come into being. When we strive to understand higher abstract laws, we have to name them and speak them before they truly come into being or manifestation. Thus concept, given form by language and verbally communicated, is a process through which creation happens. The throat chakra plays a vital part in enabling us to realize our full potential as human beings.

The sacral chakra is mainly connected to forces which might be described as 'driving' or 'dynamic' (see Chapter 6). In life, eventually, these forces find expression through our throat chakras. The sacral chakra and the throat are, after crown and root, the second most natural and strongly interactive pair within the chakra system.

The major life issues of creativity, sexuality, power and empowerment at the sacral centre demand of us responsibility. They need to find appropriate expression and communication. Responsibility, expression and communication are all attributes connected with the throat chakra. The sacral chakra *needs* the throat in order that fundamental aspects within us can find expression in living. If the throat is, in any way, an afflicted chakra, a great deal of inner frustration may develop, as the power within us will be difficult to channel and focus. If the sacral centre is undeveloped the stream of power flowing to the centre of expression (the throat) will be too weak, intermittent or diffuse. As we saw earlier in this chapter this also hinders the development of the lower will and ego at the solar plexus and the whole being may be too watery and unformed, with 'loop-backs' in the energy system.

Loop-backs

Energy loop-backs in the chakra system happen when development of any chakra is seriously impaired. Loop-backs can be particularly troublesome when they occur because of an imbalance in a major and essential chakra pairing such as that of sacral and throat. Loop-backs between sacral and throat will also affect the solar plexus and heart chakras.

If the sacral is undeveloped the appropriate energy is unavailable to the solar plexus and there is not enough impetus to bring the link energy through to the heart or throat. An important energy pathway may thus remain immature or almost unformed. What power there may be, will fall or loop back into the sacral centre, causing a build-up which has no appropriate channel through which it can find an outlet. The energy which drops back, unchannelled, can form a blockage or energy build-up in the sacral chakra itself, making it overactive. The throat, not receiving the energy it needs from its major partner chakra, will consequently be weak and underactive.

If the energy build-up remains stuck in the sacral centre the being may become very sexually frustrated, power-orientated or violent. If a proportion of the energy seeks release through the solar plexus, without being properly integrated there, the being may manifest as very self-willed or egotistical. If the excess intensity drops back into the root chakra, without being fully grounded, depression, difficulty in relating to life, or excessive materialism and disregard for natural cycles and flow, can manifest.

Physical illnesses and conditions can also be caused by chakra energy loop-backs. In the case of throat and sacral, these might be particularly: ear, throat, thyroid, lymphatic, sexual, menstrual or urinary problems.

Central column breathing (see page 17) helps to keep all pathways open, to minimize and heal chakra blockages, and prevent energy loop-backs. But eventually the essential cause of any vital hiatus needs the recognition and treatment which results from working with chakras as pairs, triads, or individually. (For more specific, individual, chakra work, see my previous book *Working With Your Chakras* in the Bibliography.)

Exercise 27 (page 176) activates the connection between your sacral and throat chakras and helps prevent the most major possible loop-back within the chakra system.

The Sacral, Solar Plexus and Throat Chakras

These three chakras are not a triad in the same way as the root, sacral and heart chakras, yet when the sacral works harmoniously with the solar plexus *and* with the throat the healthy result is a natural flow and blending between all three, forming a major chakra system strength.

Case Study: Identity Crisis

Brian had been a star pupil at his comprehensive school. He was able in every educational field and thirsted for knowledge. He was also musical, artistic and good at sport. He seemed to be one of those young people of whom it is said, 'the gods favour him'.

The crowning moment came when Brian won a scholarship to Oxford. His school, his parents, his friends and he himself were pleased and proud. With so many avenues open to him, choosing what to read at university was not easy. Eventually Brian decided on philosophy, politics and ecomomics, feeling that, with such a study behind him, the possibilities for his future career would be wide.

Though Brian's talents, and particularly his prowess on the sports field, had always made him popular and 'one of the gang' (which included young women as well as men), he had never had a serious girlfriend. His parents teased him mildly about this, but accepted that much of his time went into study and games.

The crisis came towards the end of Brian's first university year. His studies had initially gone well, but in his second term Brian realized that he was attracted to, and eventually in love with, a fellow male student. The question of being 'gay' had never occurred to him before and, though his love was reciprocated, he felt himself to be in an emotional tangle and an identity crisis. He knew that, though his parents might eventually understand, they would consider this discovery about him to be the flaw which marked the jewel. He would find their inevitable underlying disappointment very difficult to live with.

Though counselling was available at university, Brian felt so confused that he did not believe it would help him. Endeavouring to cope alone, he ended his relationship and arranged to change his course of study for his second year, so that he would mix in different circles.

In the long vacation, the fact that he needed to work to catch up on knowledge for the new course to which he had transferred gave Brian an excuse to spend long hours alone in his room. His parents felt his stress, but accepted it as relatively normal and inevitable. But the day came when he drank a quantity of wine and took an overdose of aspirin. As it turned out, this was the way in which Brian's psyche chose to call for help, rather than a carefully calculated suicide attempt. Inevitably the whole story came out and, though his parents were supportive and compassionate, Brian slipped into a deep depression and did not return to university.

So far, Brian's life had seemed mapped out – all pathways leading to what the world would term 'success'. Yet the tremendous drive of his sexuality had never been addressed and, because he was intellectually brilliant, he had automatically accepted that he would take up academic study and an academic career.

As part of the treatment for his depression, Brian spent some weeks in a therapeutic community. Here, through group therapy, psychodrama, music, creative writing and art therapy, he was helped to come to terms with his homosexuality. From afternoons spent in creative writing Brian rediscovered his love of literature and a considerable writing talent. When he was well on the way to recovery himself and had also entered into a happy relationship with someone he met at the community, Brian devoted some months of voluntary work to the therapeutic community. Eventually he decided to take a course in media studies, hoping that it would lead to openings for his writing and creative talents.

I met Brian much later in his life, when he was a successful writer but wanted to learn some meditative techniques to aid his creative processes. I have used him as a case study here, because of his identity crisis, the loop-back of energy to his sacral chakra which was responsible for his sexuality going temporarily unconscious and then plunging him suddenly into the midst of its drive for expression, and because instead of having had opportunity to find his own 'note' he had been channelled by traditional expectations and the course of events into a field where, though he was capable, he would never truly express his deeper and sensitive nature.

THE ARCHETYPE: THE WORLD

The archetype chosen for this chapter is 'The World'. We often precede the word 'world' with a possessive personal pronoun. We speak of 'my world', 'your world', 'their world', acknowledging to some extent that, whilst living together in 'the' world, there are many interacting worlds which we all, in different ways, both experience and create.

In spiritual terms the world of earth is the world of physical incarnation. It is the world where we work out much of our destiny and learn the lessons which lead us to a state of wholeness or perfection. Much of our journey is about understanding the relationship of spirit to matter and learning to balance our lives accordingly. The material world can become a spiritual trap. Denial of the material world makes us spiritually ungrounded and perhaps insufficiently aware of the lessons we came into incarnation to learn.

It is important not to confuse the world with the universe. Our world is earth, as it is portrayed on a globe map of 'the world'. The universe is rapidly opening up to us and becoming a part of our world, but it is important to be aware of this interaction and not to assume that our world is the universe. Keeping conceptual boundaries correct, and defining or re-defining our world, actually helps us relate to other worlds and planes.

In traditional Tarot divination the card of 'The World' indicates successful achievement of an aim. Drawing the card in reverse suggests over-attachment to worldly things and an obstacle to be overcome.

EXERCISES

Exercise 26
Linking the Sacral and Solar Plexus Energies

Making sure that you will be undisturbed, sit or stand with your spine straight, your body symmetrically arranged and your legs uncrossed at ankles or knees.

- Begin with central column breathing (see page 17).
- When you feel centred, let the rhythm of your breathing focus your attention into your sacral chakra. Begin to breathe in through the petals of your sacral chakra and out through its stem (five to ten in/out breath sequences).
- Change the focus of your attention to your solar plexus chakra and begin to breathe in through the petals of your solar plexus chakra and out through its stem (five to ten in/out breath sequences).
- Now, once again breathe in through the petals of your sacral chakra, but in the centre of your chakra hold your breath for a count of three before breathing the breath/energy stream up through your central column into the centre of your solar plexus chakra and out through its petals (five to ten in/out breath sequences).
- Breathe in through the petals of your solar plexus chakra. Hold the breath in its centre for a count of three before breathing the breath/energy stream down through your central column into the centre of your sacral chakra and out through its petal (five to ten in/out breath sequences).
- Finish with central column breathing.

Exercise 27
Linking the Sacral and Throat Energies

Making sure that you will be undisturbed, sit or stand with your spine straight, your body symmetrically arranged and your legs uncrossed at ankles or knees.

- Begin with central column breathing (see page 17).
- When you feel centred, use your breath to help you direct the focus of your attention. Begin to breathe in through the petals of your sacral chakra and out through its stem (five to ten in/out breath sequences).

- Change to breathing in through your throat chakra petals and out through its stem (five to ten in/out breaths).
- Return to breathing in through the petals of your sacral chakra, and hold your breath in the centre of the sacral chakra for a count of three. Breathe on up through your central column to the centre of your throat chakra and out through its petals (five to ten in/out breath sequences).
- Breathe in through the petals of your throat chakra, and hold your breath in its centre for a count of three. Breathe down through the central column to the centre of your sacral chakra and out through its petals (five to ten in/ out breath sequences)
- Finish with central column breathing.

Exercise 28
Contacting Your Sub-Personalities

The part of us which is already integrated, or which has the vision of what integration can mean, is our inner wise being. The following guided journey suggests that you connect with this being in order to support you in your meeting with your sub-personalities. The inner wise being is such a universal inner symbol that when you ask it to appear it will come, quite naturally, into your visualization. For some people the inner wisdom may take the form of an essence or presence rather than an actual personified being.

Make sure that you will be undisturbed and that you have writing/drawing materials at hand. Provide yourself with a rug or blanket for warmth, then find a relaxed but balanced and supported position for your body.

- Close your eyes . . . Be aware of the rhythm of your breathing and bring that rhythm into your heart centre, thus activating the heart energy on which to travel into your inner landscape . . . Find yourself in a meadow . . .

Activate all your inner senses, so that you see the objects
and colours, hear the sounds, touch the textures, smell
the fragrances and savour the tastes . . .

- Ask for your inner wise being or presence to be with you
  in the meadow . . . Ask that this presence accompany
  you on your journey to the place where your sub-
  personalities dwell . . . Take with you any special object,
  amulet or talisman which helps you to centre and feel
  protected . . . (See entries for 'Amulets' and 'Talismans'
  in the Glossary.)

- Somewhere in your inner landscape, maybe quite close to
  the meadow, there is a river . . . Carrying or wearing your
  talisman and accompanied by your inner wise presence,
  journey now to this river . . .

- As you walk beside the river you will become aware that
  nearby there is a quiet backwater or tributary stream . . .
  Anchored on this backwater or stream is a houseboat – the
  home of your sub-personalities . . .

- As you draw nearer to the boat you may be aware of the
  activity and noise of your sub-personalities . . .

- Stand by and observe your boat . . . What sort of boat is it?
  What is its state of repair and upkeep? What are the
  arrangements for boarding and landing?

- After this initial inspection withdraw a little from the river
  bank and find a comfortable place in which to sit while
  keeping the boat in full view . . . Choose a sun-warmed spot
  and rest your back against a tree or rock . . . Be aware of
  your inner wise presence supporting you . . .

- Ask that not more than three sub-personalities from the
  houseboat prepare to reveal themselves to you . . .

- Insist that the sub-personalities, unless they are an
  inseparable pair, and therefore really represent one
  complete sub-personality, reveal themselves to you one at a
  time . . . When you have met and greeted the first, ask it to
  step to one side as you greet the next . . . The second

personality should then step back to make way for the third . . .

- Observe and greet each sub-personality and let them also observe and greet you . . . Ask each one to tell you their story in brief (how and when they came into being, what they fear, what they require at this time) . . .

- When you have met these three sub-personalities, reflect on whether any two of them need to talk to each other, and ask your wise presence to give you advice. . . Putting the dialogue into effect is something you can do another time. Use this occasion to become aware of what might be of value to your inner growth . . .

- Before asking your sub-personalities to return to their houseboat, consider whether you are willing to make any commitment to further work with them . . . (This might involve: undertaking to return to this place for further dialogue with your sub-personalities; deciding what to do about any requests they have as to their present needs; returning to this place to allow any two sub-personalities to dialogue together; agreeing to give something to a sub-personality, which it requires, in the form of an assurance or symbolic gift and exchanging this for something you may require of it; using your creativity and the support of your inner wise presence to find ways of understanding your sub-personalities and of modifying their weaknesses and harnessing their strengths. Do not commit yourself to anything which you will be unable to follow up on in the near future.)

- Finally, thank your sub-personalities for revealing themselves and ask them to return to the houseboat, giving them any reassurance or promises of further work which you feel able to give at this time . . .

- When the sub-personalities are safely aboard, journey back to the meadow, accompanied by your inner wise presence . . .

- From the meadow return to the rhythm of your breathing

in your heart centre . . . and to your awareness of your
body, your contact with the ground and your normal
surroundings . . . Visualize a cloak of light with a hood
right around you . . . Take your pencils, pens and crayons
and record your journey.

*Note that this journey provides a chance for you to meet not more
than three of your sub-personalities. On subsequent occasions you
can ask to meet three more sub-personalities, but it is wise to limit the
number you meet at any one time. Some sub-personalities manifest
as twins or in some other way as having an inseparable counterpart.
These pairs count as one sub-personality. I have known, for instance,
a Punch and Judy, a bat and ball and a whip and top.*

Exercise 29
Reflecting on the Archetype of The World

For this reflection simply have your writing and drawing
materials at hand and reflect on what the world means to you.

- Consider your ability to balance spiritual and material
  values.
- Reflect further on the questions:
  - 'How do I taste the world? How does the world taste me?'
  - 'How do I see the world? How does the world see me?'
  - 'How do I hear the world? How does the world hear
    me?'

Exercise 30
Sounding Your Note

- Experiment with making different sounds and singing different notes.

- Sing or chant your name, rhythmically.
- Do some drumming.
- Find a Tibetan singing bowl which resonates a healing sound for you (see entry for 'Tibetan Singing Bowls' in the Glossary).
- If you have the opportunity to make sounds out of doors, the experience can be much more powerful or meaningful.

THE COLOURS

The colours for the solar plexus chakra are yellow, gold and rose.

On the positive side, yellow brings clarity and joy to life. A bright clear yellow gives mental and intellectual stimulus.

Negative shades of yellow can be depressing, make for intellectual sluggishness and negatively affect the digestive system.

Gold is the non-metallic colour and positively brings warmth and expansion. It can be very healing to the digestion.

Negative shades of gold absorb energy and have similar effects to negative shades of yellow.

Rose is the colour of rose quartz. Positively, it brings a sense of calm, comfort, security and tenderness. It brings containment for the inner child or for any disturbed sub-personalities and encourages integration.

Negative shades of rose can perpetuate the petulant child and make it difficult to connect with a sense of self-worth.

The colours for the throat chakra are: blue, silver and turquoise. They are all 'cool' colours.

Blue is a colour which calms and heals. It can help to reduce fevers. The usual shade recommended for use at the throat chakra is 'lapis blue'. This brightens, clarifies and contains.

Negative shades of blue can be too cold and without resonance. They can bring a sense of isolation and loneliness.

Silver is the metallic colour. It softens, strengthens and is protective. It brings the feminine principle to a centre which might otherwise be too activated by masculine principle.

Negative shades of silver can be 'cold as steel'. It can also generate sarcasm, cutting, hurtful remarks, and aggression.

Turquoise encourages depth and expansion. It is the colour to use if you want to reach out to wider audiences, work for the media, lecture, or write.

Negatively, shades of turquoise can be oppressive. They can generate loss of compassion and even tyranny.

The colours for the sacral chakra are orange, amber and gold (non-metallic).

Use the colours as suggested in Exercise 8 (page 42) to develop, awaken and heal your chakras.

The Fragrances

At the solar plexus vetivert and rose quieten, while bergamot and ylang-ylang stimulate. (Bergamot is an ingredient in Earl Grey tea.) Use the quietening fragrances if you have digestive problems such as colitis or ulcers, if you have difficulty when mingling with crowds or travelling on collective transport, and if you are at a transition point in your life. Use the stimulating fragrances if you have a slow metabolism, defective eyesight or fears about change.

At the throat, lavender and hyacinth quieten, whilst patchouli and white musk stimulate. People who have tense, high-pitched, nervous voices usually need the quietening fragrances, as do those who are over-talkative or over-anxious about finding the right work. Those who speak too softly or hardly at all, who are obviously under-achieving in their work and are unfulfilled but confused as to what to do about it, need the stimulating fragrances.

For the sacral chakra the quietening fragrances are rosemary and rose-geranium, and the stimulating ones are musk and amber. See page 43 for suggestions for using the fragrances.

THE CRYSTALS

Refer to page 44 and the Glossary for general guidance on using crystals. The crystals which will best help the issues considered in this chapter are:

Clear Quartz This is a universal crystal, meaning that it can be used at any chakra and to enhance or amplify any purpose or cause. Choose one with clear facets, a good point at one end and a roundedness at the other, to represent the many facets of your identity and the crystal clarity you are aiming towards.

Rose Quartz This crystal, too, can be used for most chakras and chakra work. In its 'massive' form (crystalline, but without clearly defined points or facets), it is comforting and helps to provide a good climate for transformation and integration.

Citrine A bright, clear, yellow citrine will aid the cultivation of clarity, warmth and the sense of self. It is also healing for digestive upsets.

Lapis Lazuli This aids expression of all kinds. It helps the process of co-ordination and integration within the personality, the expression of special talents, and the healing or management of deafness.

PRAYERS OR AFFIRMATIONS

The sacral chakra prayer or affirmation is:

May the unity of humanity with each other and the earth enable true creativity. May release from a sense of sin and unworthiness lead us into the full knowledge of our empowerment as co-creators, at one with, and a part of the Divine.

The solar plexus chakra prayer or affirmation is:

Through the gift of fire, let reason, logic, opinion and assimilation become truly linked to inspiration that we are not bound within limitation and separation.

The throat chakra prayer or affirmation is:

Help us to develop responsibility. May universal truth impregnate causal action so that the voice of humanity may find true harmony with the voice of the earth.

For suggestions on using prayers or affirmations, see page 45.

Chapter 8

Freeing the Spirit:
The Soul, the Spirit, Guides and Angels

Key Issues: Soul and Spirit, Higher and Lower Selves, Guides and
Angels

Chakra Pairs: Solar Plexus and Brow; Solar Plexus and Crown;
Solar Plexus and Heart

Chakra Triad: Solar Plexus, Brow and Crown

Archetypes: Guru and Devotee

This chapter will help you to:
- learn more about the relationship of soul to spirit, and higher
  will to lower will
- gain a greater understanding of communication with guides
  and angels

AREAS OF INFLUENCE

For lists of the areas of influence for the solar plexus chakra
see page 161; page 77 for the heart chakra; and page 20 for
the crown chakra.

The Brow Chakra

Location Above and between the eyes, with a stem at the back of the head

Key Words Spirit, Completeness, Inspiration, Insight, Command

Colours Indigo, Turquoise, Mauve

Element Radium

Body Higher Mental

Glandular Connection Pineal

Quietening Fragrances White Musk, Hyacinth

Stimulating Fragrances Violet, Rose-geranium

Crystals and Gemstones Amethyst, Purple Apatite, Azurite, Calcite, Pearl, Sapphire, Blue and White Fluorite

Prayer or Affirmation

We seek to command ourselves through the inspiration of the command of God. May true insight be enabled and the finite mind be inspired to a knowledge of completion.

SOLAR PLEXUS AND BROW AS A CHAKRA PAIR

The brow chakra is the window through which the flame of our spirit shines, whilst the crown chakra is the gateway to our soul.

By its very nature, spirit is difficult to describe or define. There is also much confusion about the difference between soul and spirit. In some alchemical systems (see Glossary), spirit is seen as yang or masculine whilst soul is considered to be feminine. This is a helpful working definition.

Spirit can thus be considered as pure flame, clear, direct, eternal and initiating. The spirit initiates and commands life and its evolutionary tasks. It seeks completeness, commands action to enable it, and fertilizes inspiration and insight.

Within each one of us there is a spark or essence which never gets clouded. Beyond our behaviour patterns and reactions to life, untouched by flaws of personality, character or morality, even within the most vicious criminal, this spark burns on. When we know this essence in ourselves and honour it in others, we are far less likely to be inhumane.

When the brow chakra is active, it awakens the urge to achieve complete inner harmony of body, mind, emotions, spirit and soul.

Most of us see the things of the spirit as inspirational. Yet the word 'inspiration' also means 'in-breath'. The Greek *pneuma* and the Latin *spiritus* mean both 'spirit' and 'breath'. The brow chakra, then, is also the window through which we breathe inspiration from the Greater Spirit, to fan the flame of our in-dwelling spirit.

Insight links perception with understanding and is the highest level of intuition. The awakened brow centre activates the kind of insight which goes beyond the boundaries of time and space to enable meetings with guides and angels and a wider comprehension of the imponderable mysteries.

The Sanskrit name for the brow chakra is 'Ajna' or 'command'. Through working with the brow chakra we can attain greater spiritual command of our lives.

The element for the brow chakra is radium. This is, perhaps, a difficult element for us to link with spiritual qualities since we know it as a metallic, radioactive element used in X-rays, radiotherapy and the production of luminous materials.

When asked about radium as an element for the brow centre, Gildas replied:

Radium brings power and light. It has a place in breaking down patterns in order to enable re-assembly. It has a high vibrational rate. Its symbolism at the brow centre concerns the facility of functioning on more than one level or dimension, while physically incarnate. It is about the meeting point of light and spirit in matter.

Spirit, by its very nature, is numinous. Unless the brow chakra is firmly linked with other chakras in the chakra team there is a constant danger that the spiritual seeker may develop an over-numinous relationship with life. If we mistakenly see the spiritual journey as one where we concentrate only on developing higher faculties and altered states of consciousness, the personality through which the spirit needs to shine may be too fragmented and fragile a vessel to carry the light. Hence the pairing between solar plexus and brow is an important one indeed.

The solar plexus is connected to vision, but also to identity and personality development (see also Chapter 7). When solar plexus, throat and sacral connections have been made, the powerful radium light of the spirit can truly inspire the personality and activate the aspects of spirit which are bonded in matter.

We have seen (mainly in Chapters 4 and 5) and shall see again, in this chapter and Chapter 9, how the linking of heart to its significant others within the chakra system brings wisdom and love into manifestation. Yet the perspective which spirit adds is one of pure inspiration and illumination.

Working with your solar plexus/brow pairing enhances the potential for your essential, higher and true self to illumine and inspire your integrated personality and for your harmony of being to reach a high level of expression.

SOLAR PLEXUS AND CROWN AS A CHAKRA PAIR

The main link between the brow and crown is that of soul and spirit. The solar plexus forms a pair with the brow *and* with the crown and all three form a triad. Thus the solar plexus connects to both the vision of the spirit and of the soul.

If spirit is yang, then soul is yin. It is receptive to, and integrating of, evolutionary experience. It carries the weight of all experience gathered until all karma has been cleared. During the evolutionary process the integrating thread of the soul also grows in wisdom and vision. This integrating part is the 'higher self' or 'higher will'.

The crown chakra is the window through which we connect with the higher will, and the solar plexus is the seat of the lower will. When higher and lower will are in good relationship and communication with each other, life can become easier and more meaningful.

We tend to see anything 'higher' as an authority and to project on to that authority the qualities of the judgmental, demanding and harsh taskmaster. Higher selves have had a bad press! Part of the success of the partnership between higher and lower will is that the lower will should be sufficiently conscious of itself to seek autonomy. Whilst that process is being worked out, the spiritual path can be bumpy and hazardous. But when we accept the overview, wisdom and compassionate help of the higher self, the light at the end of the spiritual tunnel appears. Our higher selves are not harsh taskmasters heaping karmic burden upon karmic burden. They long for us to be fulfilled, happy and successful in our lives and to work in cooperation with them so that evolution can proceed as smoothly as possible.

Linking the solar plexus and crown means that two important aspects work harmoniously together instead of possibly creating a polarity and pulling against each other.

SOLAR PLEXUS AND HEART AS A CHAKRA PAIR

In the journey of lower will to linking with higher will, the heart brings compassion, wisdom and tenderness to enable the formation of the solar plexus/crown connection, whilst the solar plexus and heart also form a chakra pair.

Full personality integration cannot take place unless the qualities of heart are active. The integrated being has access to heart energy and uses it in the business of life, relationships, feelings and value judgments. The inner being, and particularly the inner child, cannot be empowered until there is heart energy available to direct to the self. True self-worth is both encouraged and tempered by the heart flow, which lifts it from ego-centredness to making 'manifest the glory of God that is within us' (see page 92 for the rest of this quotation from Nelson Mandela's inaugural speech).

SOLAR PLEXUS, BROW AND CROWN AS A CHAKRA TRIAD

The ultimate goal of evolution is the marriage (or re-marriage) of soul with spirit. This can only take place when all karma has been cleared and the full nature and possibilities of life are understood. The solar plexus thus becomes an important bridge-maker, since it digests life, focuses the eye of vision into life, and enables us to attain incarnational consciousness.

Working to activate the solar plexus/brow/crown triad brings a true commitment to the conscious spiritual quest.

WORKING WITH GUIDES AND ANGELS

Connections between the solar plexus and heart, solar plexus and brow and solar plexus and crown, and the activation of the solar plexus/brow/crown triad, strengthen the energetic pathways which make communication with other dimensions safe and possible. It should be noted that communication with guides and angels is a wide topic, more fully discussed in my book, *Working With Guides and Angels* (see Bibliography).

Gildas has described the being and function of guides:

The original spark or soul comes from the Source. In order to become *like* the Source and also to ensure that the Source is not static, the soul takes on incarnation and journeys through many lifetimes in search of evolution. Gradually an overseeing, observing or higher self emerges and then each time an incarnation takes place only a part of the whole becomes personified in order to undergo the further experience which the essence requires in its search for wholeness.

When the soul thread is sufficiently evolved, the wheel of rebirth is no longer its main concern or focus. There is then an opportunity to continue on the path of evolution by being of service in different ways. Guides and communicators have agreed to aid the collective journey by sharing the less finite view and wider perspective seen from other planes of being. This is why we seek individuals on earth with whom to communicate. Our aim is to help in making the experience of incarnation less blinkered or limited in vision for you.

Guides cross the interface between planes in order to communicate. They have different concerns or aims in making their contact with incarnate human beings. For some, the main focus will be healing; for others teaching; whilst yet others will seek to inspire the artist, poet, architect, musician or writer.

Our beings on these planes are more diffuse than are yours on earth. We take on a personality so that we can have more understandable, direct and tender contact with you – but we no longer endure the limitations of personality as you do.

Belief in angels is woven into the fabric of humanity's spiritual search. From untutored reverence through to myths, tribal belief systems and every form of religious practice, angels have been recipients of prayer as well as guests at celebrations and rituals.

Angels bring us light and laughter, as well as enabling our finite minds to arrive at a wider understanding of divinity, infinity and the scheme of the universe.

Many discarnate guides are now suggesting that angels are seeking a more personal relationship with humans. They are eager to teach us about the nature of light and to help us understand the dimension of levity as well as that of gravity.

Guides are part of the human stream of consciousness but angels are not. Guides have been incarnate. Angels will never be incarnate. Guides and humans will never be angels.

The angels manifest Divine Principles or the Archetypes of Higher Qualities for us. When we seek to fulfil the potentials of human living we are dealing with angelic substance.

The word 'angel' means messenger. When interacting with angels you can send messages into the cosmos as well as receive them – the messenger service is two-way.

When asked how we could differentiate between communication which comes from angels and that which comes from guides, Gildas said:

Imagine the notes of bells. The higher, more tinkling notes are those of the angels. The lower notes are those of the guides. Together a whole carillon of bells creates many harmonies.

In order to establish communication with guides and angels we need the throat, brow and crown chakras to be open or active so that we can make our part of the journey to meet these beings of rarer substance. We must journey towards them and not just expect them to come and awaken us. We need an open heart chakra in order to communicate from our inner wisdom to the higher wisdom and so make the best use of guidance. We need an activated solar plexus/brow/crown connection in order to use guidance effectively in our lives.

Exercises 35 and 36 on pages 198–200 are those recommended by Gildas for opening a contact with our guides and angels.

Case Study: Freeing the Spirit

Marion had recently retired. An only child, born when her mother was over forty, Marion had always worked hard in order to support her ageing parents. Her father had died much earlier, her mother about two years before Marion's first visit to me.

Marion had gone on working after her mother died, because she wanted to save money for travel. She had gone from school into banking and had an executive post when she retired. The bank had moved her round a little, but she had never consented, particularly in latter years, to go too far from home. She had longed to see something of the world, but felt a strong duty to her parents and had honoured it without complaint.

Since retirement Marion had travelled to some exotic places. She came to me on the recommendation of a friend because, although her travel had been thrilling and, in some ways, the fulfilment of a dream, she still felt that she was looking for something she had not yet found.

It did not take long to deduce that what Marion really wanted was inner journeying. At first, she just wanted to know more about herself and her psychological make-up. Eventually she began to ask about guides, angels and the spiritual dimension. Never interested in conventional religion, she now began to read widely of philosophy, Buddhism and New Age writings, including channelled guidance and teaching.

Eventually Marion discovered that she could channel beautiful poetry, some of which was published in an anthology. Her story was straightforward in many ways, but opening the windows of her soul and freeing her spirit gave meaning to what might otherwise have seemed a very mundane life. Her ability to meditate and channel beautiful words gave her enormous happiness which shone from her. She confided that many friends had asked if she had acquired a secret lover in her retirement. In some ways, with psychological understanding and spiritual work, she felt she had. She had acquired an inner balance which made her complete, content and radiant in herself.

THE ARCHETYPES: THE GURU AND THE DEVOTEE

The guru and the devotee have been chosen as archetypes for this chapter because, as we seek spiritually, we often need to find a teacher. Gildas has commented that the guru and the devotee belong to the Piscean age. He sees them as self-perpetuating archetypes. The guru remains a guru and the devotee a devotee. The devotee empowers the guru, but the guru does not work towards his/her own redundancy. For the Aquarian age, Gildas encourages us to be eclectic in our search and to favour teachers who seek to empower their pupils and who are content to work towards their own redundancy.

We should not expect our inner guides to be gurus who require slavish obedience either. Our guides wish to give us another perspective, will often offer spiritual teaching and solace, but do not want to live our lives for us or for us to expect them to do so.

There is no formal exercise for contacting the guru or devotee in this chapter. I merely ask you to reflect on these archetypes and the concepts of self-responsibility and inner resources.

EXERCISES

Exercise 31
Linking the Solar Plexus and Brow Energies

Sit or stand with your spine straight, your head well-balanced on your neck, your body symmetrically arranged and with your legs uncrossed at feet or ankles, unless in a cross-legged or lotus position.

- Begin with central column breathing (see page 17)
- Use your breath rhythm to help you focus your attention into your solar plexus chakra. Breathe in through the petals and out through the stem (five to ten in/out breath sequences).
- Focus on your brow chakra. Breathe in through its petals and out through its stem (five to ten in/out breath sequences).
- Focus again on your solar plexus chakra. Breathe in through the petals of your chakra, hold the breath in its centre to a count of three, and breathe on up through your central column to the centre of your brow chakra. Breathe out through your brow chakra petals (five to ten in/out breath sequences).
- Focus on your brow chakra. Breathe in through the petals of your brow chakra. Hold your breath in the centre of your brow chakra to a count of three. Breathe down through your central column into your solar plexus chakra and out through your solar plexus chakra petals (five to ten in/out breath sequences).
- Finish with central column breathing, ending on the down-breath.

Exercise 32
Linking Solar Plexus and Crown Energies

Position yourself as for Exercise 31, above.

- Begin with central column breathing (see page 17).
- Focus on your solar plexus chakra, breathe in through its petals and out through its stem (five to ten in/out breath sequences).
- Still focusing on your solar plexus chakra, breathe in to the centre of your chakra, hold your breath for a count of three, then breathe on up through your central column and out through your crown chakra. (five to ten in/out breath sequences).
- Focus on your crown chakra. Breathe in to the centre of the many-petalled lotus of your crown chakra, and hold your breath to a count of three. Breathe down your central column to the centre of your solar plexus chakra and out through the petals of your solar plexus (five to ten in/ out breath sequences).
- Finish with central column breathing, ending on the down-breath.

Exercise 33
Linking the Solar Plexus and Heart Energies

Position yourself as for Exercise 31 (see page 195).

- Begin with central column breathing (see page 17).
- Focus on your solar plexus chakra. Breathe in through its petals and out through its stem (five to ten in/out breath sequences).
- Breathe in through the petals of your solar plexus chakra, hold the breath in its centre for a count of three, then

breathe up through your central column to the centre of your heart chakra and out through the petals of your heart chakra (five to ten in/out breath sequences).

- Breathe in through the petals of your heart chakra and out through its stem (five to ten in/out breath sequences).
- Breathe in through the petals of your heart chakra to its centre. Hold your breath for a count of three, breathe down through your central column into the centre of your solar plexus chakra and out through its petals (five to ten in/out breath sequences).
- Finish with central column breathing, ending on the down-breath.

Exercise 34
Connecting the Solar Plexus, Brow and Crown Triad

Position yourself as for Exercise 31 (see page 195).

- Begin with central column breathing (see page 17).
- Breathe in through the petals of your solar plexus chakra and out through its stem (five to ten in/out breath sequences).
- Breathe in through the petals of your brow chakra and out through its stem (five to ten in/out breath sequences).
- Breathe in deeply through the petals of your solar plexus chakra to its centre, hold your breath for a count of three, and breathe up through your central column into the centre of your brow chakra and out through its petals. Now breathe in through the petals of your brow chakra to its centre, sustaining the in-breath as you visualize the breath energy going up through your central column, through your crown chakra, down the front of your body. And breathe out as you visualize the energy going into the centre of your solar plexus chakra and then finally out through its stem (five x two in/out breath sequences).

• Finish with central column breathing, ending on the down-
  breath.

Exercise 35
Establishing an Inner Meeting Place for Work with Guides and Angels

Making sure that you will be undisturbed, with a blanket for
warmth, and writing and drawing materials at hand, sit or lie
in a comfortable, but symmetrically balanced position.

• Be aware of the rhythm of your breathing . . . Gradually
  bring the breath into your heart centre and travel into
  your inner landscape, finding yourself in a meadow . . .
  Activate all your inner senses so that you see the objects
  and colours . . . smell the fragrances . . . hear the sounds . . .
  touch the textures . . . savour the tastes . . .
• From your meadow look out at the surrounding
  landscape . . . Nearby there is a winding pathway which
  leads into hills and continues up into some mountains . . .
• You are going to take this pathway, knowing that you are
  going to a plateau which is near the top of one of the
  mountains but not beyond the tree line . . .
• Make your way to the plateau in your own time, noting the
  scenery through which you pass as you go . . .
• At the plateau take time to explore . . . You will probably
  find a source of clear running water from which to refresh
  yourself and there may be a small sanctuary or traveller's
  rest . . . There may be a place of natural sanctuary with a
  sun-warmed rock against which to rest your back and look
  out over the landscape . . . As you explore the plateau you
  are looking for a place where you are happy to sit and wait,
  with an open heart and an open expectation . . .
• When you have settled yourself in the place of your choice,

enjoy the peace ... If there is a question in your heart,
hold it there, pondering it in a relaxed way ...

- At this stage do not expect or invite a presence to be with
  you, but rather seek to establish this meeting place ...
  You have made your part of the journey ... This territory
  is yours but be aware that it is also part of the bridge to
  other worlds and planes ...
- Stay here for not more than ten minutes ... When you are
  ready to return, drink again from the water source ...
  Make your way back to the meadow ...
- From the meadow return to the awareness of your breath
  in your heart centre ... to the awareness of your body and
  your contact with the ground ... to your outer
  surroundings ... Visualize a cloak of light with a hood
  right around you ...
- Take time to record your journey in words or drawing.

Exercise 36
Drawing Your Guardian Angel Closer to you

Making sure that you will be undisturbed, sit or lie in a
comfortable but symmetrically balanced position. Have
ready a blanket for warmth, and writing and drawing materials
for recording your journey.

- Be aware of the rhythm of your breathing ... Gradually
  bring that rhythm into your heart chakra ... Travel on
  your heart energy into your inner landscape ... Find
  yourself in a meadow ... Awaken your inner senses, so
  that you see the objects and colours around you ... hear
  the sounds ... touch the textures ... smell the
  fragrances ... and savour the tastes ...
- In your meadow there is a rainbow ... You can actually
  experience the place where the rainbow begins or ends ...
  All the brilliant, translucent colours of the spectrum are

pouring down to and into the earth . . . Stand in this rainbow light and, as you experience the colours, ask that the particular colour which will help to draw your guardian angel closer to you may flood into you and bring you healing and harmony . . .

- Leave the rainbow, but, as you walk out into the meadow once more, the colour of your choice, (or the colour which has chosen you) will continue to surround you . . . Feel yourself beginning to soften a little at the edges and merge into the colour . . .

- Let the colour become soft in texture around you, like the gentle brushing and protection of an angel's wings . . . Feel lightened and protected, but also free as the colour becomes your guardian angel, gently holding you . . .

- Your angel may have more than one colour in its light . . . Let these develop and feel their protective quality . . .

- Remember a time in your life when you felt that, although you were in some kind of danger, or at risk, there was a protective influence around you . . . Thank your guardian angel for that intervention . . . Ask your guardian angel to make you more and more conscious of the protection and help which it holds out for you at all times . . .

- When you are ready to return from this experience make your journey through your meadow with the sense of your angel behind you or at your side . . . Return to an awareness of the rhythm of your breathing in your heart centre . . . Become aware of your physical body and of your contact with the ground . . . Bring the sense of your guardian angel's presence right through into your outer world . . . Remember those colours and the strong, but gentle presence of your guardian angel whenever you feel anxious or in need.

THE COLOURS

The colours for the brow chakra are indigo, turquoise and mauve.

Indigo is a colour we find difficult to perceive and describe; it is neither purple, nor navy blue. It is intense and deep, sometimes almost black, but always containing a touch of red. For chakra work it is translucent, as the colour would appear when sunlight passes through stained glass. Learning to differentiate indigo is, in itself, a good exercise for opening and awakening the brow chakra.

Positively, indigo brings peace, confidence and a sense of security.

Negatively, it can be heavy, or become associated with the 'dark night of the soul'.

Mauve at the brow centre, is dark in tone – a hue between lavender and purple.

Positively, it helps to connect the numinous with the tangible and raises the spirits.

Negatively, it can be cold and absorb energies, so creating a sense of lethargy.

Turquoise is bright – the colour of the gemstone of the same name.

Positively, turquoise feeds us spiritually and also acts as spiritual protection.

Negatively, it can cloud our judgment and make us feel distanced from life.

The colours for the solar plexus chakra are yellow, gold and rose.

The colours for the crown chakra are violet, white and gold.

The colours for the heart chakra are spring green, rose and rose amethyst.

Use the colours as suggested in Exercise 8 (page 42) to develop, awaken and heal your chakras.

THE FRAGRANCES

White musk and hyacinth quieten the brow chakra, while violet and rose-geranium stimulate it. If you have anxiety about your spiritual progress or over-zealously use meditational and spiritual practices you may over-stimulate your brow chakra, signalled by headaches in and around the chakra area. In such cases the quietening fragrances should be used to help the flow and movement within the brow to become calmer and steadier.

If you are new to spiritual development, gently use the stimulating fragrances to encourage your brow chakra to open and function well for you. For the solar plexus chakra the quietening fragrances are vetivert and rose, and the stimulating ones are bergamot and ylang-ylang. For the heart chakra the quietening fragrances are sandalwood and rose, and the stimulating ones are pine and honeysuckle. For the crown chakra the quietening fragrances are rosemary and bergamot and the stimulating ones are violet and amber.

Blending the fragrances, as suggested on page 43, will help to connect the chakra pairs and the chakra triad.

THE CRYSTALS

Refer to page 44 and the Glossary for general guidance on using crystals. The crystals which will best help the issues considered in this chapter are:

Amethyst to enhance spiritual awareness and encourage vision. It is also a protective stone, which absorbs and transforms negativity.

Sapphire to strengthen spiritual awareness and communication. It facilitates communication with guides and angels.

White Flourite to help make connections between the brow and solar plexus chakras. It helps to prevent depression and disillusionment.

Ellestial crystals To help awaken the spirit and matter and to ensure links with the highest available guidance. These cystals encourage angelic presences to be around you and in your life.

PRAYERS OR AFFIRMATIONS

The brow chakra prayer or affirmation is:

We seek to command ourselves through the inspiration of the command of God. May true insight be enabled and the finite mind be inspired to a knowledge of completion.

The crown chakra prayer or affirmation is:

Through surrender and release, let the incoming will be truly the will of God working within us and through us and leading us increasingly to knowledge of mystical union and mystical marriage.

The solar plexus chakra prayer or affirmation is:

Through the gift of fire, let reason, logic, opinion and assimilation become truly linked to inspiration that we are not bound within limitation and separation.

The heart chakra prayer or affirmation is:

In the golden centre of the rose of the heart may tender compassion be linked to unconditional love. May true detachment enable growth and continuity. Through the understanding of birth within death and death within birth may there be transformation.

For suggestions on using prayers or affirmations, see page 45.

Chapter 9

Inner Wisdom:
Getting Older and Wiser

Key Issues: Inner Wisdom, Ageing and Sageing, Fullness of Being
Chakra Pairs: Heart and Crown, Heart and Throat
Archetypes: The Sage and the Crone

This chapter will help you to:
- **come to terms with the ageing process**
- **learn more about heart-centred wisdom**
- **aid the activation and expression of the wisdom carried by your soul stem from other lifetimes**

AREAS OF INFLUENCE

For lists of the areas of influence for the heart chakra see page 77; page 161 for the throat chakra; and page 20 for the crown chakra.

HEART AND CROWN AS A CHAKRA PAIR

When we consider chakras in isolation they stand strongly for the activation of certain qualities. When they are linked to another chakra with which they form a natural pair, one chakra aspect may be emphasized, or another and deeper aspect of a chakra may emerge.

We have seen that the heart chakra is connected to feeling and feeling has been defined as a second level of emotion (see page 127–30). When heart and crown are energetically linked, the quality which emerges is that of wisdom. The wisdom of the soul calls out to and awakens the inner wisdom, and vice versa.

Gildas has said that, paradoxically, we are most likely to form a successful link with our higher guides when our inner wisdom has been activated. As we saw when discussing the archetypes of guru and devotee (page 194) the true guide does not want us to be dependent upon him/her. Like good and more experienced friends, they want to offer us the benefit of their wider perspective, without imposition, over-parenting, invasion or judgment. When we can receive their teachings, question and interpret them, use them for information, but also make our own responsible, informed decisions, guidance works well. When we *need* a guide too desperately, because we cannot cope with life, then we may go to a channel for guidance but our own higher guide will not come through until some of our crises of choice are over.

Linking heart to crown encourages us to use our support systems judiciously and helps our inner wisdom to flourish. It awakens the heart of our being in which lies that integrity which lights our path and is the core of our strength.

As this link strengthens, we often find that we have access to wisdom or even skills which we have not consciously learned. This might be said to be the positive side of karma. In other lifetimes we have learned much. Sometimes an aspect of the doctrine of many lifetimes which people find puzzling is that it seems that each time we incarnate we forget what we have learned previously and need to start again. This is because each life has new lessons but one of the great advantages of working with our chakras is that we gradually activate, or re-activate, our highest potential.

The heart/crown link is the catalyst to the sensing of our wider being. We may not remember specific past lives, but we will realize that we have access to a fount of knowledge far greater than anything we have learned by rote, patience or persistence in this present lifetime.

HEART AND THROAT AS A CHAKRA PAIR

If the heart/crown link activates wisdom, then the heart/throat connection activates our ability to know that we have it and to express it in our lives and for others around us, without being dogmatic, self-aggrandizing or patronizing, but with compassion and discernment.

Our society has lost respect for the sagacity of age. Currently the growing proportion of ageing people is considered to be a social problem and a financial burden. The elderly can feel that they deplete resources and that their life-experience means little. When this is believed strongly enough, it can become a self-fulfilling prophecy. The elderly become childlike, regressed and dependent in an undignified way.

If we respected the rich resources, particularly of a spiritual kind, which the elderly can possess, then the actual economic problems of an ageing population might be more easily resolved.

In Native American Indian tradition, the spiritual continuity and growth of the tribe depends upon the wisdom, teaching and initiation which the grandmothers and grandfathers have to give. Age is a mantle of dignity and respect. New traditions grow naturally and creatively from the old, without the disadvantage and potential wastage of youth-based innovation.

At a spiritual and soul level, and within the concept of many lifetimes, ageing and sageing have another dimension. We each have the crone or sage within us. If we can get beyond the current tendency to find the ageing process embarrassing, frightening, degrading or disgusting, then we will be better able to relate to the old soul within us and to draw on the wisdom stored in the collective unconscious of the whole of humanity (see also Chapter 11). We might even get beyond the point at which, as a family of beings, we have to repeat the same mistakes over and over again. When we contact the old soul within, our management of the personal ageing process is bound to improve.

Case Study: Living Wisely

Joan was in her late sixties when I first met her. She was distressed because she felt that her family and her grandchildren saw her as 'silly and unintelligent'.

Uneducated herself, Joan had nursed a sick husband and an ageing mother. Alongside this, she had worked hard to make sure that there were financial resources available for the sound education of her son and her two daughters. They had done well, had all gone to college or university and now had flourishing careers, good marriages, lovely homes and healthy children. They lived modern lives at a hectic pace, surrounded by computers, mobile phones and fast cars.

Joan had lost touch with her sense of accomplishment in nurturing her family's talents and in providing so well for them. She felt redundant, that she had no proper communication with the young people and that they belittled her. It later turned out that the latter was not objectively true, but it was true for her, in the moment, and thererefore had to be dealt with. In fact, Joan had also been successful in imparting a deep warmth to her children and they were as anxious about her as she was about herself.

Joan bravely came to some workshops and became interested in healing, for which she had a considerable gift. Gradually she began to offer healing and solace, and the natural counsel of an experienced lifer, to friends in the village where she lived, building quite a reputation for herself. To her amazement and delight, many young people began to gather at her home, seeking not only healing for themselves or their children, but advice on all matters from the mundane to the spiritual. They liked to be with her, found her unshockable and often repaid her in kind, by including her in family events and activities or helping, as she got older, with shopping and gardening.

Inevitably her own family noticed changes in Joan. When they came to visit there was often a houseful of people. They saw the respect in which their mother and grandmother was held and they, too, began to ask her for healing and advice.

In awakening her healing talents Joan had worked with her chakras and all the energetic connections, particularly those between heart and crown and heart and throat. As her healing flowed, so did her natural wisdom which struck a chord with the young around her, causing them instinctively to value and reinstate the crone in their village and their lives.

Joan is now older than she cares to admit, but still active, still dignified and still sought-out and respected.

THE ARCHETYPES: THE CRONE AND THE SAGE

As we have seen, our society neglects the archetypes of the crone and the sage. We pursue too arduously the fountain or elixir of eternal youth. This is partly a sign of our being out-of-touch with natural rhythms and cycles – and partly our fear of mortality and extinction.

So many aspects of life become easier to understand or to

live through when we believe in an eternity of being. The concept of many lifetimes can make us aware that no experience is ever wasted and that we are not under pressure to complete everything we want to do in one lifetime. Such beliefs make it not only easier to live, but easier to die – for we can know that our essence lives on.

The archetypes of the sage and the crone personify continuity of experience and the wisdom which endures.

EXERCISES

Exercise 37
Linking Heart and Crown Energies

Making sure that you will be undisturbed, sit or stand with your spine straight, your body symmetrical and your legs uncrossed at knees or ankles, unless using a cross-legged or lotus position.

- Begin with central column breathing (see page 17).
- Focus on your heart chakra and breathe in through its petals and out through its stem (five to ten in/out breath sequences).
- Breathe in through the petals of your heart chakra, hold your breath for a count of three in its centre, and then breathe upward through your central column to your crown chakra and out through your crown (five to ten in/out breath sequences).
- Breathe in through the petals of your crown chakra, hold your breath in the centre of your crown chakra for a count of three, and then breathe down into the centre of your heart chakra and out through its petals (five to ten in/ out breath sequences).

- Finish with central column breathing, ending on the down-breath.

Exercise 38
Linking Heart and Throat Energies

Position yourself as for Exercise 37, above.

- Begin with central column breathing (see page 17).
- Focus on your heart chakra and breathe in through its petals and out through its stem (five to ten in/out breath sequences).
- Breathe in through the petals of your heart chakra, to its centre. Hold your breath for a count of three, and then breathe up through your central column into the centre of your throat chakra and out through its petals (five to ten in/out breath sequences).
- Breathe in through the petals of your throat chakra and out through its stem (five to ten in/out breath sequences).
- Breathe in through the petals of your throat chakra to its centre, and hold your breath for a count of three. Breathe down through your central column into the centre of your heart chakra and out through its petals (five to ten in/out breaths).
- Finish with central column breathing, ending on the down-breath.

Exercise 39
Creating a Place of Inner Wisdom

Making sure that you will be undisturbed, create a quiet space for yourself and lie or sit comfortably in a position in which your body is symmetrically arranged.

- Practise central column breathing (see page 17). When you feel centred and peaceful, breathe in at the petals of your crown chakra and out through the petals of your heart . . .
- Visualize your heart chakra opening up like a rose in perfect bloom . . . Imagine travelling to the golden centre of this rose . . . In the golden centre of the rose there is a still point of wisdom and knowing . . . Find this still point and remain in touch with it for five to ten minutes . . . (If your attention wanders, just quietly keep returning to the golden centre of the rose . . .) Know that when you return you will be able to see any problems in your life from a new perspective . . .
- When you are ready, return to an awareness of your breath coming in at the crown of your head and out through the petals of your heart chakra . . . Let the petals of your heart centre gradually close in . . . Feel the contact of your feet with the ground beneath . . . Take your sense of inner peace with you as you resume your normal life once more . . .

Exercise 40
Considering the Inner Crone or Sage

- For this consideration, simply go within, without a formal guided journey . . .
- Imagine meeting with an ancient female or masculine wise figure . . .
  - What gift do you want to give this figure?
  - What gift do you wish to receive from it?
  - What question do you want to ask?
  - What does your inner ancient figure require from you?

THE COLOURS

The colours for the heart chakra are spring green, rose and rose amethyst.

The colours for the throat chakra are blue, silver and turquoise.

The colours for the crown chakra are: violet, white and gold.

Use the colours as suggested in Exercise 8 (page 42) to develop, awaken and heal your chakras.

THE FRAGRANCES

For the heart chakra the quietening fragrances are sandalwood and rose, and the stimulating ones are pine and honeysuckle. For the throat chakra the quietening fragrances are lavender and hyacinth and the stimulating ones are patchouli and white musk. For the crown chakra the quietening fragrances are rosemary and bergamot, and the stimulating ones are violet and amber.

Blending the fragrances, as suggested on page 43, will help to connect the chakra pairs.

THE CRYSTALS

Refer to page 44 and the Glossary for general guidance on using crystals. The crystals which will best help the issues considered in this chapter are:

Snowflake Obsidian Linked to the cycles of birth, death and rebirth, this stone brings stamina and wisdom.

Peacock Stone Sometimes called Bornite or Chalcopyrites, this stone aids the recall of skills which have been known and practised in another lifetime, or which are stored in the collective unconscious. This particularly applies to the revival of ancient healing skills.

PRAYERS OR AFFIRMATIONS

The heart chakra prayer or affirmation is:

> In the golden centre of the rose of the heart may tender
> compassion be linked to unconditional love. May true
> detachment enable growth and continuity. Through the
> understanding of birth within death and death within
> birth may there be transformation.

The throat chakra prayer or affirmation is:

> Help us to develop responsibility. May universal truth
> impregnate causal action so that the voice of humanity may
> find true harmony with the voice of the earth.

The crown chakra prayer or affirmation is:

> Through surrender and release, let the incoming will be
> truly the will of God working within us and through us
> and leading us increasingly to knowledge of mystical
> union and mystical marriage.

For suggestions on using prayers or affirmations, see page 45.

Chapter 10

As Above, So Below:
Spirituality and Divinity

Key Issue: Spiritual Manifestation

Chakra Triad: Throat, Brow and Crown

Archetype: The Divine

This chapter will help you to:
- learn more about the process of spiritual manifestation
- gain a greater understanding of the process of position synchronicity
- reflect on Divinity

AREAS OF INFLUENCE

For lists of the areas of influence for the throat chakra see page 161; page 186 for the brow chakra; and page 20 for the crown chakra.

THROAT, BROW AND CROWN AS A CHAKRA TRIAD

The throat chakra is a gateway chakra: the sevenfold chakra system is sub-divided into two interacting groups and the throat is a member of both. As one of the five lower chakras, it is related to an element, a developmental age and a sense. As the first of the three upper chakras, it is concerned with trans-personal expression and has connections to the higher self, spirit and soul.

When the three upper chakras are open, and in communi-cation as a triad, we often experience an increasing sense of the need to serve humanity, without living in isolation. Service to the collective becomes a necessary and intrinsic part of self-growth and awareness.

The transpersonal psychologist Maslow spoke about self-actualization. He felt that, when growth processes and neces-sary healing reached a certain point, every part of our being could find expression. The blueprint with which we come into incarnation would be actualized. Probably a totally self-actual-ized person has little need to remain longer in incarnation – and, being self-actualized, would finish the task in hand and die gracefully. However, there can be times in our lives when we feel that we are 'firing on all cylinders'. This can be cyclical, or part of the spiral of growth. Once attained it may fade again or become elusive for a while, but when we have touched it, even briefly, we know that we are capable of manifesting our full spiritual selves whilst in incarnation.

Energetically speaking, self-actualization happens when there is harmony within the whole chakra team – but it is particularly encouraged when the throat/brow/crown triad is active.

The archetype or essence of the Divine is abstract. When we personify or define it too closely we both limit it and endow it with false powers. That which is infinite cannot be defined. A religion which is built on the image of an old bearded man, sitting on a throne, writing down judgments in a huge book, has not 'come of age'. It is limited, patriarchal and immature. The throat chakra, in its triad with brow and crown, urges us to come of age, spiritually.

Religions which need many figures, both masculine and feminine, in order to express the range within the Divine, have often been rather derogatorily labelled Pantheistic – but that which is infinite must also have infinite facets which subscribe to the whole. Learning the thousand names of the Divine seems to encompass more possibilities than the vision of the old man on the throne.

SPIRITUAL MANIFESTATION

Our apparent need to control and define is an obstacle to spiritual manifestation. That which is abstract, diffuse and defies definition can only truly inspire us and aid our becoming when we let it be as it is, or consciously use open-ended definitions.

One function, then, of the crown chakra is to hold the diffuse and unnamed potential. When the crown, brow and throat are linked, there can be a constant flow of the unnamed potential from the ketheric plane at the crown, through to the higher mental plane at the brow chakra, and then on to the mental or manifestational plane at the throat chakra.

The higher mental plane is also abstract in its nature, but it is the plane on which energies from the ketheric begin to be apprehended by us and to take form. The Divine Principles move us inwardly, before we name them and use them as a life model. The angelic beings, carrying the Divine Principles into pre-manifestational form for us, touch us lightly. As these energies come through to the mental plane, they are named. Once named, they come into existence on our material plane and we work with them as archetypes.

What does this mean for us in our lives? Dealing with abstractions is not easy. I can only suggest that:

- We should not seek to over-define ourselves.
- We should never declare anything to be impossible. There seems to be much truth in the saying: 'Everything is possible under the sun.'
- We should value more and more, the art and practice of play. When we sustain an ability to play, creativity flows and we constantly explore the worlds of wonder and magic. Delight in new combinations enables discovery, from ideas through to colours, shapes and the highly manifestational world of design, furnishing, gadgetry and the way we dress.
- We should look to the world of music. Musicians and composers never run out of new combinations of notes and sounds which produce more and more harmonies to delight our ears.
- In order to let go of the insecurities which fuel our tendency to control and over-decline, we should trust that the blueprint of the Infinite is powered by love.

Case Study: Spiritual Manifestation

Joshua was mentally challenged. Not all the horrific details of his early childhood were known, but he had been physically abused and severely neglected. He was taken into care and then fostered and finally adopted by a warm and loving couple who had been unable to have children of their own.

With love, care and security, Joshua moved from being a very frightened, imprisoned child to a more confident young person reaching out to his full, if comparatively limited, potential. When he was fifteen years old, his mother consulted Gildas about Joshua's obsessive habit of ordering everything. All his possessions had to be laid out in certain patterned and ordered ways. He could fly into rages if anything was moved. Whilst this pattern related mostly to

Joshua's own room and possessions, Nesta and Mike, his adoptive parents, had honoured it, but now Joshua had begun to take more part in everyday household tasks and his need for order was impinging on them all. The cutlery drawer had become a focus for rages and tantrums and sometimes for hours spent obsessively arranging the objects in it.

Gildas felt that, besides Joshua's obvious psychological wounds and misaligned emotional body, he had lost the instinctual link to his higher-self blueprint. This link can be helped and healed when the throat/brow/crown triad is activated. In his ordering activities Joshua was not only seeking security and control in his life, but was over-defining himself. As he had entered the developmental age range for the throat chakra his need for control had been exacerbated.

Obviously we could not teach Joshua complex theories about the chakras. But he loved crystals, colours, fragrances, sounds and music. Nesta got an amethyst and an iron pyrites sun for Joshua and encouraged him to wear clothes in the blue, mauve and purple range. She mixed him his own special bath and massage oil of jojoba carrying oil, to which four drops each of lavender, white musk, rose-geranium, violet and bergamot essential oil concentrates had been added. She also gave him, at Gildas' suggestion, a tape of pan pipe music, since the clearly definable sounds of the pipes have combinations in them which resonate to the throat/brow/crown triad.

Over a period of time these treatments, plus a great deal of love and patience from Nesta and Mike, brought about a change in Joshua. Nesta particularly noticed that if she played the pipe music when Joshua started his ordering rituals, his attention could be more easily diverted or channelled into other activities. Eventually he became comfortable with far less order in his possessions and even developed a sense of humour about his need.

I have used Joshua as an illustration here, because it is easy to feel that the throat/brow/crown connection is spiritually sophisticated. Instead, it can even be developed at a relatively unconscious level, through exposure to sound, colour and crystals.

EXERCISES

Exercise 41
Connecting the Throat/Brow/Crown Triad

Sit or stand with your spine straight, your body symmetrically arranged and your legs uncrossed at knees or ankles unless using a cross-legged or lotus posture.

- Begin with central column breathing (see page 17).
- Breathe in through the petals of your throat chakra and out through its stem (five to ten in/out breath sequences).
- Breathe in through the petals of your throat chakra, hold the breath in the centre of your throat chakra for a count of three, sustain the in-breath as you move up through the central column to the centre of your brow chakra and breathe out through the petals of your brow chakra (five to ten in/out breath sequences).
- Breathe in through the petals of your brow chakra, hold the breath in the centre of your brow chakra for a count of three, then sustain the in-breath as you move the energy up through your central column, into your crown chakra and out through the top of your head (five to ten in/out breath sequences).
- Take a deep in-breath through the crown of your head, into your central column, and, sustaining the in-breath, visualize the energy going out through the petals of your brow chakra, and in through the petals of your throat

chakra. Then finally breathe the energy out through the stem of your throat chakra (five to ten in/out breath sequences).
- Finish with central column breathing, ending on the down-breath.

Sounding

Exercise 30 (page 180) gives suggestions for sounding your own note. For this chakra triad, follow those same suggestions but, as you listen to your own sounding, be aware of notes which resonate to your throat, brow and crown chakra, the full chord for the chakra triad will be harmonious.

THE COLOURS

The colours for the throat chakra are blue, silver and turquoise.
The colours for the brow chakra are indigo, turquoise and mauve.
The colours for the crown chakra are violet, white and gold.
Use the colours as suggested in Exercise 8 (page 42) to develop, awaken and heal your chakras.

THE FRAGRANCES

For the throat chakra the quietening fragrances are lavender and hyacinth, and the stimulating ones are patchouli and white musk. For the brow chakra the quietening fragrances are white musk and hyacinth, and the stimulating ones are violet and rose-geranium. For the crown chakra the quietening fragrances are rosemary and bergamot, and the stimulating ones are violet and amber.

Blend the fragrances, as suggested on page 43. (See also the case study on page 217.)

THE CRYSTALS

Refer to page 44 and the Glossary for general guidance on using crystals. The crystals which will best help the issues considered in this chapter are:

Amethyst To absorb and transform negativity and aid the making of links between chakras.

Iron Pyrites Sun To remind us of our instinctual links to our higher selves and our spiritual blueprint.

Diamond Symbolizing perfection and clarity, diamonds draw us towards our highest potential and encourage the higher will to illumine the personality.

PRAYERS OR AFFIRMATIONS

The throat chakra prayer or affirmation is:

Help us to develop responsibility. May universal truth impregnate causal action so that the voice of humanity may find true harmony with the voice of the earth.

The brow chakra prayer or affirmation is:

We seek to command ourselves through the inspiration of the command of God. May true insight be enabled and the finite mind be inspired to a knowledge of completion.

The crown chakra prayer or affirmation is:

Through surrender and release, let the incoming will be truly the will of God working within us and through us and leading us increasingly to knowledge of mystical union and mystical marriage.

For suggestions on using prayers or affirmations see page 45.

Chapter 11

All My Relations:
In Harmony with Nature

Key Issues: Inter-Species Relationships; Fairies and Nature Spirits; Morphic Resonance

Chakra Pairs: Throat and Alter Major; Alter Major and Crown; Alter Major and Root

Archetypes: Pan and Flora

This chapter will help you to:
- learn more about our interaction with other species, fairies and nature spirits
- gain a greater understanding of self-healing processes
- have hope for the growth of consciousness in humanity and understand the part each individual may play in this

---

AREAS OF INFLUENCE

For lists of the areas of influence for the crown chakra see page 20; page 161 for the throat chakra; and page 19 for the root chakra.

The Alter Major Chakra

Location Petals in the area of the nose. Positive energy centre in its stem, which is where the back of the head begins to bend round, corresponding with the 'old' or 'lizard' brain, before the division into right and left hemispheres

Key Words Instinct, Resonance, Duality, Devic Nature, Healing

Colours Brown, Yellow Ochre, Olive Green

Element Wet Earth

Sense Smell

Body Instinctual and Lower Causal

Glandular Connection Adrenals

Quietening Fragrances Musk, Cedarwood

Stimulating Fragrances Violet, Rose-Geranium

Crystals and Gemstones Carnelian, Tiger's Eye, Snowflake Obsidian, Fossils, Peacock Stone (sometimes called Bornite or Chalcopyrites)

Prayer or Affirmation

Through engagement with our Devic Nature may we move from duality and split, to oneness and unity.

THE ALTER MAJOR CHAKRA

Since the alter major chakra is a lesser-known chakra, let us consider it alone, before moving on to its chakra pairings.

An 'alta major' chakra is described in the writings of Alice Bailey (see Bibliography). 'Alta' means 'higher', whereas 'alter' means 'other'. Some Eastern yogic systems also include a chakra at the back of the head which is not related to a specific number of petals or to a Sanskrit vowel sound (as are the seven classical chakras).

With the other seven chakras there is a sequential progression from lower to higher, according to their vibrational rate and their relationship to the upright human body. The placement of the alter major is thus out of sequence. Although situated between the throat and the brow, its vibrational rate comes between those of the root and sacral chakras. Its element is a combination of earth and water; it shares the sense of smell with the root chakra and its glandular connection with the solar plexus.

Whereas the other chakras have a positive electric or magnetic polarity in their petals and a negative polarity in their stems, the alter major chakra is the only one to have a reversed polarity. The energy flow moves from the back of the head to the front (see diagram, page 7).

Working with the alter major chakra can be instrumental in awakening instinctual alertness. Energetically, the alter major is linked to the old brain cortex, or 'lizard brain'. This means that it can put us in touch with the non-verbal message system which protects us from, or warns us of, danger. This is similar to the instinct which causes rats to leave a ship or pit ponies to refuse to enter a coal-seam, well in advance of any other warnings that something is wrong. As humans, if we 'happen' to get up and leave the room just before the ceiling falls in over the chair where we were sitting we explain it away as 'lucky chance'. We say, 'my number wasn't up yet', or 'my guardian angel was working hard'. It is difficult for us to believe that these happenings come from a non-verbal signalling which can be more consciously cultivated. If this sense had not been so universally lost or dishonoured, our planet might not now be facing the threat of imminent disaster. Warnings tend only to be accepted if they have been scientifically or intellectually proven. Prophets working intuitively or instinctually are not respected and may become figures of fun.

The alter major chakra is the window through which we can connect to the phenomenon which Rupert Sheldrake (see Bibliography) named as 'morphic resonance' and linked to the 'hundredth monkey' theory. If one monkey on an island learns to wash potatoes and then teaches another, who teaches another, as soon as one hundred monkeys on the island wash potatoes, all the monkeys everywhere will start to wash potatoes without having gone through a learning or modelling process. (The figure 'one hundred' represents an optimum number or proportion.)

Jung wrote extensively about the 'collective unconscious' (see Bibliography). He theorized that everything which humans do, or have ever done, affects and impinges on each one of us.

These energies suggest exciting possibilities for the role of the individual in collective change. With sophisticated communication systems, the 'optimum number' may be more easily reached. In recent years world days of prayer, peace, meditation and humour have played a considerable role in changing our awareness and encouraging us to share resources. What is not so universally known is that working with the alter major chakra and its chakric pairs increases the efficiency of morphic resonance and the 'creative minority'. When enough people recognize this, and work with these connections, then quantum leaps will surely happen in our time.

ALTER MAJOR AND THROAT AS A CHAKRA PAIR

Connecting the alter major and throat chakras as a pair leads to an increase in our abilities to heal ourselves; to have access to past, stored knowledge (including the record of our own evolution); and to communicate with other species, including nature spirits, fairies and devic beings.

The throat chakra is a dual chakra (see page 161) and the alter major is linked to the archetype of Pan who has much to teach us about duality. Problems brought about by dualities and oppositions in life often underlie the process of dis-ease. Within each one of us there is a natural self-healing mechanism. When we are really ill this self-healing mechanism becomes depressed. Much healing, whether allopathic or complementary, aims to some degree to 'kick-start' or 'jump-lead' the self-healing mechanism.

Research shows that we can consciously influence the so-called autonomous systems of the body when we learn to activate the right side of the brain. When we engage deliberately with our self-healing mechanisms, the elementals within us are enabled to help our bodies back to health and harmony. A large factor in health or dis-ease patterns is the balance of earth, air, fire and water within our bodily systems.

Connecting the alter major with the throat chakra means that communication with our inner systems is enhanced, we can more easily hold our bodies in optimum health, and also be in touch with any developing imbalances before they become acute or chronic.

Nature Spirits

In different ways the alter major and throat chakras are connected to communication. When they work strongly together they enhance our communication with the natural world and the rhythms and life-force manifest in nature.

Comparatively little is known about the beings who are energetic guardians of the elemental and natural worlds. They are variously called devic beings, nature spirits, fairies, gnomes, elves, undines, nereids, salamanders and sprites. They have long been portrayed in stories and illustrations as part of our mythical consciousness. Devas are guardians of rivers, valleys, hillsides and trees. Fairies, elves, undines and nereids are energy beings with a sense of fun. They appear, to those who have 'the sight', in semi-human form when they want to attract attention and communicate. They are often bewildered when we do not see their flashes of light and colour or hear the tinkle of their laughter. Where there is energy, there *they* are. When all is well they work with the devas and direct their energies towards growth, fertility and abundance. When things are out of balance they are drawn to wherever the energy flow is strongest. Formed of basic energy, nature spirits on the lower levels of the hierarchy are primitively amoral and will pick up on, and accentuate, difficult as well as positive animation or interaction.

The hierarchy of nature spirits is on the same stream of consciousness as the angelic hierarchy – but there is a definite, more straightforward, evolutionary, two-way stream of consciousness amongst these beings than that within the human consciousness stream. Nature spirits and elementals are part of an energy streaming out from the Divine Source, but they also evolve *towards* the Source. The tiniest, amoral, 'dot' elementals will become fairies or undines and eventually part of one of the complex Devic forms. Devas become angels and evolve onwards through the angelic hierarchy. (For more on this, see my book *Working With Guides and Angels* in the Bibliography.)

Animals and Plants

When we are more aware of the subtle forces around us we also become aware of the role which animals and plants play in the universe. Scientifically, of course, with plants and trees we can understand the ways in which they balance the atmosphere and help to clean up reasonable levels of pollution. They are part of our food chain, as well as producing substances which are healing to our bodies. They communicate beauty and abundance to us and often inspire us to higher vision and understanding of universal patterns. When we respect, look after, and cooperate with plants we make a deeper commitment to incarnation and become more in touch with the earth and its natural rhythms and cycles.

We have a great karmic debt to animals and are collectively guilty of mistreating many of their species. We do not have to be vegetarians to be horrified at some of the conditions endured by factory-farmed animals or the plight of horses, dogs and cats who are starved or ill-treated. Only as species begin to die out do we seem to get any inkling of the value animals have in the balance of nature. Current campaigns to make us aware of the need to save particular animal species are reawakening an important awareness. If our alter major chakras had not 'gone to sleep' such crusades would not be necessary.

Gildas has spoken on several occasions of the importance of the sounds which animals make in supporting the subtle structure around us and in also helping to deal with, or prevent, pollution. The alter major/throat connection may not make us consciously hear all these subtle notes or appreciate the essential interaction of animal fragrances as part of planetary balance, but it will open us to an understanding that all factors within the natural world have a place in making the whole healthy. There are no accidents in the pattern of life. Human beings have made themselves dominant without always remembering that leadership should inspire and nourish, rather than crush and humiliate. Making the alter major/throat connection may lead us to some uncomfortable insights, but it is of the utmost energetic necessity if we are to live in harmony with all our relations – whatever their species.

ALTER MAJOR AND CROWN AS A CHAKRA PAIR

The main connection between alter major and crown is through their sharing of a subtle body. The crown is linked to the soul, ketheric or higher causal body, the alter major to the lower causal body which is a layer within the higher body.

The soul, ketheric or higher causal body holds the imprint of the intentions which we have made for this and other lifetimes. Whilst in incarnation, this layer can affect us through the subtle memories from other lives which cause us to react to positive or negative stimuli in ways which are not directly explicable in terms of our present life experience. Unexpectedly intense or so-called irrational fears, free-floating anxiety patterns, *déjà vu* experiences and exceptional giftedness are all examples of the interpenetration of the causal body into our lives.

The lower causal body of the alter major governs the rhythms chosen by our soul. Our birth will happen at a specific time and we will be preserved from death until our agreed lifespan has been reached. Awareness of, and communication with, this level of our beings, brings about a more immediate working out of the karmic laws of cause and effect, leaving less unfinished business to be balanced out in a future lifetime.

When alter major and crown are in balance, both causal layers are more integrated, and it is easier to achieve clarity about our life purpose.

ALTER MAJOR AND ROOT AS A CHAKRA PAIR

Connecting the alter major and root chakras increases our instinctual awareness. It puts us in touch with our positive animal nature, enabling us to sit more easily and naturally in our bodies and to trust them. When our living is out of tune with natural rhythms we can begin to fear the power of our bodies over us. The body has an instinctual wisdom and there is a deep sapience in dis-ease (see also Chapter 3). But when our bodies fail us, life can be complex indeed.

The connection of alter major to throat enables us to hear or apprehend the body's signallings, whereas the connection of alter major to root makes the signallings stronger and aids us in discerning, and surrendering to, our personal rhythms. When we are stressed it means that we have over-ridden those personal rhythms which are conducive to sustainable health. We do not all have the same constitution. Some of us thrive on stresses which others would find intolerable. When alter major and throat are connected we are more likely to live within our own capacities rather than striving to reach standards or norms of performance. We are also likely to be more tolerant of the patterns of others without wishing to compete or demand more.

In inner journeying it is sometimes suggested that a contact with an inner animal be made, since this signifies and symbolizes stronger connections with our natural instinctual nature. Knowing our inner 'body' power animal (see Glossary) can be helpful in the management of our bodies in today's stresses and unnatural rhythms. There is a guided visualization for this on page 236.

Case Study: Harmonizing with Nature

This case study is also written up in the alter major section of Working With Your Chakras *but I have no other which better fits the case for connecting the chakra pairs described in this chapter.*

I met James, a business executive, when I was working as a counsellor and healer in a residential natural health centre. He had become severely stressed and his blood pressure was dangerously high. He attended my daily relaxation classes and asked for some individual counselling sessions. His wife, Mary, was at the health centre too, giving James support and taking a much-needed break herself. She was desperately concerned and found her workaholic husband stressful to live with.

James found it difficult to relax. He was already wondering how to survive the remaining three weeks of the month for which he had booked. His 'normal' life consisted of a long commuter day. He took his lap-top computer and mobile phone with him wherever he went. Every journey was spent working. When he went abroad, he did not take Mary with him, nor did he allow himself time to see anything of the interesting places he visited. In the evenings or at weekends he was always to be found at his desk at home.

James had a lovely house on the edge of countryside, but never went for walks. He employed someone to help his wife with their large garden rather than get involved himself. He was reluctant to take holidays and, when persuaded to do so, the lap-top and sheafs of papers invariably went with him. On the few occasions that his wife could persuade him to go to the theatre or to socialize with friends, he was restless, irritable and abrupt.

Mary said that James only went outside on his way to the car, train or plane. She was sure that he was unaware of the seasons of the year – he wore lighter shirts and suits in summer only because she put them out for him.

When I told James that I was a healer as well as a counsellor he was surprisingly open to 'trying it out'. Perhaps he thought I could weave some magic which would allow him to go back to his old ways without making himself ill. I decided to work principally on his alter major chakra, encouraging it to open. The energy field at the back of his head felt tight, static and numb. I did some guided imagery with him, emphasizing natural scenes and the elements. Predictably, James found visualization difficult but playing quiet background music helped and he actually began to enjoy our sessions.

James was not the sort of person who would work directly with his chakras, but I taught him to massage the alter major positive polarity point gently with his fingertips. The health centre had extensive grounds, with cows and horses in adjoining fields and access to the sort of woods where the leaf-mould is thick and the scent of damp earth pervades. Mary encouraged James to walk in the woods with her and noticed that he was gradually becoming less restless and more able to converse with her in a relaxed way as they strolled through the greenery.

One day, Mary found James sitting on a bench, watching the cows chewing the cud. She sat near him and after a while he took her hand and said, 'All I really need to do is remember to watch the cows more often.' It was a true turning point. The combined treatments at the health centre were effective. James left with a much lower blood pressure reading, a determination to change his lifestyle, and a love of cows. Mary left with hope for her husband's future survival and for the quality of their life and marriage.

THE ARCHETYPES: PAN AND FLORA

Traditionally and mythologically, Pan is the king of the nature spirits and Flora his consort. They have a duality within them. Pan, in particular, sometimes appears as the eternal youth, playing his pipes, whilst flowers spring up to hear his tunes and mountains dance and sing – whilst at other times he prances around devilishly with cloven hooves, forked tail and enormous, erect phallus, creating the stuff of rape and nightmare.

Flora, though less changeable in her image, can be joyful, dancing and fertile, or negatively seductive, cruel and destructive.

When we are in tune with nature and our instincts, Pan and Flora bring us healing, harmony and celebration. They bless the earth and cause things to flourish. When we pollute the earth and deny our instincts, they rampage, wound and destroy. They are mirrors of ourselves and our relationship to natural worlds, rhythms and cycles. When we wound the earth and disrespect the natural kingdoms we eventually wound ourselves. If we see our instinctual drives, such as sexuality, as the shadow side of our natures then the shadow grows bigger than us and causes devastation.

Linking the chakra pairs discussed in this chapter helps us to keep the Pan/Flora energies in balance.

EXERCISES

Exercise 42
Linking the Throat and Alter Major Chakras

Sit or stand with your spine straight, your body symmetrically arranged and your feet uncrossed at knees or ankles, unless using a cross-legged or lotus posture.

- Begin with central column breathing (see page 17).
- Breathe in through your throat chakra petals and out through its stem (five to ten in/out breath sequences).
- Breathe in through the petals of your throat chakra to its centre. Hold your breath for a count of three, and then breathe up through your central column to the centre of your alter major chakra and out through its stem (five to ten in/out breath sequences).
- Breathe in through the stem of your alter major chakra and out through its petals (five to ten in/out breath sequences).
- Breathe in through the stem of your alter major chakra, holding your breath for a count of three in its centre. Breathe down into the centre of your throat chakra and out through its petals (five to ten in/out breath sequences).
- Finish with central column breathing, ending on the down-breath.

Exercise 43
Linking the Crown and Alter Major Chakras

Position yourself as for exercise 42, above.

- Begin with central column breathing.

- Breathe in through the stem of your alter major chakra and out through its petals (five to ten in/out breath sequences).
- Breathe in through the stem of your alter major chakra to its centre, hold your breath to a count of three. Breathe up through your central column and out through the petals of your crown chakra (five to ten in/out breath sequences).
- Breathe in through the petals of your crown chakra, down through your central column to the centre of your alter major chakra and out through its stem (five to ten in/out breath sequences).
- Finish with central column breathing, ending on the down-breath.

Exercise 44
Linking the Root and Alter Major Charkas

Position yourself as for Exercise 42 (see page 234).

- Begin with central column breathing (see page 17).
- Breathe up from the earth, through your root chakra, up your central column to the centre of your alter major chakra, and breathe out through the stem of your alter major chakra (five to ten in/out breath sequences).
- Breathe in through the stem of your alter major chakra and out through its petals (five to ten in/out breath sequences).
- Breathe in through the stem of your alter major chakra into its centre, holding your breath for a count of three. Breathe down through your central column, out through the petals of your root chakra and into the earth (five to ten in/out breath sequences).

- Finish with central column breathing, ending on the down-breath.

Exercise 45
Guided Visualization for Meeting Your Body Power Animal

According to Native American Indian tradition we each have a number of power or totem animals (see Glossary). One of them is particularly linked to our body and its health. This journey is specifically for meeting your body animal.

Making sure that you will be undisturbed, sit or lie in a comfortable balanced position with your body symmetrically arranged and your legs uncrossed at the knees or ankles, unless using a cross-legged or lotus posture. Have a blanket for warmth, and writing and drawing materials at hand.

- Be aware of the rhythm of your breathing . . . Gradually bring the rhythm into your heart centre and then travel on your heart breath into your inner landscape, finding yourself in your meadow . . .
- Activate all your inner senses so that you see the objects and colours . . . hear the sounds . . . smell the fragrances . . . touch the textures . . . and savour the tastes . . .
- From your meadow, you can see a wooded area of your landscape . . . A part of you knows where your body power animal dwells . . . Travel towards the wood and when you arrive there search for a damp part of the woods where there is a hole in the ground (perhaps by the roots of a tree), or for a damp, more rocky area where there are caves . . . Your body power animal lives either in the hole or in the cave to which you are instinctively led . . .
- Either call your animal to come out to meet you or go in to the hole or cave, taking a light with you if you wish.

Remember that, though your animal may be very wild or
fierce in the outer world, in your inner world it is your
friend and you can communicate with it . . . As you make
each other's acquaintance ask your power animal to dance
with you – a celebration of potential health, healing and
well-being . . . *(Even if you are not well, or are unable to dance
in the outer world, getting your power animal to dance in the inner
world can aid the healing process.)*

Exercise 46
Considering Pan and Flora

- Take drawing and writing materials, make sure you will be
  undisturbed and, through creative writing, poetry or
  meditative drawing, connect to the positive side of Pan
  and/or Flora.
- As you write or draw, consider your relationship to
  celebration, jollity, sensuality and your knowledge of
  natural rhythms and cycles.
- Maybe plan to celebrate a solstice, equinox or one of the
  ancient festivals (see C.J. Cooper's *The Aquarian Dictionary
  of Festivals* in the Bibliography).

THE COLOURS

The colours for the alter major are brown, yellow ochre and
olive green. They are denser tones than for other chakras but
they should still be visualized as they would appear in stained
glass with the light passing through it.

The brown is a deep brown ochre colour, with red tones in
it. Positively, it helps to link us to the earth, to fertility, natural
cycles and natural craftsmanship.

Negative tones of this colour can cause the onset of primitive fears and superstitions. They can engender primitive and forceful anger

Yellow ochre is the colour of deep mustard, often seen in lichens and tree fungi. Positively, it links us to the world of plants and herbal healing.

Negatively, this colour can be psychically toxic, making us out of touch with ourselves, our instincts and our self-healing mechanisms.

Olive green is the silvery green of the leaves of the olive tree rather than the colour of green olives. Positively, this colour brings us inner peace and strength and makes us confident in our bodies. It has no negative shades or powers.

The colours for the root chakra are red, brown and mauve.

The colours for the throat chakra are blue, silver and turquoise.

The colours for the crown chakra are violet, white and gold.

Use the colours as suggested in Exercise 8 (page 42) to develop, awaken and heal your chakras.

THE FRAGRANCES

For the alter major chakra the quietening fragrances are musk and cedarwood, and the stimulating ones are violet and rose-geranium.

Most of us need the stimulating fragrances for the alter major to help it become more open and active. These can be blended with one stimulating and one quietening fragrance from each of the other pairs to stimulate the pair connections. James's alter major chakra was quite tightly closed. His masseur at the health clinic added a mixture of lavender and amber oils to the usual massage oil.

A few people are so attuned to the elements and natural earth rhythms that they seem almost like sprites in appearance and movement or in a 'butterfly' attitude to life. In these cases the alter major chakra may be disproportionately active and the quietening fragrances should be used.

For the root chakra the quietening fragrances are cedarwood and patchouli, and the stimulating ones are musk, lavender and hyacinth. For the throat chakra the quietening fragrances are lavender and hyacinth, and the stimulating ones are patchouli and white musk. For the crown chakra the quietening fragrances are rosemary and bergamot, and the stimulating ones are violet and amber.

THE CRYSTALS

Refer to page 44 and the Glossary for general guidance on using crystals. The crystals which will best help the issues considered in this chapter are:

Fossils (polished or natural) To help us connect to morphic resonance and the wisdom stored in the collective unconscious. They promote our natural relationship with other species.

Carnelian To encourage contact with nature spirits, aid our memory of other lifetimes and help us to dream 'great dreams' (sleep dreams which have a wider relevance than the merely personal).

Turquoise To help our communication with all that is natural and also aid the connection with our body animals.

PRAYERS OR AFFIRMATIONS

The alter major chakra prayer or affirmation is:

Through engagement with our Devic Nature may we move from duality and split, to oneness and unity.

The root chakra prayer or affirmation is:

Through incarnation may spirit be brought into matter.
Through rootedness may life force be recharged and
exchanged. We acknowledge wholeness and seek to gain
and to reflect acceptance.

The throat chakra prayer or affirmation is:

Help us to develop responsibility. May universal truth
impregnate causal action so that the voice of humanity may
find true harmony with the voice of the earth.

The crown chakra prayer or affirmation is:

Through surrender and release let the incoming will be
truly the will of God working within us and through us,
leading us increasingly to knowledge of mystical union and
mystical marriage.

For suggestions on using prayers or affirmations see page 45.

Chapter 12

New Dimensions:
Death and Rebirth

Key Issues: Death and Rebirth, Chaos, New Opportunities, the Millenium, the Birth of New Archetypes
Chakra System: The New Chakras, the Base, the Hara, the Unconditional Love Centre, the Third Eye
The Archetypes: Unconditional Love, the Fool

This chapter will help you:
- learn about the more recently discovered chakras
- Understand the place of chaos in the scheme of things
- learn about possibilities for the new millennium, new opportunities and the birth of new archetypes

AREAS OF INFLUENCE

The Base Chakra

Location Petals over the pubic bone, stem at the coccyx
Key Words Retribution, Redemption, Choice, Transition, Peace, The World

Developmental Age Conception to Birth
Colours Deep Rose Red, Ruby, Purple
Element Earth
Body Causal
Quietening Fragrances Heather, Rosewood
Stimulating Fragrances Lemon Verbena, Thyme
Crystals and Gemstones Rhodocrosite, Moonstone, Rose Quartz. Rose Opal, Rubilite

Prayer or Affirmation

We acknowledge the interaction of our soul choice for retribution with our psychological environment. We seek to understand and surrender to the transition form retribution to redemption.

The Hara Chakra

Location In the auric field between the sacral and solar plexus chakras
Key Words Vitality, Power, Healing, Regeneration, Balance, God
Colours Apricot, Silver, Platinum
Element Granite
Quietening Fragrances Hibiscus, Apricot
Stimulating Fragrances Frankincense, Lily of the Valley
Crystals and Gemstones Honey Calcite, Sunstone, Iron Pyrites' Sun, Stibnite, Wulfenite

Prayer or Affirmation

We acknowledge and connect with the universal vital lifeforce. We accept our potential for health and regeneration, knowing that release from disease will bring collective self-actualization.

The Unconditional Love Centre

Location Within and extending the usual heart chakra
Key Words Wisdom, Unconditional Love, Self-Realization, Discrimination, Integrity
Colours Rose, Amethyst, Pearlized Mauve
Element Sea Water
Quietening Fragrances Orchid, Camomile
Stimulating Fragrances Geranium, Basil
Crystals and Gemstones Amethyst, Sugilite (also called Luvulite), Lepidolite, Dolomite, Alexandrite

Prayer or Affirmation

We open ourselves to the blessing of unconditional love. We accept that we are unconditionally loved. We ask that we may practise unconditional love without loss of integrity or wise discrimination. Help us to emerge from complacency.

The Third Eye Chakra

Location A vortex chakra, in the auric field, out from and slightly above the brow chakra
Key Word Beauty, Justice, Guardianship, Transformation
Colours Silvery Blue, Indigo, Magenta
Element Spiritual Fire
Quietening Fragrances Carnation, Poppy
Stimulating Fragrances Jasmine, Sage
Crystals and Gemstones Optical Calcite, Ellelstials, Herkimer Diamond, Fluorite Double Pyramids

Prayer or Affirmation

We commit ourselves to vision. In this commitment we acknowledge that the vision of the past empowers the vision of the present and that the vision of the present enables the vision of the future. In service of that vision we ask the gifts of beauty and justice so that the structures of our security may be flexible and renewable. In making gold from the dross of life and experience, may we do so without despising the dross itself.

THE NEW CHAKRAS

For some years Gildas and other channelled sources have suggested that the major chakra system needs to expand to twelve, rather than having seven or eight chakras within its team. Of course, 'new' chakras, like 'new' planets, have long been there but have remained undiscovered or unawakened. Now, as we are about to enter a new millennium, it is especially important to awaken the chakra resources which will help us find the spiritual strength to sustain ourselves through change, crisis and possibly chaos.

The new chakras do not form pairs or triads in quite the same way as those within the original major team. They form a system of their own, and it is this we need to consider and work with in our times. There are no case studies for the new chakras yet, since they are, comparatively, so newly awakening. Each one of us who seeks a spiritual perspective as we stand on the brink of quantum change is a potential case study for the new chakras.

My previous book *Working With Your Chakras* examined each of the new chakras in as much detail as possible. In this book, I want, rather, to look at the ways in which they support each other in their 'team within a team'.

Each new chakra gives us certain resources for the times in which we live. As we develop their qualities, and the energies from these chakras flow into our present energy bodies, so our very substance will change.

Whichever chakras exist for us as a collective, or as individuals, also exist within the substance of the planet on which we live. As the new earth chakras awaken, so the substance and vibrational rate of matter will change and some of our present theories of physical law and science will become redundant.

Chaos

To some of us, such new possibilities will seem exciting. To others, such predictions may bring fear and insecurity. If apparently proven laws and even our own bodies are going to change, how shall we survive the chaos which will ensue? Traditionally we fear chaos as we fear evil but, as we awaken to the potential of a New Age, we need to see it as a natural law. When, recently and excitingly, the patterns of chaos were caught on film, a new perspective on chaos had to be embraced. Its swirls and movements can be extremely beautiful; far from being completely disorganized, chaos already holds the new order which it is actively seeking, within its intricate patternings.

The new chakra energies will sustain us and give us the tools and courage to enter the chaos, find its beauty, acknowledge it as one of the wonders of Divine manifestation and emerge, ourselves, renewed and freed from the debris of the old order, into the new potential.

Death and Rebirth

All too often, when we think of death, we think of loss. We are not yet used to the realization that within all death lies potential rebirth. We too rarely speak of death and rebirth in the same breath. Yet the new chakras teach us more than ever that allowing death also enables birth. Clinging to old structures simply because we are afraid to take risks produces debris and detritus which blocks the birth channels.

New Opportunities

When we see a horizon we tend to think that it marks the end of something – it can become a boundary for us. As we look towards the symbolic horizon of the old order, we may fear that beyond it can lie only darkness and destruction. Yet, in real life, horizons move. As we journey, the horizon is constantly changing as our experience of the landscape grows greater. As we approach the place of quantum change, we must have faith that the horizons are not ultimate boundaries, but a measure of how far we have come and a sign that there is always further to go.

Gildas says that we must be as courageous as the first Elizabethan explorers who set out to prove that the world was not flat. With far fewer resources than we have now, they bravely went over the horizon, did not fall over the edge, and returned with new knowledge to the place from which they had set out, knowing that place as they had never known it before, because they were now seeing it in the context of something more than they had ever been able to imagine.

THE BIRTH OF NEW ARCHETYPES

We have seen, throughout this book, that archetypes are related to Divine Principles. As we grow able to 'discover' new chakras, new planets, new concepts, new horizons, so can we expect to discover new Divine Principles and bring them into practice. If it is time for the archetypes of guru and devotee to die (see page 194), then it is time for the archetype of unconditional love to come to full fruition. When this happens we shall be fully able to support each other as the quantum leap is made, since old hierarchies based on greed, jealousy and false power will drop away.

Perhaps another archetype, which is being born, is the positive aspect of chaos. Previously we have related only to the shadow side of this, because, by its very nature, it is so difficult to differentiate.

The Archetype of Unconditional Love

This archetype is newly awakening. We have to learn to see it not only as something we aspire to practise, but as something which encompasses each one of us. It can be surprisingly challenging and demanding to know oneself unconditionally loved. Many of us will be able to identify an inner part which would rather be punished, shaped and told what to do by a higher authority. Unconditional love for all demands that we take self-responsibility and live only from the highest within us. Scarily, this means making our own decisions and trusting in an inherent integrity to help us to know what that may be, at each step of the way.

The unconditional love centre, as a new chakra, is the energy point where we learn to receive and incorporate the energy of unconditional love. The emphasis must be on learning to receive this quality with grace. If we see unconditional love as something we must give, before we are able to receive it, then we shall be in danger of patronizing and subtly judging each other.

The Archetype of the Fool

The fool is not a new archetype, yet is coming into a new potency. When we view the fool we must question and re-question all our values and assumptions, for the fool is the one who jumps empty-handed into the abyss – and always lands on his feet. He makes us constantly question, what is innocence, what is magic and what is irresponsibility? If debated or meditated upon deeply, these are not comfortable questions to have to answer, but the coming time is going to make each one of us wish the archetype of the fool to be our true ally.

THE DIMENSIONS GIVEN BY THE NEW CHAKRAS

The Dimension Given by the Base Chakra

As the new age dawns, so karma will change. The base chakra energies, when active within our beings, enable us to leave old, retributive, 'eye for an eye and tooth for a tooth' karmic patterns behind. We shall not, in the future, be bound to the wheel of rebirth in the same way.

We choose our own karmic tasks for a lifetime, when, in the

between-life state we have reviewed the life we have just lived. We are our own taskmasters. We often choose to receive that which we (in another personality bead from the soul stem) have meted out to others. Such a choice is made when we are still attached to the old order and the old treadmill of rebirth.

Alongside unconditional love, goes self-forgiveness and a recognition that each one of us has been, and continues, on a journey of experience. All the experience which we have had, or caused, has been of benefit to the total journey of humanity; therefore we do not need to perpetuate patterns by reaping what we have sown. It is often the nature of the present karmic pattern that we cannot reap exactly what we have sown unless someone else is put in the position of sowing the same pattern so that we can reap it. This becomes a vicious pattern, a weary treadmill indeed, rather than a spiral of transcendence. We need to bring new seed into incarnation with us, learn the non-attachment to our deeds and misdeeds which is transcendence, and so allow the birth of the Divine Principle of unconditional love to live us, as we live *it*.

The Dimension Given by the Hara Chakra

The hara chakra offers us the amazing potential of regeneration. When we fully comprehend this, and allow it to course through our physical and spiritual veins, we shall have perfect choice over life and death, since our bodies will remain in optimum condition for the whole of our incarnate lifespan. We shall not age and die, but will have, instead, the responsibility of choosing when we judge our life task or service on earth to be finished or entering a new phase. We shall then make a conscious transition to the next phase of learning, rather in the same way as our guides, in their dimension, do now.

The Dimension Given by the Third Eye

The brow chakra is often confused with the third eye. Though the brow gives us spiritual vision and is necessary to the functioning of the third eye, they are not one and the same energy centre. The third eye is a vortex in the auric energy field, with energetic support links to and from other chakras.

Having an open third eye does not mean, as some people mistakenly assume, that we have instant access to past lives, future events, astral travel, shifts in states of consciousness, gifts of diagnosis and healing of disease, the ability to see auras, nature spirits and angels, and commune easily with guides. Most of these faculties are psychic in origin, rather than spiritual. A spiritual dimension can only truly be added when we cease to be diverted by the glamour of phenomena (see also page 164).

Having an open third eye simply means being able to see life from a clear spiritual perspective; maintaining hope, faith and balance in a confusing and changing world; having a concept of oneself as a responsible spiritual guardian – and having the will to develop the strength for such a task; perceiving the inner quality of others without judgment – and never losing faith in the perfection and beneficence of the divine plan in which each one of us is included. When all these qualities have been developed and, paradoxically, phenomena have no attraction for their own sake – then the phenomena will manifest anyway.

THE NEW MILLENNIUM

The changes of which our guides speak are certainly predicted to come during the first phase of the new millennium. I suspect that the dawn of the millennium itself will not be an immediate magic threshold – yet in its birth lies its potential. As the old millennium dies, we have an enormous opportunity to leave old patterns behind and make new choices. The potential for a golden age for humanity will certainly lie in the new millennium's blueprint. Collectively, we shall soon be midwives and parents to an infant prodigy. What is there, in nature, needs to be brought out and supported by nurture. When we,

as individuals, work with our new chakras we prepare ourselves
for this exciting but momentous task.

WORKING WITH THE NEW CHAKRAS

With each of the new chakras, the work, as yet, remains very
simple. These chakras need to be strengthened and awakened.
Therefore they need to have their colours breathed into them;
their crystals used (by selecting a crystal and holding it over
the chakra area for five or ten minutes); their fragrances dif-
fused into our environment and absorbed into our energy
systems; and their prayers or affirmations repeated and meditated upon.

The quietening and stimulating fragrances for each of the
chakras should be mixed together for the new chakras – as
such, they will form a balancing or awakening fragrance for
the chakra. Experiment with finding a balance of a few drops
of each, which you find pleasant and harmonizing.

Working with the Base Chakra

No specific exercise is given here for the base chakra; simply
use its colours, crystals, fragrances and affirmation as suggested
above. Doing so will help the base chakra become an active
member of your chakra team.

The Base Chakra Colours

The colours for the base chakra are deep rose red, ruby and
purple.

Deep rose red is often seen in our rose gardens. Positively,
it warms and welcomes.

Negatively, it can speak of wounding and over-vulnerability.

Ruby is the colour of the gemstone of the same name and

of deep red wine. Positively, it is a colour which leads us to seek and respect our inner depths.

Negatively, it can be a suffocating colour, absorbing everything and cutting us off from positive resonances.

Purple is bright, but less brilliant than the violet of the crown chakra. Positively, it enhances the quality of self-worth.

Negatively, it overpowers and disempowers.

As you breathe the colours into your base chakra, remember to visualize them as stained glass appears when sunlight passes through it.

The Crystals for the Base Chakra

Refer to page 44 and the Glossary for general guidance on using crystals. The crystals which will best help the issues considered in this chapter are:

Rhodocrosite This stone has a gentle energy. It promotes our ability to love the earth and to recognize the interaction of spirit with matter.

Moonstones For the base chakra, moonstones should be slightly pink in tone. They help us to make transitions and to move from retributive to redemptive karma.

Rose Quartz A comforting crystal. At the base chakra it helps to keep connections with our guardian angel alive.

Rose Opal To facilitate birth; useful for mothers during labour, but also aids the birth of ideas and new phases of life or rites of passage.

Rubilite To assist our memory of the spiritual worlds and planes. It encourages us to incorporate beauty and sacred dimensions into the things we create and the buildings we build.

Working with the Vortex Chakras

The hara and the third eye chakras have a different structure from the chakras of the usual system. They are vortices, in the energy field, supported by important energy links to other major and minor chakra points. To build these structures, see Exercise 47 on page 253 and Exercise 48 on page 255.

The Hara Chakra Colours

The hara chakra colours are apricot, silver and platinum. Apricot is the colour of ripe apricots, soft and warm in tone. Positively, it enhances the body's ability to heal itself and brings a sense of well-being. It has no negative aspects or tones.

Silver is the soft silver glow of the precious metal. It give flexibility with strength. At the hara there are no negative qualities to silver.

Platinum, though similar to silver, is rather more blue in tone. Symbolically, it means stamina and endurance.

The Crystals for the Hara Chakra

Refer to page 44 and the Glossary for general guidance on using crystals. The crystals which will best help the issues considered in this chapter are:

Honey Calcite To encourage balance; helps to strengthen the energy supports which the hara needs for optimal functioning.

Sun Stone This crystal facilitates receptivity to energy from the universal source. It stimulates self-healing abilities.

Iron Pyrites Suns These are comparatively rare forms of the pyrites family and are flat gold disks with shining rays coming from a central point. They facilitate resistance to stress.

Stibnite A useful crystal for healers, stibnite has a metallic, striated appearance. It enables a steady flow of energy to others and helps in cultivating a calm, refreshing presence.

Wulfenite This is associated with the hara because of its apricot colouring. It strengthens the auric field. It helps those in positions of authority to temper power with compassion.

Exercise 47
Building the Energetic Structure for the Hara Chakra Vortex

For this exercise it is important to be sitting in an upright position, with your back supported if necessary. Unless using a cross-legged or lotus posture, do not cross your legs at the knees or ankles.

- Begin with central column breathing (see page 17).
- Focus your attention into your sacral chakra and concentrate on letting its petals open flexibly.
- Move your awareness up, through your central column to your solar plexus centre. Let these petals open.
- Move your attention slightly upwards and to the left and locate an energy centre over your spleen.
- Move your attention over to the right of your body and feel the energy centre over your liver.
- Imagine spiralling strands of golden energy streaming from each of these centres into your auric field, and meeting at a point in front of and above your sacral chakra but below your solar plexus. Concentrate until you can feel this structure getting clear and strong. Working for a few minutes each day will be more successful eventually than trying too hard at any single session.
- When your structure is well established, you will naturally become aware of the hara vortex itself, opening, spinning and returning vitality through the spiralling lines of connection to the vital organs of your body. You do not need to close the hara centre down, it will regulate itself according to your needs.

Working with the Third Eye Chakra

The Colours for the Third Eye Chakra

The colours for the third eye chakra are silvery blue, indigo and magenta. Silvery blue has a metallic quality and is the colour seen in peacock stone (bornite or chalcopyrites).

Positively, silvery blue enhances vision.

Negatively, it is a cold colour which can breed harsh, cold detachment.

Indigo is as for the brow chakra on page 201.

Magenta is a reddish violet. It is thought to have a higher vibration than violet, which is usually seen as the highest vibrational colour in the spectrum. It is probably, therefore, the first colour in a new octave of the spectrum, to reveal itself to us.

Positively, magenta lifts the spirit. It has no negative qualities, though may be over-stimulating for some people.

The Crystals for the Third Eye Chakra

Refer to page 44 and the Glossary for general guidance on using crystals. The crystals which will best help the issues considered in this chapter are:

Optical Calcite A clear version of calcite, with a rhomboid form, this crystal breaks light into the spectrum of colour and is therefore full of rainbows. True to its name, it aids clear sight and vision of a spiritual nature.

Ellestials These are among the more recent crystal discoveries. They have a similar appearance to smoky quartz but their form is square and flat. They form close clusters and often have water trapped within them. They are crystals which inspire and encourage us to reach our highest potential.

Herkimer Diamond This is a member of the quartz family. They are diamond-shaped crystals, usually quite small and clear, as though having been polished and faceted. They are only mined in Herkimer County, New York State, and grow in liquid solution. They enhance all spiritual qualities, give vitality and encourage joy.

Fluorite Double Pyramids Also diamond-shaped, these crystals aid the development of spiritual awareness and help to transform spiritual ideas into material reality. They come in different shades, mainly white, purple, mauve and green. The white or purple are most suitable for the third eye.

Exercise 48
Building the Subtle Structure for the Third Eye

Position yourself as for Exercise 47, page 253.

- Begin with central column breathing (see page 17).
- Imagine your auric energy field, stretching out about 4–6 inches from your physical body. Sense the area where your brow chakra petals emerge into this field.
- Focus your attention a little above and beyond the petals of your brow chakra and seek an intense energy spot in your auric field, or a moving vortex of spiralling energy.
- Visualize the colours silvery blue, indigo and magenta around this area.
- Visualize a line of energy going from this energy spot or vortex into your brow chakra and through, to connect with your pineal gland (see page 186). Breathe along this line (two to three in/out breaths).
- Imagine another line of energy running from the third eye position, up to your crown chakra. Breathe along this line (two to three in/out breaths).
- Visualize a line of energy going from the third eye, through

the petals of your alter major chakra, and into its stem. Breathe along this line (two to three in/out breaths).

- Visualize a line of energy going from your third eye vortex into your throat chakra. Breathe along this line (two to three in/out breaths).
- Return your attention to your third eye point and sense it clearing and strengthening.
- Feel your feet in contact with the ground and visualize a cloak of light with a hood right around you.
- You do not need to close down the third eye vortex – it will regulate itself.

Working with the Unconditional Love Centre

This chakra, too, has a new form, since it is a chakra within a chakra. The basic meditation for opening and contacting the unconditional love centre is given as Exercise 49 on page 257.

The Colours for the Unconditional Love Centre

The colours for the unconditional love centre are rose, amethyst and pearlized mauve. Rose is a tender, but full-bodied pink. Positively, it brings a sense of security and acceptance.

Negatively, it can smother.

Amethyst at the unconditional love centre is the colour seen in paler-toned or 'lavender' amethyst crystals. This colour encourages qualities of fine discernment. It has no negative qualities or tones.

Pearlized mauve is also light-toned, with a pearlized sheen. It is the colour given out by lepidolite crystals. It is a protective colour and also encourages high aspiration. It has no negative tones or qualities.

The Crystals for the Unconditional Love Centre

Refer to page 44 and the Glossary for general guidance on using crystals. The crystals which will best help the issues considered in this chapter are:

Amethyst When chosen for the unconditional love centre, this crystal should be pale or slightly greyish. It helps the centre to awaken, whilst also strengthening and protecting it.

Sugilite/Luvulite Comparatively rare; facilitates self-acceptance and encourages the development of feelings of unconditional love for self and others.

Lepidolite A form of mica which aids self-forgiveness and release, which are often necessary before unconditional love can develop.

Dolomite To strengthen the unconditional love centre and encourage the growth of integrity.

Alexandrite To help in the cultivation of wise discrimination.

Exercise 49
Guided Visualization for the Unconditional Love Centre

Sit or lie down in a comfortable position with your body symmetrically arranged and your legs uncrossed at the knees or ankles unless you are using a cross-legged or lotus posture.

- Be in touch with the rhythm of your breathing . . . Gradually let this rhythm help you to bring the focus of your attention into your heart chakra . . . Visualize each petal of the chakra opening rhythmically with each in-breath and out-breath . . .
- Enter your own inner space and find yourself looking into a large, delicately scented pink rose . . . Notice the texture of the petals . . . Each one is tipped with a delicate touch of green . . . The centre of the rose is pure gold . . .

- The rose becomes large enough for you to enter it . . . The gold in its centre becomes a golden gateway through which you can pass . . . into a garden beyond . . . You find yourself in a rose garden, full of mauve and pink roses . . . It is formally laid out, with grassed alleyways along which to walk and wooden seats under rose arbours . . . Spend little time exploring this fragrant place and perhaps sit for a while in one of its arbours . . .
- Now you see a path which you had not noticed before and you decide to follow it . . . You leave the formal part of the garden and come to some rocks which shine with a pearly mauve light . . . Ahead of you there is a rocky archway with an angel-like figure standing there . . . As you come near the archway and the light being you know that you are welcome and that this guardian is not here to keep you out, but to welcome you in and protect you as you enter a sacred space . . .
- You can now see an amethyst crystal temple . . . As you come near, the door opens and you go inside . . . Amethyst crystals are all around you and the atmosphere is warm and welcoming . . . You feel totally vulnerable and yet totally safe . . . You know that you are fully accepted, fully seen and unconditionally loved . . . Bask in this knowledge and feeling for a while . . .
- When you are ready, retrace your steps . . . out of the crystal temple, past the guardian at the archway, back through the formal rose garden to its golden gateway . . . go through the gateway . . . and become aware again of your own breath in your heart chakra . . . Let the petals of this centre fold in, and put a star or cross of light in a circle of light over it as a blessing . . . Feel the contact of your feet with the ground and gradually ease back into your normal environment . . .

THE LAST WORD

It seems appropriate to end the book on this note – the opening of the unconditional love centre in preparation for the millennium which will bring us the changes long predicted (if not immediately, then perhaps in the foreseeable future and in the present lifetimes of many of us). Working with chakra pairs and triads and the new chakras brings energy and development not only for each of us personally, but also for the whole of humanity and the earth itself.

The Gildas Prayer

Let light from the Source shine into the darknesses of earth and bring healing

Let love from the Source shine into our hearts and bring peace and harmony

Let the force of Light, tempered with love, enter into our minds, that the things of our own creation may more truly reflect the Divine

Let light and love, peace and strength, healing and harmony bring at last that union with the Source which passes all understanding

Let understanding, born of peace and harmony, light and love, encompass the earth, now and forever. Amen.

Glossary

Alchemy This is a tradition which originated in Persia. In Europe, in the Middle Ages, alchemists were seen as being engaged on research which would enable lead (base metal) to be transformed into gold. Undoubtedly some, usually called 'puffers and blowers', undertook such research. However, true spiritual alchemy uses the imagery of base metal being transformed into gold as a basis for complex esoteric teaching about the journey and evolution of the soul.

Crystals Natural crystals, such as clear quartz, amethyst, rose quartz and aventurine, are reminders to us of the spirit which resides in matter. Crystals, used as an aid to spiritual work and healing, enhance and amplify. Crystals also have active healing energies within them. These are released when we declare our healing intention, and then use the crystal to help us focus on that intention, that area of the body or our chakras.

Crystals are readily available from many different shops, suppliers or market stalls. Use the crystal sections in each chapter to help you to decide which varieties of stones you would like to acquire. When you have found a source, rely on your intuition to tell you which, of a particular variety, is the right crystal for you.

Spend some time getting to know your crystal. Look at it carefully, handle it, admire it. When you are ready to prepare it for serious work, wait until three days before the full moon when you should put it into water containing a little sea salt. Do not do this with crystals mounted as jewellery, with synthetic cystals, or with those which feel soft or flaky – such as some pieces of lepidolite. These can be frequently rinsed in running water during this period or placed on a large, previously cleansed, amethyst cluster.

On the night of the full moon, dry your crystal on silk or soft cotton and put it in the garden or on the windowsill. Even if the full moon is behind cloud, your crystal will absorb what it needs. After this, it should be 'charged' by twelve hours of sunlight. (Behind glass is fine, but the light should shine as directly as possible onto the crystals, which should be turned regularly.) This charging can be done intermittently until twelve hours' worth of sun has been absorbed.

In a simple ceremony dedicate each of your crystals to its purpose. Light a candle, hold the stone for a while in your cupped hands, and then ask it to help in your development or healing.

(For fuller information see Soozi Holbeche's *The Power of Gems and Crystals* in the Bibliography.)

Higher Self Our higher self is, in essence, the part of our consciousness or soul which does not incarnate. The higher self has an overview of all our lifetimes and decides our task and purpose in each incarnation.

Inner Journeying Guided journeys for self-exploration require, but also enable, a slightly altered state of consciousness in which the focus of our attention may be inwardly directed. They help us to become progressively more familiar with 'what is inside' – or what is often termed the 'inner landscape'.

Through guided journeying, not only is information from within brought to the surface, but self-healing and enhancement of spiritual consciousness can become more personally directed or controlled. There is a time and tide, a rhythm or cycle in all things, but when the tide is right we need to use it as skilled surfers, rather than as flotsam and jetsam to be taken only where the wave wills. Each stage of an inner journey or series of journeys leads you a little more deeply into yourself in order to 'clear' psychological material and reveal the next steps on your spiritual path.

In the inner journeys of this book 'safety factors' are built into the method of journeying. Relaxing and aligning your physical body helps to balance your chakras and subtle energies. Though it may sometimes seem repetitive, beginning in the meadow means that there is a safe place at the edge of normal waking consciousness and the inner worlds. Before you do any serious journeying, you connect with the meadow and activate your inner senses. Before you return to the outer world you pass through the meadow, thus signalling to yourself that you are about to move from one area of your consciousness to another. If at any time you feel uncomfortable with anything in your inner world, then the meadow is there as the safe area of transition. There you can peacefully consider the inner happenings or rest awhile before you ease over into the demands of your outer world.

In the induction to each inner journey, irrespective of which chakra pair or triad it may be aimed at, you are guided to open up your heart centre or chakra. The heart energy is a particularly safe and wise energy on which to travel. Activating it ensures that your experiences will be gentle and that you will only unveil those secrets of your psyche which you are able to deal with at any given time.

Do not be tempted to use inner journeys for 'digging' into your past or memory. Accept what comes. If you are enthusiastic about psychological and spiritual unfolding, it is tempting to test the boundaries and to force blocked memories to the surface. But the psyche is very wise and reveals its depths only in an environment of trust. When you remember something during an inner journey, even if it seems very familiar or mundane, your psyche will have a reason for giving you that memory at that time. If you respect this and work with what is given, then gradually and gently the deeper revelations will also emerge. Trauma and drama are not measurements of depth or speed of growth.

Symbols used in the induction to journeys, such as a talisman or amulet, an inner wise being or a power animal, help to evoke the power, strength or wisdom in your psyche. They help you to journey wisely and to be centred as you do so. If you are at a crossroads or have any kind of choice to make during a journey, these aspects of yourself will help you find the right direction and make the right choice.

The Amulet This is similar to a talisman and has a related function. You can have an amulet as well as, or instead of, a talisman. Whilst a talisman is something that has *become* special or meaningful to you, an amulet may have been charged or blessed in some way and is usually given to you by someone special or to mark a special moment. Like the talisman, the amulet may exist in the outer world as well as the inner. It is most likely to be a piece of jewellery, a precious stone or crystal, a beautiful bottle or casket, a jewelled knife, a sword or chalice.

The talisman or amulet may remain constant and unchanging in your journeys or there may be special gifts for particular journeys. Most people who journey in the inner worlds end up with quite a collection of inner treasures!

The Power Animal The concept of the power animal has its roots in shamanistic lore. Animals can help us in our inner worlds. They protect us, guide us, mirror lessons for us, and help us to stay in contact with our natural sense of what is right, wholesome and safe. With their aid we can see in the dark, swim under water whilst still breathing, fly and glide on air currents, walk through the fire and survive the swamp or the pit. The strong yet gentle power animals of our inner worlds may be very wild or fierce in the outer. When we cross the threshold to inner experience they become our friends, they may speak to us and become our guides and protectors.

It is possible to meet animals in our inner worlds who are not friendly because they symbolize some inner conflict or imbalance, but the true power animal can always be trusted, will come when we call, track us when we stray, energize us when we are fatigued, and help to heal us when we are ill. They are recognized by the light in their eyes and their joy at being found by us, or invited into the journey.

The Talisman This may be a reflection of something which also comforts you in the outer world. For some it is their childhood teddy bear or rocking horse, conveniently miniaturized or even animated for easier travel. For others the talisman may be more archetypal or classical, like a guiding star, a staff or lantern. It does not matter what form it takes, but it must have the ability to give you a feeling of safety and comfort whenever you touch it.

The Inner Wise Presence In our good moments, when we make clear decisions or give wise, non-judgmental advice to a friend, we know that we have access to a place of wisdom within. It has little to do with personal experience and is related to a knowledge of inner potential and the potential of humankind. In inner journeys this source of wisdom becomes personified. It may be a mythological being or animal, or it may simply be an atmosphere of sacredness and love. By learning in the inner worlds that we can call this being or presence to us at will, we can be led to deeper layers of self-understanding as well as being empowered to use its strength more often and more consciously in outer life.

Karma This is the spiritual law of cause and effect (which defies 'nutshell definition'). 'As you sow, so shall you reap', gives a basic but over-simplified idea. Belief in karma goes alongside belief in reincarnation and personal, progressive evolution. The tendency is to see karma as something troublesome or heavy which needs to be overcome during a specific lifetime – but giftedness or innate wisdom are positive karmic attributes.

Psyche Analytic and transpersonal psychologies have shown how complex the human personality is. The psyche refers to the total being, with all its drives, needs, conflicts, dis-ease, health, gifts and potential.

Shadow The part of the 'I' which we do not admit into full consciousness. That which is unconscious, undefined, formless, dark, shadowy and without concept; the unknown.

Tarot An ancient form of cards which can be 'read' for the purposes of divination. The seventy-two cards form a major and a minor arcana. The major arcana consists of twenty-two archetypes covering all aspects of human experience. The minor arcana has four suits, differently named in different sets of cards, but mostly representative of mind, body, emotions and spirit. The twenty-two archetypes of the major arcana are: the Fool, the Magician, the High Priestess, the Empress, the Emperor, the Hierophant, the Lovers, the Chariot, Strength, the Hermit, the Wheel of Fortune, Justice, the Hanged Man, Death, Temperance, the Devil, the Tower, the Star, the Moon, the Sun, Judgment, the World.

Tibetan Singing Bowls These beaten brass bowls traditionally come from Tibet, where making them is an art form. When vibrated or struck, the bowls give out clear sounds, accompanied by overtones and undertones, which 'sing' on or continue resonating for an unusual length of time. The sounds are healing and often helpful in chakra work.

Transpersonal Therapy and Counselling This addresses the spiritual needs and aspirations of human beings as well as the behavioural. It concentrates on the importance of finding a meaning in life and of being creative and fulfilled in living, relating and making choices.

Yin and Yang These are Chinese words for the basic but opposite aspects of creation. Yin is receptive, feminine and dark. Yang is active, masculine and light. In the traditional yin/yang symbol one black and one white fish-like shape nestle together to form a perfect circle. The eye of the black shape is white and the eye of the white shape is black, showing that the seed of each is contained in the other.

Bibliography

Books by Ruth White
A Message of Love, London: Piatkus Books, 1989.
The River of Life, York Beach, ME: Samuel Weiser, 1997.
A Question of Guidance, Saffron Walden, England: C. W. Daniel, 1989.
Working with Your Chakras, York Beach, ME: Samuel Weiser, 1995.
Working with Your Guides and Angels, York Beach, ME: Samuel Weiser, 1997.

By Ruth White with Mary Swainson
Gildas Communicates, Saffron Walden, England: C. W. Daniel, 1971.
The Healing Spectrum, Saffron Walden, England: C. W. Daniel, 1979.
Seven Inner Journeys, Saffron Walden, England: C. W. Daniel, 1975.

Recommended Reading
Bailey, Alice. *Discipleship in the New Age*, London: The Lucis Press, 1966.
Cooper, C. J. *The Aquarian Dictionary of Festivals*, London: Aquarian Press, 1990.
————. *An Illustrated Encyclopaedia of Symbols*, London: Thames and Hudson, n. d.
Ferrucci, Pierro (disciple of Assagioli). *What We May Be*, London: Thorsons, 1989.
Heider, John. *The Tao of Leadership*, Atlanta, GA: Humanics, 1985.
Jung, C. G. *Man and His Symbols*, New York: Dell, 1968.
Krystall, Phyllis. *Cutting the Ties that Bind*, York Beach, ME: Samuel Weiser, 1993.
Holbeche, Soozie. *The Power of Gems and Crystals*, London: Piatkus Books, 1989.
Raphaell, Katharina. *Crystal Enlightenment*, Santa Fe, NM: Aurora Press, 1985.
————. *Crystal Healing*, Santa Fe, NM: Aurora Press, 1987.

Index